To Have
and
To Hold

Deborah Moggach

To Have
and
To Hold

GUILD PUBLISHING LONDON

This edition published 1986 by
Book Club Associates
by arrangement with Viking Books Ltd

First published 1986

Printed in Great Britain by
St Edmundsbury Press
Bury St Edmunds, Suffolk

To
my sister
Alex,
and to
Susi Hush

1 There is a special place behind the potting shed. Viv calls it Na-Na Land. She rules it. The ground is bald. She brings her teddy here, and her bulldozer and her police car. Sometimes she pushes them to and fro, muttering commands, and sometimes she sits there picking at her scab. When she's bored she lets Ann in, but she invents new passwords so Ann has to guess them, back to front, to prolong the longing.

Ann brings her doll, who takes up a lot of space with her frilly skirts. Viv refuses to call the doll by name, which is too soppy to say, back to front or the right way round. But sometimes she chants it, to taunt Ann, in a twee voice, higher and higher. She can make Ann cry, but the doll remains unblinking. Once Viv took off the doll's petticoat and ran it over with her bulldozer.

Viv was digging a trench. She straddled it, her skirt blowing against her legs. Sometimes she found a worm and picked it up; it twisted in her finger and she flung it out of the way. In the distance a tannoy sounded. The allotments were surrounded by factories – McVities, Heinz. With the wind blowing you could smell the soup. The far murmurs of machinery, the delivery lorries hooting, the high wire fences made these green spaces freer, airier. She was the ruler of her muddy domain. Sometimes a lark sang, high up. It was a sunny day in February.

Behind the hut the girls were silent. Viv walked round there. Three teddies were laid out on the ground and the girls were eating crisps.

'Those were for lunch,' said Viv. She looked at the teddies. 'What're they doing?'

'Sunbathing,' said Daisy.

'How boring.'

The girls munched. Viv reached for a crisp.

'When're we going home?' Daisy took back Viv's crisp and, searching the bag, exchanged it for a smaller one.

'Ann and I, we used to play for hours,' said Viv. 'Where's your imaginations?'

'When's lunch?'

'We went behind the potting shed. Your grandad's. It was called Na-Na Land. You had to cover your face and walk through a swamp and talk in special back-to-front language, and you should've heard our adventures. We made our own roads and as we went along they all closed up behind us. Sometimes we took Ann's doll along with us. It was called Bo-Bo-Angela.'

'Ugh,' said Daisy.

Rosie pulled at Viv's sleeve. She was the elder; she was eight, and as plump as Ann had been, with a sweet, wide face.

'Mum,' she said. 'Let me have a doll.'

Ann had a ding-dong doorbell. Viv loved her sister but there are some things you can never say. Beyond the door she could hear the whine of Ken's Black and Decker – Saturday sounds.

It was a street of small terraced houses, net curtains for the old residents and blinds for the first-time buyers. There was a self-respecting, Saturday afternoon air about it – a man vacuuming his car, someone painting their front door, a radio playing. Over North London the clouds had banked up, the sky darkened, and it gave the street a poised air of innocence, a toytown normality.

Viv went into Ann's kitchen and dumped some leeks into her sink. They were covered with mud.

'They'll take all afternoon to clean . . .'

'But think how organic I'm being,' said Ann.

'You feeling OK?'

Ann was three months pregnant. She nodded. The sky rumbled. She had been pregnant, too, when they'd moved into this house nearly three years before. But even Viv could no longer talk to her about this. Vegetables were easier.

'Have a beetroot.' Viv took one out of her bag. 'I hate them.'

'Why do you grow them then?'

'Some ancestral prompting. Mum leaving our tea out for us.'

'Beetroot and salad cream and the tap-tap of her high heels down the road.' Ann washed the beetroot under the tap. 'Ken likes beetroot.'

'Perhaps that's why I grow them.'

The sky rumbled again and then the rain came down; driving winter rain. It rattled on the glass of the extension room Ken was building. He straightened up and squinted at the ceiling anxiously. He was only a few yards away but dim in a haze of dust. He had saluted to Viv, through his sandstorm, but he had the air, as always, of a man who likes to get on. Time was always short. Time for what?

The kitchen had darkened. Ann switched on the light. Ken turned back to his drilling. Viv thought: shame he's so good-looking when he's the sort of bloke who takes his Advanced Driving Test.

Across the muddy sink a worm stretched, like elastic, making for the plug-hole. Viv picked it up, with Ann shuddering, and carried it out of the kitchen door.

'You'll get wet,' said Ann.

Viv glanced at Ken, who raised his eyebrows through the glass. She grinned, holding up the worm. Then she flung it into the flowerbed.

Bo-Bo-Angela. Ann had knitted clothes for her – tiny jumpers. And today, in her lounge, there was Ann's knitting lying on the settee. Nearly thirty years later and it was a tiny jumper again. This time it must be worn.

Viv walked back to her car under the black sky. She crossed the wet street, its gutters winking. All the little houses; all the hopes.

'Kids!' says their mother. 'Why do we have them?'

She snorts cigarette smoke through her nostrils and clatters around the kitchen, tut-tutting at the trails of earth on the floor. She straightens her seams, then pats her hair in the mirror.

'Course you like beetroot'; she purses her lips at herself. 'And stop squabbling, the two of you. Can't hear myself think.'

She works at the Odeon, on the till. She does it, she says, to get out of the house. Their dad disapproves but she says he'd be amazed at who's taking who to the pictures, especially the early showing, the carryings-on. Who'd have thought it in Watford? And when was money, she'd like to know, unwelcome?

When she's ready to go she looks wicked and different; when she comes home she smells of grown-ups – cigarettes and scent and indoors. Sometimes the girls go to a Saturday matinée and she calls them 'modom' in a silly voice and makes the queue grow attentive. Viv blushes, but her heart swells once she's reached her seat and thinks of her mum in her booth, her hair stiff as a starlet's.

She's late. Now she's going she smiles at them nicely and sees Ann's knee for the first time.

'What's happened?'

'I got pushed in the playground.'

'Poor pet.' She suddenly squeezes Ann's shoulders. 'Poor little pet. Was it the big bully boys?'

Ann nods.

'Dad'll be back in a tick. You get him to wash that, and don't let him off.'

She goes. The front door slams. Viv turns to Ann.

'Why didn't you tell her it was me?'

Ann shrugs and bites into a slice of bread and butter. She looks pale and good.

Viv's face heats up and she stabs at her sausage roll, hard.

Ann was two years older than Viv. She was the good

one, the plodder. At school they said she tried hard and she would get there in the end. And she did, sort of. Except Viv had skipped past her to the finishing post, long before, and the clapping had died down and some of the audience had even gone home.

'It's not fair!' Ann wailed.

This maddened their father. 'Life's not fair, young lady, and the sooner you realize that the better.'

Then he would go into the garden and bang about in his shed. Viv and Ann would stay well out of the way, watching *Bill and Ben the Flowerpot Men* on the telly. They were too young for the fairness of things.

That night a gale blew. Viv lay cupped around Ollie, skin to skin. The window-panes rattled and in the next room the girls muttered in their sleep. Even the cat was restless, shifting against Viv's backbone. Down in the street, glass splintered and a dustbin lid clattered into the road.

Viv dreamed of her trench, filled with tossing green water; it slopped to and fro, tilting like a bath, and she knew she mustn't look into it because that was not a sack of carrots that was lying there submerged. The sky was flushed pink and there was whispering behind the huts, which had grown up all around her, tall and upright, far too tall. Behind each one there was a voice, hissing to her about the sack of carrots but she was hot now and kept her hands pressed against her ears, while something warm moved against her back and there was breath against her neck and arms pulling her over and she turned over, sweaty and slippery, and it was Rosie climbing into bed with her, wheezing with asthma.

'There's horrible noises,' Rosie said, pressing close, curling up her knees and digging them into Viv's stomach.

Viv stroked her. 'It's nothing. It's just a storm.'

'It's horrible.'

'We're safe,' Viv whispered, as the slates rattled on the roof. She gripped her darling daughter.

In the city you can tell there's been a storm by the angle of the estate agents' signs. This morning they leaned all ways, making the street tipsy. One had fallen against next door's car. The sky was white and the air still, like held breath. Dustbins had spilled. Viv walked back from the Pakistani supermarket. There was something about Sundays that made her street look shabbier.

Ollie had taken the children to the park. He was irritable; nobody had slept well. Viv's head ached. In the distance a siren sounded; it would be a police car racing down the Holloway Road. From the Catholic church round the corner, bells rang for the faithful, but in this street nobody stirred. It was a row of crumbling terraced houses, four storeys high, most of them flats or else owned by the council, with large families inside them and scaffolding up, where improvements were being made. It was the sort of street where cars revved up late at night and reggae played from open windows.

But today it was cold and the windows closed. That was why Viv didn't hear her phone ringing until she was at her door-step.

It rang and rang in the empty house as she fumbled for her keys. She could see the phone through the window. Her keys had got caught in the bottom of her shoulder-bag and as she rummaged for them her carrier-bag slipped down her wrist and tipped. A carton of eggs fell on the pavement; the eggs spilled and broke.

'Shit!'

As she stared at the spilled yolks, the phone stopped.

'Catch!'

Ollie tossed the ball to Rosie. She rushed for it across the grass, but it slipped through her fingers.

'Feeble, feeble!' chanted Daisy the bully, jumping up and down.

'*What?*' Viv sat very still on the sofa. 'Oh my God.'

The front door opened, the ball bounced along the hall. Rosie and Daisy rushed into the room.

'Mum, Dad's got me Monster Munch but it's salt and vinegar and Rosie's got –'

'Shut up!' Viv turned back to the phone. She paused. 'Oh Ken, I don't know what to say.'

'Is that Uncle Ken? I want to talk to him –'

'Last night?'

'Mum, let me –'

'They've operated?'

'Mum –'

'*Shut up!*'

Ollie came into the room, taking off his coat. 'There's a large black dog outside, licking up a lot of eggs.'

He stopped and stared at Viv.

'What's happened?'

2 From where she lay, Ann was aware of little squares of light. Sometimes one was switched off and another switched on. Shapes were there; small shapes. When she blinked she could make them bigger, then they shrank. When she opened her eyes, new lights had come on; two up, three along, she could count the patterns in her head, there were little blue glows too. The shapes moved behind the windows; someone closed some curtains and time passed. Perhaps it was an hour, perhaps a month. Ann was half asleep and her mouth was dry and the baby inside her was hurting. It seemed to have been hurting for ever.

It was best to lie quite still, and sometimes, when she

opened her eyes just a fraction, blurry, she could see that it was really dark now, of course that was a block of flats outside this window, she had been lying here for ages, and a nurse had come and mouthed something at her; she must have replied politely because the nurse then went away and when she turned to the small blue glows she realized of course they were televisions, how nice, people in there. And lights were switched off and there was Ken's face beside her, very distinct; she told him she could see him quite clearly when she blinked, and that the baby hurt when she moved but it was otherwise all right, and he said something from miles away, something about the baby, and she agreed, she felt her chin move as she nodded, she said of course it would stop hurting soon, he was right, though why he was visiting her she couldn't understand, and he kept squeezing her hand.

And then next time she woke the windows in the flats were all dark, and she felt sorry for Ken in a vague rather pleasant way because he hadn't understood, and she wondered if he were all right, he must be at work now and she was at home in bed, though the walls were different. And then she thought he couldn't be at work because of course it was the middle of the night, wasn't she stupid.

And then when she woke again it was morning, and bright lights on all around her, and people lying in bed, she hadn't really seen them before. And a different nurse, a black one, was bringing her a cup of tea. And then she understood what Ken had been trying to tell her.

Ken shaved, carefully. The radio told him there was traffic congestion in the Blackwall Tunnel and a tail-back on the M 1. He listened to every word, just as he shaved with attention; he knew he must do this, he wasn't stupid, it was simply a question of lifting the razor and applying it to his cheek and the trickier bit around his moustache, he'd been shaving for, oh, twenty years now, and if he didn't do it right today he would start to alarm himself and that would never do. Now the radio told him about a cold front; the voice took it all for granted, that he would want to listen, and of course he would, and then he'd lift up the radio and take it into the bedroom while he got dressed.

There was a very faint noise but he couldn't think where it was coming from. It was a hum, or more of a faint whine; he preferred to ignore it because nobody would like to know that it came from his own head. And then he realized as he put on his shirt that it came from the phone beside the bed. Of course, he had taken it off the hook last night.

Nobody would phone him in the morning. He put it back on the hook.

On the kitchen table lay the bag with Ann's knitting in it. But he made himself a cup of tea and a slice of toast with the knitting just sitting there. He even felt a passing twinge of annoyance that the kitchen clock had stopped and he'd have to buy another battery. Ridiculously, he felt relieved that he could feel annoyed.

He was ready for work. When he switched off the radio the house was so silent that he paused a moment in the hall, listening for sounds.

He closed the front door behind him. As he did so Mrs Maguire, from next door, came out.

'Terrible, isn't it,' she said.

Ken turned. 'Sorry?'

'Terrible. We'll start getting the rats soon.' She pointed to the rubbish bags. 'We do pay our rates, don't we?'

Ken nodded.

'And what do we get for it?' she said.

'Terrible,' said Ken, and went to his car.

All along the street beside the hospital the parking

spaces were full. Viv stopped the car on a double yellow line and turned off the engine. In a perverse way she wanted to get a ticket and a small ten pounds' worth of suffering. 'Life's not fair!' her father used to shout at them, when they were too young to realize the truth. What had Viv done to deserve two strong children, with hair she could brush, that they could now brush themselves, and clever fingers, and complaints about school, and letters that they wrote, in unstamped envelopes, to the Dennis the Menace Fan Club? Two girls, with their fragrant breathing at night and their scattered Pentels on the floor which drove Viv mad because nobody put the tops on, but look what happened in the morning – the girls opened their eyes, they were alive, they had to be bullied to do their teeth.

Viv got out of the car. Today she brought flowers; yesterday there had been no time. She walked towards the hospital steps and stopped. Ken's car was parked there. She hesitated. Inside his car it was as neat as always, with his Zenith Dry Rot files on the passenger seat, just like a normal Monday. The ashtray was full.

Viv walked back to her car and sat inside it. People were going into the hospital, carrying flowers. She waited in the car, amongst the debris of her family life – mud from the allotment, crumbs, wrappers, and *My Naughty Little Sister* cassettes, all out of their boxes. Did she deserve children, that she couldn't be bothered to put back their tapes? She started to do so. Every few moments she glanced at the hospital steps, and that was how she saw her mother.

Viv hurried from the car.

'Mum!' She grabbed her arm.

Irene turned. 'Blimey, you nearly gave me a heart attack. Still, there's worse places to have one.'

'Ken's in there.' She pointed to the building. 'Let's wait in my car.'

Irene sat in the passenger seat. 'You and your mobile

16

dustbin,' she said, wrinkling her nose. 'Beats me how Ollie puts up with it.'

Viv indicated the hospital. 'I think we should let them have some time together.'

'They'll have plenty of time together when she comes out.'

'Don't!'

'I'm just saying now's the time to rally round. The poor pet. How did she seem yesterday?'

'She tried to be bright. I wish she hadn't felt she should.'

'Was it a little boy or girl?'

'I didn't ask.' Viv watched the hospital steps. Down them walked a couple, the woman carrying a new-born baby wrapped in a shawl, small as a doll. The husband carried her case, and opened their car door for her to get in.

'The poor pet,' said Irene again. 'Oh my God.'

'What?'

'Look who's here.'

Douglas was walking towards them. He, too, was carrying flowers. Viv got out of the car again.

'Hello, Dad.'

She told him about Ken. At the car door he hesitated.

'Hello, Reenie.'

She opened the back door for him and he got in.

'Well well,' he said. 'This is cosy.'

There was a silence.

Irene looked in the driving mirror. 'What's those things?'

'What things?' said Douglas.

'Sideboards. You didn't have them last time.' She turned to inspect her ex-husband properly.

'No?'

'Sideboards. Like a pop star.'

Douglas smiled. 'Nobody's compared me to a pop star before.'

'I didn't.'

Another silence. The car felt cramped. Irene took out her cigarettes and offered one to Douglas.

'No thanks.'

She stared. 'Given up?'

He nodded. Irene raised her eyebrows and looked at Viv. Viv shrugged.

'Bit late, isn't it?' said Irene.

'Nothing's too late,' he said.

'Since when have you got so healthy?'

Viv took a cigarette. 'Some things are too late.'

Irene, through her smoke, was still squinting at Douglas.

Viv said: 'For Ann, anyway.' She thought: I haven't sat in a car with both my parents for fifteen years, since they've been divorced. It takes this to do it. She said: 'It's too late for Ann.'

'She can't have any more babies.'

'Why?' said Rosie.

'Because she's had a hysterectomy, which means –'

'I don't want shoes like this, I want them without any straps and with little heels.'

'Well you can't.'

'Tamsin has and Rashida has and –'

'Shut up.'

They were sitting in a shoe shop. Rosie twitched her foot.

Viv said: 'She loved your get-well card.'

'Mum, why can't I –'

'Shut up!'

A shop assistant came up. Viv tried to exchange apologetic glances but the assistant ignored her.

'Can she try these?' Viv said, holding up a sandal. She turned to Rosie. 'Then I'll get you both some tights.' She had a strong desire, today, to buy her children new clothes.

As they walked back home she tried again.

'Ann's coming out of hospital tomorrow.'

But Rosie and Daisy were barging ahead to catch *Grange Hill* on the telly.

Viv went into the kitchen and dumped her shoulder-bag, with its crackling Barclaycard counterfoils, on the table, and put the carrier-bags on the floor. Why should they understand?

Later, however, she went into their bedroom and there was Rosie, laying her kangaroo on the floor and tucking it up in a blanket.

'What're you doing?' asked Viv.

'She's in hospital. Be quiet.'

Ken drove Ann home. She was silent. In the hospital it had been hard to find things to say. He had saved up stories for her, stories from work, but they were mostly the alcoholic adventures of Bob and Al, the chippies who talked the most, and they sounded sordid in the telling so he had stopped.

In the next ward there had been babies crying, quite distinctly. Ann had had to listen to that all day. Probably all night too, though neither of them had brought the subject up. There were so many things that could not be mentioned; he hadn't realized how much of their life was concerned with the future, with building for a family. He couldn't even talk about the extension because its real, unsaid name had always been a playroom, a child's room facing the sun and connecting to the kitchen. So he had told her about the car breaking down, which really wasn't much of a topic. He had wanted to make her smile. He had wanted to tell her about surveying the house in Wainwright Avenue, how he'd been shining his torch into the gaps in the lath and plaster and all the time some little girl, an inmate of the place, had been tying his shoe-laces together. He had wanted to tell her how the lady of the house had come in to ask him about the extent of the rot, and how he hadn't been able to move. But he couldn't tell her this. So they had sat in silence, and he had held her hand and asked her about the food. And she had said that soon she would be out of there and she wanted to come home.

They drove towards Finsbury Park. It was 3.30 and the schools were coming out. A lollipop lady stepped into the road and Ken stopped the car. Children, holding their mothers' hands, crossed the road. Blue anoraks, red anoraks, a little boy dropping some paper and his mother smacking him. Ken switched on the radio.

'. . . *and now, with news from Beirut, here's our correspondent . . .*'

He twiddled the dials, revving the car. It seemed to take an age for the children to pass; didn't they understand? He glanced at Ann's profile.

He ushered her into the hall. The house was neat and tidy, as if they were visitors.

'Cold?' He put her case down.

'I'm fine.'

'I put the heating on.' He felt the radiator.

She nodded and went into the lounge.

'You've been cleaning,' she said.

'I'll make us a cup of tea.'

'Shouldn't you be back at work?'

'Not yet.'

When he came back with the tea, she was sitting on the settee. He wished she had a book or a magazine on her lap. Even just for his sake.

'Thought we could have a dekko at these.' He sat down next to her and opened the brochures he'd brought. 'Have a biscuit. Look.' He turned a page. 'This place, you have your own villa, balcony, strange Greek plumbing, the works. Levkas, that's just below Corfu but not so spoiled. A touch of the vine-shaded tavernas, and we could have a bash at windsurfing.'

The brochure lay on her lap. After a moment she turned the page. It lay there, open.

'Or we could try Kos.' It said: *Family villa, sleeps six, reduction for children.* He turned the page, the next, then the next. 'Or what about a bit of culture, what about Florence?'

'That would be nice.'

There was a silence.

'Look, I'm not going back,' he said.

'Course you must.'

'I'm staying here,' he said. 'With you.'

'Please Ken. I'm all right.'

Another silence.

'Please go,' she said, her voice sharper.

Ken paused. She sat there, turning the pages. He stood up. She didn't move. Then he went to the door.

She raised her head. 'I'm sorry,' she said, her voice low.

'Annie!'

'I'm so sorry.'

'Don't ever say that!'

He moved towards her, but she turned back to the brochure. He looked at her brown hair, neatly brushed, bent over the photographs. He went out to his car.

Ann put away the tea-mugs and the uneaten biscuits. The house was silent. She had wanted so much to come home, but now she was here she felt like a guest.

Opening the cupboard door, she caught sight of a glimmer of plastic behind the saucepans. It was hidden away, wedged at the back. She pulled it out. It was the bag of baby's knitting.

Now she was alone she pulled out a chair, quite deliberately, sat down at the table, and started to cry.

3 Two young girls are at the beach. It's a perfect
summer's day; nothing must spoil it. Viv wears
one of those bobbly nylon bathing suits, its bottom
rubbed ochre with sand. She is standing beside
her father, who is skimming pebbles over the
water. He chooses the flattest he can find and gives it to
her. His arm around her, he shows her how to do it.

'That's it,' he says. 'That's the way.'

Viv throws it.

Ann sees the pebble and comes up to them.

'It sank,' she says.

'No it didn't,' says her father. He passes Viv another
pebble and Viv throws it. 'Bravo!' he says.

'That one sank too!' cries Ann. 'It didn't jump at all.'

Her father takes no notice. Viv grimaces at Ann. This
time it is Viv who finds him a flat stone, and this time it is
he who throws it, with a flick of the wrist so that it skims
one, two, three times. This is quite right for a dad. But
Viv hadn't done it right.

'I saw she didn't!' Ann says again. It's so unjust that
her voice squeaks. She looks at Viv's slender, stork-like
legs, her smug buttocks rubbed with sand; she looks at
her father's neck, reddened by the sun.

'It's my turn,' she says. She stands next to them. She
too wears a bobbly swimsuit, like blisters on her, but she's
tubbier. It's only this summer, now she's ten, that she's
realized this. She picks up a flat pebble and throws it. Her
father has lit a cigarette; he has lost interest. And anyway
her pebble, of course, sinks.

They are newly married now, and the four of them are
on holiday in Devon. It is another perfect summer's day
and they are beside a river; khaki water dappled with
sunlight. Ken, who is good at these things, is making a
fire; he requires concentration as he pyramids the sticks
and the women are staying away. Ollie, who says he enjoys
being subservient, is fetching pieces of wood for him.

Ann, in her swimsuit, is sitting on the river bank, dabbling her feet in the water.

'Go on!' calls Ollie. 'Don't be a sissy.' He went to public school and sometimes it still shows, though not often.

Viv is standing at the water's edge. She is wearing a flowery, second-hand dress and holding her swimsuit. The sun catches the cloudy mass of her hair. She is as slender as a deer, caught unawares. But Ann is her sister and knows no adult is unaware.

Ken blows on the flame and straightens up, standing to look at his fire. Suddenly Viv pulls off her dress and her knickers and walks into the river.

'Christ, it's freezing!' she calls, and the men turn. She slips into the water and swims, gasping and laughing. 'Come on, Annie!'

But Ann sits there. She finds a stick and tosses it into the water which is now ribbing out, in circles, from Viv, who swims round and round, her long body yellow under the surface. Ann tosses another stick; it rocks in the water, rocked by Viv's larger waves.

'It's wonderful!' calls Viv. 'Come on.'

But Ann sits there, tossing twigs. Ollie is fetching wood; Ken has turned his back and is busying himself with the fire.

Finally Viv steps out, naked and dripping, her hair hanging wet down her breasts. High up in the trees a bird calls. She hurries over to the fireside, grabs a towel and sits down, her arms around her knees.

'Mmmm . . .' She edges nearer to the warmth and passes Ken a stick. He takes it from her and puts it on the fire. Then he turns away, his back to her, and starts blowing at the flames.

'It's lit already,' Viv says.

That night, in their bed-and-breakfast place, Ken makes love to Ann. He bites her shoulder and presses her into him, startling her with his passion. The room is black, she can't see his face and he doesn't say a word. He grips her tightly, hurting her sunburn.

The next morning Ollie tries to pay for them all.

'Of course not!' Ken's voice is loud in the little hall.

'It's only one night,' says Ollie. 'It's my treat.'

'Out of the question.'

Ann and Viv exchange glances, behind the men's backs. The four of them stand there as Ken finds his wallet. Against the flocked wallpaper hangs a barometer; it indicates: *Thunderstorms Ahead*.

Viv bent over and pulled the washing out of the machine. It was Sunday morning. She yanked at the damp, tangled lengths, the shirts entwined with each other, the socks plaited.

Ollie came up behind her and caressed her breasts. She pulled out a pair of dungarees, their fasteners clanking in the empty drum.

'Turns you on, does it?'

'What?' he breathed into her ear.

'Seeing me subservient.'

'I just feel physical in my track-suit.'

'Well go and be physical with your mates.' Ollie was going to play rugger.

He rubbed his face against the back of her head. 'You're my mate.'

She nudged him away and lifted the basket of clothes on to the table. 'Sublimate it on the playing field. That's what it's for.'

She started sorting the clothes into piles. He watched her.

'I know what you want,' he said.

'Tell me.'

'To be taken by force. You've always liked rough trade.' He sighed, and picked up his sports holdall. 'I'm just too well-bred.' He looked at his watch and started for the door.

'Listen,' said Viv. 'I've been thinking.'

He put down his holdall. 'I hate it when you say that. What do you want – a divorce? A child? A goat?'

'No. Why don't you ask Ken to join your team?'

'Ken?' He stared.

She nodded. 'He's been awfully depressed. Ann says so. He hasn't been working on his extension or anything. People are sorry for her but they forget about him. You know how buttoned-up he is.'

'On our team?'

'Why not? It might cheer him up. You're only a bunch of wanky journalists. He's fitter than the lot of you.'

Ollie paused. 'You ask him.'

'Why? I'm always doing everything.'

'He might think I was being – oh, condescending. You know how touchy he is.'

'But do you think it's a good idea?'

Ollie hesitated, then shrugged and nodded his head. She kissed him goodbye, and slid her tongue into his mouth.

Ann wondered what was missing from work and then realized: nobody told her any jokes. She had been back nearly a week now and they were all so kind, but if only they realized that the way they were careful made her lonely. She silently urged them to be normal; how long would it take? She had a sweet tooth and sometimes used to bring in peanut butter and jam sandwiches for lunch. In the past they'd groaned at this but now nobody teased her.

And there had been some alterations. Frances, the most homely, used to have a photo of her husband and son on her desk but now it had been removed. Ann wanted to say: please put it back; don't save my feelings.

And even Janine, who was not the type, made an effort. On Friday morning she was on the phone:

'Simone, you do what your nan says! You play up and I'll give you what-for!'

But when Ann passed the desk her voice sank to a whisper.

She found comfort in numbers, which never let her down unless the computer developed a fault, and that at least was nothing to do with an anxiety to please. Cool numbers blipping on to the screen, two and two equals four, they did, how simple, thousands slotted together to create more thousands, plus percentage interest. They worked, they were just, there was a bottom line that added up, then it could all be put away, you could clear your head and forget about it and start on the next. If she kept her eyes down and worked from one half-hour to the next, it was possible to look up and find that already nearly a morning had passed.

Late on Friday afternoon Derek called her into his office. He held up the mortgage application forms for Ferncroft Road.

'Janine did these, didn't she?'

Ann hesitated.

'Did she?'

Ann nodded.

'We must do something about that girl,' he said.

'She's got a lot of problems – you know, child to support, mother who's –'

'I know, I know.' He raised his hand. 'But don't we all. She's daffy, Ann, like half the girls here. Course she's got problems but look at you, how you've been coping.'

Ann was silent. Derek lit a panatella. 'Don't think I haven't noticed,' he said. 'That sunny smile hasn't fooled old Derek.'

Ann took the papers. 'I'll do them on Monday.'

'Can't trust them, Annie. Not like you.'

'I've just been here longer.'

'And it's not just me who's noticed. I think there may be some good news coming your way.'

26

'Why?'

'Know I went to the Dinner on Tuesday?'

Ann nodded.

'Heard some encouraging noises about our Annie here.'

'Really?'

'Don't look surprised. Though that blush is very becoming.'

'What did they say?' she asked.

'You'll find out. And now we know you won't be leaving us –' He stopped, and cleared his throat. 'Sorry.'

'Don't apologize.'

'Didn't mean to –'

'Don't be careful, please,' she said. 'Everyone's been so nice but sometimes I feel like screaming.'

He indicated the door. 'Don't do that or they'll think I'm misbehaving.'

It was five o'clock. Derek stood up and started to sort his papers together. He opened a drawer and took out a video cassette.

'Not another one,' said Ann.

'My dear, the weekend looms.'

'How's Mary?'

'The same, Annie. Just the same.'

Ann got up and took the mortgage form. 'And the boys?'

'Fine, fine,' he replied.

She looked at the cassette. 'What's it this time?'

'*The Sound of Music*. Trouble is, it always makes Mary cry.'

The cloakroom was tiny and Janine took up most of it. She was pulling on a satin skirt.

'Doing anything this weekend?' she asked.

'Just seeing my sister,' said Ann, edging past her to get her coat.

'She the one with all the kids?'

'Only two.'

'Seems like more. Always have to change the blotters when they've paid a visit.'

'Why?'

'They draw on them. Rabbits and stuff.'

Ann smiled. 'They keep rabbits.'

'Bet their rabbits don't wear ballet skirts.'

'The drawings do?'

Janine nodded, and started applying lipstick. 'Doesn't look like you, does she?'

'Everyone says that.' Ann edged back with her coat. 'So who're you seeing tonight?'

'Never guess where I met him. On the escalator. I'd got me heel stuck.'

'Thought you were seeing that frozen-food chap.'

'Him?' Janine pursed her glistening lips, inspecting them in the mirror. 'He's in Hull, getting a new company car.'

'While the cat's away . . .'

Janine looked at Ann in the mirror. 'Know something? I think you're perking up.'

The man in the pet shop was weighing up coloured gravels and putting them into plastic bags. Ken stood inspecting the tropical fish. He knew it was ridiculous, but nowadays he delayed going home. He knew he shouldn't.

'Look at them rats.'

'Not rats. It's gerbils.'

Two boys were behind him. 'Hoi, look at that one!'

'Dirty bugger.'

The man called across: 'You two – out!'

'What, us?'

'You.'

'We're with him.'

One of the boys moved over beside Ken. The air smelt of fruit gums. 'Hey mister, what's that one?'

28

'That one there?' said Ken. 'Isn't she a beauty. She's a Mozambique Mouthbrooder.'

'What?'

'So called because she incubates the fry in her mouth.'

'Yuk.'

'Marvellous, really.' He gazed closer. 'There's a world in miniature in there. See those bright little ones, like flashes of light?'

'Which?' The fruit breath came closer.

'Those. Guppies. Started with guppies when I was . . .', he looked at the boy, '. . . about your age. Every penny of my pocket money.' He turned back to the swaying weed. 'Young and eager,' he said.

The rasp of a match. The boy lit a cigarette.

'Out!' called the man.

Scuffling together, both boys left.

The man was now marking up prices on lumps of rocks. 'Thought you were their dad.'

'Oh no.'

'Cheeky sods.'

'No, nothing to do with me,' said Ken.

My dear, the weekend looms. There was Derek, with his house near the golf course in Potters Bar, and his species roses and his sad wife and his two bounding boys – Ann had seen their photograph. Their Saturday morning T V gave Mary a headache and their schooling cost him an arm and a leg. Freckled faces, smiling. There was Frances, creamy and content, who'd do her Sainsbury's shopping while her husband followed with the pushchair. He'd made the child's birthday cake this year, uneatable sponge but who cared? There was Mrs Maguire next door, Ann could hear her now, shouting at her children. How did they all fit into that house, with her husband unemployed and home all day? There was Janine. On Saturdays her ex came round; he took Simone out and then the little girl got stomach ache because he was trying, according to Janine, to buy her love with sweeties, and when Simone had a tantrum on Sunday then Janine knew who to blame it on. She said once:

'You know Annie, sometimes I envy you.'

'Why?'

'Just you and Kenny. Snug.'

Ken, his back to her, was standing at his aquarium. He was suspending a plastic bag in the water to equalize the temperatures. In the bag was a fish.

'Always feel like I'm making tea,' he said.

'Why?'

'Dunking the tea-bag.'

Ann laughed.

'That's a nice sound,' he said.

'What is?'

'You laughing.'

She paused. Then she continued sewing – one stitch, two. She kept her voice normal. 'It's something . . . well, I've been thinking about.'

'Tremendous news and about time too. You've been working there long enough.'

'I don't mean the job business. I mean something else.'

'What?'

She stopped sewing. 'But I don't know what you'll say.'

'Try me.'

'Can't you guess?'

'Nope.'

She kept her eyes on him – the luminous fish, blocked by his shoulder; his pale blue shirt; his stocky body that she thought she knew so well. She looked at the intent back of his neck. Was he listening? 'We could adopt.'

There was a silence.

'Ken, say something.'

Bubbles rose soundlessly in the aquarium. He didn't turn. 'I don't know what to say.'

'Have you thought about it?' she asked.

He nodded.

'You have?'

'Oh yes,' he said, 'I've thought of precious little else all week.'

'Really?' Her heart quickened. She went over to him.

'Yes,' he repeated.

'I could do it, I could love it, I –'

'Ann –'

'Black or white or brown . . . it would be ours.'

She stood beside him. Then he turned. 'I'm afraid . . .' He stopped.

'Don't be afraid. We'd both love it. We'd –'

He said slowly: 'I'm afraid you have a larger heart than me.'

There was a silence. The fish swam on serenely, their tails flicking.

Later that evening he went for a run. He thudded past pubs, their lit windows, the roar when the doors opened. He thudded past houses, their glowing, curtained interiors, the changing flicker of their TVs; he veered off along the high street, his breath rasping now . . . past the shuttered shops and the drifted litter and the all-night minicab office, a blare of neon and radio . . . past the take-away kebabs and chips, a glimpse of plants and chrome, a whiff of grease . . . oh, the whole sordid city, it passed in a jagged blur; how his feet hurt, how his lungs ached, the freezing air rasping in and out like a saw . . .

. . . He ran until he was running along unknown streets, under a railway bridge, past the stench of urine, and then buses were passing and lights dazzled and he thought his lungs would burst.

Then he sat down on a bench. It was cold and wet. He buried his head in his hands.

4 That night Ann dreamed she had a baby called Jonquil. She wheeled the carrycot to the supermarket; it was Saturday and crowded and she had a lot of shopping to buy if only she could remember it all. She knew time was getting short and her sister Viv was expecting her – she was waiting for her somewhere far outside London.

She loaded up her trolley. People pushed past her, voices chattered behind the aisles, her watch was ticking loudly and she must hurry. She paid for her shopping and took the bags down the street to the car. It was not until she had driven a long way, right out into the countryside, that she turned to the back seat and saw it was empty. She had left the baby behind.

She drove back, fast. She knew that Jonquil must be gone; someone must have stolen her by now. The supermarket had grown larger in her absence; it was in a different street, with trees outside. The aisles stretched for ever, the whisperings were louder, as if the packets of Persil were talking, and her legs were so heavy as she ran, and sometimes she heard mewlings and she knew now that babies must be there, not just Jonquil but other babies – she could hear them – but why did nobody take any notice? She tried to ask people but no sound came out of her mouth; her lips moved but people just stared at her as if she were mad; and as she ran her limbs were so heavy, as if her body was filled with sand, and just around the next corner she must surely find her. But there was nothing. No baby. Just aisles of shelves. And squashed amongst the tins, poking out like tongues, wedged here and there, she found plastic bags of knitting.

Viv's hair was bunched up on the top of her head and fixed with a child's red plastic clip.

'Come in, excuse the chaos.'

Ann followed her into the living room. 'Looks the same as usual.'

Though she only lived half a mile away she had not been to Viv's house for several weeks, not since she had gone into hospital, and she felt the old reactions rise like a taste in her mouth. It was almost reassuring, in a world which had changed so utterly, to find some familiar feelings left. She gazed around with a mixture of awe, exasperation and a kind of bemused envy. It was a large room, the whole ground floor, with the kitchen at the back, overlooking the garden, and a bay window overlooking the street. 'Lived-in' could be one description; Ken called it squalid, but that was after he had once risen from the settee and found a piece of buttered toast sticking to the seat of his trousers.

Breakfast had not been cleared away and the table was strewn with Sunday papers. There was a half-eaten croissant on the floor which Viv picked up and absentmindedly ate as she switched on the kettle. The walls were crowded with pictures – Indian hangings from Viv's mystic sixties days and an explosion of children's drawings: stiff-haired apparitions with spider hands, called Mummy and Daddy. There was a ripe smell of soiled sawdust from the hamster's cage on the dresser, and the pegboard was covered with reminders to Ban Cruise Missiles, buy bog roll, and use the services of Dyno-Rod Plumbing and Emergency Drain Clearance.

Ann started clearing away the breakfast plates.

'Sit down,' said Viv.

'I'm not an invalid any more.'

'It's not your mess. You've come to lunch.'

'I want to do it.' Ann filled the sink. The windowsill was cluttered with plants, parsley in a jam-jar of yellowish water, and some lanky mustard and cress growing from a saucer of cotton wool. Through this she could see the garden. She thought of her dream, and Viv waiting for her in the countryside, and how years ago Viv had waited for her behind the potting shed, in the bright sunlight of their childhood. Then she thought quite distinctly, for the first time in actual words: I can give a childhood to nobody.

'Here, let me do it.'

Viv was there, moving her aside and taking the brush. Ann had not started the washing-up.

'Sorry.'

'You dry.'

Ann said: 'Where are the girls?'

'Mucking about outside.'

'Don't you ever worry?'

'Worry?'

'That they'll get lost?'

Viv stopped, her hands in the water. 'Remember when I left Rosie in the greengrocer's?'

Ann thought for a moment, then she nodded. 'She was very young. I suppose you just couldn't believe you'd had one.'

'Something like that.' Viv nodded. 'How's it been at work?'

'Nobody told me any jokes.' She looked around. 'Where's the tea-towel?'

'Over the hamster's cage.' Viv pointed to the dresser. 'He only comes out at night, so they cover him up to make it dark. So he'll wake up.'

'But if he's covered up they can't see him.'

Viv laughed. 'They haven't figured that out yet.'

Ann lifted the tea-towel from the cage and peered in. 'He's asleep.' They laughed.

Suddenly Ann felt such a longing that it took away her breath. She sat down.

'What's the matter?' asked Viv.

Ann pretended she had seen something on the floor, and had just sat down to pick it up.

Viv fetched the coal from the cupboard under the stairs. As she loaded the scuttle she remembered: she had lost the girls in Spain.

34

Last summer . . . a wide, empty beach. She and Ollie arrived there early and left the girls for half an hour while they went back to their hotel to unpack. When they returned the beach had filled up with people, thousands and thousands of them. The girls had been swallowed up in the crowd of sunbathing bodies, none of whom spoke English. It had taken them two hours to find the girls, sitting quite still and shuddering with tears.

She shuffled some coal on to the fire and said: 'It was a nightmare.'

'I had a nightmare last night,' said Ann.

'What about?'

'I can't remember.'

Viv sat on the table, swinging her legs and drinking a glass of wine. The meat was beginning to hiss in the oven but she hadn't bothered to start the vegetables yet. She always did things at the last moment, whereas Ann would have peeled and prepared them all beforehand. How dull she seemed to herself, when she was with Viv. But then that had always been the case. Viv seemed to suck the colour from her. She should have become used to it now.

On this momentous Sunday, before everything changed for ever, she remembered looking at Viv swinging her legs in her faded jeans. Her messy hair pulled up on the top of her head, artfully artless; her charming face – a snub-nosed prettiness which men had called kittenish until she answered them back; that indefinable air she had always had, like many beautiful women, of being in the possession of a secret. It wasn't just her looks. Heads turned towards her like flowers towards the sun. She made others, by comparison, seem half-asleep. Even more beautiful women looked blanker; her life came from within. Ann could bear this; she had told herself so many times. For didn't she love her?

And besides, she had a husband of her own, who liked the way she prepared vegetables beforehand. And who said, infrequently but with some feeling, that he loved her.

'Wonder what they'll talk about?' said Ann.

'You can't talk, playing rugger. That's the point.'

'It's ridiculous – all these years they've hardly ever been together.'

'We've been there, that's why. And you know what we're like.'

Ann looked at her watch. 'Better lay the table.'

'Don't be subservient.'

'They'll be hungry,' said Ann.

'You sound just like my sixth form. They're becoming so docile. It's because we're doing *Jane Eyre*. They're getting worried they'll be a failure in men's eyes.'

Ann paused. 'I feel a failure.'

'Don't ever say that!'

'Ken doesn't say so, of course –'

'I'd kill him if he did.'

'He doesn't. It's me.'

'Oh Ann.' Viv jumped off the table and came towards her. But at that moment the front door burst open and the girls ran in.

'Hello Auntie Ann.' Rosie came up and hugged her.

Ann pressed her face against Rosie's cheek. Eight years old and she still smelt new and fragrant. Sweet, slow Rosie, whom she secretly loved the best, though she would never admit it to a soul. She turned to Daisy, and pulled something out of a carrier-bag. 'It's your turn this time, Daisy,' she said, giving her the dress she had been sewing this past week. 'I do hope it fits, you're growing so big.'

Daisy put on the dress; it was pink and frilly. She jumped up and down in front of the mirror.

Viv inspected her daughter. 'What a wonderful frock. You look like the heroine of a Georgette Heyer romance.'

Stung, Ann said: 'I do read other books, you know.'

'I know.'

'Not just those ones.'

'Just taking the piss.'

Ann frowned. 'I wish you wouldn't say that. Anyway, you read them too. Before you became the local intellectual.'

'Wasn't much competition in Watford,' laughed Viv. She looked around. 'Once I believed in romance. When anything was possible. Before all this.' She smiled. 'Remember reading them under the bedclothes? Remember *Belle of the Ballet*?'

'Ah yes . . .'

'With her tip-tilted nose and light dusting of freckles . . .'

Daisy said: 'Mum, why can't I do ballet?'

'Because you do dance.'

'I want to do ballet, in a ballet dress.'

Viv said: 'Ballet's regressive.'

'What?' Daisy climbed off the settee and wandered into the garden.

Viv said to her sister: 'Remember *Photo-Love* and *Valentine*? I loved Elvis because he was so oily and sexy.'

Ann said: 'I loved Cliff Richard.'

'That's because you were nice. Nice girls loved Cliff.'

'Nice girls who knew how to sew.'

They smiled.

Ann went on: 'Remember Dad caught us reading *Valentine* behind the shed?'

'He thought it was dirty and gave you a walloping.'

'Ah yes . . .'

'You always got the wallopings.'

'I was oldest,' said Ann.

'It wasn't fair, picking on you. Dad never was fair.'

Ann paused. 'I didn't mind.'

'I did.'

'You didn't!'

Viv paused. 'Well, I do now.'

There was a silence. Faintly, the girls' voices came from the garden. Viv drained her wine. 'It's not fair.'

'What isn't?'

'Life. He was right.'

'Fathers are supposed to be.'

There was a silence. Ann couldn't speak with the girls so near and the men soon returning. Besides, how could Viv help?

In the next street the church bells started ringing. Ann laid the tea-towel back over the hamster's cage. When she was younger she had had a hot, teenage love affair with God. None of her family had ever gone to church and so she had carried on her secret conversations in the dark. She had bargained into the blackness and prayed under the bedclothes. When she had had bad thoughts about Viv she had submitted to her own punishments, squeezing her belt knotches too tight. She had feared God with a passion so fierce it had made her dizzy, and she had starved herself to feel dizzier.

The church bells rang and Ann reached into her carrier-bag and brought out the trifle. She had made it that morning, piping whorls of cream around the top and decorating it with cherries. When had she lost her faith? It seemed like yesterday. She put the trifle into the fridge for lunch and thought: once I believed in God. Now I believe in food.

'. . . And he comes panting through the snow,' said Ken, 'puffing and panting, and she opens the door and says, "Where's the salami?"'

There was a roar of laughter. Ollie ate a handful of peanuts and thought: it's wonderful what a scrummage in the mud will do, followed by a pint. Such simple male reassurances. Living with Viv, he needed them.

Diz, the captain, leaned over and whispered: 'Where did you find him?'

'Who?'

'Our Kenneth here.'

'He's my brother-in-law,' said Ollie.

38

Diz stared. 'He's not!'

Ollie nodded. Over at the bar, Ken started another joke. He was one of the few men Ollie knew who improved with alcohol. Viv said he was like a car you had to hand-crank to get going, but once the engine was started it could outrun the lot of them. That was in her more polite moments.

'He's a natural,' said Diz. 'Can you bribe him to join the team?'

'He's not used to rugger,' said Ollie. 'He's a soccer chap.'

'That calibre, who cares?'

Ollie looked at Ken with new respect. And he could crack a joke. Put someone in an unfamiliar place, and after fourteen years they could still surprise you.

The front door slammed.

'Oh oh, here they come,' said Viv. 'Our Action Men.'

Ollie and Ken came in. Ken carried an off-licence bag, and they wore the sheepish look of those with three pints inside them.

'Good game?' Ann asked.

Ken nodded. 'We won.'

She smiled. 'How marvellous.'

He took a bottle of wine out of the bag. 'A modest contribution.' He looked at Viv and Ann. 'And what have you two girls been doing? Yackety-yak?'

'Christ,' said Viv.

'Watch it,' said Ollie to his brother-in-law.

Ken turned to him. 'They're angry with us. We're in the doghouse.'

'No,' said Viv, a cigarette between her lips as she drained the sprouts. 'I think you're sweet.'

Ken looked disconcerted. Ann willed him to take care.

'So he comes charging down the field,' said Ken.

Ollie turned to Viv. 'That's that twit from the *New Statesman*.'

'But you two saw to him,' said Viv.

'Tall bloke,' nodded Ken, 'built like a beanpole. No muscle on him.'

'Whereas you,' she said, 'small but perfectly formed . . .'

'Sorry about my height, Viv,' he said stiffly, 'but I do keep myself in trim.'

The girls came in. Ollie raised his eyebrows at the dress. 'Wow Dais, you look like a middle-aged gospel singer.'

'Ollie!' said Viv.

They sat down to lunch. Ken glanced at the clock; this was one of Viv's three o'clock starts.

'I refuse to be intimidated,' said Ollie. 'In this murky, uncertain world, rugger's good clean fun.'

'It's the last remnant of your poncy school,' said Viv, 'I've got rid of all the rest.'

'Anyway,' said Ollie, 'it's the only exercise I get.'

Viv said: 'The only exercise I get is sex and the stairs.'

Ollie laughed. Ken looked at her warningly. 'Little ears, Viv.'

Ann said quickly: 'What about school? That's exhausting, surely?'

'That's nerves,' said Viv, 'like being on stage.'

'And your allotment?'

'That's backache.'

Ollie turned to Ken: 'They were brought up in a bungalow.'

'I know,' said Ken. 'What do you mean?'

'Don't ask me,' he said, and added darkly: 'I'm sure it affected them.'

Viv said: 'Twelve acres in Hertfordshire sure affected you.'

Ann smiled at them. 'Children!'

Viv turned to her. 'We thrive on class warfare, Ollie and me. It's the dynamic of our marriage. We're a microcosm of contemporary Britain. I climbed up from my class, with aspirations.' She pointed to Ollie. 'He climbed down from his, with guilt.'

Ann smiled. 'Stop pretending you quarrel on these elevated lines.'

'It's usually much more sordid,' said Ollie. 'Like who's going to make who feel resentful for not being helped to clean the kitchen.'

Ann looked around. 'Seems you've spared yourself that one.' They laughed. Daisy leant forward and took a potato.

'Er, Daisy love,' said Ken, 'there's a spoon for that.'

Ollie turned to him. 'So you think you'll join our team?'

'You've seen it,' said Viv. 'Typical middle-class bunch of wankers. Softies, lefties, media men. Belligerent yet indecisive.'

'The only thing they can play with are words,' said Ollie. 'We need you.'

'I too have opened a book,' said Ken. 'Despite the cloth cap and overalls.'

'Ken!' Ann put her hand on his arm.

'Don't be so touchy,' said Viv, leaning forward and grabbing a potato from the bowl. 'So male. He doesn't want you as his bit of rough. You're good.'

'You haven't seen me play.'

'I've seen the others,' she replied. 'Anyone'd be good compared to them.'

'Thanks,' said Ken.

'And I can tell by that muscle tone.' She ran her hand across his chest. He stiffened. 'I'm allowed to feel you. I'm your sister-in-law.'

Ollie laughed. 'She's always doing that. I call it touching people up. She calls it body language.'

Ken smiled and ran his finger across his moustache. He always did that when he was uneasy. Then he said: 'I'd be delighted to join your team, if they'll have me.'

Ollie raised his glass. 'Let's drink to that.'

★

Ollie went into the hall to get some more coal. Viv joined him as he scrabbled in the cupboard.

'I wish you hadn't said that,' she hissed.

'Said what?'

'About Daisy's dress. It was bloody rude. Ann made it for her.'

'It was only a joke.' Grunting, he lifted up the coal scuttle.

'You were making fun of her,' said Viv.

'But you do,' he said. 'Her prim little house and her Scenes of London place-mats.'

'I'm allowed to,' hissed Viv. 'I'm her sister.'

'And?'

'Sisters can do it. Other people can't.'

Ollie looked at her. 'And I'm "other people"?'

''Fraid so.'

Ken and Ann sat, with their cups of coffee, in front of the fire. Ken gazed into the flames. 'Had one of those gas-effect things in the pub. It fooled me.'

'Listen, Ken.' She lowered her voice. 'Don't get angry . . .'

'What?'

'You shouldn't criticize their children.'

'What do you mean?'

'Ssh!' she hissed. 'I mean, when Daisy took that potato.'

'Why shouldn't I? It was bloody bad manners. Anyway, you do.'

'What?'

'You put the girls right,' he said, 'and quite properly, in my opinion.'

'That's different,' she said.

'Why?'

'I mean – well, Viv's my sister.'

'So? They're my nieces. If I don't, who else will? In this madhouse.'

'Ssh!'
Ollie and Viv were returning.

It was dusk by now, and Viv and Ann had left the two
men to do the washing-up. They wandered along the aisles
of the garden centre, the rain pattering on its roof. Beyond
the displays of coiled hoses rose up palm trees, shiny and
tall, and cascades of ferns. The place had a white, hard
light. Ann thought of the supermarket in her dream and
the hot pulse of her search. Why had she been searching
for Viv?

'The dizzying possibilities,' said Viv's voice beside her.
She was inspecting a rack of seed packets, and lifted one
out. *'Produces a rich profusion of sky-blue blossoms,'* she
read out, *'from earliest spring to the first frosts.'*

Ann smiled. 'You believe it?'

Viv nodded. 'Every year." She put the packet back.
'It's optimism. Or stupidity.'

'Or faith.'

Viv had come here to buy seed potatoes for her allotment. They wandered on.

Ann said: 'Last night I dreamed of a baby called Jonquil.'

Viv stopped. 'What a lovely name.'

She looked at Ann, then led her to a bench. It was
white, wrought-iron, with a price-tag. They sat down.
For some moments Ann didn't speak. She was realizing –
later she remembered her exact thoughts – that one day
she must bring herself to buy plants for her extension
room because that would now be its purpose. It would
probably look quite decorative and, as Ken said, whatever
they used it for, it couldn't fail to increase the value of
their house.

She said: 'I think I'm going mad.'

Ken wiped a plate dry. 'Hope she doesn't go mad at
that place.'

'Annie?'

'Her and her Access card.'

Ollie passed him a bowl. 'Ann never goes mad, surely.'

'Not alone.'

'Ah, but under the evil influence of her sister . . .'

Ken rubbed the bowl dry. 'Well, Viv's the one with the green fingers. Things grow, for Viv.'

Ollie nodded and passed Ken another bowl. Ken looked through the foliage at the garden. He willed Ollie not to start talking. Ollie liked asking the sort of probing questions that made Ken's armpits hot.

Ken cleared his throat and pointed to the rabbit pen. 'I see there's some new arrivals. How many this time?'

'Eight.'

'Breed like rabbits, eh?'

Ollie nodded. 'The kids are getting blasé about the Miracle of Birth.'

Ann said: 'I didn't think it could get worse, but it does. Every day. Nothing means anything. I wake up . . .' She paused. 'There's Ken beside me but he seems miles away.' They were sitting on the 'For Sale' bench. Ann turned the price-tag over and over in her hand. 'He can't help.'

'No,' said Viv.

'Nobody can. Not him, not you.'

'I wish I could.'

Ann took a breath, then said in a rush: 'Yesterday I was watching Mrs Maguire in her garden. She's always screaming at her children, and I looked at her back view, her big broad back, she had her legs apart, and I hated her. I did, Viv. I hated her for taking them for granted. I felt I was going mad.'

'You're not mad!'

'He won't talk about it, you see.'

'And he won't consider adopting?'

A couple strolled past them, pushing a trolley of peat bags. Ann and Viv sat in silence.

Finally Ann said: 'No.' She paused. 'He minds.'

'I thought he would.'

'Whose it is.'

Viv nodded. Ann fiddled with the price-tag. 'He does love children.'

'I know.'

'Even though he may be, well, severe sometimes. But that's because he wants the best for them.'

Beside her, Viv nodded. She rummaged in her bag and brought out her cigarettes.

Ann said slowly: 'He was so excited this time.'

'I know.'

'Telling everybody. He even told the neighbours and you know what he's like with them.'

Viv nodded, and blew out smoke.

'That's what's made it so difficult. He's clammed up. If we could share it, if I knew he felt it too. This feeling of . . .'

'Of what?'

Ann paused. 'Emptiness. Nothing being worth doing.'

Viv drew on her cigarette. 'Worse than last time?' she asked finally.

Ann thought for a moment. 'Yes.'

A couple passed, the man holding the hand of a little girl.

Ann said: 'She'd be that age by now.'

Viv nodded.

Ann said: 'I still think of her, every day.'

'So do I.'

'Even though she was hardly there. Hardly born.'

They sat in silence. Viv smoked the rest of her cigarette. They had seldom spoken about Ann's stillborn child, and there seemed even less to say now. After that birth, three years ago, there had still been hopes of another. Viv gazed down at her potatoes; they lay in their string bag like a clutch of eggs. She dropped her cigarette and ground it out with her foot.

'Just emptiness,' said Ann.

Viv put her arm around Ann, who sat there stiffly.

Then Ann said: 'He could still have one, of course.'

Viv nodded. There was another silence. A man passed, wheeling a sack of peat. An assistant passed, holding a bunch of keys. They watched a woman stroll by, carrying a fern in a pot.

'If only it was that easy,' said Viv.

'What?'

Viv pointed. 'Buy a baby and take it home.'

Ann's voice rose: 'Ready potted.'

Suddenly they both started to laugh hysterically. They sat there side by side, shaking and hiccuping, gasping for breath. Viv felt her sister lean against her at last, her shoulders jerking; the tears started to run down their faces.

The garden centre was closing. Above the glass roof the sky had darkened. Customers averted their eyes from the sight of two women, sitting together and now weeping.

The church bells were ringing for the early evening service. Ollie sat on the settee, reading the *Sunday Times* Colour Magazine. Ken furtively glanced at the clock: six. He willed Ann to hurry up. He felt a kind of queasy loneliness. At first he thought it was the result of all that drink but at last, with surprise, he identified the feeling as homesickness. He hadn't felt it so strongly for years. There was something about this place that unsettled him and made him long for his own safe lounge. He stood at the bookshelves, leafing through the *Portable Orwell*. Despite Viv's preconceptions he had actually read some Orwell and had always admired the passion of the man. At least Ollie had stopped talking.

Daisy wandered in and said: 'I can whistle now.'

'Can you?' He closed the book. 'Show me.'

She whistled.

'Excellent,' he said.

'Can you whistle?'

'Of course.' He whistled 'Hills of the North Rejoice', a tune that never failed to stir him.

'What's that?' she asked.

'A hymn.'

'What's a hymn?'

He stared. 'You don't know?' He looked at Ollie, who was busy reading. He turned back to Daisy. 'You don't know any hymns?'

She shook her head.

Ann unwrapped her plant and put it on the windowsill. Ken was sitting in the armchair reading the *Sunday Express*. From behind the page he asked: 'What's it called?'

'What?'

'The plant.'

'I don't know.' She looked at the label. 'Can't pronounce it.' She threw away the cellophane. 'I just liked it.'

He turned a page. Then he said: 'They don't know any hymns.'

'Who don't?'

'Your nieces. Isn't that sad?'

She looked at him. 'But you're an atheist.'

'Agnostic actually.' He turned another page. 'I still think it's sad.'

She nodded, and turned back to look at the plant. It had little buds coming. She couldn't think of anything to do. It was becoming familiar, this feeling of panic. Nine o'clock in the evening and there was nothing in the world which seemed worth the effort. The only way to quell the panic was to tell herself: it's Sunday evening, that's why.

She wanted to ask Ken if he felt the same. But then she realized: if he did, it wouldn't make any difference. And that gave her the greatest fear of all.

★

Viv lay awake. It was the dead centre of the night. Beside her she heard Ollie's regular breathing; she heard the stirring of her children in the next room. The creaks and sighs of an old house; how many children it must have kept temporarily safe. She heard a car hooting. She heard her father's voice, shouting at Ann: *Life's not fair, young lady, and the sooner you realize that the better!* Ann, as young and tender as Rosie, her sweet wide face perplexed, for how could anyone bear to tell her the truth?

Down in the garden a cat yowled. The house breathed with its sleeping souls; she thought of Ann, washing her doll's petticoat and hanging it up to dry, forgiving Viv who heard her murmurings under the bedclothes at night, speaking to a God she had to believe existed, for where else could one find the rightness of things? There had to be a rightness, otherwise one just believed in tossing a coin, and who could survive believing in a cruel flick of the wrist?

A bed creaked and in the doorway stood Rosie in her Mothercare nightie. She rubbed her eyes and came over to Viv.

'I had a horrible dream,' she said.

'Come here.'

Viv pushed back the bedclothes and Rosie climbed in, as she so often did.

'I dreamed there were lots of long men . . .'

'Ssh . . .'

She put her arms around Rosie and smoothed the hair from her forehead. But her daughter wouldn't be calmed; she turned her head from side to side.

'And then one of them dropped down from the tree . . .'

'Ssh . . .'

She willed Rosie to close her eyes. She must smooth it all away, because in a few years it would no longer be possible.

★

That's nerves, like being on stage. All the next morning
Viv mouthed the words. Never had she felt such an act-
ress, standing in the classroom with the faces in front of
her and her eyes on the clock. Later she could remember
nothing she had said, it had passed in a blur until lunch-
break and she was driving the car to Wood Green High
Road.

She parked opposite the building society. For a moment
she sat there, her throat tight. Now she had made up her
mind she felt a curious, hot shyness. But she also felt that
she had just woken up. She got out of the car.

'What's the matter?' Ann stared at her through the glass.
'What's happened?'

Viv stood at the window like a customer. She felt she
should write down her news and slide it through, like a
cash withdrawal. She would see Ann unfolding the piece
of paper; she would see Ann's face change.

'Nothing's the matter,' she said. 'Come out to lunch.'

'What? Can't hear through this glass.'

'Are you free for lunch?'

Ann nodded and went to get her coat. A minute later
they were getting into Viv's old Peugeot. On its bonnet
someone had traced, with their finger, I AM DIRTY.

Viv did not start the engine. Ann sat beside her.

'I've been thinking,' said Viv.

'What about?'

'I've been thinking all night and I don't know why I
didn't think of it before.'

'What?'

Viv paused. 'About the baby.'

Ann stared at her. 'What baby?'

Viv said: 'It's so obvious.'

'What is?'

'I'll have it for you.'

'Have what?'

Viv said slowly: 'The baby.'

There was a silence. Later, Viv remembered watching a

traffic warden walk towards the next car, starting to write in her book. She remembered a blur of red buses.

Ann said: 'What did you say?'

'I'll have the baby for you.'

5 Never had an afternoon taken so long to pass. At last it was four o'clock. The bell rang, doors slammed, voices echoed along the corridors. Viv hurried back to the staffroom but Madeleine, as usual, was on the phone.

'. . . Of course I'm ready for a relationship,' she was saying, 'but not a commitment. Look I can't talk now . . .'

But she would. Viv fidgeted nearby. She felt big with her news, blushing with it. She clutched her ten pence, hot in her hand.

Harold, who worked with her in the English Department, came in and went to the lockers. He paused and turned round.

'Viv dearest, I might be an obliging chap but I draw the line at correcting your homework.'

Viv stared at the lockers. 'Christ. Sorry.'

She removed her books from his locker and put them into her own, one below. 'My mind's gone,' she said.

He patted her shoulder. 'Don't worry, we're all suffering from terminal fatigue.' He looked at her more closely. 'Or have 4b been practising their sharing skills and passing you some of their substances?'

Viv laughed. Madeleine was still on the phone.

'Bright-eyed one,' he went on, 'are you going straight away or do you want a cup of tea?'

She looked at the phone. She had to ring Ollie. 'Er, I'll stay a moment.'

'I'm not rejecting you,' Madeleine was saying, 'I'm just saying I've got to prepare my tests tonight.'

'. . . What a bunch of tarts,' said Harold.

'What?'

'I said, guess who I saw in the pub last night with guess who?'

Alan, their Head of Department, came in.

'Dare I tell him?' asked Harold.

'Don't worry,' said Alan. 'I'm inoculated. The I LEA does it for free.'

'I was telling Viv, I saw the cream of our womanhood, Eileen and Yvonne from the Upper Sixth, in the pub last night with the schoolkeeper.'

'Don't blame them,' said Viv. 'He's got a lovely little bum *and* he comes with a free house.'

'Know something, Viv Meadows?' said Alan, half joking, but you could never be sure. 'You're worse than the lot of them.'

'She's being very skittish this afternoon,' said Harold. 'I think 4b slipped her something.'

Madeleine put the phone down. Viv darted to it.

'Ollie? Hello. Listen, will you be late? What's happening tonight?'

Ollie said he was going to a gallery opening – one of the staff photographers had a show. 'What's up?' he asked. His voice seemed faint and crackly, as if he were a hundred miles away. She wondered how she could ever tell him.

'Oh, nothing,' she said. 'See you later.'

Ken was still out, visiting sites. Ann put down the phone. If only she could simply hear his voice; though what she could tell from his voice she had no idea. She just wanted to know he was there, and that at some point she could speak. It was 4.30. She pictured him tramping up and down some rubble-strewn house, innocent of her news and therefore incomplete.

Derek came over to her desk. 'Er, Annie.'

'Yes?'

He showed her a sheet of paper. 'There's a little

something here that puzzles me. You worked this out?'

She nodded. 'Just now.'

'Correct me if I'm mistaken, but shouldn't these,' he pointed, 'be in hundreds?'

She stared at the paper. 'I am an idiot.'

'Don't be silly. Rather a relief really.'

'Why?'

He touched her shoulder. 'To see that even you can make a mistake sometimes.'

Faces stared. They grimaced, they grinned. They pointed their fingers at her. Their hair was spiked and their cheeks painted: tattoos, swirls. Sometimes their chests were bare; that was when they were African tribesmen. Sometimes they wore chains and pins; that was when they were punks. Viv moved from photo to photo, pretending to look. She tried to feel casual.

'All this narcissism.' Diz came up behind her. He was Ollie's magazine editor.

She pointed to the photos. 'These?'

'Us.' He indicated the guests: smiles, glistening lips, small whoops of laughter. 'Who's looking at the pics?'

'I am,' she lied. Now she saw Ollie.

He came over, eyebrows raised. 'What're you doing here?'

'She couldn't resist these beautiful bodies,' said Diz.

'Don't inflame her,' said Ollie. 'You're heading for trouble.'

Diz passed him a glass of wine. 'Half an hour with the Pentels and you too could be an art object.'

'Sex object.' Ollie sipped. He looked at Viv over the rim of his glass. She smiled and wished she hadn't come. 'She wants something. I know that look.'

Diz refilled Viv's glass. She drank. 'I just felt like it,' she said. She wanted to shout her news and silence the room. She wanted never to tell anybody.

★

Giggling, they stumbled into the hall.

'Where're the kids?' Ollie asked.

'Julie's got them for the night.'

They went into the living room and she started pulling off his jacket.

'Hey, what're you doing to me?' he mumbled.

'Come on, now's our chance.'

'You're pissed. This is rape within marriage.'

'You're always going on about knee trembles.' She pulled him on to the sofa, unbuttoning his shirt.

'I knew you were turned on by primitive men.' She gave up with the shirt and pulled it over his head. His voice came out muffled. 'All gay, you know, those tribes. Poncing about – ow,' as she yanked, 'poncing about with their little mirrors.'

Viv got his shirt off and silenced his mouth, kissing him. She ran her cold fingers down his back, feeling him flinch. She would heat him up.

'Women are just for reproductive purposes,' he muttered, lifting himself up so she could slide his trousers off. 'Just bodies, just wombs...' She pulled off his shoes. 'Just duty ... it's only what I'm doing, after all ...' She eased off his underpants ... 'Just doing my duty ...'

She flung aside a child's shoe and climbed on him, pushing back his head. Over on the dresser the wheel scraped as the hamster, now wide awake, went round and round.

'Candles,' said Ken, nodding appreciatively. He sat down. 'We ought to do this more often.'

'You like it?' The lights were low. Ann lifted the lid from the *coq au vin*. 'Ken, I wanted to ask you something.'

'Tell you what. Let's be really romantic.'

He jumped up and went over to the music centre. He searched amongst the records and held up a Simon and Garfunkel. 'Remember when we first heard this?'

She nodded.

'At Bob and Jenny's.' He smiled. 'There you were, looking through the records and feeling as spare as me. In that red dress with the things on it.'

'Listen, Ken –'

He switched on the stereo. The lights fused.

'Blast!'

Viv and Ollie lay on the sofa, their limbs damply locked. Clothes lay strewn on the floor. There was silence, but for the scrape, scrape of the hamster.

'Primitive enough for you?' asked Ollie at last.

'Ollie. I've got something to tell you.'

'Oh no, you *were* buttering me up.' He gestured at the clothes.

'No. I just feel . . . so excited. Shall I tell it to you straight?'

'Go on. Get it over with.'

She laid her head on his chest. Her cheek felt his thumping heart. She said: 'I want to have a baby for Ann.'

'What?'

She lifted her head. 'It suddenly seemed so obvious. It'd be like having a baby for ourselves.' She paused and then spoke, her voice low. 'I could do it, Ollie. We could do it.'

'You want to what?'

'Have a baby for her. We've worked it out. I could take a couple of months off work, then breastfeed it for six weeks and –'

'We? Who?'

'Me and Ann. We had lunch today.'

'You can't be serious.'

'I am. I've never been so serious in my life.'

He moved her back and stared at her. At last he said: 'What?'

54

She took a breath. 'It's possible, Ollie. I know I could do it. What do you think it must be like for her? The finality? The hopelessness?' She spoke slowly. She had rehearsed this scene all day, but now she couldn't remember how she was going to put it. 'She thinks she's going mad.'

'It's you who's going mad.'

'Just when she thought that this time, at last, it would be all right.' She sat up, beside him. She looked at his watchful face, his brown, messy hair. 'What do you think it must be like, seeing our children grow up? Everybody's children?'

They sat there. A car passed in the street; the hamster scraped.

'Ollie, it's actually possible to help her, to change somebody's life. Don't you see?'

He didn't reply.

She spoke in a rush. 'You and me, we're always talking. Words, words, that's all anybody does. Well, at last we can actually *do* something.' She lifted her hand and turned his face towards her. 'Don't you see how lucky we are, how unfair it is? Don't you see we can do something about it, just because I'm a woman?'

'You can't.'

'Just because I'm a woman,' she said again. 'I can choose to. There's a marvellous freedom about it.'

'Free? Being pregnant?'

She nodded. Her whole body concentrated – every fibre, every nerve. 'Listen, Ollie.' She cupped his face in her hands but he jerked away. 'It can be done.' She spoke urgently. 'It can.' She searched his face; she could tell nothing from it.

'Think I'll put on my underpants.' He moved aside, reached down and pulled them on. It sealed him away and made her more naked. He sat down again on the other end of the sofa.

She looked at the floor and thought: which way will he

55

turn? At this particular moment she had no idea. It was as if she had met him ten minutes ago. It shocked her, that he could be so unfamiliar, when for fourteen years he had been her best friend.

'You are an extraordinary woman,' he said at last. 'And I thought I knew you.'

She fumbled amongst the clothes for her cigarettes and lit one. She blew out the smoke. 'You do.'

'You want us to have a baby, and then just give it to Ann and Ken?'

Suddenly she grabbed his hand. 'Isn't it a wonderful idea? Isn't it exciting?' His hand didn't move. 'We're always going on about – oh, how we should break down the old systems, nuclear families, how we should be experimental –'

'Ah, so this is an experiment.'

'No!' she shouted. 'It's real!' She stopped, and adjusted her voice lower. 'It could be,' she said softly. 'If we let it.'

He shook his head. 'Extraordinary woman.' He was half smiling, but that made her uneasy. 'Why don't we save the bother and just give them Daisy?' He raised his eyebrows, his voice jauntier. 'And throw in a set of place-mats and some Green Shield stamps? And come to think of it, the milkman looks a lonely sort of chap, we could give him Rosie – no –' he held up his hand, his voice rising – 'no, we'll hold an auction for her, plenty more where she came from –'

'Ollie!'

'We'll put ourselves in the Yellow Pages and say we'll deliver anywhere in the London area.'

'Ollie.'

He stopped, breathing heavily. Then he started to laugh. Warily, she smiled. He leaned forward, shaking, and put his head in his hands. She gazed at the bumps of his backbone, at his long lean thighs. He could be sobbing or he could be laughing. It unnerved her that she couldn't guess which.

56

'Ollie,' she said gently. 'Talk to me. Tell me what you think.'

He stayed sitting there, his head buried. Finally he looked up. His face had changed; as if it had collapsed and been reassembled.

'Know something, Viv? I haven't dared tell you, all these years.'

'What?'

He stayed gazing at her. Finally she dropped her eyes. He said: 'You frighten me.'

Ken stood on a step-ladder in the hall, fiddling with the fuse box. Ann held up the candle.

'Blasted bloody thing,' he muttered. 'Just one of those days.'

'Poor Ken.'

'Screwdriver please.'

She passed it to him.

'My godfathers, what a day. First Bob prangs the van, then there's a gas leak at that place in Willesden. Panic stations. Then – wait for it – but who gets a flat tyre?'

'Oh no.'

'Muggins here.'

The lights came on. She sighed and blew out the candle. How could she talk to him now?

'Sorry.' He climbed down from the ladder. 'Ruined that lovely meal.'

'It's not ruined,' she lied.

She told him in the darkness, in bed. She prayed into the blackness that he would listen, that he would simply let her finish speaking. She pushed her feet round and round the cool edges of the sheets; the electric blanket was on and she was hot. She thought: how can I think about being hot at a time like this? She thought how in the past she had bargained with God under the sheets, long ago now, and how Ken's body had moved into hers – oh, how

57

many hundreds of times? *With my body I thee worship.*
Under this sheet they had pressed their warm limbs together. Mouth to mouth, life had begun.

She began.

'Ken.'

'Mmm . . .' He shifted drowsily.

'Ken, I must talk to you.'

'Now?'

'There never seems to be the right moment.'

He turned over. 'What is it?'

'It's about this baby business.'

He paused. 'I'm sorry, Ann. I just can't do it.'

'It's too late anyway. I rang an adoption society.'

'What? When?'

'Yesterday,' she said. 'The latest age for a woman is
thirty-five. That gives us less than a year.'

'You sure about this?'

'Yes.'

'Can't be. I'll phone them up.'

She said, 'It's too late.'

'It can't be!'

'You refused anyway.'

'But . . . oh Annie.'

'It doesn't matter,' she said.

'It does!'

'It's too late, it doesn't matter.' She took a breath. 'At
least, it needn't matter.'

'What?'

By now her eyes had become used to the darkness and
she could make out his shape beside her. But she kept her
gaze on the ceiling. 'Would it seem like adoption if Viv
had the baby for us?'

She turned to look at him. Beyond his head she could
see the green numbers pulse on their digital clock. 11.51
changed to 11.52.

He said: 'You're joking.'

'I'm not. Nor is she.'

58

She felt his hand move to her forehead. He stroked her. 'Annie darling, just get some sleep.'

'She means it.'

Suddenly he sat up and switched on the light. She blinked. His face stared down at her.

'What's she on about?'

'She means –'

'She been up to her tricks?'

'What?'

'Putting ideas into your head?'

'No. She's thought it out.'

'Oh yes?' His voice rose squeakily. 'Funny sort of thinking. Still, I wouldn't put anything past her.'

'Ken –'

'You're far too sensible to listen to her.'

'But we've talked! She's offered to. She'll have it, and breastfeed it –'

'That's enough!'

'But –'

'Let's not hear the sordid details.'

'Don't get angry. I'm just . . .' She looked at his reddened face.

'You two, sometimes . . .' He paused. 'What've you girls been up to?'

'Don't call us girls.'

'What the hell's she playing at?'

'I'll explain –'

'Explain tomorrow.'

'But –'

'Not now. Please.' He put his arms around her. His voice softened. 'Look, I didn't mean to shout, but I just don't like to see you upset. It's you I'm worried about, darling.'

He stroked her arm, pushing up the sleeve of her nightie. She flinched, but lay still. He went on stroking; he shook his head, smiling faintly. She wished he would stop looking at her like that. But she must not move.

59

'You've been through so much,' he said. 'Let's forget your sister for a bit, put it all out of our minds.' He kissed her cheek. 'You're the one I love, remember.'

She willed herself to put her arms around him. For the first time in their marriage, as his hand slid down her breast, she felt like a whore.

She leaned over him and put out the light.

Babies are crawling over each other, piles of babies. They are whimpering softly. Chubby, bendy limbs and bright eyes. The room is as high and blue as the sky. Won't they get chilly? Viv searches through the babies, panic-stricken. They are naked and they all look alike. On each arm – oh how soft those arms are – on each there is a tattoo, and she must learn how to read them, because one baby is hers. But when she looks closely, the tattoos are just squiggles, meaningless. She knows that somewhere she must find her own name. That baby will be hers, but time is running short and she must get it out of here. She must get it home.

She woke abruptly. She was damp with sweat. The house was silent and she knew her girls were gone. She pushed Ollie but he stayed asleep. She shook his shoulder.

'Ollie! Where are the girls?'

He turned over. 'At Julie's, remember?' He sat up and put on the light. 'Got to get them before breakfast.'

They looked at the clock. It was half past four. He turned off the light and lay back.

A moment later she thought he had gone back to sleep. But she was wrong; the duvet dragged as he turned over, away from her. He spoke with his back to her, his voice surprisingly clear.

'Viv.'

'What?'

'Don't you see?'

The duvet shifted as he turned his head and then moved round again to face her. His knee knocked against hers.

'Sorry,' she said. It was too dark to see him clearly; as the girls were away they had turned off the landing light.

'One fact, in all this, seems to have escaped your notice,' he said.

'What do you mean?'

'You know perfectly well that . . .' He stopped, sighed, and spoke again. 'That once you had a baby, *if* you had one . . .'

A silence. 'What?' she said.

'You'd never bear to give it up.'

There was another silence.

'You know that,' he said. 'Don't you?'

6 All over London people were going to work. It was a damp, mild winter morning. Girls gazed out of the windows of buses; they rubbed their hands on the misted glass. Cars revved up in traffic jams; from them came the mixed chatter of their radios. The city's heart beat, quickening. It knew nothing of Ollie's head, which ached from the previous night's cheap wine and disorientating talk. He was swallowed up as he descended into the Underground. The man standing on the escalator in front of him knew nothing; how surprising that it was all the same. Ollie gazed at the uncomprehending back of the man's neck and turned to look at the advertisements for bulging underpants and American musicals – *Fourth Great Year* – and then a photo of a woman's face and the words *Pregnant and Worried About It?*

Ken entered his office, a Portakabin in the works yard. Archie was already there, sifting through the mail.

'What a day,' said Archie. 'What a bummer that was. I

go home and I wouldn't have been surprised if my old lady told me she's expecting quads.'

'Quads?' asked Ken, hanging up his coat.

'If she is, she's keeping it dark.'

Ahead of Ken lay a day of banter, and four site visits, and orders from the depot. How could it sound so normal?

Viv sat beside Yvonne, whose essay she was reading. Yvonne smelt of eau-de-Cologne and cigarettes; it made Viv queasy.

Mr Rochester is macho, she read, *like a volcano which is about to explode.* She pointed to the page. 'Shouldn't that be "erupt"?'

Yvonne shrugged. By turning her wrist unobtrusively, Viv could see her watch. Ten minutes before the end of the lesson. Then she could phone Ann and find out how Ken had reacted. Did he erupt or explode? Dare she phone at all?

Ann tried to phone Viv, but the first time there was no reply in the staffroom and the second time someone told her that Viv was still teaching. Ann tried to concentrate on her work.

The next time she looked up, there was her father. He was standing at one of the customer windows. She jumped up and hurried over.

'Dad!' She smiled through the glass. 'This is a nice surprise.'

'Just thought, well, I'd pop round.'

She stared at him. For one moment she thought that he must know and that he had come here to talk about it. But that was surely impossible. She hurried round to the interconnecting door and unlocked it.

'Trying to keep me out?' joked Douglas.

'Awful, isn't it?' she said, indicating the electronic lock.

He came into the office and looked around. 'Like the décor.'

'We had it done up – oh, three years ago. Would you like some coffee?'

'Putting you out?'

'Of course not.' She smiled at him. She saw little of her father, and even then it was mostly at Viv's house.

He pointed to the customer windows. 'I should be out there.'

'Of course not.'

He paused. She poured the coffee. 'What I mean is . . .' He took the cup. 'Well, there's something I'd like to ask you.'

'What about?'

'A little . . . business matter.'

She stared at him. 'Oh.'

'I'll come straight to the point. What's the chance of me getting a mortgage?'

'Goodness.'

She stared at his creased face and grey hair. Her mum was right about the sideboards.

'You going to buy your flat?' she asked.

He stirred his coffee, gazing into the cup. 'Not exactly. I was, well . . . thinking of moving.'

'How exciting.'

'Just thinking.'

'Where?'

'Nothing's finalized yet.' He put aside the spoon and looked up. She thought: it's years since he's looked at me and actually asked me a question. 'So what do you think?'

'It depends on the size of the loan and the repayment period,' she said.

'It wouldn't be out of the question, for an old dog like me?'

'If you give me more facts I'll make some calculations.'

'Think you can put in a word for me with what's-his-name, Derek?'

'I can look into it.'

'You can?'

She smiled at him. 'It is my job.'

'Yes, of course.' He smiled at her hurriedly. She knew that at that exact moment, now he had the facts, he would get up to leave.

He rose to his feet and put down his unfinished coffee.

'Do us a favour, love . . .'

'Yes.'

'Keep this to ourselves, just you and me.'

They went out into the road. He kissed her lightly on the cheek.

'You're a good girl,' he said.

She stood there watching him as he walked away, heading for the shopping precinct. Once he turned and, seeing her still there, waved; then he walked on. She watched him until he was out of sight, and then she watched the passers-by who replaced him. What was he up to?

Perhaps she would wake up and realize he had never visited her, and that Viv, a day ago, had never sat in that grubby car across the road and spoken those words. Her morning felt dislodged.

Back in the office Janine came up. 'Been looking for you,' she said. 'Your sister just phoned.'

'Blast!'

Janine raised her eyebrows. 'Keep your hair on. She says she only had a minute and she'll phone later.'

It was not Dad's fault, of course. Still, Ann felt a wave of what she told herself was simply irritation.

Ann was not yet home. Ken looked at his watch and poured himself a lager. He wandered around the lounge, then switched on the TV.

'Mom, Dad's outside and he says he has some important news.' A cute American child tugged at his mother's apron. *'Honey,'* she said, *'why can't he tell me himself?'*

The child answered: '*He has this problem getting out of the car.*'

Canned laughter. Ken flipped the channels.

'*We spoke to Dr Gupta who is himself blind and who has made a study of –*'

Ken switched off the TV and stood beside the window. The plant she had bought on Sunday was already beginning to droop. He felt the soil: wet. Ann was always over-watering; that was what her sister said. Viv's plants somehow managed to thrive on neglect.

He felt the usual prickling sensation. What a relief it had been to come back here, to home sweet home, on Sunday night. He drained his lager and put the glass down on the table. It rattled; he realized with surprise that his hand was shaking.

The gate clicked. He looked out of the window. Ann smiled at him, startlingly near, as she unlocked the front door.

'Hello.' She came into the lounge. 'You're home early.'

'You spoken to Viv?'

She nodded.

'Ah.'

'I told you, Ken. She's serious.'

'He's in on it?'

'No. It was Viv's idea.' She sat down on the settee. He remained standing beside the window.

'I can just imagine them,' he said, 'like we're some deserving case.'

'Of course not –'

'Telling all their friends. Probably put it in that magazine of his.'

'Ken –'

'Remember when we all went to Salcombe and he tried to pay the hotel bill?'

'It's not like that!'

He felt his voice rising, but he couldn't stop it. 'Think they can give it to us like a Christmas present?'

'No!'

He lit a cigarette, keeping his back to her so she would not see his hands. 'What exactly is she planning to do? It's against the law, you know. I suppose she hasn't thought of that. Like those women in the papers.'

'No – it'll be unofficial –'

'Will? It will, will it? All fixed, eh?'

'No! We need to talk.'

'We do not need to talk!' he shouted. 'We're going to forget all about it!'

He drew deeply on his cigarette, staring at her plant. Two buds had fallen off.

He said: 'Tell you something. I'd rather adopt a baby than have theirs.'

'But we can't! I told you, it's too late!' She started sobbing – a noisy, rasping sound he hadn't heard for years. 'It's all right for you, you can have a baby with anybody – that woman in accounts –'

He swung round. 'Ann!'

Her face was wet and red. 'With what's-her-name at the Youth Club. If we got divorced –'

'What?'

'– you could start all over again!'

He hurried over and sat down beside her, but she got up.

'What's this about divorce?' he said.

She stared down at him. 'You say you're worried about me – I mustn't distress myself, I mustn't let Viv upset me – but all you're really thinking about is yourself, and your stupid, *stupid* pride!'

He tried to grab her, but she pulled away.

7 The next day was blustery and sunny. It sent the blood singing in Viv's veins; she felt muscular and happy, as if anything were possible. It was the first of March. The wind blew away her doubts as she dug the earth, bending to pull out the strings of couch grass. She flung them aside – petty, pale strings, they could not beat her. Nothing could. She smelt tomato soup, and when she lifted her head she could see the dizzying sky.

Words: she flung them aside. All the talking, these past two evenings – the words scattered on the wind. She remembered standing in the garden centre just a few days ago – it seemed like another year now – and saying *anything's possible*. How much had she realized it then? *You can make things happen, if you believe it.* Ann's face, turning to her, blanched in the strip lighting, her cardigan buttoned up as if it were possible to keep herself for ever safe and sad. *Viv, you've always been able to make things happen.*

Viv dug a shallow trench and took out her packet of broad beans. She pressed one, and then another, into the earth, planting them in a zig-zag. This was the part that satisfied her the most. Then she clomped back to the beginning again, her rainbow gumboots weighed with mud. In the distance she could hear the shouts of her children; for once they were not bored here, they seemed to be possessed by the same energy as herself.

The beans were buried. She straightened up and saw the flash of blue anorak as the girls chased behind the huts. Then she turned towards the car park and saw Ken.

He was walking towards her. She stood still. He was not yet within earshot so she could say nothing, which made her blush. Out of the corner of her eye she could see him, stepping over the puddles. He looked incongruous in his business suit. He made his way around the runner-bean poles, with last year's rags still fluttering from them.

At last he was near enough.

'Hi!' she called.

'Hello.' He came up to her and looked around. 'I was just passing. Thought I'd drop in.'

Just passing? She gazed at the distant factories. She smiled at him encouragingly.

'Working on a house near here,' he said. 'Saw your car over there. Seeing there's no school today. Read about it in the papers.'

She nodded.

He said: 'Surprised you're not joining in.'

'The demo?'

'Being so political.'

'Didn't feel political today.' She smiled again, and bent down to her carrier-bag. 'Want an orange?'

'Er, no thanks. Sure I'm not interrupting?'

She shook her head. 'Been longing for an excuse to stop.'

There was a pause. He turned his head. 'Coming along.'

'You haven't been here for ages, have you?'

'Not since the thistles. You've put a lot of work into this place.'

'When I start something I can be very determined.'

There was a silence. They stood there, watching the browning under-leaves of the sprouts rustle in the wind. His shoes were frilled with mud.

'Smell soup?' she asked.

'Now you mention it.'

She pointed to the factory.

'So much for the natural life,' he said.

'Lots of my girls work in there. Whenever I smell soup I feel a failure. All these years I've taught them and they end up tinning minestrone.'

'You're not to blame.'

She sighed. 'Words. All those words and it didn't do them a blind bit of good.'

68

'Don't say that.'

'I got out, you see. If I hadn't got brains I'd be working in there.'

'Rubbish.'

'Till they get married, of course, and have babies.'

The words hung there, refusing to blow away. She looked at her gumboots: silly swirls of green and orange. The mud on them looked more honest. Ken cleared his throat. She opened her mouth to speak. Instead she said: 'Want a conducted tour?'

He bowed. 'I'd be delighted.'

She walked ahead along the path, and paused at the expanse of earth.

'Broad beans in there,' she said. 'Need a lot of manure, broad beans.'

Out of the corner of her eye she could see him nod politely. She pointed to the further stretch of earth. 'That's for lettuce and carrots.' She paused. 'Not much to see yet.'

'It's very interesting.'

'In fact, not anything.'

They came to a stop. She took a breath, then she turned to him. 'Ken –'

In the distance a hooter sounded. 'Is that the time?' He looked at his watch. 'Duty calls.'

'Ken –'

'Must be toddling.'

Before she could speak he had turned and was hurrying away down the path. She didn't watch him; it felt like an intrusion, for them both.

She hadn't begun to peel her orange. She dug her fingernail into its skin, angrily.

Ann's shoes pinched, so she had taken them off. They were beige high-heels, with ankle-straps; she had bought them on impulse the day before. They were far too expensive. Their solace had been temporary. She sat at her desk and glanced at the clock: 1.15. Derek came out of his office, putting on his jacket. He paused at her desk.

'Aren't you going out?'

'Waiting for Ken,' she said. 'We had a vague lunch date. Only looking at video recorders.'

'Don't get the one I got. Keeps doing the wrong thing. There you are, all set up, supper on your lap, switch the damn thing on and it's the second half of middleweight boxing.' He smiled. 'Not conducive to marital harmony.'

Ann glanced at the clock again. 'Perhaps he's forgotten.'

'Ken never forgets.'

'No,' she said, doubtfully.

'Not our Ken.'

Derek went out. Ann, wincing, put on her shoes in readiness.

1.25. Ken ordered a second pint. The pub was shabby, but he deserved a depressing room. Through the frosted glass he could hear the traffic in Willesden High Street. It was the nearest pub to the allotments.

Pinned behind the bar was a photo of a bare-breasted girl, advertising K P nuts. Her gaze followed him, challengingly, wherever he looked. He lit yet another cigarette.

The girls had finished their picnic. They ran off again. Viv, feeling restless, wandered along the allotments, looking at other people's neater plots. An old man in braces was double-digging a trench; she had never double-dug, though her gardening books told her she should. How blameless he looked. Was he too elderly, now, for confusions? This morning she had felt strong and supple; now she knew nothing, and the thought of digging tired her.

Overalled figures were sitting in the factory yard. Viv

went up to the wire fence and saw Mo, whose sister Tracey was in the sixth form.

'Stupid bitch,' said Mo, sitting down on an oil drum. 'You'll be seeing her Friday?'

'Second period,' said Viv. 'If she turns up.'

Mo passed her some chewing gum, through the wire, and sat down again. 'Told you she's living with this bloke?'

Viv nodded.

'The milkman calls her madam, when she answers the door in her dressing gown. Then five minutes later out she trots in her school uniform.'

Viv grimaced, undoing the silver paper around the gum.

'Sisters,' said Mo. 'Nothing but trouble. You got any?'

'One.'

'She got a fella?'

'She's married.'

'Like him?'

Viv shrugged, then nodded.

Mo said: 'Mean he's boring?'

Viv chewed for a moment. 'Not exactly boring,' she said, picturing Ken. 'Predictable.'

1.40. Ken drained his third pint. Behind him there was a clatter. He jumped. But it was only somebody winning on the fruit machine.

He stubbed out his cigarette and stood up.

How simple to be old, in braces. You double-dig your trench and then it's time for tea. How simple to be young, and sitting behind the hut with your bulldozer. In Na-Na Land everything is possible; you can ride on a horse which sprouts wings just behind your thighs, they bump you as they flap and you can hear them creak. You bully your sister to come with you, as if you're just going down to the shops. Or you simply squeeze your eyes tight and watch

71

the pin-pricks jostling behind your lids, and soon it's time for tea.

Viv sat on the grass beside her hut and lit a cigarette, which did her more damage than tea. Just before Ken appeared, she remembered looking at her watch and thinking: five to two, I ought to go home and do some shopping. Then she looked up and there he was, walking towards her in his dark suit as if the reel of film was being replayed.

This time she jumped up and met him.

'Viv,' he said. 'We must talk.'

She glanced around. Her neighbour, just a few yards away, was examining his space. He could do that for some considerable time.

'Come into the hut,' she said.

As they moved towards the hut the girls came running up.

'Uncle Ken!' they shouted.

He fished in his pocket and brought out two packets of peanuts. 'Why don't you be chipmunks?' he suggested. 'Run off – no, scamper off – and have a peanut picnic.'

Ann sat in the sandwich bar eating a bowl of salad. Her shoes hurt. Outside, shoppers passed. At the bus stop, people joined the queue; the next time she looked up a bus was drawing away and the people had gone. The sun shone; as everyone had observed all morning, it felt like the first day of spring.

Ken slotted one flowerpot into another. He was half turned away from her. The hut was small, and if he turned to face her they would nearly be touching.

'Viv, I'll come straight to the point.' There was a silence. He slotted the flowerpots into a tower. 'I don't know what to say.'

'Tell me what you feel. What do you feel?' She couldn't

watch him. She looked at the floor, with its debris of old *Beanos*.

'I feel . . . oh, it's so difficult.'

'Look, Ken. We both love Ann.'

He nodded.

'Very much,' she said.

'Yes.'

'It's possible to make her happy. It's perfectly possible to do it.' She spoke faster. It was up to her. 'I can have children. Only too easily.' She wished they could sit down, but there was nothing to sit on. 'It's unfair, isn't it? In fact, I've spent most of my adult life trying not to have them. Like at college, remember?'

'What?'

'University. The abortions.' She stared at him. 'Didn't you know?'

He shook his head.

'Ann never – ?'

'No,' he said.

'Perhaps she thought you'd be shocked. Anyway I did. Two. I suppose I was a bit carefree. Still, it's all in the past.'

He was standing beside the shelf. He picked up a matted mass of string and started to untangle it. 'I've never talked to you about, well, anything like that.'

'Funny, isn't it,' she said.

'There's not the occasion, is there?'

'Even when . . .' she paused. 'Even, you know . . .'

'Yes.' Ken's fingers worked at the string.

She said: 'Even during that awful time, when we could've come closer.'

He nodded.

'Anyway,' she said. 'That's over.'

'Over, but not gone.'

'Of course not.' She stared at the muddy comics. 'Never will be. We shan't forget her, Ken. She was born; she was a proper person.'

73

Ken looked out of the small, smeared window. Behind him, the door was ajar; it creaked to and fro in the wind but she did not dare close it. She couldn't move. She looked at the sunlight on his moustache.

He said: 'I held her, you know.'

'I know.'

'They let me hold her for as long as I wanted. She was all there, Viv. All in working order.' Far away a train passed. The neighbour had started to whistle. 'She was perfect.'

She put her hand on his shoulder. 'Oh Ken . . .'

'Anyway, so this last time we thought that everything was going to be all right. I really believed it. I thought – it's not possible to – well, it couldn't. Who'd let it happen again? Who could be so – ?'

'Ken!' She gripped his shoulder. 'Don't think about it! Think about the future. We won't deny the past, or pretend it never happened. Ken, I can have babies as easily as – plums falling from a tree. I've never felt ill – I've been disgustingly healthy. I've sailed through my pregnancies. When everyone else was moaning, I was loving it. I even found the births . . . wonderful. Powerful.'

She stopped to catch her breath. She felt illuminated; she felt hot to her fingertips. She stayed gripping his shoulder, willing the girls to stay away.

'I know,' said Ken. 'But –'

'But what?'

'I couldn't possibly have you do it.' He looked at her. 'I couldn't.'

'I can! I *want* to.' She moved her other hand to his shoulder and pulled him from his string. They stood there, face to face. 'You don't have to feel guilty, or beholden. You really don't.'

'I wouldn't want that.'

'No. Well don't then.'

'I just want the best for Ann. I want her to be happy. Like she was.'

'We can make her.'

'We?'

She paused. Outside, the whistling continued. She felt herself taking a breath – could he hear it? She said: 'You don't want it to be Ollie's child, do you?'

There was a pause. Finally he said: 'Want me to be frank?'

'Not much point, otherwise.'

He shook his head. 'No, then.'

'Thought not.'

'It's not that – you know. I don't want to sound –'

'You want your own child.'

'Yes,' he said simply. 'I do. Very much.'

They stood there in silence. Behind him rose his tower of plants pots. He said: 'But how?'

'Oh, there must be ways.'

'But what?'

'I don't know – ways and means. Methods.'

'What?'

'Oh, artificial whatsits.' She shook her head. 'Look, that's not important. The important thing is that it's possible.' She paused. 'Now we know we can do it.'

They stood there, looking at each other. Finally she took away her hands. She had left dusty fingerprints on his shoulders.

The *Capital* office was in Covent Garden. It was an open-plan room, designed to fearlessly display its own digestive and nervous systems. The heating pipes were painted pink and lime-green, in a soon-to-be-dated high-tech style, and they hurt Ollie's eyes. He had a headache again today. He and Viv had been up half the night again, drinking and arguing.

Ellie, the new girl from the switchboard, stopped at his desk and gave him a package.

'Ugh.' She sniffed it.

'Brie. Thanks.' He paid her.

'You look awful,' she said.

'Thanks a lot. Haven't had much sleep lately.'

She raised her eyebrows. She had wiggly blonde hair tied back with a ribbon. 'Sounds interesting.' She sighed. 'You have all the fun.'

'Who do?'

'Journalists.'

'Where did you work before?' he asked, and bit into his sandwich.

'DHSS. Come dinner time they all took out their knitting.'

'Sounds a gas,' he replied.

'Now you see why I came to London.'

'You fixed up yet?'

She nodded. 'Got myself a room. Got it from one of our small ads.'

She left him and went over to the switchboard. Diz said that with her wholesome Lancashire accent she gave the place phone credibility. Diz also said that Ollie's housing piece was late and he'd better pull a finger out, old son, as the copy date was Monday.

Ollie put his head into his hands.

Viv dumped the cabbage into the sink and washed the mud off her hands. Her father had dropped by; she wished she could be alone to think about the conversation with Ken.

'Any slugs?' asked Daisy, poking at the cabbage leaves.

Rosie went up to Douglas. 'Want to see my cut?' she asked, pulling up her trouser leg.

'Er, later love,' he said. 'Look what Grandad's got.' Coins jangled as he rummaged in his pocket. He gave the girls some money. 'Why don't you two pop round the corner and buy yourselves some' – he lowered his voice – 'sweeties.'

'Dad!' Viv glared.

The girls ran out of the front door. Viv thought: everyone's bribing them today. Douglas sat down at the table and she put on the kettle.

'Viv, lovey, I've been wanting to have a little chat.' He cleared his throat. 'I expect you think I'm just a crusty old bachelor, past all that sort of palaver . . .'

She stared at him.

He went on: 'You know, since your mother and I . . .'

'What's happened?'

'What would you say if I told you, well, I was giving it another whirl?'

'You're not!'

'Don't look so horrified.'

'I'm not,' she said. 'Christ.'

He nodded. 'There's life in the old dog yet.'

She stared at him – his worn, familiar face, his unfamiliar sideboards. Today he wore a tie, too.

'Who is she?' she asked. 'Where did you find her?'

'At the club.'

'Your Thursday place?'

He nodded, and started to push around the crumbs on the table. 'She's a divorcée too. Most of them are, of course, apart from the widows.'

Viv felt dizzy. 'What's she called?'

He raised his hand. 'One thing I must tell you. She's not English.'

'What is she?'

'She's from Vienna but you could hardly tell. She's called Vera.'

'Where does she live?'

'Swiss Cottage at present, but we're thinking of buying a little place of our own.' He stopped pushing the crumbs, and looked up. 'Well?'

She came over and laid her cheek against his balding head. This was uncomfortable. He stood up and she put her arms around him. 'Congratulations.'

'You don't mind?'

'Why should I?'

'Well – your mother –'

'Dad! That was years ago.'

'I'm the luckiest man alive, Vivvy. She makes me very happy.'

The children came in, their jaws working. Rosie went into the garden and Daisy went over to the sink.

Later, when their grandfather had gone, Daisy called out to Rosie:

'Sweeties! Look!'

Rosie came into the kitchen and Daisy passed her a plastic bag. A moment after taking it Rosie screamed and dropped it on the floor. Inside were no sweeties; only slugs.

She makes me happy. Viv thought of her father and an Austrian divorcée – how fascinating it would be to meet her. She thought of Ken's face as he stood in the dusty little hut and she gripped his shoulders. *We can make her happy*. It could be done. One person actually had the power to change somebody's life.

Once, when they were children, she had called Ann out to the garden. 'Look Annie, I've got some blackberries!'

Ann had come out into the garden. She was wearing her blue spotted dress, Viv could remember every detail now: the bald patch on the lawn, where she stood holding out the plastic bag; the washing on the line.

'Got some blackberries for you!'

'For me?' Ann came nearer.

'They're a present.'

Ann hesitated. 'Promise?'

'Promise.' Viv held out the bag. 'Come on.'

Ann took the bag and screamed. Inside, it was moving with black slugs.

It had taken her all morning to collect those slugs. Unlike Ann, she didn't mind touching them. When Ann had fled into the house, crying, their father had found the whole thing hilarious.

78

Viv washed the cabbage at the sink and thought: I will make her happy now.

Ann poured the blackcurrants from their freezer bag into the flan case. As she did so, she heard the front door and Ken's step in the hall.

He came into the kitchen. 'Hello.' He kissed her on the cheek. 'Mmm. Looks good.'

She didn't reply. He went to the sink and poured himself a glass of water.

'Thirsty?' she asked.

'Had a drink at lunchtime,' he said. 'Knew I shouldn't.'

'Why?'

'Couldn't do a stroke all afternoon.'

Ann started whisking some cream. She could see him refilling his glass. After a moment she stopped the motor and said: 'Who did you have a drink with?'

'Nobody.' He put down the glass. 'What's the matter?'

'Nothing.' She started the motor and went on whisking. The cream started to wrinkle. He rinsed the glass and put it on the draining board. She stopped the motor. 'I just thought . . .'

'What?'

'Just thought you were having lunch with me.'

He stared. 'I am an idiot.'

'Doesn't matter.'

'It does!' He came towards her. She picked up the flan and put it into the fridge.

'Had to meet somebody,' he said.

She closed the fridge door. 'Thought you were alone.'

'Afterwards. Had to meet somebody afterwards.'

'I'm sure it was important.'

'It was,' he said.

'That's all right then.'

He paused. 'It was your sister.'

She stopped. 'What?'

'I went to see Viv.'

'Finish your supper!' said Viv to the children. 'Else I'll have to eat it.'

Idly she spooned up some baked beans and put them into her mouth.

'What's for pudding?' said Daisy, going to the fridge.

Viv ate some cabbage. The girls never ate cabbage; she put it on their plates just to make herself feel better. Perhaps by simply seeing it they'd mysteriously absorb the roughage.

'One more mouthful,' she said, but they weren't listening. She finished off their baked beans. 'I'll get fat.'

'Where's Dad?' Rosie asked.

'Late,' Viv mumbled, her mouth full. She carried the plates to the sink.

Just then the front door opened and Ollie came in.

'Hi folks!' He grabbed Rosie and lifted her into his arms.

'She'll get indigestion,' said Viv, thinking what wonderful fathers men can be when they haven't had to look after their children all day.

'Higher!' cried Rosie, and Ollie turned her upside down. Peanuts scattered on the floor.

'Whoops,' said Ollie.

'Uncle Ken gave them us,' said Daisy. 'I ate mine.'

'She scoffed hers,' said Rosie, as she got lowered to the floor.

'Rosie always *keeps* everything,' whined Daisy.

'Uncle Ken?' asked Ollie.

'I'll clear it up,' said Viv, getting a dustpan and brush.

'Ken?' said Ollie.

'What a mess,' said Viv, sweeping up.

'When?' asked Ollie.

'He told us to be chipmunks,' said Daisy.

'Come on, kids. Bed.' Viv threw the peanuts into the bin.

'Today?' asked Ollie.

Daisy said: 'He told us to have a peanut picnic.'

Viv went to the stairs. 'Come on. Bed! You little pests.'

Ken washed his hands and rubbed a flannel over his face. He paused for a moment, looking in the mirror. Some streets away an ambulance passed, its bell ringing. He waited until the sound faded; he never used to notice ambulances. Then he noticed the dirty marks on his shoulders and rubbed them off.

He went down to the kitchen. Ann was opening the oven door; she had her back to him. He sat down at the table.

'You went there specially?' she asked.

'No, I was working –' He stopped. 'Yes. I went there to find out what your mad sister's actually on about.'

'What happened?'

'We chatted about . . . well, how she thought it might be done.'

'How?' She turned. Her cheeks were pink.

'Oh, various ways . . .'

'You think – it might . . .?'

'Happen?'

'Do you?' She stood there, holding the casserole. She looked small and eager, with her big oven gloves.

He paused. 'I don't know.'

'Can we do it?'

'I don't know!' He heard his voice rising to a squeak. 'Let me think about it!'

Ollie went into the bathroom. Through the wall he could hear the murmur of Viv's voice as she read to the children. Her voice rose to a West Country bellow: '*You kids, stay off moi land!*' She was taking her time.

The sink was full of water; submerged in it was a drowned teddy. He lifted it out; it was waterlogged. He threw it into the bath. He started to wash his hands and then, suddenly, he plunged his face into the cold water.

He lifted up his dripping face, gasping, and rubbed his hair with a towel. He thought: now why did I do that?

When he got downstairs he poured himself a gin and tonic and wandered around the kitchen. She hadn't started making the supper but this might be a sign that he should. With Viv, one never knew.

He had finished his drink by the time she came downstairs.

'Wish they wouldn't ask for that stuff,' she said. 'Nearly as bad as Enid Blyton.'

'So he came to the allotments?'

She nodded, and fetched herself a glass. 'Christ, I need a drink.'

He watched her getting the ice. 'So what did he say?'

'Ken?'

'No, Dustin Hoffman.'

'We just talked.'

'Viv!'

She said: 'You know, we've never really talked, Ken and me. All these years.' She poured a large amount of gin into her glass.

'What did he say? What did you say?'

'Don't interrogate me!' She undid the tonic bottle; it hissed. 'I don't ask where *you've* been.'

'That's different.'

'I don't ask who you've had a drink with.'

'That's not important,' he said.

'Who was it then?'

'Someone from the office.' He sat down on the arm of the sofa. 'Ellie, a new girl. I took her to a wine bar.'

'He just came to the hut.' She drank.

'You arranged it?'

She shook her head. 'He just arrived.'

'With his bag of peanuts. What did you talk about? Your sprouts?'

'For a bit.' She raised her eyes, holding up a piece of lemon for his gin, but he shook his head.

'Sounds like a conspiracy to me,' he said. 'Bribing my children, secret meetings . . .'

'It wasn't secret.'

'I have a funny feeling I'm being left out of things.'

'You're not!'

The stairs creaked. Rosie stood there in her nightie.

'You're shouting,' she said. 'I can't get to sleep.'

Viv slipped off her kimono and climbed into bed. Ollie lay there, reading *Private Eye*. He turned the page. She waited a moment, then she touched his cheek.

'Sorry I shouted.'

He put down the magazine. 'So am I. I'm sorry.'

'We're both a bit . . . you know . . .'

He nodded, then he leant over and turned off the light. He turned back and put his arms around her. Then he started nuzzling her neck. 'Mmmm . . .'

She kissed him. He tasted of familiarity and toothpaste. His hand slid down her breast. 'Viv . . .'

'Mmm . . .?'

'I've got a suggestion.'

'What?' she murmured, then lay still.

He moved his hand down between her thighs, and breathed into her ear. 'Let's start on that baby now.'

She lay rigid. He went on stroking. Finally she said: 'Ollie . . .'

'What?'

'There's something I've got to tell you.'

'Mmm . . .?' He was still stroking her.

'It's about my talk with Ken.'

His hand paused. 'Yes?'

She said: 'He wants it to be his child.'

8   It was Sunday; post-rugger. The changing-room was noisy and smelt of damp men. Ollie stood in the shower cubicle, drenching himself, and sang at the top of his voice:

'Love, oh love oh careless love,
Taught me to weep and it taught me to moan,
Taught me to lose my happy home . . .'

Ken was showering in the next cubicle. Suddenly Ollie stopped singing and shouted:

'So you want to impregnate my wife?'

He rinsed himself and stepped out. Ken also stepped out, wrapping a towel modestly around his waist. With another towel he rubbed himself dry.

'Did you say something?' he asked.

Ollie wrapped his towel around his hips. 'I just said: "*Funny thing, life.*" '

Ken smiled. 'You mean, fifteen grown men kicking around a bit of leather?'

'Something like that.'

He looked at Ken's chest: packed and muscular, with a pair of good, broad shoulders and a surprisingly thick growth of hair. He remembered Viv running her hand over it and laughing: *Small but perfectly formed.* He had known Ken for years but he had never really looked at him.

Diz came up and tweaked Ollie's ear. 'Bit aggressive, weren't we, bully boy?' He indicated Ken. 'He is supposed to be on our side.'

Ollie said: 'Me, a bully?'

Diz ran his hand over Ollie's chest. 'No, you're all soft and liberal.' He turned to Ken. 'Take note. A prime specimen of lapsed-radical, twentieth-century man. Note the equivocal slope to the shoulders, the privileged lack of muscle tone . . . a body wasted by introspection. Note, however, the one over-developed organ . . .'

'What's that?' asked Ken.

'The social conscience.'

'Sod off, Diz,' said Ollie.

'I'm allowed to humiliate you. I'm your editor.'

In the pub Ken tried to buy the drinks.

'Let me –' said Ollie.

'No, please –'

'Come on –'

'No –' Ken nudged Ollie away and offered a tenner to the barman. 'What's the damage?'

As Ken paid, Ollie murmured: 'Curious phrase, isn't it?'

'Isn't what?'

'"The damage". What, exactly, is the damage it means?'

'Search me.'

Ken passed out the pints.

'Dart-board's free,' said Diz. 'Come on.'

'Look, Ken –' began Ollie.

Ken was moving away. Ollie touched his arm; the beer rocked in his glass. 'Ken –'

'What?'

'We must talk, the four of us.' Diz had moved away; Ollie kept his voice low. 'Viv and I've talked, and if we're going to go through with this –'

Ken stared at him.

Ollie nodded. 'She's told me.'

Ken paused. 'I see.'

'Bit of a shock, but . . .'

They both drank. There was a pause.

'I can understand,' said Ollie. 'No, really. I know how you feel –'

'Look –' Ken glanced around at the crowded bar.

'How about Tuesday?' said Ollie. 'You could both come round and have supper.'

'Er, Tuesday's Youth Club.'

'Wednesday then?'

Ken nodded. They paused, then they walked over to the dart-board.

'Stop talking rot,' said Diz. He pointed to Ollie: 'Bet you always pick our Kenneth's brains.'

'What about?'

'Your house.' He turned to Ken. 'You must've learnt by now that journalists have a divine dispensation to get everything free.'

'Oh shut up,' said Ollie, and took the darts. He aimed, and hurled them at the dart-board.

Diz laughed. 'Steady on, Ollie-baby.'

Ollie came into the kitchen, put down his briefcase and stared.

'Good Lord, we're not expecting the Queen Mother.'

Viv was on her knees, scrubbing the front of the kitchen units.

He laughed. 'Know something? You look like a proper housewife.'

'Stop standing there. Come and help.'

'You haven't worn that apron since they were babies.'

'Sweep the floor.' She looked at her watch. 'They'll be here soon.'

He took off his jacket and fetched the broom. 'It's only your sister and her husband, you know.'

'Hurry up.'

He started sweeping the floor. When he got to the dresser he pulled it out from the wall. Reaching down behind it, he picked something up. 'Fossilized toast!' He inspected it closely. 'I'd say circa the late seventies. Ah! And here's the earring that redheaded slag lost at our party, remember?'

Viv didn't reply. She was taking out the groceries and muttering: 'Watercress, tomatoes, now where's the sodding coriander?'

'Look!' he said. 'Trish and Alan's change-of-address

card. No wonder they took offence. Think I'll designate this a site of archaeological interest.'

She didn't laugh. 'Coriander, coriander . . .'

He straightened up. 'This is ridiculous!'

She rifled amongst the packages. 'It's somewhere here.'

'We're not on display! We're not a bloody shop window.' Suddenly he grabbed a Pentel and went up to her. 'Stand still.'

'What're you doing?'

'Close your eyes.'

She was wearing a white plastic Mothercare apron; they had bought it together. On it he started writing, in large letters. 8 O-LEVELS, FERTILE, –

'What're you doing?' She twisted her head down.

SOUND TEETH –

She pushed his hand away. 'Ollie!'

He put his hands on her shoulders and shook her. She was damp from her work.

'Look, Viv, you don't have to do all this. Don't you see?'

'What?'

'How lucky they are?' He stared into her pink face. 'How bloody lucky?'

She paused. 'Don't be aggressive with them.'

'No.'

'Don't be angry with Ken.'

He gazed at her as he had gazed at Ken, following the lines of her face, looking at her thin shoulders under her T-shirt. Ken had looked surprisingly strong; Viv, he realized, had lost weight. She had always been slender but now, in her labelled apron, she looked about twenty years old, and frail.

He said: 'I promise I'll behave.'

'This evening must be a success.'

He nodded. 'God help us . . .'

7.45. Viv had rubbed the marks off her apron and hung

it up. The table was laid. She had even found the real napkins Ann had once given her. They looked well pressed, because they had never been used.

8.0. 'Hurry up, Ollie!' She called upstairs, leaning on the banisters. He was right; of course it was stupid to be so jittery.

Back in the kitchen she paced around the table. She was wearing her loose lurex harem trousers, the sort of garment you could hopefully curl up in and relax.

Ollie joined her in the kitchen. They drank a gin and tonic.

At last she asked: 'Should we phone?'

'Ken's never late.'

She lit another cigarette, annoyed with herself because she wanted to save up any cigarette-smoking for when Ken and Ann were there.

8.15 . . . 8.20. 'Bad for the nerves,' said Ollie.

'Bad for the *bœuf en croute*.'

He raised his eyebrows. 'Surrogate motherhood's going to be an expensive business.'

8.35.

'Perhaps they're late,' said Ollie, 'because they know we're always late.'

The bell rang. They jumped.

'You go,' said Viv.

'No, you.'

'Wimp,' she said.

She went along the passage and opened the front door. Ann stood there. Viv looked beyond her; Ken must be parking the car.

Ann said: 'He's not coming.'

The three of them sat at the table, eating bean salad. Ken's empty place had not been cleared away; Ollie said he might have second thoughts.

'I called him a coward,' said Ann. 'I shouted at him. It was awful.'

Viv poured them some more wine. 'I still don't understand. Is he going to go through with this or not?'

'I don't know. All he said was it was too private for one
of your big heart-to-hearts.'

Ollie gestured round the room. 'What does he think?
We're on *Candid Camera*?'

'He's shy, you see,' said Ann.

'Shy?'

Viv nodded. 'Course he is. That's why he gets so aggressive.'

Ann looked at them pleadingly. 'He's not a coward
really. He'd be the first over the trenches.'

Viv smiled. 'But you don't have to talk then.'

Ollie mopped up his vinaigrette with some bread.
'There's so much stuff we've got to talk about . . .'

'I know,' said Ann. 'The legal side, the money side. He
wants to discuss those.'

'Why the hell isn't he here then?'

'Ollie!' Viv glared at him.

Ann paused. 'You know perfectly well why.'

'Why?'

'Because you make him feel inferior.'

'We don't!' said Viv.

Ann nodded. 'It shows.'

'What does?'

'The trying.'

Ken knelt on the kitchen floor, mending the ironing
board. He banged in a nail. Beside him, spread out on a
newspaper, was the broken teapot he'd been meaning to
mend for months. He would get on to that next.

While Viv poured out the coffee, Ollie went over to the
fridge and brought out a bottle of champagne.

'Let's drink this anyway.' He opened it, and filled three
glasses. They raised them. 'To this generation, and the
next.'

Viv said: 'And the older one too.'

'What?' asked Ann.

'Dad and Vera.'

Ann put down her glass. 'What?'

There was a silence.

Viv said: 'Hasn't he told you?'

'Told me what?'

Viv stared at her. 'Oh God.'

'What's happened?'

'I presumed he'd told you by now.' Viv paused. 'He's getting married again.'

There was a pause as Ann took a sip from her glass. 'No. He hasn't told me.'

'Oh hell,' said Viv.

'He hasn't bothered to tell me. All he's bothered to do is ask me for a mortgage.'

Nobody spoke. They gazed at the empty bowl in the middle of the table. Some scrapings of cream remained in it, and a stray glacé cherry.

Ann made a faint hiccuping sound, then Viv realized it was not that: she had started to cry.

Viv jumped up and knelt beside her. 'Don't.'

Ann raised her streaming face. 'He doesn't love me –'

'He didn't mean to –'

'Oh I've always known that, of course I have! It's just ... oh, nothing's any good. Ken can't even bother to swallow his pride and come here, just because he's embarrassed, but why does that matter, for God's sake? Why does it matter if it's his baby, it's only a little mechanical business, everything else seems so much bigger than that, but the trouble is he doesn't seem big enough for it, probably none of us are! Everything seems so empty –'

'Don't –' started Viv.

'– All these years, all these miscarriages, and my darling little girl who was hardly there but she *was*, she was there, she was mine, I held her, she was all perfect,

90

except she never moved, and what's the point of anything, what's the point of lovely meals like this and kind
sisters and even Ken being loving because he is really,
but nothing's any use, it doesn't mean anything when I
can't have a child!'

Ann stopped, hiccuping for breath. Viv and Ollie stared
at her. She fumbled for a handkerchief but she couldn't
find one; Viv grabbed the napkin and wiped Ann's face
with it, her poor wet eyes, and then her nose.

There was a silence.

Then Viv said: 'Listen, Ann. Whatever happens, I'll
have this baby for you.'

Ollie spoke for the first time. 'She will.'

'Leave Ken to me.' Viv wiped Ann's eyes again. Ann
hardly ever wore mascara but she had worn it for this
evening; her cheeks were streaked. 'I'll take him out and
get him drunk and tell him what we're all going to do.'

Ann turned to face her. 'Will you really?'

Viv nodded.

9 Madeleine, as usual, was on the phone. Today
she kept her back to the staffroom and spoke in a
whisper. Viv gazed at the broad bottom in
the faded jeans. She resented Madeleine for
using the phone, yet she felt grateful to her for
delaying things. She sat down on the sofa beside Harold,
who looked up from his *Guardian*.

'Trevor wrote me a note today saying could he go to the
toilet, spelt TOYLUT. I said he could go to it when he
could spell it so he changed it to BOG.'

Viv laughed. Harold pointed to the newspaper. 'There's
a post here in Norfolk, Grade 2. Would they be fresh and
innocent in the fens?'

Viv shook her head. 'They just keep it in the family.'

'Don't think I can stand the hormone level here much longer. Very unsettling for a middle-aged chap.'

'Poor Harry.' Viv stroked his head and glanced at the phone.

'Just seething with sex. What's the name—oh yes, Tracey. The one who babysits for you. Apparently she threw up in biology this morning.'

'Did she?' Viv thought of Mo's conversation, at the allotments.

'Must be the excitement of seeing a nude frog. Then there's that little incident behind the kitchens. Honestly, Viv, when I go home and tell Louise about my day the kids ask why I'm speaking in French.'

Madeleine left the phone. Viv jumped up and rummaged in her bag. 'Harry darling, could you lend me 10p?'

He gave her a coin. 'Chivalry, though terminally ill, is not yet entirely extinct.'

'You're a pet.'

She went to the phone and dialled. She was wearing her striped jumper and felt ridiculously hot.

'Hello,' she said. Ridiculous. She had never, in her life, rung Ken at work. 'Is Mr Fletcher there?'

He was. She asked him out for a drink.

Viv sat at the kitchen table, correcting exercise books. She heard Ollie's footsteps coming down the stairs. He stood in the doorway, holding his overnight bag.

'Listen to this,' she said, '*Mr Rochester is a real man, with a bad temper and broad shoulders and smouldering eyes.*' She closed the book. 'Perhaps he could fix our guttering.'

Ollie laughed. 'You've been inflaming them again?'

'She goes on like this for half a page. What Harold calls tumescent prose.' She stood up. 'You off then?'

Ollie nodded. 'I've said goodbye to the girls. So you're seeing Ken tomorrow?'

Viv nodded.

'We're both doing our bit, aren't we? You for the childless and me for the homeless.' He was going to Liverpool for a housing piece. He paused. 'I do admire you, you know.'

'Hey, what about love?'

'I'm not allowed that now.'

'Spiritually you can.'

He smiled. 'Thanks a bunch.'

She put her arms around him. 'Be Petrarchan. For a month or two you can just write me sonnets and pass them to me in bed.'

He rested his cheek on the top of her head. 'Are we mad?'

She turned up her face and kissed him. 'I love you for this.'

Ann drained the potatoes, grimacing at the state of Viv's sink. She looked at her watch.

Finally Viv came downstairs. She was wearing a knitted apricot two-piece.

'Crikey!' said Ann.

Viv looked anxious. 'I wore this for my interview at school.'

Ann laughed. 'It's not you, Viv.'

'I've been hours trying things on. What shall I wear for your husband?'

Ann started mashing the potatoes vigorously. 'Whatever you feel comfortable in. The first thing you find on your bedroom floor.'

Viv went upstairs.

'And hurry!'' Ann called. 'You know how he hates waiting.'

She called the girls in to supper and went on mashing the potatoes. Squashing the lumps, she remembered Viv as a teenager, zipping on her long white boots. Those boots.

They had always shared a room. Ann would be sitting on her bed, doing what? She could never remember. What Viv was doing was getting ready. Struggling into her boots, buttoning up her suede miniskirt which was grubby but who could afford to get it cleaned? Bending over her inadequate mirror, pencilling Twiggy lashes underneath her eyes. Sixties warpaint. Sometimes she borrowed make-up from her mother's dressing table.

Late at night Viv would creep in. Creaks from the floorboards. Her efforts to be quiet of course always woke Ann; besides, she wanted to hear. A groan, as Viv unzipped her crippling boots: *beauty before comfort*. A sigh from the eiderdown as she sat on the bed and whispered about what she'd done, with who. The stifled giggles that made their chests ache. Viv smelt of scent and risks.

Viv appeared again, dressed in a T-shirt and a floral skirt.

'Better?' she asked.

Ann nodded.

Viv came over, dipped her finger in the mashed potato and sucked it. 'Ken always says I look like a tramp. Or a site foreman.'

Ann laughed. 'Not true. He told me once I ought to take a tip from you.'

'He didn't.'

' "Be bolder," he said.' She moved away and shouted upstairs: 'Rosie! Daisy!'

Ken wore a sports jacket and the pink tie he'd worn on Christmas Day; his hair was sleek and still wet. She greeted him, wishing the pub wasn't so empty. He jumped up to get her a drink.

'You stay,' – she indicated his glass. 'You haven't finished.'

'Please, let me –'

'Ken –'

'Please.'

'All right. Pint of Burton's please.' She sat down, smiling. 'For strength.'

'Where's Mum gone?'

'I told you. She's having supper.'

'But why's she having supper with Uncle Ken?'

'Why not?'

'Why don't they have supper here?'

'Come on. It'll get cold.'

They sat down. Daisy looked at the chicken. 'Yum. Mum never cooks us this.'

'Doesn't she cook you a proper tea?'

'Not all this stuff. Where's she having supper?'

'Look, I'll show you something.' Ann took Daisy's fork and stroked it along the mashed potatoes. Then she lifted up some peas and scattered them on the top. 'We used to do this, your mum and I, when we were your age.' She started to sing: *'We plough the fields and scatter the good seed on the land . . .'*

'What?'

'For it is fed and watered by God's almighty hand.' She stopped. 'It's a hymn.'

'Oh, a hymn,' said Daisy.

'Sorry about the other night,' said Ken.

'Doesn't matter.' She sipped her beer.

'The meal, all that trouble.'

'Listen, Ken. I'm going to go to a lot more trouble than that.'

There was a pause.

'So how's school?' he asked.

'Fine. Look, Ken . . .'

'What?'

She was silent. She took out her cigarettes and offered him one.

95

'I'm trying to give them up,' he said.

'So'm I.'

They each took a cigarette. He rummaged for his lighter.

'Here.' She took out her matches and lit his.

'Thanks.'

They sat there, blowing out smoke.

She said, at last: 'I feel like a first date.'

He didn't reply.

She said: 'We ought to talk about clinics.'

'Isn't this illegal?'

'We'll pretend we're married.'

He looked at her. 'They wouldn't believe us.'

'Leave it to me. I'm a wonderful liar.'

'Wouldn't they want to see documents, certificates –'

'Don't worry. We'll sort all that out.'

He paused. 'One thing we must sort out . . .'

'What?'

'Money. I'd rather settle it with you –'

'I've told you, Ken. You're not paying me to have your baby!'

He looked around, swiftly.

'Nobody's listening,' she said.

'There's such a thing as compensation.'

'Ken . . .'

'What?'

'Don't feel guilty, don't feel beholden. It's dangerous.'

'What?' He looked at her, alarmed.

'You end up resenting the person. Even hating them.'

'I won't! I'm just . . . so grateful.'

She put her hand over his. 'There's no such thing as a selfless act. I *want* to do it. Get that into your thick head.' He didn't reply. She smiled. 'Come on. Let's have another drink. Let's get plastered.'

'Come on. Bed.'

Ann led the girls past Viv and Ollie's bedroom. She

96

glanced inside. It looked ransacked, as if a burglar had decided nothing was worth taking. Clothes lay scattered over the bed: gold trousers, leather skirt, the second-hand, flowery dress that Ollie said made Viv look like a nymphomaniac charlady.

Ann closed the door.

The pub was filling up. Ken finished his third pint.

'I'm starting to enjoy this,' he said.

'Let's go and eat.'

He stared. 'What about Ann?'

'I'll phone her up,' said Viv.

'. . . and the Prince took the magic goblet and drank from it. And as he drank, a wonderful thing happened; he grew young and strong again, and his wounds healed. In the forest the birds started singing and the flowers opened. The Prince strode through the woods, looking for his lost Princess –'

The phone rang. Ann put down the book and hurried into Viv and Ollie's room. She sat down on the bed.

'Viv! How's it going? How is he?' Ann whispered, even though there was nobody to hear. 'No, we're fine. Yes, do. Stay out as long as you like.' She paused. 'Good luck.'

Smiling, she put down the phone. She was sitting on the protruding buckle of a boiler suit. When she got up she found it had laddered her tights.

'Sit this side.' Viv patted the seat. 'Such is the womblike nature of their lighting I can hardly see you over there.'

Ken got up and moved next to her.

'Still,' she said, picking up the menu, 'the best curries in London.'

After a moment Ken said: 'Ann's a wonderful woman, Viv.'

'I know.'

'Never a moment's bitterness.'

'What about?'

'Here you are,' he said, 'straight A's in your exams and you never did a stroke of work.'

She smiled. 'I did when nobody was looking.'

'I remember coming to tea once –'

'Used to get out the best cups for you –'

'And there you were,' he said, 'with your school pullover back to front.'

'Sexier like that.'

'You'd had your ears pierced and your dad blew his top.'

'Very protective, Dad.'

'Of you.'

She paused. 'Of me.'

There was a silence. He looked down at the menu.

'University, kids . . .' he said. 'No, there's no sweeter-tempered lass than Annie.'

She put her hand on his arm. 'You needn't convince me, Ken. I think you're very lucky too.'

They sat silently, listening to the sitar musak. Slightly drunk, she had the sensation of the maroon room echoing and receding, of conversations endlessly repeated. The other diners seemed to be speaking in whispers, but that was probably her imagination. To them, Ken and herself must look like just another couple.

She pointed to the menu. 'Fancy something mild? That one, that's nice. Lamb cooked in yoghurt, very subtle . . .'

'Sounds nice,' he said. 'But I think I'll have rogan ghosht, some keema nan, and I wouldn't say no to some dhal and dahi.'

She looked at him in surprise.

He turned to her, raising one eyebrow. 'Ah,' he said.

'Ah what?'

'You've always thought I was a meat-and-two-veg chap, haven't you?'

She paused. 'Of course not.'

'I, too, have lived it up in the odd subcontinental nightspot. I too have had a misspent youth.'

98

'Have you?'

He smiled. 'No. Just came to these places with Ann.'

They laughed. She thought of themselves a couple of hours ago, and the blurring, confidential gift of alcohol.

'Used to go to the pictures,' he said, 'then we'd come to a place like this.'

'Like us. Now.'

He nodded. 'I felt . . . if we went to a film first, we'd have something to talk about.'

'Oh Ken . . .'

'You've never had that problem, have you?'

'What?'

'Self-confidence.'

'Course I have.'

He paused. 'Sometimes I'd write down interesting topics and put them in my wallet.'

She smiled. 'Kenny . . .'

He looked at her. 'Know something? Never told that to a living soul.' He turned to the tablecloth. 'Never been . . . spontaneous, like you.'

'Pretty spontaneous to tell me now.'

'Must be learning.' He aligned the salt and pepper pots, side by side. 'You think I'm pretty boring, don't you?'

'Don't be stupid!'

'Boring old Ken with his D I Y and his boring old job –'

'No!'

'And his boring old tropical fish. Don't know how Ann can stick him.'

'Ken!'

He paused. 'I think it's boring too.'

She stared at him. 'What?'

'My job. I see the lads horsing around, but I'm not one of them, am I? But I'm not management either, not a high-flier, don't want to be. Don't want a golf handicap.'

'Glad about that.'

He looked up. 'Know what I want? I want to run my own little garden centre.'

'Really?'

He nodded at her, his face solemn. 'Oh I'm full of surprises.'

She nodded, smiling. 'So why don't you?''

'It's a big risk. I'll have to . . . well, see how things turn out.'

'You mean, if we' – she corrected herself – 'if you two have a baby.'

He nodded. 'Won't be the best time to give in my notice.'

'So if I get pregnant, you'll have to stay in your boring job.'

'But I won't mind, will I?'

'Why not?'

'Won't mind anything,' he said simply, 'if there's a child.'

Ollie had spread his papers over the bed. He could make a hotel room look as if he had lived in it for weeks.

He put on the kettle for a cup of tea. He didn't want one, but he liked to use the tea-bag and the midget pot of denatured milk. On the T V, a game show was in progress. A track-suited woman, of ample build, was trying to hammer one of those test-your-strength machines. Her husband watched anxiously.

'How's Joyce doing then?' asked the compère.

'She can't get it up.'

'Thought that was a husband's problem.'

The audience roared. Ollie switched off the T V. Outside the window loomed a darkened Liverpudlian office block, too near. Suddenly he felt even lonelier. He picked up the phone.

Ann woke. Her neck ached; she had fallen asleep on the settee. She thought it was the doorbell that was ringing: in her dream Viv was trying to get into her own house.

It was the phone. She picked it up.

'Ollie! No – it's me, Ann.' She looked at her watch. 'No, not yet. It's a good sign, Ollie. They need to, well, have a chat. No, I'm fine. Tucked up. No, really . . .'

She put down the phone and looked at her watch again. Then she lay back on the settee, her eyes open.

Viv and Ken came out of the restaurant. Viv staggered; they had finished with brandies.

Ken said: 'Forgotten where we parked the car.'

Viv giggled. 'You? Mister Advanced Driving Test?'

Ken looked up and down the street. 'Round the corner somewhere . . .'

They were near Paddington Station, in one of those shabbily wakeful areas that surround mainline termini. She took his arm. 'Let's be companionable.'

They walked along slowly. 'Sleazy, isn't it?' he said.

She nodded. They passed an all-night Wimpy bar, and then the black windows of Genevieve Sauna and Massage.

He said: 'You like this sort of all-human-life-is-here sort of place, don't you?'

She nodded. 'I like a bit of sleaze.'

'Thought so.'

She turned to him. 'Don't you? Just a teeny corner of you . . . hitherto unack-' – she hiccuped – 'un-acknowledged?'

'Perish the thought . . .'

A woman passed them. Viv nudged him. 'Bet she's one,' she whispered.

'A you-know-what?'

Viv nodded.

Ken said: 'Let's play Spot-the-Tart.' They paused outside a late-night supermarket. A woman stood inside, looking at the shelves. 'Two,' he whispered.

They walked on, slowly.

'Three,' said Viv.

'Her?' Ken looked at a middle-aged woman on the other side of the road. 'Surely not.'

Viv nodded. 'Another one can tell.'

'Another what?' He sounded alarmed.

'Another woman.'

'Ah.'

They laughed.

He said: 'Bet you played I-Spy with Ann.'

She nodded. 'Did you?'

He shook his head. 'Nobody to play it with.'

'Poor Kenny.' She ruffled his hair. 'Poor only child.'

'Four.'

They turned to look at the passing woman.

'Four,' agreed Viv, clutching his arm.

'At school they said you could always tell if a girl had – you know . . .'

'Done it.'

'Done it,' said Ken, 'if she wore a charm bracelet.'

'Did anyone?'

He nodded. 'Brenda something. She was in the next desk in Geography. She kept asking me why I was staring.'

She laughed. 'Make any headway?'

'Me? I was petrified.'

They had arrived at the car. She hugged him, burying her face in his jacket.

'Oh Ken, you're so . . .'

'So what?'

'Sweet.'

He paused, in her arms. 'Don't want to be sweet.'

'What do you want to be?'

'Masterful. Dangerous.' He paused. 'Spontaneous.'

They stayed, their arms around each other, leaning against the car. In the distance, men guffawed and a car door slammed. Behind them, in the main road, a bus passed, its windows lit and empty.

In a low voice she said: 'Let's be spontaneous now.'

'What?'

'Want to be spontaneous?'

'How?'

She said: 'Look behind you.'

Ken disentangled himself from her arms and turned. 'What do you mean?'

She spelt out the lit sign on the front of the building. 'H–O–T–E–L.'

He looked at the place. It had once been a row of terraced houses but had now been converted into a shabby commercial hotel. In the ground-floor window a sign glowed: *Central Heating. H and C in all Rooms.* He said: 'So?'

She kept her voice low. 'Ken, let's not go to that clinic.'

'What?'

'You know . . .'

Now he understood. He stared at her. She remembered, later, how the neon light shone on his moustache. She remembered the silence.

'Come on, Ken.'

'But –'

She took his hand. 'Come on!' Half-elated, half-appalled, she looked into his eyes.

'We can't!' he said.

'Isn't it better, this way?'

'But Viv –'

Suddenly she dropped his hand. 'Sorry. Mad idea.'

There was a silence. Standing beside the car, they gazed at each other. She turned away. It was a cold night but she felt the heat rise in her face. 'Don't know why I said it.'

'Mad.'

Blushing, she went round to the passenger door of the car. She kept her eyes on its roof. She heard him insert the key into the driver's door, then it must have got stuck because he stopped. She waited. She longed to be home, and closing her own front door behind her. How could she have been such an idiot?

'Come on then,' he said.

She looked across the car. Ken was still standing there; he hadn't moved.

'What?'

'I said, come on.' He looked across at her, directly, his eyebrows raised. She said nothing.

Then he walked round to her side of the car and took her hand.

'But –' she stopped. They stared at each other.

He held her hand and they crossed the road, stopping to let a taxi pass. Still holding her hand, he pushed open the door into the hotel foyer.

10

A hand was stroking his brow. Ken woke, suddenly. Ann was sitting on the bed; sunlight shone through the curtains.

'You'll be late for work,' she said.

He stirred and groaned.

'That was Viv on the phone,' she said.

'What?' He sat up.

'It's OK. She's rung off.'

'What did she say?' he asked sharply.

'She wants to see you at lunchtime. She's made an appointment at a clinic.'

'A clinic?'

She nodded. 'She'll phone you later, at work.' She smiled. 'Feel awful?'

He nodded. 'Hangover.'

She paused. 'Ken, I'm so happy.'

'What?'

'She told me.'

He stared. 'Told you?'

'You know, that you're going to do it.'

'What?'

'Go through with it.' She stroked his forehead again and leant over to kiss him on the cheek. 'I'm so proud of you. Don't look like that. I am.' She got off the bed and pulled open the curtains. Sunlight flooded the room; Ken flinched.

'Now there's no turning back,' she said.

Harold met Viv in the corridor and walked with her to the staffroom.

'And how's Viv this sunny morning?'

'Awful,' she groaned.

'What's the matter?'

'Hangover.'

'Naughty naughty.' He nudged her. 'I usually give a detention for hangovers.'

Ann knocked, and went into Derek's office.

'Here's the surveyor's report,' she said. She sat down, wincing.

'What's up?' he asked.

'Nothing.'

'Come on, Annie.'

She indicated her neck. 'Just my, well, this bit.'

'Poor Annie.'

'Slept on a settee,' she said.

He stood up, and came over to her chair. 'Let Doctor Derek get to work.' She sat still and he started massaging her neck. She thought: nobody ever does it quite right but one always murmurs 'aah, lovely' . . .

'Mmm, lovely,' she murmured.

'I hope, I mean . . .'

'What?' she asked, her eyes closed.

'No, none of my beeswax.'

'Come on.'

'This wasn't, er, the result of marital strife?'

'Oh no,' she said. 'Babysitting.'

'Ah.'

'No marital strife,' she said.

He went on massaging.

'You can do it a bit harder if you like,' she said politely.

He kneaded her shoulders. 'Mary used to love this. In the good old days.'

'Derek . . .'

'Sorry. Out of court.'

'No,' she said. 'I was just babysitting for my sister. All above board, dirt-resistant, stain-free, fully washable above board.'

His hands stopped. He looked at her in surprise. 'What do you mean?'

She shrugged. 'Don't know.'

'Strange creatures,' he murmured.

'Who are?'

'Women.'

She stood up, preparing to leave. 'Stranger than men?'

Viv tracked Harold down in the stockroom. She linked her arm with his and laid her head on his shoulder.

'Harry . . .'

'What's all this in aid of?'

'Dear darling Harry . . .'

'All right. I will.'

'What?'

'Elope.' He put down his books. 'Come on. No more Trevor, no more Darren, no more 4b, the little wankers.'

'Listen –'

'We'll drink life's cup to its dregs.'

She squeezed his arm. 'Listen, I promise I'll elope with you tomorrow if you'll just –'

'Oh-oh.'

'I've only got one class this afternoon, and you're free then.'

106

'Oh no.'

'And they're only carrying on with their project. Please, Harry!'

'Take your horrible class?' He sighed, and picked up his books again. 'And I thought you were offering me your body.'

'Hair of the dog,' said Ken, bringing his pint to the table. He sat down and passed Viv her orange juice.

The same tune was playing on the jukebox; the pub was empty, except for a cluster of businessmen at the far end.

'Well,' she said, 'here we are again.'

He nodded and took a gulp of his beer. Then he wiped the froth off his moustache and addressed the table: 'Don't know what to say.'

'Don't worry.'

He paused. 'I'm sorry.'

'I'm not.'

He looked up at her sharply. Then he said: 'Is, er –'

She shook her head. 'He's still in Liverpool.'

There was a pause.

'Got off your classes all right?' he asked.

She nodded. Then she looked around. 'Feels wicked in the middle of the day.'

'What does?'

'Being here.'

He nodded. There was another silence. What could they say now? The previous evening had felt so different.

He looked down at the table. They were sitting beside the window. In the daylight his skin looked grey, as if he had not been outside for weeks. He said: 'I feel so guilty.'

'Don't! Look Ken, I –'

'Ssh!' He frowned, looking behind her.

She turned. A large woman with frizzed black hair was approaching them; with a jolt Viv recognized Suzi, an American friend of hers. She'd had a perm. She carried a holdall, and her two companions were heading towards the bar.

'Well hi!' Suzi came up to Viv and Ken. 'Thought I recognized you. Am I disturbing anything?'

'No,' said Viv. 'This is my brother-in-law Ken.'

She grinned. 'That's OK then. Hi Ken.'

Ken half rose; she shook his hand. He sat down again.

Viv explained: 'Suzi taught drama at my last school.'

Suzi turned to Ken. 'So you're married to Viv's sister?'

'Yes. Er, can I get you –?'

'No thanks.' Suzi indicated the bar. 'I'm with them. Mind if I just show Viv something?'

'Please do,' he said.

She pulled up a chair, sat down and rummaged in her holdall. She found a rolled-up poster and held it up. It showed a mushroom cloud and the slogan INVEST IN WHAT FUTURE?

'Great, isn't it?' said Suzi. 'Only came through today. It's specially designed for banks, building societies, places like that.'

'It's terrific,' said Viv.

Suzi turned to Ken. 'Powerful, isn't it?' Ken didn't reply and she turned back to Viv. 'How many can you take?'

'Oh, fifty.'

Ken looked at Viv. 'You're going to stick them up?'

Viv nodded, and said to Suzi: 'His wife – my sister – she works in a building society.'

'Terrific,' said Suzi. 'She can –'

'I don't think she will,' said Ken.

There was a pause. Then Suzi said: 'Hey Viv, I've got some wonderful news. They've taken my book.' She turned to Ken: 'My magnum opus. My baby.'

'That's marvellous!' said Viv. 'Who's publishing it?'

'This women's collective in Limehouse. Very feisty.'

'What's it about?' Ken asked politely.

'Gender bias in the school situation.'

'When's it coming out?' asked Viv.

'End of the year. We'll throw one hell of a party, you must both come.' She grinned. 'This is advance notice for nine months' time, so you can't say you're busy.'

Viv looked swiftly at Ken and then grimaced. 'Well . . .'

'What?' asked Suzi.

Viv recovered herself. 'Well, you can't predict what might be happening.'

'I get you,' said Suzi. 'Yeah, I agree. With these lunatics in charge, who can predict anything?' She stood up. 'I'll leave you to it.' She rolled up her poster, said goodbye and went to join her friends.

Ken turned to Viv. 'You going to stick those up?'

Viv nodded.

'It's against the law, you know. Flyposting.'

'You think it's criminal?' she asked.

'Yes.'

'I think it's criminal to threaten the human race with extinction.'

'Viv!'

'We're not doing this for fun, you know. We're not hooligans.'

He raised his eyebrows. 'My dear Viv, nobody wants war.'

'Don't dear me!'

He sighed and took a gulp of beer. 'Know what really gets on my wick?'

'Tell me.'

'You and your' – he gestured towards the bar – 'friends there, your muddle-headed, self-righteous, dungareed ninnies thinking they have a monopoly on peace. It's so condescending!'

'You're the condescending one.'

'You label yourselves, doing bloody silly things like those bloody silly posters. You put people against you.'

'At least we're doing something, instead of sitting on

our backsides. For Christ's sake, Ken, what sort of world do you want your children to grow up in?'

'I haven't got any children.'

She twitched her shoulders, blushing. 'What I mean is, don't be such a fascist.'

'You don't even know what "fascist" means.'

'I know one when I see one.'

He raised his hands in despair. 'There you are, in a position of responsibility, infecting children –'

'Infecting?'

'Infecting them with your half-baked –'

'Two of my friends have gone to prison for their beliefs. Catch *you* doing that!'

Ken stared at her. She thought he had seen somebody else come into the pub, but then he said: 'This is appalling.'

'What?'

'We can't quarrel now.'

'Why not?' She grinned. 'We always disagree. I feel better now.'

He tugged at his moustache, and looked down at the table again.

'Don't you?' she asked.

He didn't reply, he just gazed up at her with the sort of stricken look she had seen on the faces of her children, especially poor Rosie when she was being taunted.

She put her hand over his. 'Look Ken, I've got something to tell you.'

'What?'

She took a breath. Then she fumbled for her cigarettes. 'I rang an AID clinic. Ken, they were horrified. They won't even see us.' Now it was she who looked down at the table. 'They said, as things are, nobody will. It's up to us.'

Viv stood at the hotel window and looked down into the street. *Key-cutting ... Ear-piercing ... 24-Hour Mini-*

Cab Service . . .Opposite, there was a slot-machine arcade called *Family Amusements.*

'Nice day out for the family,' she said. 'Take them to a Paddington video parlour.'

There was no reply from Ken, who stood near the door. In the next room a lavatory was flushed. She heard the sound of Ken putting down the carrier-bag, and then the creak of the bed as he sat down.

'No tarts this afternoon,' she said, not turning.

'What?'

'No women on the prowl. Looks so blameless today. Think he recognized us, that ferrety man at the desk?'

'He must be used to this sort of thing.'

She laughed. 'Think so?' She moved away from the window. Out of the corner of her eye she could see Ken sitting on the bed.

'What sort of person,' she asked, 'would come to a place like this?'

'Commercial travellers.'

'Lonely people.' She paused. 'Well, here we are.' She moved nearer him and picked up the carrier-bag. She took out the half-bottle of Scotch she had bought. 'Better get this down. Don't want to.' She held up the bottle and smiled at him. 'Close your eyes and think of –'

'Don't want to think.'

'No.'

He paused, then he got up and went over to the basin. 'I fear we have a one-glass situation.'

She laughed and unscrewed the bottle-top. He held out the tooth-glass and she poured some Scotch into it. 'And here,' she said, passing it to him, 'is some gender bias.'

He smiled slightly. He held up his glass. 'Cheers.' He drank a little.

'That's better,' she said.

He raised his eyebrows. 'You always behave like that after an Indian meal?'

She nodded. 'Blame it on the biriani.' They smiled. Then she said: 'Ken, she'll understand.'

'Why?'

'She just will.'

'How do you know?'

'I just know.'

He passed her the glass. She sipped, flinching.

'Viv . . .'

She put down the glass. 'Look, let's pretend we've just met. We don't know anything about each other except we quite like Bell's whisky.'

He sat down on the chair. 'It's all rather complicated, isn't it?'

'Let's be simple then. Lie down and take your clothes off.'

He stared at her.

She patted the bed. 'You can keep your underpants on.' She started undressing. 'Lie down, face down.'

He took off his shirt, his shoes and socks and then his trousers. He lay down on the bed, face down. She stood beside him, in her underwear, and started massaging him.

'Relax. That nice?'

He nodded.

'You're still not relaxed.' She went on, kneading his shoulders and rhythmically rubbing his spine. 'That's better. Ah, you've got a little mole here. Didn't see that last night.' He grunted, lifting his head. She pushed his head down and went on massaging. 'Terrific muscle tone.'

'Thank you.' He lay still for a moment, then he muttered: 'So this is what he does.'

'Who?'

'Ann's boss. He gives her massages.'

She stopped in surprise. 'Like this?'

'I rather think they're fully clothed. But then perhaps she was lying.' He paused, face down. 'Perhaps they're catching.'

'What are?'

'Lies.'

She lay down beside him. 'Ken . . .'

'What?'

'Don't think about Ann,' she said gently. 'Not now.'

He shook his head, in the pillow.

She smiled. 'I only want you for your body. Nothing wrong in that, is there?'

He didn't reply. She stroked the back of his neck. 'It'd be complicated otherwise.'

He nodded. 'It would be horribly complicated.'

Suddenly he sat up, dislodging her hands. He pushed away from her and grabbed his trousers.

'Ken!'

He started pulling on his trousers. She grabbed him but he pushed her off.

'Ken –'

'There must be another way.'

'Listen Ken! This is simplest –'

He pulled on his socks. 'No!'

'The others'll understand –'

'Don't be so *thick*!' He stared at her.

'What do you mean?'

'Oh Viv . . .'

'What?'

He looked at her. 'For an intelligent woman you can be bloody stupid.' Suddenly he stopped, half-dressed and exhausted. He sat slumped on the bed, his head bowed. She paused, then leant against him tenderly.

'I know how you feel,' she said gently.

He turned to look at her. 'You so sure?'

She nodded. Then she whispered: 'Trust me.'

She put her arms around him and kissed his dry lips. She pressed his face to hers and stroked the back of his head. He buried his face in her hair and they fell back together against the pillows.

★

'Auntie Ann gave us mashed potatoes and chicken and cheesecake with curranty stuff in it.'

'Well I'm giving you toasted cheese.'

'Boring, boring.'

'Sit down.'

'Wish she was our mum.'

'Shut up!'

The phone rang.

'Oh, hello Ollie. Do I? No, it's nothing. Just irritated with the kids.' She sat down on the hard arm of the sofa and rubbed at a ladder in her stocking. 'Last night? Oh, it was fine. I'll tell you about it – you'll be back tomorrow, won't you? What? No – I said it was fine. Look – must go, the kids are knocking over – 'bye.'

She put down the phone. The children looked up from the table.

'We're not knocking anything over,' said Rosie.

'You lied,' said Daisy. She started chanting: '*Liar, liar, knickers on fire –*'

'Shut up!' shouted Viv.

'*Hang them up on a telephone wire!*'

Ann carried in the warmed plates. 'This is a treat.'

She had laid the table in the lounge. Ken lifted out the containers from the carrier-bag.

'Don't like to see you slaving away in the kitchen,' he said. He laid out the containers on the table. They were hot; he sucked his fingers.

'And these,' she said, touching the vase of tulips.

'Just a bunch of flowers,' he muttered.

They sat down. She unpeeled the lid from one of the containers and breathed in the aroma. 'I feel so spoilt.'

He looked at her sharply. 'Don't!'

'What?'

'Nothing can spoil you!'

She gazed at him curiously. 'What a funny thing to say.' She paused, and went on unpeeling container lids.

'Haven't had one of these for ages, have we? What's this?'

'Bhuna ghosht.'

'What did you and Viv have last night?'

'Can't remember. Mutton mughlai, that sort of thing.'

She tore off a piece of nan bread and ate it. 'Don't you mind doing it again?'

'What?'

She indicated the meal. 'When you had it last night?'

He shook his head. 'Want some prawn thing?' He passed her the container and she took some.

She smiled. 'Remember that ancient waiter with the squint?'

He nodded.

She said: 'Remember when I ate that whole chilli by mistake?'

'And that stuff ran down your face.'

'It was Viv's,' she said, spooning out some dhal.

'What?'

'Viv's mascara,' she said. 'I'd borrowed it. Didn't usually wear mascara.'

They ate for a moment in silence. Then she said: 'I'm so glad, Ken.'

'What?'

'That you got on. What's happening about the clinic?'

He tore off a piece of nan and laid it beside his plate. 'She's looking into that.'

She smiled. 'I'm glad it's going to be your child. You must realize that.' She took a sip of beer. 'It makes it so much better.'

He spooned some yoghurt on to his curry and swirled it around: beige swirled into brown. He looked up. 'Know something?'

'What?'

'Those days, I remember looking round that restaurant and thinking something.'

'What?'

'That I was the luckiest man there.'

She smiled and put her hand on his arm. 'You don't have to say all this, you know.'

'Why not?'

'You just don't have to.'

She ate for a moment in silence. Ken ate a little; he was not hungry. Suddenly she laughed.

'What is it?' he asked, startled.

'That.' She pointed. He looked down at the table. Small pellets of nan lay scattered beside his plate. 'You used to do that when we were first going out,' she said. She looked at him and smiled. 'That's because you were nervous.'

Ann lay in bed reading her book. A March gale was blowing outside; rain spattered against the window.

Ken took off his dressing gown and climbed in beside her. Ann read aloud: '*Mark saw Candice through the party throng. Their eyes were riveted together.*' She laughed. 'Ouch!'

She closed the book and put it on the bedside table. Ken lay on his back, looking at the ceiling.

He said: 'Ann.'

'What?'

'About the clinic . . .' A gust of wind blew the rain against the glass; the window frame rattled.

'What about it?'

He paused. Then he turned his head. 'Nothing.' He put his arms around her and stroked her. Then he started kissing her passionately.

Gently she pushed him away.

He moved back. 'What is it?'

She shook her head. 'Nothing.' She paused. 'Must be all that curry, made me sleepy.' She touched his brow, and then turned and switched off the light. 'Blame it on the biriani.'

'What?' In the dark, his voice was sharp.

'Remember "Blame It on the Bossa Nova"? Viv and I

had another version.' Softly she sang: '*Blame it on the biriani* . . . then it got rude. Funny, isn't it?'

'What is?'

'We hadn't a clue what biriani was but it sounded very wicked.' She paused. 'Silly, wasn't it?'

He spoke into the darkness. 'Why?'

'Couldn't be anything wicked about a biriani, could there?'

They lay there, side by side. Then she leant over and kissed his cheek. 'Night-night.'

11 'Here's your horrible Brie stuff again.' Ellie sniffed a package and put it on Ollie's desk.

'Thanks.' He gave her some money.

'So how was Liverpool?' she asked, as he unwrapped the paper.

'Lonely.'

Since he had been away she'd put a pink streak into her fringe. The rest of her hair was tied up with a bit of lace. She picked up the copy of *Capital* which lay on his desk.

'Mind if I nick this for lunch?' she asked.

'That's incest.'

'What is?'

'Reading something you work on.'

'I don't work on it,' she said. 'I only answer the phone.'

He took the magazine from her and leafed through it. 'Well, Ellie, what do you want? A lesbian co-operative? A growth workshop? One waterbed, slightly foxed?'

'A fella.'

He stared at her. 'What?'

She blushed. 'Oh heck . . .'

He opened the magazine at the Lonely Hearts page. 'You don't need this bit.'

'Who says?'

'I do.'

Still blushing, she said: 'Why not, Mr Knowall?'

He gestured at her. 'Well . . . just look at you.'

She turned to go. 'Knew you'd take the mickey.'

'Wait.' He searched down the columns and read out: '*Wanted: warm, sensitive, non-smoking cat-lover* – you love cats?'

'Yes.'

'Good. *Nice legs essential . . .*' – He leant back, looked at her legs and nodded – '*. . . for long-term relationship.*'

She held out her hand. 'Give it to me.'

He shook his head and read: '*Virile estate agent seeks freehold lady.*'

'Ugh.'

'You can have a *slim, shy guy* – no, he's gay. Or a *well-built graduate* – no, he's gay too. Here's a *caring electrical engineer* – ah, and a *professional man* – as opposed, that is, to an amateur man like the rest of us.'

She laughed. 'You're daft.'

'You're the daft one. You really going to reply to one of these?'

She shrugged. 'Got any better ideas?'

'What about – oh, clubs? What about the people here?'

She grimaced. 'They're all –'

'– into L T Rs.'

'What's that?'

He grinned. 'Living Together Relationships.'

She nodded. 'They're all married.'

'Or married.'

She sighed and took the magazine. 'Think they're all weirdos?'

Ollie raised his eyebrows and bit into his sandwich. 'No weirder than the rest of us,' he mumbled.

During the night the gales had blown away the clouds. It was a clear, sharp day. The puddles winked in the gutters; lorries passed with a hiss. Viv sat in the car, her palms damp. It was 1.15; she had been waiting for twenty minutes but she realized she was still clutching the wheel. A bus passed; sunlight flashed on its windows. On the other side of the high street stood the row of shops. The Archway Building Society had a new poster in its window; from this distance it looked like a family on a beach: happy and tanned, no doubt. Two children, it was always two.

1.20. She had come on impulse. Soon she must get back to school. Another bus passed. The door opened, but it was only a customer coming out.

She had had to come. She couldn't bear it any longer. She thought: I could switch on the radio. But her hands didn't move.

The door opened again. This time it was Ann. She came out, buttoning up her jacket, and looked up at the sky. Viv's heart thumped. But another girl had come out with Ann; she wore a pink coat. She said something to Ann and they both laughed. Then they turned to the left and walked down the street together.

Viv opened the car door. She waited a moment, gripping the handle. Ann and the girl walked along briskly; after a moment they were swallowed up in the lunchtime shoppers.

Viv closed the car door. Slowly, she put the key into the ignition and drove away, back to school.

Tracey sat on the desk, smiling dreamily. Her face was floury with powder; there were bumps over her chin. It was the afternoon break and the room was empty, except for Viv, who sat on the next desk.

'Hope it's a little girl,' said Tracey.

'This is terrible,' said Viv. 'Look, I don't want to be schoolmistressy but –'

'Don't even mind throwing up.'

'What're you going to do?'

'He buggered off, you know. My bloke.' She was still

smiling. 'Couldn't see him for dust but I don't care. Not now.'

'But what about your A-levels?' Viv wanted to shake her, to shake off that smile.

'Did you feel like this, with yours?'

'Listen, Tracey. You're one of my brightest girls –'

'They give you a flat, with a baby.'

'But what about your future?' said Viv. 'Your career –'

'What, be factory fodder like Mo?'

'No! You're clever, you could –'

'Leave off.' Tracey eased herself off the desk and started for the door. 'Thought I'd be able to tell you. Of all the idiots here.' She paused. 'Thought you'd understand.' She sighed theatrically. Her hair was greasy; she suddenly seemed matronly for her years. Viv got up but Tracey opened the door. 'You stick to *Jane Eyre*,' she said, her parting shot, and closed the door gently, as if more in sorrow than in anger.

Ollie let himself in and put his suitcase down in the hall. Strange, he thought, how the house always seemed altered, even after a couple of days. Roller skates on the carpet, from an unknown voyage down the road; Viv's crumpled dress, to go to the cleaner's; phone messages stuck in the mirror, and a Roneoed letter from the girls' school announcing no doubt either a teacher's retirement, contributions welcome, or a jumble sale, jumble welcome. It was all the same as ever but shifted, as if normality was shattered shards in a kaleidoscope that were shaken up each day to settle in an altered pattern. The house was silent.

He went into the living room. For a moment he thought it was empty. He looked around: the morning's breakfast in the sink, the table piled with exercise books, a Sainsbury's carrier, an empty crisp bag on the floor. The evening sunlight shone through the straggling windowsill plants. He looked at a single empty tea mug, and a fag-end in a saucer, both given poignancy by the absence of the person who had finished with them.

Then he noticed that Viv in fact was in the room. She was lying on the floor under the sofa; her head was hidden. He gazed for a moment at her patched jeans (*Nuclear Power? No Thanks* on her buttock) and her purple jumper. Hadn't she heard him come in?

'That bad, is it?' he asked.

'What?' She sounded muffled.

'Reality.'

'Hi,' she said, and then: 'Bloody Bertie.'

Ollie looked at the dresser. The hamster's cage was open.

'Why don't they ever shut his cage?' He turned back to Viv's legs. 'Come on out and I'll fix us a drink. I want you to tell me all about it.'

'What?' asked the muffled voice.

'Ken and you. Everything.' He went to the fridge and took out the ice. He pressed the rubber compartments; the ice clattered into the tumblers. He glanced again at Viv's motionless legs. 'You know,' he began slowly, 'I was thinking, while I was away . . .' He went to the tap and refilled the ice tray with water. 'I might have joked about it, and got angry but it was only, well, you know . . .'

She didn't reply. He looked at the dirty soles of her trainers.

'. . . embarrassment,' he went on. 'There's something about, well, the mechanics. But it struck me in Liverpool . . .'

'What did?'

'The enormity of it. What you're doing. It's what one means by . . .' He cut two slivers of lemon and paused, turning to look at her legs. '. . . By an act of love.'

Still no reply.

'Come on,' he said. 'Tell me about it, blow by blow.'

'It was all right. Quick!' She shifted under the sofa. 'There he is! Head him off!'

Ollie hurried over and crouched down at the end of the sofa. 'Where?'

'Brute!'

'What?'

'I'm talking to Bertie,' she said. 'Quick!' She rummaged under the sofa.

Crouching, he asked: 'What do you mean, "all right"?'

'Got you!' She wriggled backwards from underneath the sofa. Her face was red and her hair messy. She held up the hamster and spoke to it: 'You and your unquenchable thirst for experience.' She took him over to the dresser and put him in his cage.

Ollie passed her a gin and tonic. 'Let's sit down.'

She sat down at the table. 'Tracey's pregnant,' she said.

'Is she? Tell me about it.'

'She's going to keep it.'

'Not her,' he said. 'You. What happened? Have you found a clinic? Will you have to pretend to be married?'

She nodded, pushing the ice around with her finger. 'There's this place in Harley Street.'

'Harley Street? What did they say? Will you have to go into little cubicles?'

She paused. 'Look Ollie. I promised Ken I wouldn't . . .'

'Wouldn't what?' He stared at her.

She lit a cigarette. 'It's all so . . . undignified. He wants us to, well, respect his privacy.'

'He is a pompous twit.'

'He's not!' To his horror, her eyes filled with tears.

He jumped up and sat down beside her. 'Darling . . .' He put his arm around her but she pushed him away.

'I didn't mean to upset you . . .' he said.

She rubbed her nose, sniffing. It was not like her, this. She wouldn't look up. 'It's all so . . . difficult.'

'Vivvy darling . . .'

'We'll talk about it later,' she said.

He nodded helplessly.

★

Viv moved away from Ken; their skin made small, sticking sounds. She fiddled with the radio knob beside the bed. It produced crackles of static, then faint music.

'Blimey,' she said. 'It works.'

She turned up the volume. It was 'Land of Hope and Glory'.

'Oh dear,' she laughed. 'How proper.'

She turned the knob and the music changed to the faintest reggae, as if transmitted all the way from the West Indies. She felt Ken shift as he reached to the side for his cigarettes. It was the next day; the lost, at least losable, time between five and seven. She had left the girls with Julie down the road and said she was going shopping. She must remember to buy something on the way home. This was her most fertile time of the month and, as she had whispered to Ken over the phone, they might as well take advantage of it. Though it felt disconnected, to say these words to him, what made her feel more unlikely was phoning him at work, never at home. It was ridiculously hard to ask for Mr Fletcher. She thought of her children, sitting at the table, their eyes round. *Liar, liar, knickers on fire.* She didn't think of her children.

She said: 'I'm getting quite fond of this awful room. Wonder why they always give us the same one.'

Ken didn't reply. He offered her the cigarette packet. She took two, lit them and passed him one.

'That's nice of you,' he said.

'You ought to do this. Like in the movies. It's very smooth.'

'I'm not very smooth,' he said. He paused and looked at his watch.

'I'd better lie still a moment,' she said.

He looked at her. It was the first time for half an hour that he had met her eye. He was a surprisingly resourceful lover, and tender, but he kept his face buried. Was he comparing her with her sister?

Then his expression changed as he realized. 'Ah,' he said.

'Strange, isn't it?' She smiled. 'Years ago I'd be jumping

123

up and down, trying *not* to get pregnant. Now I'm lying here, willing it to work.'

He frowned. 'Viv . . .'

'What?'

'I wish you wouldn't, well, be so clinical.'

She raised her eyebrows. 'We're supposed to be clinical, aren't we?' He was silent. She added: 'Not that it isn't . . .'

'What?'

'Rather nice.'

He paused. 'Is it?'

'Isn't it?' She smiled. 'In fact, it could become a habit.'

Suddenly he put his head in his hands. 'Oh God.'

She touched his shoulder. 'You promised,' she said gently. 'No "oh Gods".'

Ken didn't move. She looked at his bowed back, at the hand covering his face. His muscularity made him look all the more helpless, but she did not dare hold him. She said: 'Just think of your body as separate. Men are good at that.'

He spoke through his fingers. 'Are they?'

'Fuck 'em and forget 'em.'

His head jerked up. 'Viv!'

'Come on. Haven't you ever done that? Before Ann?'

There was a pause. Ken drew on his cigarette. At last he said: 'I'd only, you know, the once . . .'

'No!'

He nodded. Down below, in the street, there was a traffic jam; she could hear cars hooting, the slamming of a door and angry shouts. Early evening noises. Through the net curtains there was grey daylight; the upstairs solicitor's office opposite, an unpromising place lit with strip light, went dark, as the light was switched off. It was nearly time to go.

She heard Ken take a breath. 'I went on this biking holiday to Belgium,' he said.

'Belgium?'

'Well, it's flat.'

She smiled. She wanted to ruffle his hair but she should know by now he didn't like that; he would consider it patronizing.

'Anyway,' he said, 'she was German. I thought it would be easier if I didn't speak the language. It was on this camp site. It was awful.' He stubbed out his cigarette and passed her the ashtray. She balanced it on her blanketed stomach. Outside, the hooting continued. 'Someone shone their torch in, and all the noises . . .'

'Multilingual screwing?'

He shook his head. 'The couple in the next tent, they were English and they were arguing about her mother, and how she ought to be put into a home now she was incontinent.'

She burst out laughing and ruffled his hair; she couldn't help it.

'Not very conducive,' he said. 'I'd never seen a naked woman before, my mother was very . . .'

She nodded. 'I know.'

'Or even sort of naked. Except for Brenda.'

'The one with the charm bracelet?'

He nodded. 'Brenda would, well, show you, for five bob. Which was a lot of money.'

He stopped. Opposite, the solicitor's light flickered on again; somebody must have forgotten something.

'Go on,' she said.

'So I washed our neighbour's car, and polished it with wax, and got the five bob. Well, I paid her, and she showed me, in the boiler room, and do you know what?'

'What?'

'Next day my neighbour pranged his car. A write-off. I felt terrible.'

'Why?'

He paused. 'I thought it was the wrath of God.'

She didn't know whether she should laugh. She concen-

trated on the window; opposite, the lights were again
switched off. The room was gloomy now the daylight was
fading.

She said: 'What did Ann say?'

'What?'

'When you told her?'

He turned to look at her. 'I didn't.'

'Why not? It's a wonderful story.'

'I couldn't.'

'Why?'

'She's my wife.'

She couldn't help herself this time; she burst out
laughing. 'You are an extraordinary person.'

'Don't say that!'

'Why not?'

He turned away. 'I'm not in a test tube.'

There was a silence. At the basin the tap started dripping; it had a life of its own. She said gently: 'I'm sorry,'
and got out of the bed. With her back to him she pulled
on her briefs and then, swiftly, her dress. She turned: 'Do
I look a mess?'

He gazed at her. He said: 'You look very young.'

She buckled up her belt. 'You don't have to say that.'

'Can't I?'

She didn't reply. She wished he would get up. She
pulled on her tights; how can one do this fetchingly?
Impossible. She should have worn stockings again. She
started brushing her hair.

'So do you still believe in the wrath of God?' she
asked.

He hadn't moved. 'I don't know,' he said. 'I don't know
anything any more.'

She ran her fingers through her hair and shook her
head to make it curly. She felt she was sitting on a silent
stage. 'Well don't worry,' she said.

'What do you mean?'

She gestured around: the dripping tap, the darkening

window, his clothes heaped on the chair. 'This room must never have known such worthy sex.'

He stared at her. She could no longer see his face clearly. 'Worthy?' he asked.

'Isn't that the word?'

'Is it?' He gazed at her, still not moving.

Ann was cutting up liver; the strips slumped on to the wooden board. In the early years of their marriage she had got Ken to do this for her; she couldn't bear to feel the slippery, wet bonelessness of the stuff. Besides, she had liked him protecting her and smiling at her disgust. But she had pulled herself together; squeals were less charming in one's thirties. Or was it that he had stopped offering? He used to hover around her in the kitchen, busying himself with something, as if the air in the other rooms were thinner with her absence. But wouldn't one be a fool to expect that to last through fourteen years of marriage, a flat and then a house, several thousand meals?

Seven o'clock. The radio pips sounded; it was only then that she realized the radio had been speaking all this time and she hadn't heard a word. She looked out into the garden; it was smaller than Viv's, and paved because Ken had said you couldn't keep a lawn this size. Tubs stood around the walls, spaced as regular as sentries; they glimmered white and attentive. In them, wallflowers had faded in the evening gloom. April had come in cool and blustery.

Above the wall Ken had fixed a trellis; it unsuccessfully screened Mrs Maguire's washing – gently rocking Babygros and Mr Maguire's enormous underpants. She thought: there is no mystery in my garden. How barren and self-respecting it looks. She felt herself flush with shame, for hadn't she herself helped Ken to make it that way, working beside him, clearing rubble and laying slabs?

She felt tired and old and her fingers were bloody. It

had seemed a long day; strange how much more exhausting work could be when one's mind was distracted. She heard the front door click. Ken paused in the hall, clearing his throat. He always did that, when he was looking at the letters. She only realized that now.

Behind her, he entered the kitchen.

'Hi,' he said. He never said 'hi', he said 'hello'. Or had she just not noticed? What else had recently escaped her, that she must now rewind and inspect with her sore eyes? New words; old clearings of the throat.

She half turned. He was carrying his sports holdall.

'Sorry I'm late,' he said. 'Had a swim.'

She turned back to the liver. 'You don't have to explain, you know.'

A silence. 'What?' he asked.

Her knife was sharp; the liver parted, pink, soft as butter, as she cut it. She said: 'Exactly where you've been.'

'But I have been swimming! Look!'

He came up to her, grabbed her free hand and pressed it on to his wet hair. She pulled her hand away, showing him her bloody fingers.

'Ugh!' he said.

'Sorry.'

'Sorry.'

She had finished slicing the liver. She put on the tap, a little turn of the cold, a little turn of the hot, and washed her hands under the water.

'Ann . . .'

She went on washing.

He said: 'It's about this clinic business. There's something I've got to tell you.' He paused.

'Don't.'

He stared. 'Don't what?'

She spoke swiftly: 'Don't tell me.'

He looked at her. 'What do you mean?'

'I'd rather you didn't spell it out.'

'But –'

'It might relieve you . . .' She spoke more gently, and turned to address the sink. 'But I don't want to know.'

There was a pause. He cleared his throat. 'How did you . . .?'

'I guessed,' she said. 'Remember, I've known you an awful long time.'

'But –'

'*Please!*' She swung round.

He gazed at her. 'Don't you care?'

'Of course I care. What do you think?'

He sat down at the table and ran his hands through his hair. It stood up in spikes. 'Oh God.'

'But this is more important than how I feel,' she said. 'Or how *you* feel. Do you understand?'

He stayed sitting there, gazing at the cruet.

She said: 'And after all, it'll soon be over, won't it?'

There was a silence.

'Won't it?' she asked.

He nodded.

She turned back to the sink and rinsed the chopping board; then she washed up the knife. 'Just promise me one thing,' she said. She stared out at their little garden. Of course she loved it. She said: 'If this is going to work, I don't want you crawling in like a dog that expects to be beaten.' She dried the knife on the tea-towel. 'I won't beat you.' She moved over to the units and opened a drawer. 'But please don't say how grateful you are.' She laid the knife in the drawer, with the others, and closed it.

Ollie closed the Kelly's Street Directory. There was an odd, echoing sensation between his ears, as if his skull had swelled.

Ellie passed him, and paused at his desk. 'Found what you were looking for?' she asked, pointing to the Kelly's.

He nodded, slowly, and stood up. 'You going to lunch?'

'Hey!' Ellie's flushed face flew past him. He pushed

harder. She was sitting on a child's roundabout, her bleached hair flying. 'Hey, stop it!' She put out her boot; it scraped as the roundabout slowed down.

She jumped off, breathless. 'You must've been a right bully once.'

He nodded. 'I used to pull the wings off little girls.'

'Well, keep your hands off mine,' she said, smoothing down her skirt. 'They're the only pair I've got.'

He didn't smile. She looked at him curiously as they walked out of the playground and down the street towards the piazza. It was warmer today; a watery sun shone on the yellowed stone columns. Ollie led her to a cocktail bar and they sat down at an outside table.

When the drinks came she looked in her glass and said: 'Like fruit salad in here.' She took out a cherry and ate it.

'Like it?'

She took a sip and grimaced. 'Tastes like the stuff me mum gave me for my tonsillitis.'

There was a pause. Then he said. 'You come from a happy family, don't you?'

She shrugged, and nodded.

'It shows,' he said.

'How?'

'You know how to trust people.'

She raised her eyebrows, but he didn't say any more. Instead, he indicated her drink. 'I'll get you something else.'

She put her hand over her glass. 'I want to be wicked and sophisticated.'

'Don't!'

'What?' She stared.

'Stay as you are.'

She looked at him in surprise. They sat there in silence. Ollie finished his drink; she sucked a mint leaf. Down the piazza, a group of people started shouting. Ollie jerked his head in their direction. 'Is that street theatre or are they just pissed?'

130

'What do you mean?'

'Just a Covent Garden joke,' he said.

She grinned. 'You seem to be cheering up.'

He paused. 'Only because of you.'

In the staffroom, teachers were taking out their lunch. Harold opened a can of Tizer. It hissed. He stared at it and said: 'Now why did I buy this?'

Madeleine looked out of the window at the watery sunshine and said: 'It almost feels like spring.'

The room hummed with the desultory monologues of those who have worked hard all morning. Harold settled behind his *Guardian*.

'Never guess who's taking up the cello.'

'Who?'

'Shane.'

'*Shane?*'

Mr Masterman, who did not resemble his name, dozed in his corner. Miss Hasnain, who was new, wrote some notes. Adam, who taught games, lit a roll-up. Just then there was a knock on the door.

Harold called out: 'Go away!'

There was a pause, then another tap.

'No!' said Harold.

Finally he sighed, got up and opened the door.

'Christ,' he said. 'Sorry. Thought you were a kid.'

A woman stood there: pleasant, forgettable face, now anxious. Pale pink lipstick; neat brown hair; buttoned two-piece. Spotless kitchen; inhibited in bed; Catherine Cookson reader. Nice legs, bet nobody told her; dull shoes. He tried to guess, in a flash, whose mother she must be. He always did this but he was usually wrong. 'Come in,' he said.

She looked around. 'Er, is Vivien Meadows here?'

He shook his head. 'She had to go home. Gas man cometh, she said.'

'Ah.'

'You've got a child in her class?'

'No,' said the woman. 'I'm her sister.'

He looked at her. 'Gosh.'

She stood there, undecided. He pointed to the phone. 'Give her a ring; she should be there by now.'

The woman thought for a moment, then rummaged in her handbag for some change. Yes, thought Harold: could be. Shorter, of course; not so pretty; not the style. But nice mouth like Viv's, no wonder he'd noticed the lipstick. The sort of woman, rounded and complete, who could sit in a staffroom for years and not be noticed, but when one did one found her a pleasant surprise. Two kids: Bruce and Sally. Not a tooth filling between them, and they wrote thankyou letters on Boxing Day.

Harold watched her at the phone and, thinking of his own children, sighed.

Ken stood at the window. Viv lay on the floor, face down, doing press-ups. Today it was the next room to what now seemed their usual.

She lowered herself up and down. 'Only a hotel,' she gasped 'would ever think of having a mustard and maroon carpet.'

Ken, who was putting on his tie, looked down at the shops. *Keys Cut, Ears Pierced.* He thought of Viv at sixteen, having her ears pierced; he flinched at the damage. Keeping his voice light, he turned and said: 'I once saw a sign saying, "Ears Pierced While You Wait".'

She collapsed on the floor, laughing.

He said: 'Wouldn't have much choice, would you?' He looked at her as she lay on the floor, pale and slender. She wore red lace briefs; today, for the first time, no bra. He said loudly: 'Go on!'

She went on with the press-ups. 'How many do *you* do?'

'Thirty.'

'Jesus.' She went on, gasping. He turned away. She stopped and said: 'My body's starting to feel different, I'm sure it is. It feels fitter.'

He gazed at the dusty window-pane. 'Mine feels different too,' he said.

'How?'

There was a silence. Then he said: 'It feels alive.'

In Viv's empty living room the phone was ringing. Finally it stopped.

Viv, still breathless, pulled on her jeans and jumper. She sat down again, leaning against the bed. Ken hadn't moved from the window.

'It's so peaceful here,' she sighed, closing her eyes. 'No phones, no noise. Like we're in a calm bubble. Uncomplicated. At home, everything's such chaos, everybody yelling, the girls wearing odd socks because I can never sort them out.'

Ken turned from the window. 'They do look a bit of a mess.'

'What?' She opened her eyes.

'The girls.'

She stared at him. 'You can't say that! We're not married.'

There was a silence. Somewhere in the building a door slammed. 'Of course we're not,' said Ken at last. 'It was stupid.'

She struggled to her feet and hurried over to him. 'Ken –' She put her hand on his arm; he jerked away.

'I've no rights,' he muttered. 'No rights at all.'

'Come here.' She touched him again; he pushed her off.

'You really know how to hurt someone, don't you,' he said. 'Calm, is it? Nice calm bubble? So delightfully uncomplicated?' His voice rose; he flinched at his own shouting. 'Well listen to me, Vivien Know-it-all Meadows, you college miss, think you're so clever, let me tell

133

you something. It's bloody complicated!' He roared out the words at her. 'It's utter bloody chaos!'

They stared at each other, appalled. Then he grabbed her and kissed her, hard. She turned her face away but he wrenched it back. With one hand he pulled up her jumper; he pushed her towards the bed. She stumbled, gripping him, and fell back on to the blankets.

Ann sat on the bench opposite Viv's house. The sky had clouded over as if the sun, after shining fitfully all day, had finally become dispirited by the world it had illuminated.

In fact it had started to drizzle. Ann shivered. Viv's car appeared and stopped outside the house. Viv climbed out, just like any mother, with the girls. Ann heard raised voices as the children protested about carrying the shopping in. Viv wore a new pink track-suit. She went into the house with the girls. How could Ann speak, with them there?

But then Viv reappeared, without the girls, to fetch the last bags. Blameless teacher, housewife, mother. How blamelessly harassed she looked. As she unloaded the bags she noticed Ann. She slammed shut the car door and hurried over, crossing the road and jumping the low wall into the playground.

'Ann!' she gasped. 'How nice to see you. Come in, it's raining.'

Ann didn't move. 'I tried to phone.' She indicated the track-suit. 'Never seen you in one of those.'

'Trying to get fit.' Viv smiled, still out of breath. 'Come on.'

Ann shook her head. She paused, then said: 'I just wanted to say I know what's happening.' After repeating the words to herself all day they came out pinched and bright, like stage dialogue.

Viv stared at her, then she moved forward and sat down, heavily, beside her.

'I don't want to talk about it,' said Ann. 'All I wanted to ask, in case I put my foot in it – does Ollie know?' She turned. Viv's hair was sparkling with rain; she shook her head slowly. Ann looked down at Viv's pink-clad thighs, speckly now. She stood up. 'Must go.'

Viv jumped up. 'But –'

Ann smiled at her and indicated the track-suit: 'It's not your colour,' she said kindly.

Ollie looked at his watch. 6.30. Across his desk lay scattered the transcripts for his drug abuse piece. All afternoon he had told himself he must start editing them. But the typing seemed so wearingly dense, like a code he no longer had the urge to decipher. When alarmed about this he told himself it was just the effect of three cocktails at lunchtime. That was simple, wasn't it?

He stacked the transcripts to one side. He must go home. It unnerved him that he feared to open his own front door. What would she be doing? Making the children's supper, wearing her familiar jeans? How could he bear to speak?

He paused at the switchboard. Ellie turned.

'Who's it to be tonight?' he asked.

'*Fun-loving accountant.*' She grimaced. 'I'm meeting him in that wine bar you took me to once.'

He thought: I can chat to Ellie, I can banter. I can sound normal. He asked: 'How're you going to recognize him – carnation in his buttonhole?'

She shook her head. 'He says his glasses are broken, so I can tell by the sellotape.'

Ollie laughed. He thought: see, I can laugh. Ellie can't tell there is anything wrong.

He turned to leave. She said: 'You OK?'

He replied: 'I'm fine.'

He closed the front door behind him and put down his briefcase. It was raining steadily now; he was wet. For a

135

moment he listened, attentive as an animal sensing danger. Far upstairs he could hear the girls' voices; for once they seemed to be playing in their bedroom. From the living room came the rattle of crockery.

He went in. Viv, in a pink track-suit, stood at the sink, washing up. She turned, smiling.

He stood in the doorway and said: 'You haven't been to that clinic, have you?'

His voice was toneless. He watched her expression change.

'What?' she asked.

'You heard me.'

She stood there, clutching the sponge. 'What do you mean?'

'Just been checking the facts.'

'What facts?'

He lowered his voice. 'You're a lying bitch.'

'Ollie!'

'There's no number three hundred and whatsit in Harley Street. I've checked in Kelly's.'

'But –'

'Should've tried a bit harder to get your story straight. I might have believed a do-it-yourself kit.'

She moved forward, but stopped at the table.

'Ollie,' she said.

'You did it yourself, didn't you? Your way. Four bloody weeks you've been at it.'

'Listen –'

'You've been screwing him, haven't you?'

'No,' she said. 'I –'

'You've been screwing him.'

There was a silence. Outside, the rain pattered on the concrete. He willed her, with all his heart, to say no.

Finally she said, in a low voice: 'Don't put it like that.'

He paused and looked at her. Her cheeks were pink. He wished he was still at the office and that he had never come home. He wished he could do it all again, and come home, and simply not ask her. His heart shrank, cold and beating. He said: 'What would you prefer?' He put on a cod Parisian accent: 'You made love?'

'No!'

He paused. 'You didn't?'

'No.' She stopped. 'I mean . . .'

'What?' he asked. 'You mean yes.' He spoke softly. 'I have been stupid, haven't I?'

'No!'

'Really stupid.'

'Ollie, please try to understand –'

'Fun, was it?' he asked.

'Please!'

'Exciting?'

'Ollie!'

'Good, was he? Good at it?'

'Look –'

'Bet he couldn't believe his luck. After all these years of fancying you.'

'He hasn't!'

'Don't be stupid. You've noticed all right.'

'He's married to my sister!'

'Exactly.'

'He's part of the family!' She still stood at the table, gripping its edges. He moved away to the front window and stood staring out at the rain and the motionless swings of the playground.

He said, without turning: 'He knows I know?'

'We haven't talked about that.'

'*We?*' Oh, nice. Already a couple, are you?'

'No!'

Ollie ran his finger along the dirty woodwork of the window. 'Christ, he must be laughing.'

'He's not!'

'Little prick.'

'He's terribly worried,' she said.

137

'Laughing at poor old Ollie, the cuckolded husband. Stuck here while he shafts his wife.'

'It's not like that!'

'Even bought him a drink last Sunday,' he said. 'The turd.'

'Ollie, you must understand –'

'Where do you do it? No, don't tell me.'

'A hotel.'

'How delightfully sordid.' He rubbed his dirty finger on his trousers, and faced her. She sat, slumped, at the table.

'No,' she muttered, 'he –'

'Got a little ring, have we, from Woollies?'

She raised her head. 'It's not like that –'

'Who pays?'

'He does.'

'Creep.'

'Ollie,' she said. 'This isn't helpful.'

'All that stuff about the clinic –'

'But –'

'Lies, lies.' He couldn't bear to look at her. He turned back to the window. 'There I am, being all supportive, saying what a noble thing you were doing, and you just let me babble on, you little bitch –'

'Ollie don't!'

She started sobbing. His own window-pane blurred. 'Poor Viv,' he said, his voice thicker. '*You* can't bear it.'

'I'm only trying to have a baby.'

'What? Immaculate Conception?'

'No!' she cried. 'It's reproduction.'

'*I* call it adultery.'

He wiped his nose on the back of his sleeve, turned round and grabbed the car keys from the dresser. Without looking at her, he walked out of the house.

'Ollie!' she called, opening the front door. But he was already in the car and fumbling with the key.

★

138

Ellie sat in the wine bar, sipping her orange juice – the real thing, with bits in. At the next table sat a man in glasses, but they were red ones and he'd put his Filofax on the table. Ollie had instructed her about those, and how they went with *kir* and *spritzers* and having little labels on your clothes and being aware. Anyway, this bloke was talking to a girl with a terrific profile and a lot of back showing; now where did you get a tan in April?

Ellie took another sip. She wished she smoked. Anything to look busy, and she'd read the drinks list about twenty times.

Somebody pushed past the chairs and stood at her table. She looked up. It was Ollie. He was breathing heavily and his face was damp. So was his hair.

'Come on,' he said.

'But you haven't got glasses.'

He didn't smile. He looked awful. He took her hand. 'Come on!'

She stood up, bewildered. He led her out; the chairs rocked as they passed.

Ann was in her garden. It was dark, but when she looked up the sky was lurid pink, so pink it hurt her eyes. The trellis had grown taller, and rattled. Down below, in the garden, someone was hiding behind the tubs, which were now as big as urns, on stalks. In the gloom she could see Viv's skirt behind one of them. Viv darted to another.

'Come on, Annie! Look what I've got!'

She was a little girl again, and she held out a plastic bag.

'Come on, Annie.' Her voice wheedled.

Ann refused to look. She felt angry, but it took her a moment to realize why. Then she knew that Viv had hidden Bo-Bo-Angela; she'd buried her under one of the urns.

'Look what I've got for you!' Viv's voice rose to a taunt. 'Cowardy-custard!'

Ann refused to look. Her garden had grown so black and cramped; around it the trellis was so tall and noisy.

Viv darted behind another urn and held out the bag. It glimmered in the gloom. But it wasn't right; there couldn't be a doll in there, it was far too small. Besides, wasn't Bo-Bo-Angela buried?

Viv darted out and pulled at Ann's sleeve.

'Shut up!' Ann heard herself shouting, from a long way off. Her throat hurt. 'Shut up! I hate you!'

Viv pummelled at her. Ann pushed her away; how big Viv had grown now, and strong.

'I *hate* you!' Ann shouted, gripping an arm that was far too hairy. And then she opened her eyes and of course it was Ken, leaning over her.

'Darling,' he said. 'You all right?'

She stopped, perspiring and breathless. She was in bed; it was dark. In a small voice she said: 'Sorry.'

12 It was the next evening. Ollie came downstairs, opened the fridge and took out a can of lager. Viv was lying on the sofa, her eyes closed. She had put a Beethoven sonata on the record player – one of his own serious records dating from before their university days. He had never heard her play it before. She looked pale. On the dresser, Bertie went round and round on his wheel. How many miles had he travelled since this time yesterday? Nothing had changed in his little sawdust world.

Ollie held up the lager. 'Want one?'

She shook her head. 'Asleep?'

He nodded. 'I read them that right-on story you bought. About the single parent with the one white child and the one black one.' He sighed and sat in the armchair. 'Sometimes I feel lonely for Ladybird Books. Peter and Jane and their nice parents who look as if they've never had sex.'

'Or problems,' she murmured.

'Or problems.' He drank from the can. 'Her in her apron and him with his pipe. I've got this funny feeling she's never fucked her brother-in-law.'

Viv smiled faintly. 'Want to bet?'

'I don't want to know.'

'You know what they say about the Famous Five.'

'No!'

There was a silence. The piano played. He thought: we must look so peaceful.

She said: 'Am I undermining your security?'

'Just a little, lately.'

She opened her eyes, and sat up. 'Oh Ollie . . .'

He took another sip. 'Still, I can always write about it in that novel I never get around to.' He paused. 'Does Ann know?'

She closed her eyes again and lay down. He watched her. She nodded.

'You're all in on this together?'

She shook her head. 'You needn't get paranoid.' She opened her eyes again and sat up. 'Don't you see, none of this is important. When it's over we'll forget it's ever happened.'

He drained his can and put it on the floor. Then he sighed. 'You can be very stupid.'

Her eyes widened. 'What do you mean?'

'Come on, Viv. Is this going to go on? What are your plans?'

'We haven't made any yet.'

He laughed flatly. 'Too busy humping?'

'No!' Her cheeks were pinker now. She ran her hand through her hair. 'But, well, there's no point in coming to a decision till next month, when I'm fertile again.'

'And then you'll go on with this affair.'

'It's not an affair!'

'Sneaking off to some seedy hotel.'

Her voice rose. 'Want us to do it here?'

'Don't be disgusting!'

They stared at each other. The music finished; the stereo clicked. Round and round the hamster wheel scraped. She said, more softly: 'Ollie, this must be the most selfless sex in the British Isles.'

He sighed and lay back in his armchair. 'Oh dear Viv, you radical women are all the same. Desperately simple-minded. The stronger your beliefs, the narrower your imagination.'

'What do you mean?' She stared at him.

He said: 'Your sister has been jealous of you all her life.'

'That's not true!'

'You're prettier, cleverer –'

'No –'

'*And* you can have children.' He paused, his eyes averted. 'And her husband has always wanted you.'

For a moment she didn't speak. The room was quiet; even the hamster had stopped. Then she said: 'That's not true.'

He nodded. 'And you've played on it, haven't you, Vivvy. Eh?' His voice grew oily. 'Sort of forgetting to put on your bathing costume when you swam in rivers, oh dear, scatterbrain.'

'Don't be stupid. It's nicer like that.'

'Then there's the way you quarrel –'

'He's such a bigot.'

Ollie kept his eyes closed. He smiled, feeling sick with himself. 'It's a form of flirtation. You needle him, you get him all excited. It's very sexual.'

'That's ridiculous.'

Suddenly Ollie opened his eyes and sat up straight. 'He's an innocent, Viv. He's putty in your hands.'

'Don't be stupid!' She sighed. 'I'd hoped you'd be more ... large-spirited. You and your ideas about – oh, re-structuring society and open marriage and everything. But scratch the surface and know what you are?'

142

He was still smiling. 'Tell me.'

'An ordinary jealous male, thinking of his male pride and his male dignity.'

Ollie raised his eyebrows. 'Scratch the surface,' he said slowly, 'and *you're* a slut.'

There is a giant step between suspicion and action. Once the action is taken you have stepped into another room and closed the door behind you. In this room the furnishings are different and strange. You cannot return.

Viv was thinking this the next Monday. It was the Easter holidays now and the girls were in the garden, squabbling over the old plastic tractor they both thought too babyish to ride on till the other one wanted it. How entirely normal it all seemed. On the windowsill were jammed her seed trays, the same as every year: stout little cabbage seedlings, their palms outspread; green threads of cornflowers with their seed husks still clinging. On the radio a phone-in droned, just like a normal Monday; she wondered why the callers always sounded so whiney and always came from Ashford. She also wondered about her aching breasts, and the faint queasiness she had been feeling for a week, and how long exactly had it been since her last period.

But there is all the difference in the world between wondering, uneasily, and actually walking to the chemist's and buying a pregnancy testing kit. Asking for it in those words, hearing your voice speaking them, passing across real pound notes (no, she would have to write a cheque) and bringing it home.

She put the carrier-bag on the table. To reassure herself she had also bought mundane items like bath cleaner and toothpaste. She had only been out a quarter of an hour, to the Holloway Road; in her absence the girls had come in and installed themselves in front of the TV, where they were watching a demonstration of nuclear physics and still squabbling. Nothing seemed changed; yet the room was altered by the fact that she had acted, and now there was a Boots bag on the table.

And by the time the real children's programmes had come on that afternoon, she had found out she was pregnant.

It was Tuesday morning, and Ken gazed out of the window at the works yard. He looked at the stacked timber and the Portaloo and thought: can I phone yet?

He hated even saying the words to himself. He looked at his watch. 10.15. By now he (*he*) must have gone to his magazine office. But what if he were ill, or writing at home today? These thoughts should not even be crossing his, Ken's, mind. He was starting to behave like – no, he would not say.

The steps outside thudded and Bob and Al came in, wearing their dusty overalls and jostling each other at the door.

'– Nice little slagette,' Al was saying.

'Where did you give it her?' Bob asked, grinning.

'In me dad's van.'

Ken cleared his throat and put out his hand for their chits. Al wiped his nose on the sleeve of his overalls and said: 'Honest, Kenny, I seem to have this terrifically sensual body, drives them mad.'

Ken didn't reply. He felt hot. He tried to concentrate on the chits. Looking up, he said: 'Fourteen lengths of two-by-fours? This for Forsythe Road?'

Al nodded.

'Seems a bit excessive,' he said. As he looked down at the figures he could see the two men nudging each other. He went on, ticking off the items with his biro. 'Sand and cement . . .' He ticked, and then looked up. 'Twelve gallons of Treatment? You used all that?'

'Blimey, Ken,' said Al.

Ken cleared his throat again. 'Just trying to keep the record straight. Keep things in order.'

Bob opened his eyes wide. 'Don't look at us.'

'See, boys,' said Ken, 'there's been a lot of petty losses. I'm not blaming you, mind. But bits here, bits there –'

'Bits on the side,' grinned Bob.

Ken paused, his biro in mid-air. His shirt felt tight.

'Where were we, Thursday afternoon?' Bob asked him, leering.

Ken's throat was dry. He shrugged and looked down at the papers. Out of the corner of his eye he could see Bob put his finger on the side of his nose.

'Don't worry,' said Bob. 'See no evil –'

'Look, lads.' Ken indicated his watch. 'Better get a move on.'

When they were gone he lit a cigarette. His hands were trembling. He looked at his watch: 10.30. He dialled.

Thank goodness, Viv answered. He cleared his throat again and asked: 'Just wondering if it was still, you know . . .'

'On? Fine.' Viv's voice sounded faint and crackling. 'Suzi's taking them to the Unicorn Theatre, so we've got the whole afternoon.'

He put down the receiver and sat there, gazing down into the yard. Their voices had been as hushed as conspirators'. He thought: when Ann told me she had to go to Swindon today, to see the new computer, I didn't think: how nice for you; how interesting; how instructive. I thought: I might not feel quite so bad, with you out of London.

He stubbed out his disgusting cigarette, violently.

This time they were given their original room. They sat side by side on the bed. Ken passed her a paper bag.

'Bought us these,' he said.

She looked in the bag and shook her head, grimacing. 'No thanks.'

'I thought you liked apple strudel.'

145

'Not today.' She passed back the bag to him. 'Go on, you have one.'

'No thanks.'

They sat there in silence. Then she put out her hand and caressed his knee. He didn't move.

'This is the worst bit,' she said gently. 'Isn't it?'

He nodded.

'Look, I'll begin,' she said. She leaned over and took off his jacket. 'You do one and I'll do one.'

Still he didn't move. She paused, then she got up and pulled off her T-shirt and jeans. Underneath she was wearing a pink, lacy one-piece thing. He looked away quickly. 'That's nice,' he said.

'Ollie bought it.'

He shifted. 'Oh.'

She sat down beside him. Then she sighed and asked: 'Aren't we allowed to make this real?'

He didn't reply. He heard the sigh of the silk as she crossed her legs. A fly buzzed against the window-pane. He put his head into his hands.

'Cheer up, ducks.' Viv's voice had changed. 'You'd like one of the other girls?'

He shook his head and spoke into his hands. 'I'd like you.'

'That's the ticket.' She ruffled his hair. 'It's always hard the first time, isn't it? Sorry, fourth, fifth time.' She started unbuttoning his shirt. 'Still, we pride ourselves we run a friendly establishment here; we really care for our customers.' She threw his shirt aside and leant down to pull off his shoes. 'Specially nice respectable gents like yourself; nice class of shoe.' She flung them aside and pulled off his socks. 'I'd expect you're an executive, am I right? And very nicely built too; you keep yourself in trim, I dare say.' She stroked his chest. 'Mmm . . . bet you're a terror on the rugger pitch, bit of a terror in other departments too, I wouldn't be surprised . . .' He lifted himself up and she started pulling off his trousers.

146

'Hmmm . . . yes, I thought so . . . you're not as shy as you look –'

'Viv!'

'What?'

He pulled her to him and cried out: *'Don't!'*

'This is a nice idea,' said Ann, as the waiter showed them to a table. Ollie had chosen a Greek restaurant near Charlotte Street, where he often came to lunch. She looked around at the lurid Mediterranean landscapes on the walls. 'Very authentic. When Ken and I went to Corfu it was all Watney's on tap and Birmingham accents.'

Ollie laughed. 'And the food's warmer here.'

'Ah yes. Lukewarm moussaka.'

They sat down. She was wearing a paisley blouse. Her brown hair was brushed, conker-shiny. If he blinked, she could be an unknown woman. For the first time he noticed the faint lines on her forehead, and at the corners of her mouth. He said: 'I don't think I've ever had a meal alone with you in my life.'

'No.' She smiled. He thought: she often smiles, very sweetly, but she hardly ever laughs.

She inspected the menu. He thought how people became fixed at first glimpse. The first time he met her, he'd come down from Keele University with Viv for the weekend and they had had lunch at Ann's flat. Viv had dropped the casserole and Ann had apologized. Ann became fixed as someone who presumed to be wrong, who busied herself with meals, who had a wide, pale, settled face, as if matronly before her time. He looked at her again, now in her mid-thirties, and thought with surprise: she looks younger now. And more tired, and rather more interesting.

She said: 'Nothing much we can do at the moment, is there?'

He shook his head. 'We're waiting in the wings.' He indicated the menu. 'What shall we drink?'

147

'Let's have a bottle of wine. Let's live dangerously.'

He smiled and thought: without Viv, she looks prettier. Viv is like a virtuoso violin; when it's removed one hears the rather nice tune of Ann, the accompanying piano.

'Why are you smiling?' she asked.

He couldn't tell her, so he said: 'Dangerously?'

She nodded. 'I'm learning.' She paused, watching some people come into the restaurant and sit down. She said: 'Viv was the expert at that. I'd be asleep, and she'd creep in and tell me all about it. Once, she'd been out with a Maltese waiter and she came home with love-bites all over her neck. It was a heatwave, and next day Dad said: "Why're you wearing a scarf in June?"'

Ollie laughed. 'She told me about that.'

Ann ate an olive. 'Ken's never bitten my neck.'

'Were you envious?'

'No.' She paused and took out the stone. She put it in the saucer. 'Yes. Oh, I didn't want to be bitten by a waiter, but . . .' She shrugged. 'It wasn't just boys, it was the risks. The danger.' She took another olive. 'The fun.'

The waiter brought the wine and filled their glasses.

Ann smiled. 'Whenever we had chips for tea she'd gobble hers up, and I'd save mine till last. So she'd see me eating them and be jealous. But they never tasted the same.'

'Why not?'

'They'd gone cold.'

Ollie burst out laughing. 'Oh, she's always lived in the fast lane, chip-wise.' He pointed to the menu. 'Go on, have some today. Make up for lost time.'

Ann didn't look at the menu. Instead she asked: 'Do you mind?'

'About all this?' He paused. 'No.' There was a silence. She looked down at the menu. He said: 'Yes.'

She nodded. 'It's worst for you. You don't gain anything at all.'

He asked: 'Do *you* mind?'

'I thought I didn't, but . . .'

'But what?'

She shrugged. 'It's silly.'

'What?'

'It's just . . . I saw them yesterday. And I wish I hadn't.'

Ollie froze. 'Yesterday?'

'I'd come from Paddington Station, and I was going to the bus stop. I saw them coming out of their, well . . .' She took another sip of wine. 'They didn't see me.'

For a moment, Ollie couldn't speak. He felt his scalp prickle, as if his skull were going to burst.

He thought: *You lying bitch. You told me you'd stopped.*

Ellie had taken the day off work. She sat in her room with a cloth over her head, inhaling Friar's Balsam. Funny, she thought: you can always tell you're ill when you start to miss your family. She breathed in deeply. She even longed for her little brother, so maybe she'd got flu.

Nobody told you how lonely London could be. Outside, the street was quiet. Her room was above a parade of shops in Crouch End but in the afternoons there were just a few mums with pushchairs. In Covent Garden, on the other hand, the people were all in Golf convertibles, with accompanying passengers, or else they were overweight and from Ohio and asking her the location of streets she'd never heard of.

She thought she heard the bell ring, but she decided it was just her imagination and her blocked head. But it rang again, twice. She removed the cloth, put on her dressing gown and hurried to the window. She opened it and looked down.

It was Ollie. He waited below. Her stupid heart thumped, and she noticed for the first time that his hair was thinning on top. She'd never seen him from this angle, he usually towered above her.

'Coming!' she called, and rushed to the mirror. Her

face was pink and damp; her eyes piggy. Too late. She ran down the stairs and let him in.

'I had to see you,' he said.

'It's O K,' she replied. 'It's only a cold.'

He put his arms around her.

'That'll get the tongues wagging,' she said, trying to laugh.

'What?'

'If you started sneezing too.'

'Ellie –'

He stopped. He looked terrible. She led him up to her room. It looked so exposed, with her smalls soaking in a bowl and her Soup-for-One packet not thrown away. To divert his attention she pointed to her collection of china and glass cats on the mantelpiece.

'See,' she said. 'I *am* a cat-lover.'

He didn't reply. He sat down heavily on the bed.

She asked: 'What is it?'

He paused. 'I feel so lonely.' His voice sounded strangled.

'Here, let's have some tea.' She went over to the kettle.

'No thanks. Just had lunch.'

'What nationality?' It was one of their routines.

'Greek.'

She removed her inhalation bowl and sat down beside him. 'You can't mean that.'

'What?'

'You're lonely.' She pointed to her copy of *Capital*. 'There's always a warm, non-smoking lesbian.'

Ollie smiled thinly. He said: 'I shouldn't have taken you out, should I?'

She looked down at her slippers. 'No, but . . .'

'I shouldn't.'

'What've we done? A couple of lunches. An evening at the pictures. I'm just a shoulder to cry on.'

He said: 'You're not.'

'I am.'

150

He turned to her and started stroking her damp hair, pushing it back from her face. She said gently: 'Don't.' He went on; he hooked a strand and laid it behind her ear. She said in a low voice: 'You're married. You've got two lovely little girls.'

He said: 'Remember what I said, about trust?'

She nodded. She remembered every word he'd said to her.

'About you being able to trust people?' he said. 'Believe in them? You do, don't you?'

She shrugged.

'That's why I want to be here,' he said. He touched her face. 'I shouldn't be.'

'No,' she said.

He got up and went to the door. He did it so abruptly she was left off-balance.

'What're you doing?' she asked.

'Must go.' He opened the door.

She got up and pulled at his arm. 'You could at least tell me why.' He stared at her. She glared at him. 'You come barging in here,' she said, her voice rising to a croak, 'you don't even have the decency to tell me why, and then you bugger off.'

He moved away and leaned against the door frame. Her throat hurt, her head throbbed. She glared at him.

'Can't you understand why?' His voice was quiet now. She turned away; she could not bear to see his face. He said: 'I must go before I do something stupid.'

He moved away and went down the stairs. She shut the door, went over to the bed and sat down. Ridiculously, she burst into tears. She must have a temperature.

She told herself: don't be daft. She got up and filled the kettle. Her inhalation was lukewarm now; she would have to make some more. She held up the bottle; she couldn't keep her hand steady and the writing was dancing – yes, *two tablespoons*. She removed her bowl of smalls from the sink and rinsed out the balsam basin.

The kettle had just boiled when there was a knock on the door. She opened it. He took her in his arms; she held him tightly. He was crying too. They stepped back, staggering, off-balance, into the room.

It was Easter Sunday and suddenly hot. Flies buzzed over Viv's compost heap; the bushes rustled as Ollie hid eggs. Ann sat on the rabbit hutch and watched him. He seemed preoccupied. She had thought it was just her fault at lunch on Wednesday – that she never brought out the best in anybody, and that his wit would have flowered with Viv. But he seemed just as tense today. She watched him squatting down to insert a small silver egg into a crack in the wall, and she wondered, with sudden pain, if Ken would ever hide Easter eggs for their child, like this. If, indeed, they ever had one.

Ollie stood up and glanced swiftly at the kitchen window. She had always found him attractive in a lanky, feminine way. An appealing man. Helpless. The antithesis of Ken. She remembered when the Meadowses had first moved into this house, years ago, and she had offered to make them bedroom curtains. Ollie had come downstairs with the measurements; he had no tape measure and he'd told her: 'Seven Penguin books by thirteen.' She remembered Ken's bemusement.

It was so hot, almost thundery. There was an oppressive feeling in the air; even the girls were subdued. Ann went in to help Viv, who was moving around the kitchen as if asleep at the controls. Their father and his fiancée were expected for tea. Ken, thank goodness, was still outside, fiddling with the car.

'What can I do?' she asked. She hadn't seen Viv since the day of the pink track-suit and she felt grateful that the girls were in the room – they were sitting in the front end of it, so they couldn't see where Ollie hid the eggs.

'Not much to do,' said Viv. 'Dad wants it to look all informal.'

Not hard to look informal here, Ann would have joked at any other time. She sat down with the girls and opened their *Beezer* annual. But instead of seeing the cartoons she saw Ken and Viv, unreeling again like a stubborn piece of film: they were walking out of the hotel towards the car. Ken had parked on a yellow line and he had a parking ticket. It was so unlike Ken, that. For the moment it hurt more than anything else.

'Another piece?' asked Vera. She had brought along a *Sachertorte*, a speciality of Vienna. They were all sitting at tea.

'No thanks,' said Ann. 'I'm getting so fat.'

'Nonsense.' Vera turned to Ken. 'A man, he likes a woman to look like a woman, don't you, Kenneth?'

'Yes,' said Ken. 'But she should watch her weight.'

Ann looked at him sharply and turned to Vera. 'I'd love another piece.'

Vera cut it for her. She was a tall, well-groomed woman with the sort of handsome face that looked as if it had suffered. There was a stillness about her that impressed Ann. Her father, by contrast, had grown as skittish as a schoolboy.

'I have heard so much about you,' said Vera, turning to Viv. 'I may call you Vivien?'

'Of course,' said Viv. She shook her head at the cake. She had eaten nothing.

'And your little girls,' Vera went on. 'I feel so happy, that we are buying a flat nearby here. I hope we shall be getting to know each other. Families are so precious.'

There was a silence. Ollie sneezed.

Vera said to Viv: 'You should give him some oil of camphor.'

'It's his cold,' said Viv.

'Pardon?'

'He doesn't want me fussing over him.'

Ollie nodded. 'It's my cold.'

153

There was another silence. Ann looked outside. In the garden, the two little girls, clutching their plastic bags, were searching for the eggs.

Douglas cleared his throat. 'It's a lovely little place. Hope you'll come round.' He turned to Ann. 'You too, of course. We both thought: better have a clean sweep.' He cleared his throat again. 'New start.' He held out his plate for some cake. 'Well, I for one enjoy being spoilt. High time too. All those years of baked beans.'

'My darling,' said Vera. They gazed at each other with such naked love that Ann had to turn away. She looked at the sunlit garden.

'Found them all?' asked Douglas.

Ann nodded. 'They're climbing over the wall. I expect they're going to count them in front of the children next door.'

'They're beautiful, aren't they?' said Vera. She turned to Ken. 'You know, Kenneth, I always love the children. I wanted them, but my first husband – it wasn't possible. So this great joy was denied me.'

'Vee –' said Douglas.

'I just tell them that I understand,' said Vera. 'If we are a family we should be open together, don't you think?'

There was another silence. Ken was tearing up little bits of silver paper – wrappings from an Easter egg. Ollie sneezed again.

'Think it's flu?' asked Douglas.

'I'm fine,' said Ollie.

'It's the change in the weather,' said Ken. 'Suddenly it's summer.' He went on shredding up the paper and rolling it into little balls.

Ann said sharply: 'I wish you wouldn't do that.'

Viv stood up and fetched the kettle. 'More tea, anybody?'

Ann turned to her father. 'So where are you holding the reception?'

'A nice hotel, we thought. Any suggestions?'

'Ask Viv,' said Ollie suddenly.

Douglas turned to him, surprised. 'Why?'

Ollie said: 'Viv's the hotel expert.'

Douglas turned to Viv. 'Are you?'

'No!' she said.

Nobody spoke. Vera looked from one face to another. Then Viv went to the garden door and closed it. She turned round. 'I've something to tell you,' she said. 'I'm pregnant.'

Ken's hands stopped shredding. Ann didn't dare move.

Vera was the first to speak. 'What wonderful news!'

Their father said: 'Well, well.'

Vera turned to Ollie. 'Why didn't you say? Here I was, chattering along –'

'I didn't know,' said Ollie flatly.

Ann jumped up and hugged Viv. For a moment Viv didn't respond, then she put her arms around her.

Ollie's voice asked: 'How long have you known?'

Viv spoke into Ann's hair. 'A week.'

'A week?' asked Ken.

Viv gently pushed Ann back and went to the table. She sat down. Ken hadn't moved; he was staring at her.

Their father leaned over and said jovially, to Ollie: 'Bit of a shock, eh?'

Ollie turned to Viv. 'Good of you to let me know.'

There was a pause. Ann, standing beside the sink, looked at them all sitting motionless at the tea table. The moment was transfixed. There was the scrape of a match as Ken lit a cigarette.

Viv turned to Ollie. 'I was going to tell you first, but then I thought: this is a family affair. I wanted to wait till we were all here. Because this belongs to everyone.'

Her father looked around the table. 'Have I missed something?'

Viv said to Ann: 'You tell them.'

'Me?' asked Ann.

'It's your business now, as well as mine.'

155

Ann felt the warmth spread into her face. She tried to speak, and began again. 'You still mean it?'

Viv nodded gravely, and turned to her father. 'I'm not keeping the child,' she said.

Douglas stared. 'What?'

Vera asked: 'You're not going to have the baby?'

'I'm going to have it,' Viv began, and stopped. She looked at Ann.

Ann cleared her throat. 'But she's going to give it to me and Ken.'

Douglas, wreathed in Ken's cigarette smoke, looked at Viv. 'Come again?'

Vera turned to Ollie: 'Do you –?'

'Yes,' said Ollie. 'I know about it.'

Douglas spoke loudly. 'Is this April the first, by any chance?'

Ollie said: 'It's not my baby.'

'It's Ken's,' said Viv.

Ann remained at the sink. She felt as alert as an animal, poised between joy and fear. She hardly breathed.

Her father looked from one face to another and said finally: 'What've you all been up to?'

'I was artificially inseminated,' said Viv. Ollie turned, sharply. Ken stayed still.

'What?' said Douglas.

'It's Kenneth's baby?' asked Vera.

Viv nodded. 'Ken's and mine.'

'I have read about this in the newspapers,' said Vera.

Douglas turned to Ken. 'You paying or something?'

'Dad!' said Viv. 'I'm doing this for love.'

Ken said: 'Of course there'll be proper compensation –'

'For love, Dad,' said Viv sharply. 'Something you might not understand.'

There was a noise at the back door. They all froze. Rosie and Daisy were in the garden. They banged on the glass; their heads appeared, hair flying, as they jumped up and down. They looked like apparitions from long ago –

156

how much time had passed since they had climbed over the wall?

Viv rose and let them in.

It was so hot in the garden. Viv stood for a moment, breathing in the scent of next door's lilac. The blossoms lolled heavily over the wall, as if inspecting her – fragrant and incurious. How peaceful it was. She looked back at the house. Through the window it all looked like a normal family gathering: Ollie washing up, the girls' laughter rising inside the room; her father's deeper voice. She took her time emptying the peelings into the compost heap.

When she turned back, Ken was behind her. She looked at him: his square, masculine face, flushed now; his helpless hands hanging at his sides.

He spoke in a low voice. 'There's something I need to know.'

'What?'

'On Wednesday, when we . . . you know . . .' He glanced back at the house. 'You must've known you were pregnant.'

She nodded.

He asked: 'Then why?'

She looked down. The compost heap was built of bricks; in one of the cracks she could see something shining. She picked it out; it was an egg the children had missed. She gave it to Ken. Then she shrugged, trying to look casual. 'I suppose I just wanted to.'

She moved back towards the house. He remained standing there, holding the egg.

'Didn't you?' she asked, and hurried back into the house.

Vera was sitting on the sofa, her hand outstretched. On either side of her the girls were inspecting her ring.

'. . . and these are little diamonds,' she said. 'The jewels of love.'

Rosie touched them. 'Are they proper ones?'

'Cost enough,' said Douglas. His colour was high and his voice loud. He stood at the mantelpiece and glanced at Viv as she came in.

'Don't listen to your grandfather,' said Vera. 'He has no romance in his heart.' She looked up at Douglas, and smiled.

Rosie said: 'Mum, why haven't you got a proper ring? Why didn't you have a proper wedding dress?'

Viv put away the compost bin. 'It was my sort of proper.'

'Some bloody kaftan,' said her father.

Daisy said: 'Auntie Vera wants us to be her bridesmaids.'

Vera nodded. 'I'm seeing them in the most pale green, like new little leafs.'

'Leaves,' said Douglas sharply.

Viv went over to the dresser and took out her purse. She said to the children: 'Run along and get some crisps.'

'They've just had tea,' said her father.

The girls grabbed the money and ran out into the hall. Viv called after them: 'Eat them in the playground, else you'll have to wash up.'

She turned back. Ken had come in from the garden; he stood beside the sink. 'Can I help?' he asked Ollie.

Ollie shook his head. 'Too many cooks.' His apron had come undone at the back. Viv longed to tie it up, but she knew she couldn't.

She turned to her father. 'Don't tell anyone. We haven't decided anything, we haven't even talked. I just wanted you to know.'

Vera smiled at her. 'I'm so happy.'

'Are you?' asked Viv.

'It is a very beautiful thing to do.'

Viv looked at the Austrian woman. She felt expanded, lighter. She felt herself smiling, for the first time. 'Are you?' She moved forward and sat down on the sofa beside her. Her father still stood at the mantelpiece. He was fiddling with some bits of Lego.

He turned and spoke sharply to Vera: 'She's joking, Vee.' There was a silence. 'In poor taste, I grant you, but –'

'I'm not!' said Viv.

'In fact it's disgusting,' he said.

Ann spoke. 'She means it, Dad. We all do.' She had stopped even the semblance of drying up and sat down at the table.

Douglas stared down at Viv. 'That's Kenneth's baby in there?'

Viv nodded.

He went on: 'And how does your husband –'

'It's not mine,' said Ollie. He had turned from the sink and stood there in his Mothercare apron. The front was blurred bluish, where the Pentel marks had been wiped.

'Excuse me,' said Douglas, 'but how do you know?'

'It's not,' said Ollie.

Douglas's face was deep red now. He turned to Ken. 'You, young man. How could you?'

'Dad!' said Viv.

'My own daughter!' he went on. 'It's like incest.'

'Don't be stupid,' said Viv. 'We're not related.'

'Don't get uppity with me, young woman, just because you've been to college –' He stopped for breath.

Ann went nearer him and said sharply: 'Dad! Will you listen? It's over, it's done. It was all perfectly decent.'

Ollie spoke. 'Perfectly,' he said.

'In a clinic,' said Ann.

'A clinic,' said Ollie.

'And quite frankly I think it's rather prurient to enquire too much about that particular aspect.'

There was a pause. Vera had taken Viv's hand. Nobody moved. Then Douglas said: 'You must all be out of your bloody minds.'

Viv turned to Vera. 'You seem to understand.'

Vera nodded. 'I understand.'

Viv spoke to her father; he loomed above her. 'Vera called it beautiful.'

'Ah,' he said, 'but there's one difference.'

'What?'

His voice rose. 'You're my daughter, not hers.'

Beside her, Viv felt Vera stiffen. She looked up at her father. 'Listen, Dad. I love Ann. She's had a raw deal, and nobody should know that better than you.' Everyone was silent. Viv took a breath and went on. 'I'm doing this for love. We all are. You call it disgusting. Do you know what I think is disgusting?' She paused. Her father didn't answer. She went on, her voice rising. 'Do you? The way you've loved me more than Ann. That's a terrible, terrible thing to do to a child.' Her hand felt slippery with sweat; she took it from Vera's and looked up at her father's red face. 'God knows I'm not perfect – I've had abortions, I've been unfaithful to Ollie, often, I'm a terrific liar, I'm bossy and inconsistent and, oh, lots more . . .' Breathing heavily, she turned to Vera. 'You must be enjoying this, here's family life.' She turned back to her father and spoke urgently: 'But none of this is as truly wicked as making a child feel a failure. There's no prison sentence long enough for that and yet it's not even considered a crime.' She stopped, breathless, and then hissed: 'Now isn't *that* disgusting?'

Nobody spoke. From the playground came the faint sounds of children yelling. In the street a car passed. Then Ollie started clapping.

Viv frowned at him. He said: 'I mean it.'

Vera turned to her. 'You can't say that to your father.'

'I had to,' said Viv. She willed her heart to stop thumping.

Vera went on: 'But it's no wonder he has favoured you more than Ann when –'

'*Vera!*' her father bellowed.

They all stared at him.

Viv turned to Vera. 'What do you mean?'

Her father shouted: 'Shut up, you stupid woman!'

Vera burst into tears. She bent over her knees, sobbing. 'Now look what you've done,' he said.

Viv put her arm around Vera, whose shoulders were shaking. Ann moved over quickly, taking out a hand-kerchief. She sat down on the arm of the sofa, comforting her.

The doorbell rang. Nobody moved. There was no sound, except small hiccups from Vera.

The bell rang again. Finally, Viv jerked her head at Ollie. He left the room; they heard him walking along the hall, then opening the door. There was a chatter of voices and Irene came in.

She stumbled on the mat. 'Whoops,' she said merrily.

Behind her came Frank. He was a plump, benevolent man with corrugated grey hair. He smiled and nodded at Viv.

Irene saw her ex-husband and raised her eyebrows. 'Hello, Doug.'

'Hello,' he said.

Viv said hastily: 'Er Mum, this is Dad's fiancée, Vera.'

Irene looked at Vera, who was blowing her nose. 'She looks happy about it.'

'Mum!' said Viv.

'Pardon me,' said Irene. 'We've been celebrating. Doug, this is Frank; he runs the salon.' Irene worked at a hair-dresser's.

'Hello, Frank,' said Douglas.

'Glad to meet you,' said Frank, stepping forward and putting out his hand. Douglas shook it.

Viv spoke to her mother. 'I thought you were going to –'

'Venice,' said Irene, nodding. 'Just popped in, didn't we, to bring these.' She put two large Easter eggs on the table. 'For the girls,' she said. 'Where are they?'

'At the shops,' said Viv.

'And to show off me frock,' said her mother, swirling round for them all. She wore a dress with large red poppies printed on it.

'Lovely,' said Viv, going to the kettle. 'Have some tea. Frank, do sit down.'

Her mother grimaced. 'Can't we have something a bit more festive?'

'Of course,' said Ollie. He went to the fridge and took out a bottle of white wine.

Frank laughed. 'She'll be too sloshed to get on the plane.'

'Well, you only live once,' said Irene.

Frank took out a packet of panatellas and offered one to Ken, who shook his head, and then to Douglas.

'No thanks,' said Douglas.

'Mind if I do?' asked Frank.

Viv fetched the glasses.

Irene, who was looking at Vera curiously, sat down beside her on the sofa. Vera moved a little, to give her room. Irene asked: 'So where's he taking you for your honeymoon – Southend?'

'Crete,' said Douglas loudly.

Vera looked up at him, surprised. 'Where?'

'Crete,' he repeated. 'Well, why not?'

Irene looked at him with interest. 'You have changed.'

'As you said,' he replied, 'you only live once.'

Viv looked from her mother – petite and beady-eyed, like a bird in flowery plumage – to her father, who looked larger than ever, and flushed, as he stood at the mantelpiece. She wondered what Vera was seeing, now. The Austrian woman sat on the sofa, still and dignified, gazing from one face to another. She wore a sombre but rather beautiful brown silk dress. Beside her, Viv's mother looked garish. Viv thought: who in this room do I actually trust? She passed out the glasses of wine; the scent of it made her queasy.

Frank leaned towards Vera and asked conversationally: 'Have you visited Venice?'

162

'Course she has,' interrupted Irene, and turned to Vera. 'She's from Vienna, aren't you?'

'It is very lovely,' said Vera.

'Vienna?' asked Frank.

'Venice,' said Vera.

'So I've heard,' said Frank.

Irene took a sip of her wine. 'See Venice and die.'

Viv passed her father a glass. 'That's Rome.'

'Is it?' asked Frank.

Viv nodded. 'See Rome and die.'

Ollie, passing by, muttered to her, 'It's Naples,' and sat down.

'It isn't,' said Viv.

Her mother giggled. 'Well anyway, it's not Southend.'

Vera looked around confused. 'Where is Southend?'

Viv smiled. 'Quite near Crete.'

'Pardon?' asked Vera.

Silence fell. Ollie started humming under his breath and picking at the frayed seam of his jeans. Viv frowned at him. Ken stood against the draining board, drinking.

Irene turned to Vera and said: 'That's a gorgeous outfit you're wearing.'

'Thank you,' said Vera.

Douglas nodded. 'She made it herself,' he said, pointing at Vera with his wineglass. 'She's a professional.'

'Mmm,' said Irene, feeling the material between her fingers. 'Lovely little shoulders. So you get paid for it?'

'Course she does,' said Douglas.

'A proper dressmaker,' said Irene. Then she looked at Vera. 'Say, will you make something for me?'

'Look –' began Douglas.

'I mean it,' said Irene. 'You can see she's handy with a needle and I'm rushed off my feet.'

Vera smiled. 'I would be delighted.'

Douglas said: 'Vera, I don't –'

'Oh shut up.' Irene glared at him. Then she raised her glass. 'Let's have a toast.'

163

Vera raised her glass. 'To Vivien,' she said.

Irene turned and stared at her. 'Viv? Why?'

Viv said hastily: 'No, here's to everyone.' She had poured herself some orange juice. She raised her glass. 'Heaven knows, we need it.'

The guests were gone. Ollie paced the room, pouring the dregs of other people's wine into his glass. He drank, then looked at Viv.

'Why didn't you tell your mum?'

'Not with Frank there.'

'She'll be hurt,' he said.

'She's tough.'

Ollie stood at the window. In the playground, children were sitting on the swings. He saw his two daughters sitting on top of the climbing frame. They didn't move. Perhaps they were having a conversation; perhaps they were dreaming. He could hear nothing, even from the boys playing football; the scene looked blameless in the luminous evening light.

He said: 'You're the tough one.'

He went to the table and swept Ken's tiny silver balls into his hand. He put them into the bin, which was stuffed with wrapping paper, and started wiping the table. He went on: 'You're in your element, aren't you?'

'How?' asked Viv. She was lying on the sofa, her eyes closed.

'Using people.'

'I'm not using people, I'm being used. Look, I'm pregnant!'

'Call that being used?'

'What?' she asked.

'I call it playing at God.'

She sat up. She looked pale, but that was going to make no difference to him.

'You've got us all dangling now, haven't you?' he said.

'Don't be ridiculous.' She stood up and came over to

him. 'Don't be vile to me now,' she whispered into his hair. 'Come on, let's go upstairs. It's been weeks.'

'No.' He moved away. He looked at the clean table; now that was done, there was nothing else left to wipe.

'We can now,' she said. 'I'm pregnant.'

'No!'

'Ollie.' She stood at the other end of the table, looking at him. 'I love you. I'm not using you.'

'That what you say to Ken?'

She shook her head. 'That was just sex.'

'And the others?'

'You knew about them,' she said.

'You used people for our marriage.'

'Haven't you, sometimes?' She raised her eyebrows.

'No!' His voice had risen to a silly squeak. He hated himself. He hated her. And she was even smiling.

'We can cope,' she said.

'That's your speciality, isn't it?'

'What is?'

'Coping!' He spat out the word and strode out of the room, banging shut the door behind him. He hurried up the stairs, his face burning and his eyes filled with tears. A small part of him said: these exits are getting ridiculous. Another part of him said: aren't you the one with something to hide?

13 In his lunch-hour Ken stopped to buy some wine. He had been working on site that morning, as one of the chippies was off sick and nobody else was remotely capable of doing the job. Not that he didn't, secretly, enjoy doing it. When he opened the off-licence door he noticed his grimy hands.

Ollie and Viv were coming over that evening to Talk.

Inside the shop, Ken looked at the bottles. Ollie's parents were the first – and so far the last – people he had ever met who had a wine cellar. It went with the wisteria and the two labradors with bad breath. Ollie himself, of course, knew enough about wine to pretend he knew nothing, and was always over-effusive about the stuff Ken produced.

He stood at the shelves, undecided. There was a special offer on Frascati, the same wine Ollie had given them at Easter. On the other hand, what about Chablis? Double the cost, what the hell. He remembered the hotel at Salcombe: Viv suntanned, in a red spotted dress that showed her shoulders, Ollie folding up the wine list and grinning at the waiter as if he'd known him for years. *Let's have some frightfully overpriced Chablis.* And the waiter, dammit, smiling back.

Ken walked to his car with the two bottles of Chablis. Opposite the off-licence was Peter's Pet Store. The last time he had been there, looking at the fish, it was – oh, well before any of this had happened. He had felt like a middle-aged man; he had felt worn but unused.

How could he bear to face any of them? With or without Chablis?

He opened his car door and then stood still. Shoppers passed, unconcerned. The sky remained grey. The bin nearby remained stuffed with McDonald's cartons. But he knew, now, that nothing would ever be the same again.

Of course he knew this, but how chancily these things creep up and pounce. Only now did it hit him. Viv was going to have his baby. He had to lean against the car, he felt so dizzy.

Ann laid out the bowls of peanuts and looked around the lounge. The fact that she had gone to the trouble of setting her hair made her feel nervous. Don't be foolish, she thought. Don't panic.

Ken had only just come in from work. He was in the

kitchen, washing his hands. She remembered a TV production of *Macbeth*: how Lady Macbeth kept washing her hands. What was it she was trying to clean?

Instead of asking this she said: 'What is it?'

'Timber preservative. Can't get it off.'

She smiled. 'At least you won't get dry rot.'

He didn't reply. She went up behind him and put her hands on his shoulders. He flinched, and moved aside for a scrubbing brush.

She said: 'Ken, please don't.'

'Don't what?'

'Always push me away.'

He didn't turn, but held up his hands. 'I'm filthy,' he said.

'What's happened?' Ann stood in the hall, staring at Viv: her eyelids were swollen and red; a tear slid down her cheek.

Viv blew her nose. 'Just a cold.' She pointed to Ollie. 'His.'

Ann breathed again, normally. 'Come in and sit down,' she said. 'Sure you're OK?'

'Fine.'

Ollie said: 'We've all got to take care of her now.'

Ann looked at him sharply. They sat down. Viv looked around the room with the curiosity of a newcomer. What was she seeing, and with whose eyes now? Ann realized, with a feeling like liquid draining from her stomach, that Viv would never again be simply her sister.

Ken came in with the wine. Viv inspected her fingernails. Ann looked at Viv's bent head; her curly hair pulled up with butterfly clips.

Ollie said: 'Ah, Chablis.'

Ken sat down and cleared his throat. 'What we've got to decide is, who to tell and what to say.'

Nobody replied. Viv blew her nose again, then raised her head. 'We'll tell them the truth.' She screwed up her

167

Kleenex into a ball, aimed, and threw it into the waste-paper basket.

Ken said: 'Is that wise?'

Ann asked: 'What'll you tell the children?'

'That I'm having a baby and giving it to you.'

Ollie, who was leaning over for a handful of peanuts, stopped. 'But who's having the baby?'

'Me and . . .'

'You and who?' he insisted.

'We'll tell them everything,' she said.

'Will we?' Ollie asked. He ate his handful of peanuts in one gulp and looked at her.

'We believe in telling the truth,' she said.

'Do we?' he asked.

There was a silence. They all looked at the aquarium. The fish flicked luminously to and fro, as if an aquatic paintbrush was busy. Viv took out her cigarettes and lit one. Ann shifted in her seat. Viv caught her eye and stubbed it out.

'Sorry,' she said.

'Don't be sorry,' said Ann.

Viv looked around at them all, her red eyes wide, and asked: 'Why should we hide anything?'

Viv was in the kitchen, finding the kitchen roll. She pulled some off and blew her nose.

Ken came up behind her. 'Viv –'

'Stay away!' she cried.

He stared.

She tried to smile. 'Don't want to catch my cold, do you?' she asked, and went back into the lounge.

Ollie looked at the glass coffee table, with its brass edges. He looked at the framed reproductions of Degas dancers, and then he looked at Ken's veneered units. It was all so known, yet today entirely unfamiliar. He thought: none of this is happening.

He gazed into the aquarium but what he remembered was the soft skin on the inside of Ellie's thighs. He remembered, yesterday, sitting in her room while she played the recorder, grave and simple as a child. He remembered, afterwards, touching the corners of her mouth with his tongue.

Vera and Douglas's new flat was in a mansion block, up towards Highgate. It was one of those buildings with a bit of landscaping out front and some fancy Edwardian brickwork. Perhaps it reminded Vera of lost splendours.

Now she stood, poised on the pavement, as a removal man carried a table from the lorry. 'Oh be careful!' she said. 'It's very fragile.'

'Look, lady,' he answered. 'I'll do my job and you do yours.'

She pointed. 'There is a scratch.'

He ignored her and carried it towards the entrance hall.

She turned to Viv. 'Some men, they are such brutes.'

Viv laughed. 'But look at the muscles on him.'

'What?'

'Doesn't matter.' Sometimes Viv missed her mother. 'Leave them to it,' she said. 'Come and have a cup of tea.'

On the way back they met Ann, shopping. They walked to Viv's house together. It was a calm, grey day. If Viv had known then what was going to happen, she would have felt it as the stillness before the storm. As it was, she just felt that air of significance that hangs over a day when someone is moving house.

Vera sat down, sighing. Like many well-groomed women, an outsider had to look at her twice before they realized she was exhausted. Viv went over to the kettle but Ann stopped her.

'Let me.'

'I'm not an invalid,' said Viv.

'Still feel sick?'

Viv nodded. 'A bit.'

'Wish I could feel sick for you.'

They both made the tea and sat down at the table. Vera said: 'Your father, he is in such a temper.'

'Moving's bad for the blood pressure,' said Viv.

'Shouting here, shouting there,' said Vera.

Viv asked: 'Does he shout at you?'

Vera sipped her tea, and then said: 'All men shout. Because they do not get in touch with their feelings, in here.' She touched her breast.

Viv asked: 'The other day, why did he get so angry?'

'Pardon?' asked Vera.

'When you were here. Why did he get so angry with you?'

Vera sipped her tea and said, after a moment: 'Oh, it was nothing.'

'But he made you cry,' said Viv. 'In front of everyone.'

Vera said: 'It was me to blame.'

Viv sighed. 'He can be very violent.'

'No!' Vera shook her head, frowning.

Ann said: 'He can.'

'You don't understand!' Vera spoke loudly.

'We do,' said Ann. 'We know him, we're his daughters.'

Suddenly Vera burst into tears. They stared at her, appalled.

'I didn't mean . . .' began Ann. 'What is it?'

Vera fumbled in her bag and brought out a handkerchief. Ann went over and sat beside her.

'I can't say,' said Vera.

'Tell us, please,' said Viv.

Vera raised her swollen face. 'It's not my business,' she said. 'I come here, into this family, I am an outsider. I want to belong, to be part of this, and now –'

'You are!' said Ann.

170

'All the barriers,' said Vera, shaking with sobs. 'All the secrets.'

'You mean the baby?' asked Viv.

'No,' said Vera. 'Not the baby.'

'What is it?' asked Ann.

Vera turned to her, and then to Viv. 'It's you.'

'Us?' asked Viv. 'But you're welcome here, we're delighted –'

'No!' said Vera.

'You are!' said Viv.

Vera blew her nose. They sat there, watching her. She put away her handkerchief and shut her bag with a click. Then she said, in a low voice: 'He was wrong.'

'Who was?' asked Viv. 'About what?'

'Wrong for never speaking, all these years.'

'Who do you mean?' asked Viv.

'Your father.'

'What hasn't he said?' asked Ann.

Viv asked: 'He hasn't told you something?'

Vera looked at them both. 'It's you he hasn't told. The two of you.'

There was a pause. Ann said: 'You must tell us. Please.'

Vera took a breath, then stopped. She looked at them both, again, as if making up her mind. Then she spoke. 'You are not real sisters.'

A moment passed. Then Viv whispered: 'What?'

Vera didn't reply. She simply gazed at them, as if in pain.

'Go on,' said Ann.

'Your mother, she is the same,' said Vera, turning to Ann. 'But Douglas is not your father.'

14

Ann is standing in Sainsbury's. She thinks: I'm always shopping. Why am I always shopping?

The packets bewilder and depress her. The light is so bright; it hurts her head. There are shelves of what is simply water, bottled. She wants to laugh, but she can't. She'd make a noise and everyone would look. The planet is silting up with empty plastic bottles that once contained water. Where does madness lie?

She must move on. She walks past yoghurt pots with Mr Men on them, leering at her. She is filled with fear because she can't make up her mind what to buy, but if she admits this the panic will get worse. Better never to speak, even to yourself. Besides, soon you might be talking out loud. In her dream she thought she knew what she was seeking. She cannot shake that dream away; it has lingered for weeks, like a taste at the back of her mouth, where the thinking begins. She had only found bags of knitting, squashed into the shelves. How large and echoing that supermarket had been; she shivers to remember it. Those silly mewlings. She had never found out what she was looking for. Now she knows that she had never deserved to.

A man passes; he is about sixty. He turns away from her to look at the meat – chops, sliced across the bone. Red and moist. Somewhere, there is a man of perhaps sixty who is her father. She feels she is walking on a moving floor; it is sliding beneath her feet like those rubber walkways at airports, and she wants to get off. How clean the sawing is – through the bone, the nerves and the flesh. Someone felt the pain; but on the other hand, who can tell?

She feels weightless, and bereft, and very, very tired. She also feels queasy, as if the bulk of her internal organs have been surgically removed. But she finishes her shopping, because she must remember that she is workable still.

*

'Can I help you?' asked the stylist.

'Is Irene Smith here?' asked Ann.

The young man looked in the book. 'Have you got an appointment?'

Ann shook her head.

'She's got a space at three o'clock,' he said.

'She's my mother.'

He laughed. 'Sorry, I'm new.'

'But I'll take the three o'clock space,' said Ann.

Ann sat at the mirror. She wore a wrap; she felt like a patient about to undergo an operation. She hadn't been to the salon for a year; the place had been redecorated with palms and wickerwork. Frank and her mother stood behind her.

'So he popped the question in Venice,' said her mother. 'He said, can we be VAT-registered together?'

'What?' asked Ann, looking at her mother in the mirror.

She pointed to Frank. 'He's made me his business partner. Aren't you proud of your mum?'

Ann didn't reply. Her mother pursed her mouth – such crimson lipstick – and touched Ann's hair.

'So what's it to be?'

'Just do something,' said Ann.

'What?' She raised her eyebrows.

'Cut it all off. Do anything.'

Irene smiled. 'At last she says so. You leave it to Mum.'

'I want it bleached in streaks.'

'Smashing.'

'And permed.'

'Can't do both,' said her mother. 'Bad for the hair.'

'To hell with my hair.'

'Annie!'

Frank said: 'So it's carte blanche, is it?'

Irene lifted strands of Ann's hair and let them fall. 'She's always had stubborn hair,' she said. 'When she was small we had such fights about her plaits. All those rubber bands you had then. One day I couldn't stand it any more and I cut them off with the kitchen scissors, snip snip. Remember, Annie?'

Frank laughed. 'And you still trust her?' he asked Ann. 'A mother who's been so cruel?'

'I hated them,' said Ann.

'What?' he asked.

'My plaits.'

She felt her mother's hands on her head, tilting it first one way, then the other. 'I'd say all this off,' said Irene, 'and here, and layered for lift.'

'She's got a nice bone structure, hasn't she?' said Frank. 'Takes after her mum.'

'No I don't,' said Ann.

'You do,' he said. 'You just can't see it.'

Her mother spoke. 'Like I've always said, Annie, you've got the potential, always have. Just got to make the best of yourself.'

Frank touched Ann's head. 'A light perm here, in my humble opinion, just for body.'

'Do what you like,' said Ann.

Frank turned to Irene. 'Wish they were all so amenable,' he said.

'Must go,' said Ollie, twisting his hand so he could look at his watch. This was tricky, as Daisy had his hand splayed out on a piece of paper. She was tracing around his fingers.

'You're always going out,' she said.

Viv shot a look at Ollie; she did shoot it, like a dart. She too was trapped by their offspring. Rosie was tracing around her hand.

Daisy went on: 'You're always shouting.'

'What?' said Ollie.

'You and Mum.' Rosie went on tracing. 'You've got dirty fingernails.'

'Sorry,' said Ollie. 'What's all this for, anyway?'

'Our collection.'

'Well,' he said 'get a move on.'

'Where *are* you going?' Viv asked.

Rosie interrupted: 'You make Mummy sick too.'

'What?' asked Ollie.

'We've heard her.'

Both girls started making retching noises. Daisy, who had learnt to belch on demand, did that too.

'Shut up!' shouted Viv.

Ann's hair hung wet around her face. Her mother started snipping.

Ann said: 'I saw Vera last week.'

'Oh yes?'

'We had a talk.'

Her mother said: 'Never thought he'd go for somebody like that.'

'Why?'

'Always said he didn't like mousy women.' She tilted Ann's head. 'That's better.' She went on cutting, snip, snip. 'Still, you know your father.'

'No I don't.'

'Contrary old git. Once he gets an idea –'

'He's not my father,' said Ann.

Her mother's hand stopped. She looked at Ann in the mirror. 'What did you say?'

'Dad's not my father.'

Her mother didn't reply. She stood there, the scissors hanging in her hand.

'How could you not tell me?' said Ann. 'All these years?'

Irene cleared her throat. Her lower lip trembled; Ann had never seen that expression on her face before. Her round blue eyes stared at Ann in the mirror. She said: 'Your father and I – I mean Douglas and I – we decided to let bygones be bygones.' She looked around. 'Can't talk here.'

'So you were pregnant with me when you got married.'

Her mother nodded. 'He was ever so decent, Dougie. He said: who was to know? He said, we'll bring it up just like – I mean you – just like you was his.'

'He didn't, did he?'

'What?'

'Bring me up like I was his.' Ann looked at the reflection of her mother. 'He never did.'

The children had run outside. Ollie stood in the hall, holding his briefcase.

Viv asked: 'Shall we tell them it's your child?'

'And let them think I'd give away my own baby?'

'Well *I* am,' she answered.

'They'll starting having nightmares about packing cases.'

'What does it matter who the father is?' she said. 'You or Ken.'

'One day it'll have to know. Let's hope it takes it better than Ann.'

He moved towards the door.

She said: 'You off?'

He nodded. 'Just got to look up some things at the office.'

'I see.'

'Back in –' he began.

She finished for him: '– a couple of hours.'

They looked at each other. He opened the door, and left.

Viv went back into the kitchen. She stood at the table, looking at the drawings of their two ghostly hands.

Ann looked at herself in the mirror. She was transformed; there was no other word for it. Her hair was short and streaked and feathery. She looked new; she was a whole new person with whom Ann must become acquainted. She looked a great deal prettier.

She got up and went to the desk. There were only two

customers left. She had already written a cheque; she gave it to her mother, and with it three pound notes.

'Annie!' said her mother.

'It looks very nice.'

Irene pushed the money back at her. 'You ninny.'

Ann left the money on the desk and turned to go. Irene grabbed her sleeve.

'Don't go,' she said. 'Look, we're closing in a moment. Stay and we can talk.'

Ann shook her head. Then she realized she was still wearing the wrap. She pulled it off, grabbed her coat and left the salon.

Ann stood at the bus stop. A chill wind blew. Mothers, laden with Saturday shopping, waited in the queue. In front of Ann stood a small boy, eating chips from a Kentucky box. He gazed up at Ann, and then offered her a chip from his carton. She smiled, hesitated and took a chip. The boy's mother saw and slapped his hand.

The sky was darkening; soon it would rain. Ann's exposed neck was cold. Beside her was a showroom of brass beds, bathed in spotlight; on the glass were pasted signs saying FINAL REDUCTIONS. She waited. She looked at the head of the little boy in front of her. He had been given a crew-cut; the fuzz barely blurred the shape of his young skull.

She waited, as everyone else waited, to go home to their own lit rooms. But when her bus came she stepped aside and, after a moment's pause, walked back towards the salon.

'Oh, he was a laugh,' said her mother. Her voice had softened. 'Above the Gaumont they served teas, and you could dance. I'd go with my friends from the depot and he'd give them all a whirl but he always came back to me.' She touched her own cheek. 'He called me Petal because of my skin.'

The salon lights were off. People passed in the street, unaware of the two women sitting on the styling chairs. They were drinking, out of salon mugs, some liqueur that Irene had brought back from Venice.

'What did he look like?' asked Ann, her voice still cool.

'Lovely hair. Springy. Lots of it.'

'What colour?'

'Stubborn though, like yours. Chestnut.' She lifted up the bottle to pour some more. 'Sambucca, only you're supposed to put in a coffee bean and light it. It's an Italian custom.' She sighed. 'It does take me back.'

'Did you love him?'

Irene looked at her daughter. 'Oh pet,' she said. 'Think I didn't?'

Ann paused. 'What was his job?'

'Toys. He was a representative for what's-its-name, you know.'

'I don't know,' said Ann. Her mother tried to offer her more drink, but she shook her head. 'I don't know anything.'

'Anyway. Something or other. He used to wind up these silly little ducks and make them walk across the floor.' With her fingers she demonstrated on the shelf. Her pointed red nails walked past the laid-out combs.

'Did he know about me?' Ann asked.

Irene shook her head. 'He changed his job, Archie did, and went up north.'

'Where?'

'Stockport.'

'What was the firm?'

'Something.' Irene frowned, trying to remember.

'What?'

'Cobbs. That's right. Cobbs Brothers. I thought of going with him but he'd never said anything, and the morning he left, he brought me round this silly rubber monkey and I knew it was no good.'

'Why?'

'Wouldn't have worked. He was like a child, Annie.'

'So he doesn't know I exist? And you don't know if he does?'

'Thirty-five years, pet,' said her mother. 'He might be dead.'

'No.'

'Probably got grandchildren now.'

There was a silence. The street noises seemed muted, as if they came from far away. Ann ran her hand along the chrome rim of the styling trolley. Finally she looked up: 'Why didn't you tell me?'

'It was Doug's idea. See, he knew I was in the club when he proposed, but he was so good about it. I mean, in those days it was different. It would've been a scandal. But he said he'd take you on.'

'He didn't really,' said Ann.

'Didn't what?'

'Take me on.' She turned back to the chrome and rubbed it with her finger. 'He hated me and I never knew why. And you never told me.'

All week Viv tried to speak to Ann, but her sister had retreated. Yes, she said, she had talked to their mother but she didn't want to go over it all again. No, it would be better if Viv didn't come round. Not just now.

Ever since childhood Ann had been capable of doing this – curling up in a corner and pulling down the blinds, all the while staying extra polite. Viv had tried all her ploys, from teasing to shock treatment, and experience now told her that none of them would work, they would only upset Ann all the more, and there was nothing to do but wait.

Besides, she had problems of her own. It's unnerving how small London can be once things are going wrong, as if an unseen hand, against all your wishes, moves you in the direction you least want to take. Summer term had started and on the Thursday, after school, she drove into Covent Garden to pick up some posters from the printer's. Surely it was just chance that she happened to park in one particular street, some distance from Ollie's office.

One can recognize lovers by the way they sit. When they are side by side it's easy. But when they sit opposite each other it is unmistakable too – not just by the way they hold their gaze but by their mirrored gestures. Ollie and the blonde girl both sat with their heads resting on one hand, while their other hands rested on the table. If she were closer she could have seen that their fingers did not quite touch. It was a sunny afternoon, and they were having tea and cakes.

Her second reaction followed swiftly on the shock: she was thankful that the children were not there. They didn't have to see their father. Nor would she have to keep chatting to them brightly as they went up the street, as if she was perfectly all right.

It took Ann days to dare phone Directory Enquiries. Finally she did it from work. For some reason the bright normality of the office made it marginally easier.

It was no good. There was no such firm as Cobbs Brothers in Stockport. If there had been, it no longer existed. The reedy voice of the British Telecom girl tried to be helpful – 'Cobbetts Limited?' she said. 'Electronics Engineers? Or there's a Cobbs, Hawkins and Colefax, Solicitors?' Thirty-five years ago; no wonder.

Ann thanked her and put down the phone. She knew now why she had not dared before.

'Have I told you,' asked Derek, 'how much I like the hair?'

'Thanks,' said Ann. They were sitting in his inner sanctum. He was looking greyer than ever nowadays. In the mornings his hands trembled; when he passed sheaves of papers to the girls, they exchanged grimaces.

'Don't know what I'd do without you, Annie,' he said. 'You're not like the others. You're reliable.'

'Don't say that.'

He looked at her in surprise. 'Why not?'

'Just don't.' She stopped, then added: 'Please don't rely on me.'

He paused. 'Anything the matter?'

She shook her head.

He shifted the pencils on his desk, laying them beside his golfing trophy. 'Annie, this might not be the time to ask, but . . .' He stopped.

'But what?'

'Well, I know that you quite properly . . . give me my marching orders. But what I was wondering was, well . . .' He coughed, and neatened up his biros. 'Well, do you just think of me as some sort of a father figure?'

She stared at him. 'Of course not!' she said, louder than she meant.

Everyone considers themselves a coward, in one way or another. Ken had flunked the dinner with Viv and Ollie but, as was observed at the time, he would be the first over the trenches. Ann remembered coming home to find the broken ironing board, teapot and kitchen cupboard fixed, his own mute way of making amends. He refused to let her thank him.

Her own cowardice dismayed her. All weekend she put off making a decision, and by Sunday night she felt as brittle as glass. She snapped at Ken; she felt an impatient disappointment with herself, like a headmistress looking at a pupil more in sorrow than in anger.

On Monday she made up her mind. Douglas worked at the Gas Board headquarters, and she left work early to wait outside, like a grieving spy.

He appeared on the steps, soon after 5.30, and walked down the road. She followed his familiar back. He went into a greengrocer's shop.

He waited in the queue, pulling a carrier-bag out of his pocket. She went up to him.

'Hello,' she said.

'Well well!' He swung round. 'Caught in the act.'

'What?'

'Being domestic.' He lowered his voice: 'I'm learning, see.' He looked at her, his head on one side. 'You've done something.'

'What?'

'Your face looks different.'

'It's my hair,' she said.

'Ah. And very nice too.' He gestured at the piles of fruit. 'Want to give me some advice?'

She shook her head. 'I want to talk.'

They sat in a café opposite the greengrocer's. A bun lay untouched on Ann's plate. The café owner, a beefy Italian, was quarrelling with the waitress, who looked like his daughter. His voice was so loud that for a moment Ann couldn't hear what Douglas said.

He repeated it. 'I'm sorry.'

'It's a bit late for that,' she replied.

'We thought it better, your mother and I –'

'That you'd pretend to be my father?'

'I was!' he said. 'I brought you up. It's that that counts.'

'You think so?' She thought she could challenge him by holding his gaze. Instead she looked down at the table. It was a chequered formica.

'Look Annie,' he said, 'you're going to bring up somebody else's baby. You're going to call yourself its mother.'

She shook her head. 'I'll tell it.'

'You so sure?' His half-smile maddened her.

'I'll tell it the truth.'

'When?' he asked.

'When it's old enough.'

He paused, then he scratched at his whitening sideboards. He looked up at her, and said: 'You think that'll make it happier?'

'What?'

'It makes you happier to tell the truth, because you're that kind of person. But you've got to think of the child.'

'You just thought of the scandal.'

'Ann!'

'You did.'

'Don't say that,' he said. 'Please.' He pushed the bun towards her, but she shook her head. 'Think the truth does you any good?' She didn't reply. He began again: 'Look, we had our ups and downs, but so does anybody.'

'Call them that?'

'What?'

'Ups and downs? You always favoured Viv, you were always nicer to her.' Her voice rose. 'She was the one you made the little chair for, remember, and it was me who'd always wanted one, she hardly ever sat in it. And she was the one you let push the lawnmower, you never let me, and I was the oldest, and you were always shouting at me.' She stopped for breath.

'Annie –'

'And all those years I never realized the reason. You hated me because I wasn't yours.'

'No,' he said. He sighed and inspected the table. He hadn't touched his cup of tea. He looked up at her directly: 'No, I loved you. I always considered you mine. But if I favoured Viv it was because . . .'

'Because what?'

'Because she made me happy.'

There was a pause. Then Ann said: 'I didn't?'

'Life's not fair, love, and it's nothing to do with who your parents are. Some people . . . life smiles on them because, well, they make people smile around them.'

'And what was wrong with me?'

'Nothing.' He leant over and put his hand on her shoulder. 'Come on, lovey. Let's put the past behind us.'

183

'I can't forget it.'

'Forget Archie,' he said. 'He's not your dad.'

'He is.'

'Not really.' He squeezed her shoulder. She didn't move. Then he said: 'He's given you nothing. Not even the shouting.'

At the greengrocer's he bought a bunch of flowers, chrysanthemums, and gave them to Ann. She went home.

Ken wasn't back yet. She went into the kitchen. Her little house seemed so quiet. Outside stood the skeleton of the extension, forever half-built.

She unwrapped the flowers from their damp paper and found a vase. She ached with self-disgust.

She was just about to put the flowers in the vase when she stopped. Instead she threw them away, jamming them into the swing-bin. Their silly heads got caught, so she pushed them down.

15 It was the third week of the summer term. School had finished for the day and Viv and Harold were waiting in the staffroom; they were supposed to be having a meeting with Alan, their Head of Department.

Viv looked at her watch; she glanced out of the window. The sky was blue; her car waited in the empty car park. In the heat, the school railings shimmered. 'Wish he'd hurry up,' she said.

Harold leered. 'Off somewhere exciting?'

'Mmmm.' She nodded, closing her eyes.

'Where?'

'My cabbages.'

He laughed.

She added: 'Got to pick up the kids first.'

'You're a strange woman.' He leant over to pat her knee. 'Half siren, half earth-mother. Think I'll set you as a special topic.'

She asked: 'How's Louise?'

He sighed. 'You're a woman. Tell me, Viv, what is it they want?'

'What's up?'

'Can't keep them happy.' He sipped his tea. 'Trouble is, you see, she wants another child.'

'Another one?'

He nodded. 'Just when we're getting on our feet. She's gone all funny again.'

The door opened and Alan came in. 'Sorry I'm late,' he said, and sat down. He looked from one of them to the other. 'I wanted to fix a time for our planning meeting. Got to sort out the autumn curriculum, and which of you'll be taking the Lower Sixth.'

Harold groaned.

Alan asked: 'You two worked it out yet?'

Harold replied: 'I have broached the subject but . . .'

'But what?' asked Alan.

Harold pointed to Viv. 'This lady is prevaricating.'

Viv felt herself blushing. 'Sorry,' she stammered, 'I didn't mean . . .'

Harold laughed and turned to Alan. 'I think she's planning on doing a bunk.'

There was a pause. Alan turned to Viv. 'You're not leaving?'

'No!' she said hastily. 'No, of course, I just –'

There was a tap at the door. They all stopped.

'Who is it?' called Alan.

The door opened. On the threshold stood Ken.

Children are perverse creatures, possessed of a sixth sense. When you're trying to do something else, they hang around you all day, whining that they're bored. The moment you need them beside you for moral support they

185

spring into creative life and dash off elsewhere, engaged in the sort of lengthy imaginative game you longed for them to do at any other time but this.

Such were Viv's thoughts as she walked across the allotments. 'Don't get your feet muddy!' she called out helplessly, as Rosie and Daisy rushed off. Though it had rained heavily the night before, this was not the sort of stricture she would normally shout, but she was too flustered to simply let them go. Beside her, Ken trudged along the soft margins of the path. He was wearing his business suit; when she tilted her head slightly she could see the dark blur of his legs. She wished her children were here.

He said, again: 'I'm sorry to barge in like that.'

'I told you. It was a relief. I was getting into difficulties.'

He asked: 'Can we go into the hut?'

She searched for her key. The sun was hot, but it seemed too confidential for her to take off her jumper. She opened the door and went in. The place darkened as he stood in the doorway.

'Why won't you see me?' he asked.

'I do.'

'I must see you.'

'Well, here I am.' She sat down on a bucket and took off her shoes. He watched her as she started pulling on her gumboots. She paused as he moved in a step, and closed the door behind him.

He spoke in a low voice. 'You've been avoiding me.'

She looked up. 'We've all got to meet. When I start looking pregnant we've got to decide what to tell people.'

He fingered his moustache. Then he turned away and inspected the packets on the shelves. 'At Easter you said . . .' He paused. 'You said you'd been unfaithful before.'

'Watch out!'

'What?'

She pointed to the packet he was holding. 'Slug bait.

They die in glistening heaps, like a horticultural Last Judgement.'

He put the packet back. Still he didn't turn. 'Why did you say that?'

'Because it's true.'

'Were you just trying to tell me I was, well, just like one of the others?'

'You're not like one of the others,' she said gently. 'You're the father of my child.'

She willed him to stop. The hut was cramped and so hot. Her heart knocked. She wondered if she should simply pick up her hoe and walk outside.

'Just playing, aren't you?' he muttered, with his back to her. He was standing against the window, his head haloed by the cobwebs that hung on the panes of glass.

'What?' she asked.

'Those other men.'

'Ken,' she said. 'It wasn't often.'

'Why then?'

'Because Ollie and I –' She struggled for the right words. 'We believe in adventure. Life's short, it's to be lived and explored. You may not understand –'

'Why not? Because I've got such a boring little marriage?'

'No!' She paused. 'Faithfulness . . .' She pushed away the sight of two people sitting in a street café. She said: 'Faithfulness is nothing to do with two bodies rubbing together in the dark –'

'Don't be crude!' He spoke abruptly; the cobwebs swayed with his breath.

'It's being honest.'

'You and your honesty,' he said. 'That's just a game, like the rest.' He turned and stared at her. 'You play with people, you use them –'

'Think it's playing when I throw up every morning?' Her voice rose. 'When I have to lie to my children about why I'm being sick, and then I'll be swelling up, and having to give up my job, and saying God knows what to people, and carrying a baby that I know will never be mine? Think that's playing?' She stopped, breathing heavily.

His eyes didn't move from her face. He gazed at her; then he turned away and spoke to the veiled window. 'You played with me.'

'You haven't been listening,' she said. 'You're just like Ollie.'

'You and your striptease.'

She paused. 'That was just a joke.'

'Exactly.'

She tried to steady her voice. 'Sex is supposed to be fun.'

'Specially when you do it after you know you're pregnant.'

She paused and looked down at her gumboots, encrusted with last week's mud. 'I'm sorry.'

'Just two bodies rubbing together in the dark,' he said. 'You used me.'

'Men do it too.'

There was a silence. Then he said: 'I don't want you to tell people.'

'What?' She stared at his back.

His head was bent. 'That you're its mother.'

She took a breath. 'What do you mean?'

'Ann and I'll just say we adopted it.' He was lighting a cigarette. He blew out the match. 'I don't want people to know that the mother of my child's a whore.'

Her heart thumped against her ribcage. For a moment she believed this must be a dream. They were caught, like the Sleeping Beauty, in this cobwebby little room, now wreathed in smoke. Suddenly she would shake her head, the mist would clear and none of this would have happened. She would be outdoors, hoeing the chickweed.

And he wouldn't be speaking now, in that low voice. 'You're in my blood, Viv.' He wouldn't be saying this.

188

'You're part of me, you're all of me. I wake up aching for
you, the taste of you in my mouth, the feel of your skin –'

'Don't!'

'You're everywhere I breathe. It's getting worse. Viv,
I've tried to stay away, I've tried to pretend it's not
happening –'

'It's not!'

'Yesterday I parked outside your school. I had to. I sat
there and I saw your car, your lovely grubby car. I looked
at the school, at all those windows, and do you know? I
was happy, for the first time in weeks, just because I knew
that behind one of them was you.'

'Ken –'

'I'm ill, Viv,' he said. 'I'm ill with you.'

She cleared her throat. Her heart, like a rock, was locked
inside her. She felt drained of breath. She said, in a quiet
voice: 'You mustn't say all this.'

'Viv, I want you.'

Suddenly he stamped out his cigarette and went down
on his haunches, down there beside her. He grabbed her
shoulders; his fingers hurt. The bucket rocked, then fell
over as he lifted her to her feet. He kissed her, pressing
her against the shelves. Behind, the tower of plant pots
shifted. Then she heard her children's voices outside,
calling. She pushed him away.

He suddenly gave up. He stood limply; she couldn't
bear to see him. He put his arm against his face, hiding it,
shielding his face as people do when near an explosion.

Quickly, she let herself out of the hut, so her children
wouldn't guess that anything had happened.

You have to concentrate, when shelling broad beans. It
looks mindless, but if you are feeling disturbed you are
inclined to get the two heaps of beans and pods confused.

Viv was picking out the beans from the compost bucket
when Ollie came in from work. He kissed her lightly on
the neck.

189

'Sorry I'm late,' he said. 'Had to go to the Public Record Office and look up some stuff.'

She didn't turn. 'You're being very thorough lately,' she said, picking out beans.

'What?'

'In your research.'

There was a pause, then Ollie went out into the garden to greet the girls.

It was a golden evening. Ann stood for a moment in her small paved garden. Ken had re-planted the tubs with geraniums; they glowed in the evening light, blood-red. If she narrowed her eyes, like she used to when she was small, they blurred to blobs. Next door the Maguire children shouted to each other; there was the scraping sound of their trike being dragged across the concrete. Through the open window came canned laughter from their TV.

Last night she had dreamed, again, of this garden. To dream the same setting twice unnerved her. This time the extension had been finished, but it was much taller than she had expected and its glass was milky. She had been standing in the garden – empty this time, with no white urns – and she had been banging on the glass, but she could not get in. Nor could she see in, as its window were opaque. Someone was inside there, she could hear them breathing, but they didn't, or wouldn't, hear her. She had banged and banged. She realized when she woke that the breathing, of course, had simply been her husband, lying beside her.

Someone flushed the lavatory chain; the drains rushed. She turned to go in. As she did so she noticed Ken's shoes. They had been put outside the kitchen door. She picked them up; their soles were caked with mud.

She put them down again and went into the kitchen. Raising her voice, she called: 'Did you go out on site today?'

From the lounge Ken called: 'No, I told you. Stuck in that blessed office . . .' He went on: '. . . checking all those blooming chits, that's why I was so late. Drives me round the twist, Annie.'

'Poor Ken,' she said.

'What?' he called.

She shouted: 'Poor Ken!'

She looked again at the shoes. She could just see their toes, jutting round the kitchen door.

'. . . not to be trusted,' his voice went on. 'There's someone on the fiddle there . . . The lying, the dishonesty . . .'

She closed the kitchen door, clicking it carefully, and went back to her cooking.

In London there are so many buildings that you can seldom see the setting sun; hours can elapse between its sinking out of sight behind the rooftops and its final departure. Meanwhile, and for a soft, darkening time afterwards, you can at least see the luminous sky.

Viv had thrown the bean pods, and all the rest, into the compost heap. She stood for a moment on the lawn; her feet were bare and the grass already damp with dew. Around her rose the houses. Windows were open; she could hear reggae music. Up above her the sky was streaked, towards the west, with dissolving ribbons of blue. At the kitchen window Ollie stood, washing up. What a good husband he looked, with his sleeves rolled up. She reflected, yet again, how normal her household looked, how normal all those other windows looked in all those other impenetrable homes.

She went in, and put the bin back in the cupboard.

Ollie asked: 'So she's left school already?'

'Tracey? Yes.'

'The silly twerp. So bloody irresponsible.'

Viv shut the cupboard door. 'At least she has the excuse of youth.'

Ollie didn't reply. Viv put her pile of exercise books on the table and sat down.

'She's not a grown man,' she said.

'I do have eyes in my head.'

She replied: 'So do I.'

She looked at Ollie's back. He turned. 'Now what's that supposed to mean?'

'I'm not stupid,' she said. She looked down at the exercise books. *Sharon Thompson, Leroy Marks* . . . the names danced. She cleared her throat. 'Shall I tell you the signs?'

At the sink, Ollie stood still. 'What?'

She took a breath and spoke carefully, as if she had rehearsed this. She had rehearsed it. 'Over-eagerness to explain where you've been. Over-exuberance with the children. Shiftiness with me. Guilt-induced ardour in bed –'

'Unreturned,' he said.

'Not surprisingly.' She paused and went on. 'Over-scrupulousness in emptying your trouser pockets. Sudden knowledge of the current pop scene. Endless lunch-hours that end with you nipping into the toy shop and salving your conscience by buying the children elaborate toys, except you forget to get the batteries that go with them –'

'I'm sorry,' he said. 'I'll get some tomorrow.'

She rearranged the exercise books, aligning them exactly, edge to edge. She said: 'It's never been like this before, has it? We've always been open about it. It was like a game and only we knew the rules. We were in it together, weren't we? Besides' – she tried to talk lightly – 'it was always material for that novel you're always meaning to write.'

'When I don't have to earn our living,' he said.

'Half our living.'

'Half.'

He had turned to the sink. She thought: I'm always talking to men with their backs to me. 'This time though,' she said, 'what seems more than a little tactless –'

'Spare us the staffroom pedantry.'

'– is the question of timing. Now doesn't seem quite the time to choose.'

Ollie didn't reply. He seemed to have been standing like that at the sink for ever, facing the windowsill of leggy geraniums and the spotlit Fairy Liquid bottle. The whole thing seemed stagy, as if it were happening to someone else.

'Ollie and Ellie,' she said musingly. 'It sounds faintly comic, like a music-hall routine.'

'I can't help that.'

'Love's like that, isn't it? Sudden, blinding, unpredictable.'

'Viv!' He smashed the washing-up brush into the sink. Suds flew.

'Up to now we've always been honest,' she said sadly.

'Oh yes?'

'Yes.'

He said: 'You weren't honest about Ken.'

'That was different.'

'You lied,' he said. 'You told me you weren't sleeping with him.'

'I had to lie.'

'Why?'

'Because it *wasn't* a game,' she said. 'It was serious.'

'Exactly.'

'No – serious because there was a baby involved.'

'So serious you couldn't stop yourself screwing him even after you knew you were pregnant?'

'Ollie!'

'Secret assignations in the allotment?' He turned and faced her. 'The girls told me. He was there today, wasn't he?'

Suddenly she smiled. She felt buoyant. 'Is that all it is?' She jumped up and went over to him.

'What?'

'A little game of tit for tat?' She tried to embrace him but he moved aside and left her at the sink.

He stood flat against the fridge. 'I'm fed up with being manipulated.'

'What?'

'It's all OK nowadays, isn't it, for women? It's called taking destiny into your own hands. It's called being strong, independent women. You're not called bossy any more, or pig-headed, or downright selfish –'

'Selfish? To have a baby for my sister?'

'You say you're at the mercy of your wombs, you're oppressed because you're female, but what you do is as old as time, and just as devious.'

'What is?'

'You use your femaleness, you use your wombs!' He slapped his aproned stomach. 'But the difference is that now we poor sods can't answer back.'

'You and I – we can. We've always talked.'

'Yes!' he shouted. 'Because we can't do anything else.'

'That's crap.'

'I'm fed up with talking,' he said. 'It's a substitute for feeling.'

'Is it?'

'I speak from experience, dear.'

'Don't dear me.'

She sat; he stood. They were both close to tears. He said: 'I've become an empty vessel filled with theories. Mostly yours. I don't know how to live.'

'Spare us the B-movie stuff.'

'So you can have your beefcake –'

'What?'

'He's a real man, isn't he?' Ollie leered. She couldn't bear to see his face like this; she turned away.

'Don't be stupid,' she said.

'You've always wanted that, and now you're getting it. It's called reverting to your origins.'

'Don't start that!' she warned.

'All this radical stuff is just skin deep,' he spat out, his face ugly. 'Underneath you're a conventional working-class girl who wants a ballsy, macho man to fix your guttering and screw you rigid. I've watched you and Ken for years, well now you've got him eating out of your hand –'

'Shut up!' she yelled, sobbing.

'And everyone's saying how selfless you're being, too –'

'*Lay off!*'

She jumped up from the table and tried to slap his face, but he pushed her away. She stumbled against the dresser.

'*Ollie!*' she yelled, her hand shielding her belly.

16 Ann was putting away the shopping. As she opened the cupboard door she heard the click of the front door. She paused and went on, lifting out the packets and storing them with a now self-conscious care. She thought, with sadness, how for years she had welcomed that returning click. How he, if he were home first, must have welcomed hers.

Ken came into the kitchen and paused inside the door. 'Just changing,' he said. 'Squash tonight.'

She was kneeling at the cupboard. She stood up, pulling her skirt down over her knees. She thought: when you are unhappy, you don't want to look revealed – your legs, anything. She gestured at the skeletal extension. 'Builders nowadays,' she said. 'So unreliable.'

He frowned. 'But it's me who's building it.'

'Can't trust them,' she said.

'What?'

'They just disappear.' She hated her own light tone. She made herself half smile. 'Don't do any work for weeks.'

He patted his pockets for his cigarettes. He was smoking more heavily nowadays. 'Sorry, Annie. Look, I'll get going again this weekend.'

'Now it was different in the old days,' she said. 'Builders were a hundred per cent then, solid gold.'

'Look, I promise –'

'Promises, promises,' she said, walking past him. He moved aside. In the doorway she turned and said lightly: 'I promise to build the extension, I promise to love and cherish . . .'

She left him and went into the lounge. She wanted him to follow, and yet she dreaded it. When he did, she picked up her Miss Selfridge's bag and started to go upstairs. He moved aside for her and pointed to the bag.

In a jovial voice he said: 'We have been going mad lately.'

'Mad?' she asked, her hand on the banister.

'I just mean . . .'

She indicated the bag. 'I can spend my money how I choose –'

'Of course. I just –'

'I do earn my living.'

'Can I see it?' he asked.

She lifted the dress out of the bag. It was yellow and silky, with thin shoulder-straps.

'I say,' he said, 'won't you be a bit chilly?'

She gazed at him. 'Thanks.'

'I mean it's lovely . . .' He stopped. She put the dress back into the bag. 'Where're you going?' he asked.

'I'm going out tomorrow.'

'Who with?'

She stood there, one foot on the stair, and closed her eyes. 'He's tall and dark,' she said dreamily, 'and he doesn't say, won't you be chilly, he says, ah, your shoulders are smooth as butter and your arms are soft and downy and the back of your neck as tender as a child.'

There was a silence. 'Annie –'

'I too can live a fantasy life,' she said.

'Look –' He stopped.

'Look what?'

'Look, love, I know it's all been upsetting, your dad and everything –'

'Think it's just that?' She stared at him.

Head bowed, he shuffled his foot, pushing down a loose edge of the hall carpet. Then he looked up. 'Actually, who *are* you going out with?'

'The girls from work.'

'Ah,' he said. 'I won't be in anyway. Youth Club.'

She asked: 'Think you're still suited to the job?'

'Which job?'

'Being the moral guardian of the flower of our youth?'

He stared at her. There was a silence. She was about to say: just going to hang this up. But she realized that he too was going upstairs, to change. Their bedroom would be too small for the two of them. How sad that was.

She hung the carrier over the banisters and went into the kitchen. She heard the house creak as he went upstairs. There was always something one could be doing in the kitchen. Scrub scrub, wipe wipe, cook cook.

There was hardly room to stand in the cramped cloakroom. Certainly not enough room to change clothes, but Ann had managed it, all bumping elbows. Janine was the expert at miracle changes, emerging like a sniggering butterfly.

Stuck around the basin were postcards from last year's holidays: a Greek donkey from Frances, a Spanish beach mushroomed with sunshades from Cora, who had since become impregnated by a motorbike mechanic and left the office, and the Leaning Tower of Pisa from Janine, embellished with lewd biro speculations. Tonight she herself was one of the girls. She felt reckless; she had a teenage stomach ache – not that she had done much of this as a teenager, that was Viv's speciality – but she'd done enough to know.

She looked at her shorn, streaked hair. She wore big earrings for a *piquant* effect. She leant towards the mirror and outlined her lips redly. For the first time in her life she wanted to get drunk. She thought: I never felt like this, even when I lost my babies.

She went back into the office. Derek, who was just going home, raised his eyebrows. 'Good Lord, it's Audrey Hepburn.'

Janine sneered: 'Give over, Grandpa.'

He inspected Ann in her yellow dress. 'You look . . .'

'Sexy,' said Janine.

'Very pretty,' he said.

'She's coming out with us.'

He turned to Ann. 'What's all this in aid of?'

'Search me,' smiled Ann. She hooked up her slipping strap. Search her, she truly didn't know.

Trish nudged Janine. 'You wearing those panties you bought?'

Janine nodded, and said to Derek: 'They're called M.'

'M?'

'Get M on, get M off.'

They all laughed. Derek said: 'Well, old stick-in-the-mud will wend his weary way.'

'That's right,' said Janine. 'It's under-30s night.'

'Under-36s,' corrected Ann.

'Sorry, Mrs Fletcher,' said Janine in a posh voice. She turned to Derek. 'Hurry up and you'll catch *Gardeners' Question Time.*'

Derek started to leave and paused at the door. 'Lock up, will you?' he asked Ann.

She nodded. She hated herself for her new hardness of heart, that she did not feel sorry for him. He left.

Janine turned to her. 'You're my flatmate, right?'

'Right,' said Ann.

'And you're certainly not married.'

198

Ann grinned. 'Certainly not.'

Just then the phone rang. Ann answered it.

'Hello, Viv.' Her stomach tightened. 'No, I can't. I'm sorry, I'm just going out. What? Look, we'll talk about it.' When? Viv was asking. 'Soon,' said Ann. Her stomach hurt, her heart hurt. Viv spoke; she replied: 'You want me to be frank? No, I can't trust you. I can't trust you and I can't trust my own husband and I can't trust anyone in my bloody lying family. Must go.' She put down the receiver. Nobody else had heard; they were gathering their things together.

Janine came up to her. 'Chin up.'

Ann obediently raised her chin. Janine got out her perfume spray and squirted Ann's neck.

Ann's head spun; the music thumped. Most of the Top Ten was unfamiliar to her, though she recognized some of the tunes from car radios in traffic jams. Lights flashed above her, and below too; there were bulbs beneath the dance-floor, sheathed in frosted glass. It made her unsteady, as if she were dancing under water.

Bodies bobbed around her. She was sweating and her stomach ache had gone. A man was dancing opposite her; he jiggled from side to side, pumping his arms like pistons. He leant towards her, she smelt his aftershave; he shouted over the music: 'Where're you from, then?'

She shouted back: 'Nowhere.' She had lost Trish and Janine in the crowd.

'What?' he shouted back. 'What did you say?'

She paused, swaying. 'Stockport!' she yelled.

She thinks: I'm drunk. I'm sitting in a strange man's car. The ashtray is full; there is an empty Benson and Hedges packet and two parking tickets on the floor. He turns her face to his; he breathes into her mouth.

The evening has been so long that by now his aftershave is familiar to her. His name is Ted, she knows that much.

He looks younger than she is and he has a soft, dimpled face. A mother's boy on the loose; he doesn't really want to be here either.

They are parked near Leicester Square; people brush the car as they pass. She lays her hand on his stomach; beneath the shirt it's surprisingly hard. Her head spins; she wills herself be be kissed so that they don't have the obligation of speaking.

Her mouth opens against his, he tastes of cigarettes. His tongue darts behind her teeth. It probes like the dentist. She repeats to herself: I love you I love you, and suddenly she starts giggling, trapping his tongue.

He draws back, alarmed. If he weren't sitting here, doing this, he would probably be a kind man. He asks: 'What's the joke?'

'Nothing.'

She silences him with her mouth, and moves his hand to her breast. He grunts. Stupidly, her dumb body is aroused.

Even Viv sometimes changed the sheets. She was doing so, bending over the bed, when she heard the doorbell ring. The children answered it. She heard footsteps on the stairs and then her mother was in the room.

'I've got a bone to pick with you,' she said, shutting the door behind her. Her hair looked challengingly newly set. 'Why didn't you tell me about this baby?'

Viv sat down on the bed. 'I'm sorry.'

'Why did you keep it secret?'

Viv replied: 'Keeping secrets is something we all seem good at. Except you kept yours for thirty-five years.'

'Don't be sarky with me.' Irene stood at the basin. Abstractedly, she took out Viv's earrings and Rosie's trick pimple. She frowned at the small circle of plastic and put it in the soap-dish. 'You told your father and his lady-friend. Know who I heard it from? Her. She comes into the salon this morning to measure me for a frock, for their blooming wedding, and she thinks I *know*. Never felt so humiliated in my life.'

'I'm sorry,' said Viv. 'I haven't been able to tell anyone yet.'

'Why not?'

'Because I don't know what to tell.' She put her head into her hands. 'None of us seems to be speaking to each other.'

'Why not?'

'Ann's terribly upset about . . . you know.' She looked up. 'And about Ken.'

'Ken?' asked her mother.

Viv gazed through her fingers at the woven matting of the floor. A hairclip and a piece of Lego were trodden into it. 'He says he's in love with me. It's only because I'm having his baby.'

'Oh no, I've noticed for years.'

Viv looked up. 'Really?'

Irene put the earrings on the chest of drawers. 'Don't tell me you haven't noticed the way he looks at you, like a blooming spaniel. Why do you think he bought a house four streets away?' In the mirror her eyes caught Viv's. Viv looked down at the matted matting. 'You may think I'm stupid but not much escapes old Reenie.' There was a silence. Then she asked: 'What about Ollie?'

'He thought he could take it but he seems to be cracking up too. We had a terrible fight last week.'

'Blimey.' Irene came over and sat beside her on the mattress. Viv thought: it's years since she's been up here.

Her matrimonial bed looked suddenly exposed. Near the head of it, the mattress was stained. Dried whitish round the edges, the stains were from milk that, years before, had leaked from her own breasts. She looked away and spoke to her mother's red high-heeled sandals. 'So I haven't told anyone, not even you.'

'What a bunch of ninnies. Four grown people, with a

201

better education than I ever had, and look what a mess you're in.'

'You see, we said we wouldn't make plans until I was pregnant, and now I am –'

'– all hell's let loose.'

Viv leant limply against her mother's shoulder. It felt plump and scented. She had forgotten how small her mother was; she herself felt big and bony and helpless.

'Well,' said Irene. 'At least it's brought you back to your old mum.' She leant forward and searched in her bag for a handkerchief. Neither of them had one.

Viv, half laughing, rubbed her eyes. 'Is this stupid?'

'Uh-huh. But you'll be all right. You're tough, like me. It's your sister I'm worried about.'

'Really?'

'She's mad to get saddled with a baby and that boring husband anyway. She ought to get out and live a bit.'

'You think so?'

'I went through it too, remember. Stifling marriage to a stifling bloke. Look at me now. Never been happier.' She stood up. 'You're not the only women's libber around here, you know.'

Viv stood up too, wiping her nose on her sleeve.

'Come on,' said her mother, picking up the clean sheet. 'I'll give you a hand.'

'Talking, that is, of women's lib.'

Her mother grinned. They billowed the sheet out; it rose and then sank, gently, around the bed. Sheeted, the bed looked wider, and empty. They tucked in the edges.

Ken sat in his office, trembling. He had just snapped at Archie, the store foreman, for the simple reason that Archie had told him a mildly disgusting joke about two prostitutes and a corkscrew. The poor man had been startled by his response.

He thought: I'm not myself. But those weren't the right words; he knew that as he thought them. In fact he felt more himself than he had ever been in his life. He felt peeled; stripped and bare and shivering. Loud noises startled him; traffic confused him. He went into shops and couldn't remember what he'd wanted to buy – he, Kenneth. Then there was music. He had always loved it; at home he had a large record collection. But now music sank into his heart, spreading warm as honey and then suddenly filling him with the most insupportable pain. That morning he had turned on his car radio and the sound of a violin had pricked the back of his eyes with needles.

Everything moved him. Across the yard, sunlight glinted on the stacked pipes. He had sat here for years and he had never noticed how, when the wind blew, the poplar tree behind the depot shook into silvered fragments. It was a beautiful tree, waiting there to be watched. Yet below it – how could they? – they guffawed about cork-screws.

He thought: I'm not myself. I'm going mad. He must be going mad, because he was dialling Viv's number. It was the middle of a working day and nobody would be there. He was mad because he just wanted to hear the phone ringing in her home. In some imbecilic way he felt closer to her if he caused the phone to sound in her living room.

He laid the receiver on his desk. He could hear the faint ringing. He could picture her room, her scattered mess. Perhaps her empty coffee mug would be nearby.

He lit yet another cigarette and, the receiver lying near him, dear to him, he attempted to get on with his paperwork.

'My mouth feels like a lizard's latrine,' said Janine, drinking her coffee. She had been out again, to the nightclub they had all visited the week before. Ann was now her confidante – about the inadequate performances of the men she met, about her daughter Simone's tantrums

203

and her mother's hypochondria. Three months ago in this office, the voices had stilled when Ann had come into the room and nobody had told any jokes. How much had changed since that time, they had no idea. They probably put it down to a new haircut and an unknown man who caressed her bottom on a dance-floor.

Janine shifted in her seat and inspected the computer print-out. This was because Derek was in sight; he had popped his head around his office door.

'Er, Annie.' He beckoned. 'Would you like to step in here a moment?'

Ann went in. Mr Fowler, the Managing Director, had been closeted with Derek all morning. He was a gloomy man with a military moustache.

Derek closed the door behind Ann and showed her to a chair. 'You know, Ann, that I mentioned a while ago that I might have some news for you?' There were beads of sweat on his forehead. 'Well, Mr Fowler has just confirmed it.'

Ann gazed at Mr Fowler. He said: 'Mrs Fletcher, I'd just like to sound you out . . .' He took out his pipe and tobacco pouch. 'We've kept it under wraps till now, but you should be the first to know.'

For a confused moment Ann thought: which of my secrets have they heard?

Mr Fowler stuffed some tobacco into his pipe. Whether or not a man is managing director, with a pipe he can make everybody listen. He can pace his routine until they fidget with insecurity. Finally he said: 'Derek is being transferred to Head Office, and that leaves his post vacant.'

Ann stared at Derek. 'You're leaving?'

Derek cleared his throat. 'It's for, well, personal reasons.'

Mr Fowler said: 'We'd like you to know, Ann – may I call you Ann? – that our estimation of you and your abilities is very high, and Derek has of course confirmed this. You've a steady head on your shoulders, but also that

204

something special, that certain flair –'

'Tony, you're making her blush,' said Derek.

'We're always on the lookout for good women managers,' he went on, 'and in fact our record hasn't been bad in that respect. Last year we promoted two women . . .' He stopped and struck a match.

Derek let out a yelp of laughter. 'Actually, they're both on maternity leave.'

Through dense smoke Mr Fowler said: 'We have hopes they'll return. However, in your case –' He stopped, suddenly frowning, and looked down at his dead match. 'Anyway, Derek and I have had a chat and I've popped over today to, well . . . To put it plainly, we'd like you to consider taking over this branch.'

Ken sat in his car. He had to drive to Ridgeway Avenue to check on how the lads were progressing with the damp-proofing. That was what the old Ken told him. The old, un-whole, un-alive one.

He must do his job, he knew that, but he would make a detour, first, past those school gates. Just to slow down, just to look.

As he drove, the word hit him: adultery. That sound was so ugly; he pushed it down, out of sight. Besides, it was hideously inaccurate. Nobody had felt like this. If they had, how could they bear it?

The sun blazed on the school windows. It hurt his eyes to look. The dull modern building was aflame with her.

'It's a big commitment,' said Derek.

Ann nodded. The pipe smoke made her feel sick. Through the haze she heard Mr Fowler speaking.

'If you'd like to go away and think it over . . .'

She shook her head. She felt, rising within her, the familiar reckless despair. Why not take the job? There was no hope in anything else. Stupid of her to have ever believed there was.

She turned to Mr Fowler, or Tony. 'No,' she said. 'I'll take it.'

'Really?' asked Derek. 'Are you sure?'

She nodded. They all stood up and shook hands.

17 It was the hottest June for years. On the roads the tarmac blistered; children wrinkled it up, pushing it with their sandals. In fumy high streets women sought refuge in the beige chill of Marks and Spencers. Plants drooped in cracked flowerbeds; policemen perspired in shirt-sleeves. People, as always, complained. At Viv's school, bosomy sixth-form girls lay on the grass like porpoises and came into classes reddened.

In the two households the windows were opened to catch the breeze, sunlight flooded the front rooms in the mornings and the back rooms in the afternoon, work was done and strawberries eaten but nobody spoke. Nobody spoke because they feared the answers. It is always easier to be distracted by other things, and there were plenty of them. Ann's new job began, within two weeks of the meeting with Mr Fowler, and she started bringing home work in the evenings. Zenith, the firm that employed Ken, became even more damaged by the recession and crises kept him busy; besides which, he disappeared for lengthy lunch-hours nobody knew where, and then there was his Youth Club, for which his wife had questioned his fitness. He seemed much preoccupied and, startling Ann, shaved off his moustache. His bald face looked vulnerable. Viv, still slowed by nausea, was involved with school exams and her thirsty allotment and caring for Rosie, who suffered not only asthma but hay fever too, worse than ever this summer, as if infected by something troubling in the air besides pollen. Each of the four was subdued by guilt, as if a lid had been lifted, revealing, within, unwelcome mirrors they preferred not to inspect. And all the time a child grew remorselessly, innocent of the tumult it was causing. It lay, suspended in rosy silence.

Perhaps, who knows, Ollie felt the most guilty. One day, coming home from work, his children rat-tatted him with invisible machine guns. He escaped upstairs.

Instead of hanging cherries round his own girls' ears he hooked them around Ellie's. As the two of them came in from their lunch-hour he took them off and popped them into his mouth.

Diz met him and remarked: 'You look all flushed and replete.'

'It's just the sun,' said Ollie. 'Look.' He unbuttoned his shirt to show his sunburn. 'I've got a red V.'

Diz said: 'How Blackpool.'

'Watch it,' said Ellie. She left for the cloakroom.

Diz said: 'I've never seen such a sexual glow.'

'Will you stop making snide remarks?'

Diz paused, then said: 'Only when you stop coming in late, my son, and taking two-hour lunches, and spending a fortune on phone-calls to your wife. You do have a job here, this isn't just a telephone exchange, even if you are shagging the switchboard operator.'

'Ssh!' said Ollie, looking round.

'And you'd better pull a finger out with the theatre section. It's late.'

Diz was right. Ollie's work was suffering. He had lost that chancy precision with words upon which he had built his career. Troubled at home, he no longer had the confidence to write, and expect ears to listen. When he himself was behaving so badly, how could his words be worth even the paper upon which they were typed? *Words, words!* he had shouted at Viv. What did they possibly mean? They were just a sleight of hand, a trick of the wrist. Viv stood there, carrying within her an alien growth, and he flinched from looking into her eyes.

It was worse, of course, with his marriage. He could tell himself it was going through a bad patch. The words were such clichés that they might have sounded reassuring, but they didn't convince him. On the other hand, to admit, even silently, that his marriage was breaking up would be too painful, and besides, then something must be done. The old door would close and he would be in a new room, there would be no turning back. Until then, like a TB sufferer who tells himself he simply has a slight cough, until the day comes when he starts spitting blood and can no longer avoid naming his own disease—until then Ollie spent more time with Ellie, lying on her bed during those stuffy evenings while she rubbed cream into his sunburn and soothed his heart. He knew he deserved to be machine-gunned by his daughters.

It was not until the beginning of July that Ann walked past Viv's house. Until then she had taken a detour home from work to avoid the street. She hadn't told Viv about her promotion, though no doubt Ken had done so during one of the long tête-à-têtes that kept him so frequently out of the house – these trysts being described, for Ann's benefit, as 'troubles with the Hornsey Road site' or the all-purpose 'crisis at work'. When he spoke of his day, she froze. Nobody knows, until it happens to them, how terrible it is to find your husband is capable of lying.

But she could bear it no longer and one evening walked past. Quite apart from anything else, she had been painfully missing her nieces.

As she had expected, they were playing in the street. Her heart quickened. They detached themselves from their friends and ran up.

'Auntie Ann!' cried Rosie. She took her hand and started pulling her into the house. 'I've got a newt.'

'Is your mum here?' asked Ann.

'She's gone to the shops.'

208

Ann paused in the living room. She felt weak, both from relief and disappointment. She was led to the newt. The room was in even more of a mess than usual. On the pegboard was pinned a chart, with tasks to be done: Washing Up, Feeding Rabbits, and the names of Rosie, Daisy and Mum.

She pointed to it. 'Why's your dad not there?' she asked. 'Isn't that sexist?'

'He's always out.'

'What?' She stared at Rosie.

'With his girlfriend.'

'Girlfriend?'

Daisy said 'They took us to McDonald's. She ponged.'

'What of?'

'Perfume,' Daisy yowled. 'Ugh. Smelly Ellie!'

Both girls started chanting 'Smelly Ellie!'

The next day Ann rang Ollie at work but he wouldn't speak, except to say that he knew he was behaving badly but Viv didn't want him, she never had, she'd finally achieved her ambition and made him redundant. He sounded belligerent and drunk.

Phoning Viv was harder. Despising herself, she put it off until the next week. It was a great deal easier to manage a building society than to dial that familiar number.

'I didn't know about Ollie,' she said at last. 'I'm so sorry.'

'Come round to lunch,' said Viv. 'We must talk.'

'Can you manage? Shall we have lunch here?'

'Of course I can manage,' said Viv.

Ann put down the phone. They had arranged it for Saturday. Ken, she knew, would be coaching the Youth Club team, so he wouldn't know where she was. At times she thought of the man in the car, and wondered why she only felt the smallest tweak of guilt.

★

Ollie had now taken to spending some nights with Ellie, and had gradually changed into almost a visitor at his own home. He was not at the ringing-bell stage, but he did hesitate upon the doorstep. When crises strike there are those who confront and those who escape, and it will only take a crisis to reveal them. At university he had been heavily into drugs, releasing himself into heightened oblivion. Not blurry – people thought that who'd never taken them – but sharper. He knew he was being weak, but that didn't make him feel any better.

He was no longer presumed to be in on a Saturday, just 'mucking about', as the girls put it – reading *Private Eye*, getting his dry-cleaning, attempting perhaps yet again to find the bits for their Scalextric. Now he was inclined to take them out for treats. Though the household knew about Ellie, the official reason for his absence was that he was trying to get to grips with his novel, an explanation that the girls seemed to accept with the surprising *sang froid* of the young.

On Saturday he came to the house and the girls leapt up like puppies.

'Take us to Hamley's,' they said. 'You promised.' They had always been mercenary, but recently – either from circumstance or natural development – they had become worse.

'I thought Windsor Safari Park.' He eyed Viv, who stood at the liquidizer. The table was laid for two.

They started whining. 'We went there last time.'

'This time we'll bribe a monkey to sit on our bonnet.' Viv passed him the car keys; the girls ran outside. He looked at the table, raising his eyebrows. 'What's all this in aid of?'

She pushed the liquidizer. It whirred. He waited.

'What?' she asked.

'Our Kenneth coming to lunch?'

She paused. Sunlight slanted through the window. Her skin was pale and sheeny. 'You'd like that,' she said. 'Wouldn't you? Salve your conscience.'

'Who is it?'

'Ollie.' She rested against the kitchen unit. 'I need no longer tell you who it is. It is no longer your business. My gazpacho belongs to me and whoever I decide to share it with.'

'Look, I –'

'It's Ann.'

'Ann?'

She poured the pink liquid into two bowls and started chopping up parsley. She didn't look up. 'You might prefer me to have an adulterous little *déjeuner à deux*, but I'm actually having lunch with my sister.' She spoke with the clipped tones in which he pictured her addressing an errant fourth-former. 'Just one thing,' she went on, scraping the knife across the board and pushing the parsley on to the bowls. 'Are you going to be in tonight? Where're you going to rest your troubled little head, in the study or in your love-nest in that delightfully soignée locale known as Crouch End?'

'Shut up.'

She sighed. The sunlight touched her shiny face. 'You may be finding yourself, or paying me back, or suffering the male menopause, or whatever it is you're doing, but there's one thing I'd like you to realize.'

'What?'

'Life has to go on. I don't mean this,' she pointed to her stomach. 'This is going on whatever us stupid fuckers are doing. What I mean is . . .' She paused. She spoke with the precision of a prepared speech. This made him feel even more guilty. 'What I mean is, while you're out there finding true love, there are children to be looked after, washing to be done, hamsters to be cleaned out, car to be MOT'd, milkman to be paid, dentist to be gone to –'

'Affairs to be had?'

'Oh go on!' She spat the words out. 'Go to your funfair,

play around with your silly little girlfriend; you're just a child.'

He paused at the door, the car keys hanging from his finger. 'I'm certainly not a man,' he said theatrically. 'You've seen to that.'

He pocketed the keys and went off to his monkeys.

Ten minutes later there was a ring at the door. For a mad moment Viv thought it was Ollie, transformed into a gentleman caller who would woo her afresh. But it was her mother.

'You're looking peaky,' she said. 'You weren't like this with the others.'

'I know,' said Viv.

'Still, this one's different, isn't it?' She looked around. 'Where is everyone?'

'Er, they've just popped out,' Viv lied. 'Shopping.'

'Thought I'd see how you were. Must go back in a moment, I'm up to me eyes.'

'At the salon?'

Viv shifted from one foot to the other, willing her mother to leave. It was one o'clock.

'Oh look,' said Irene, inspecting the table. She smiled. 'Told you it'd be all right, didn't I?'

'What?'

'Knew you were a softie at heart.'

'What do you mean?'

'Just you and Ollie, is it? You usually forget.'

'What?' asked Viv.

'Your wedding anniversary.'

There was a pause. Viv realized the date. 'Ah,' she said.

'Fourteen years,' said her mother. She pinched Viv's cheek. 'So underneath those dungarees there beats a heart.'

'Two hearts, actually.'

Her mother laughed. 'What about the kids?'

'What?'

'Oh, little garnishes too.' She popped an olive into her mouth. 'You celebrating tonight? Want me to take them off your hands?'

'No really –'

'All right, be like that.'

'I don't mean –'

'Won't come often, that sort of offer,' she said. 'Not from me, anyway. Probably will from Vera. It's called sucking up to your step-daughter. She'll be taking out the kids and stuffing them with sack-whatsit –'

'*Sachertorte.*'

'She'll be giving him a heart attack.' She paused. 'Still, perhaps he'll die happy.' She stood up to go. 'Men,' she said. Her friend Frank was gay. 'All men want is chocolate cake and no questions.'

A few minutes later Ann arrived. Because she had seen her so seldom, it still gave Viv a shock to see her new haircut. Shorn, her sister carried herself with poise.

She took a summer pudding out of the carrier-bag. 'Hope it's OK,' she said. 'Haven't made one of these for ages. Don't seem to bother with puddings nowadays.'

Viv uncorked the wine and poured her a glass.

'Thanks,' said Ann. They were as polite as if they had just met.

Viv sat down. 'How's work?'

'I can't switch it off.' Ann sat down. 'I bring it home with me.'

'How awful.'

'It's not.'

'What?'

'I wouldn't bring it home if it was awful.'

'No.'

Ann said: 'I like facts and figures.'

They sipped their wine. Never before had Viv longed

so much for a cigarette; she had an emergency packet, but she didn't like to bring it out in front of her sister.

'How're you feeling?' asked Ann.

'Fine.'

There was a pause. Viv got up to fetch the bread. At the dresser she turned. 'You really want to know?'

'Yes.'

'Tired and aching and bloody terrible. Only stopped throwing up last week. I always thought other people were being pathetic when they described their pregnancies.'

'Have you seen a doctor?'

Viv shook her head.

'You should,' said Ann.

'Never have time.'

'Don't be silly.'

'Look,' said Viv. 'It's my business.'

'Is it?' asked Ann.

Viv looked at her. 'Isn't it?' There was a pause. Then she said: 'I presume it is, as you've gone and got yourself promoted.'

'Can't you see why?' said Ann loudly.

Viv didn't answer.

'Do sit down,' said Ann. 'You've made this lovely food.'

Viv moved towards the table and sat down. Ann watched her. They dipped their spoons into the soup.

'Just shows,' said Viv. 'One can't count on anything.'

'I used to think I could,' said Ann.

'Me too.'

Ann paused and put down her spoon. 'I used to think I could count on Ken.'

Viv looked up and stared at her. 'I'm not seeing him.'

'Wish I could believe you. Wish I could believe any-thing.'

'It's true! I've spoken to him a couple of times on the phone, that's all.'

Ann tore off a piece of bread. 'Funny, isn't it then, that he's always out.'

'Frightfully funny, but it's nothing to do with me,' said Viv. 'I've been busy being sick.'

Seconds ticked by. There was no sound, except a rustle from the cage as the hamster turned in his sleep. Ann glanced up. She had the look she wore when she was a child – the creased brow, the cloudy eyes as she struggled with her own distrust. The world tricking her, as Viv used to do for fun. As her parents had done in earnest. When she discovered about her father she had said to Viv: *They've taken away my childhood.*

'Believe me,' urged Viv. 'God knows, we're all in a mess. At least we can get that bit straight.'

She didn't move. They were sitting opposite each other, the wine bottle between them. Then Ann's face cleared. Magically – as if her features melted – she smiled. Then she started to laugh.

Across the table Viv started laughing too, with a squeaky edge of hysteria. They both laughed until they felt emptied. Finally they simply sat there, limp, shaken by a few residual sobs. Viv leant over, took Ann's glass and filled it with wine.

'So do shut up,' she said. 'And get sloshed.'

There was a thunderstorm in the night. The next day the streets were fresh and the rubbish sluiced away. Along Viv's road the cars sparkled. She came out of the newsagent's with the girls. All three of them were sucking ice lollies. She felt better than she had done for weeks.

As they walked up the hill towards Highgate, they met Douglas and Vera, who were window-shopping in the Holloway Road.

'Dad!' she called. 'I was coming to see you. I've got an idea.'

'One of your mad ones?' he asked.

She threw her lolly stick into the gutter. 'The wedding, next month. Is it too late to cancel it?'

Her father stared. 'What?'

'Cancel the hotel reception and have it at my house?'

'Your house?' asked Vera. She looked bronzed and startled.

Viv nodded. 'I want to give you a party.'

'Well well,' said her father. 'That would be nice.'

'You could manage?' asked Vera. 'What about Ollie?'

Viv shifted to the other foot. 'Oh, he'll like it too.'

Viv always thought her clearest on the allotment. The windy spaces blew away her doubts; the cabbages, leathery and grey, were her multitude of supporters. Her jumbled home dwindled; stopping her car, with a scrunch, on the cinder parking-place, she felt simpler and lighter.

She had had no doubts that urgent day when she had stood in the hut with Ken, telling him it could be done. Nor that day, weeks before, when she had straddled the earth and smelt the soup and felt capable of anything.

It was on the Tuesday, after school, that she finally decided it was time to tell the children. Now she was happier about Ann, there was no point in delaying it. She was watering the rows of plants; the spray sparkled in an arc. She raised the hose and watched the mist leap against the sky, and then somebody was tugging at her skirt.

'I'm bored,' said Daisy.

'Don't be silly.'

'I want to go to Windsor Safari Park.'

'You've just been. Why don't you play with your teddies?'

'They're asleep.'

'My teddies never slept.' She had finished watering. She dragged the hose back to the tap, watching the water leak into the ground, and turned off the current. The girls were hanging around at the door of the hut.

She said: 'I've got something to tell you.'

'I want some crisps.'

'Listen. I'm going to have a baby.'

216

They stared at her. 'A real one?' asked Rosie.

'Hope so. Now listen.' She squatted down. They stood in front of her. 'I always try to tell you the truth, to treat you as proper people. So listen carefully.' She paused, looking at their faces. Daisy was picking at some mud on her knee. 'You know that Ann can't have children and how that makes her sad?' They looked at her, their faces blank. 'Well, I'm going to give her this baby.'

'When?' asked Rosie. 'Now?'

'When it's born. So she can have a baby to bring up, that'll make her as happy as you make me.'

'But you're always shouting at us,' said Daisy.

Viv ignored this. 'What you must understand is that it's not as if we'll be giving the baby away and never seeing it again. It'll be part of the family. One big family. Isn't that marvellous?'

They gazed at her. Daisy scuffed at a small ridge of earth. 'Where'll it live?' asked Rosie.

'With Ken and Ann.'

'In their house?'

'Yes.'

'They'll make it wash its hands before tea,' said Rosie.

'Quite right too,' said Viv.

'They're all strict.'

'Listen,' said Viv. 'It's all going to be wonderful. But don't tell anyone yet. *Anyone*. It's our secret. Ann and I made up our minds properly on Saturday, when you were at Windsor Safari Park.'

Daisy wailed: 'I want to go to Windsor Safari Park!'

'Oh shut up,' said Viv.

'If we go home now,' said Daisy, 'will you buy us a Cornetto?'

Viv sighed and climbed to her feet. She thought of all the agonizing the four of them had gone through, thinking of this moment. She thought of something Ollie used to quote to her: *Adults are deteriorated children*, and she wondered: are they? Sometimes adults seemed rather more sensitive. She rolled up the hose and considered the *sang froid* of the young.

It was the last day of the summer term. In the staffroom a few teachers were still packing up. Madeleine took a card off the noticeboard.

'Nobody wants my yoghurt maker.' She took off another card. 'Nobody wants my kittens.'

Harold said: 'Try again in September.'

'They'll be having kittens of their own by then.'

'Ah,' sighed Harold. 'These whirlwind holiday romances.'

Madeleine laughed and went to the door.

'You patched it up with Dave?' Viv asked her.

She nodded. 'We're going on a walking holiday in Cornwall.'

'Don't get corns,' said Harold.

'Corny,' groaned Viv.

'Trouble with holidays,' said Harold, 'you need a holiday to recover.'

Madeleine asked him: 'You're going to that caravan park again?'

'Please. Leisure Centre.' He nodded. 'Once again I'll be staying in a blot on the landscape.'

' 'Bye,' said Madeleine. 'See you next year.'

She left. Harold and Viv were alone. He was ready to go, but she seemed to be waiting for something. He asked her: 'You still don't know where you're going?'

'Nope.'

'That's what I like about you.'

'What?' she asked.

'Impulsive. I should live like you, never planning –'

'I do plan!' she said abruptly.

He put down his bag of books. 'Sure you're O K?'

She nodded.

'I've been worried about you.'

'I know,' she said.

'Where's the old Viv? I need her.'

'Why?'

'For her dirty limericks. I'm letting the side down in the pub.'

Suddenly she embraced him.

'Mmmm . . .' he murmured.

'What?'

'Something to get my arms around.'

She struggled free, awkwardly.

'No, it's nice,' he said. 'You feel quite womanly.'

'You like them fat?' she asked, trying to keep her tone light.

'I don't have a lot of choice.' He sighed, and reached for his carry-all. His large, leathery face looked tired.

She said: 'You've meant a lot to me this term.'

'I try to oblige.'

She paused. 'Will you do something for me?'

'That depends.'

She asked: 'Will you forgive me?'

'For what?'

She spoke seriously. 'For not treating you like a friend?'

He frowned. 'What are you talking about?'

'Nothing.'

Suddenly she hugged him again, to hell with her size. At that moment the door opened and Alan came in.

'Whoops,' said Harold. 'Caught again.' He released Viv. 'Just some departmental negotiation.' He kissed Viv on the cheek. 'You look after yourself,' he said, and left.

Alan sat down. Viv went over to the tea cupboard and looked inside. 'No milk.'

'Never mind.' He patted the seat beside him. 'You said you wanted a chat.'

'Not a chat. A talk.' She stood beside the pin-pricked wall where the timetable had been. She felt sad that she

219

had to tell Alan, whom she liked less than Harold. Alan was younger and more successful. He had a pencil-thin jazzman's beard, and ambition had made him pompous.

He said: 'I think I know what it's about.'

She froze. 'How?'

'These things filter out, Viv.'

'What things?'

'What you've been up to,' he said. As she stared at him, he ran his finger around his jawline. 'I've had complaints.'

'What about?'

He paused. 'Look Viv. You're a terrific teacher and you have an exceptional rapport with the kids. But for that very reason you can be dangerous.'

'What?'

He patted the chair again. She moved forward and sat on the arm of the sofa.

'Because they listen to you,' he said. 'They trust you.'

'What are you talking about?'

'I'm sorry to bring it up now, but perhaps you can mull it over during the holidays. I'm talking about your, well, political and feminist propaganda. Particularly with the girls. Apparently they go back home and start spouting all this stuff about male exploitation and' – he winced – 'body fascism. Look, I'm all for giving kids a choice of the options, but you've honestly no right, particularly as many of them really aren't career material. Viv, I don't want us to turn out a hoard of discontented subversives.' He stopped.

Viv said: 'That's not the reason I wanted to talk to you.'

'No?'

'I wanted to tell you I'm pregnant.'

He stared at her, then burst out laughing. 'You, pregnant?'

'I haven't told anyone else. Please don't.'

He was still chuckling. 'I thought you looked a bit plump but –'

'But what?'

'You!'

'I've had them before,' she said crisply. Crisper than she felt.

'I know, but you've always said that stage was over, you were devoting yourself to your career, part of our team, women can choose, etcetera. Just what you tell the pupils, in fact.'

'I know.'

'Well,' he said, 'I guess congratulations are in order.'

'Sort of.'

He raised his eyebrows. 'What do you mean?'

She shifted on the arm of the sofa. She had told Ken: *I'm a wonderful liar.* She gazed down at the threadbare rug. Once she had dug up her father's potatoes and put the tops back in the earth; the next day they had stood beside the drooped leaves and she'd told him, with such utter conviction that she convinced herself, how the boys next door must have climbed in and done it. That had been easy.

'Look,' she said, 'I just wanted to give you official notice that you should make arrangements for a supply teacher.'

'When?'

'December.' She tried to smile. 'I'll tell it to be born at Christmas so it won't be too disruptive.'

'Supply?' he asked.

'I'll be coming back afterwards.'

'Sure?' he asked. 'What about the baby?'

She looked down at the rug. 'I've got some sorting out to do this holidays,' she said. 'There are problems.'

'Medical?'

'Domestic,' she said.

'Ah.'

She took a breath. 'Ollie's not the father.'

221

For the first time in the four years she had known him, she saw Alan blush. It was almost worth it for this. First the tips of his ears went pink, then it spread. 'You mean . . .'

'It's not his baby.' She told the faded staffroom rug: this isn't lying, it's simply omission.

Alan ran his hand again around his jaw. 'Forgive me for prying,' he said, and stopped.

'What?'

'It's not, by any chance . . .' He paused, and then spoke precisely: 'Harold's?'

She stared at him. '*What?*'

'Harold's baby?'

She burst out laughing. She wobbled on the sofa arm, losing her balance. Alan blushed pinker and inspected his fingernails.

At last she gasped: 'For such a self-righteous prig you do have a filthy mind.'

Ollie should never have gone to the loo. Or Viv should never have gone to the gym. If they hadn't, Ellie might never have found out. Yet, anyway.

Viv, influenced by Ken, was trying to keep fit and had enrolled in a chic ladies' gym in Covent Garden, where for various reasons the others were slimmer than she was and dressed in pink and emerald leotards, like sheeny skins. One day there was nobody to look after the children and she left them with Ollie, who was going to take them to lunch.

First, though, he went to the lavatory, and as they lay on the rubberized flooring environment of the *Capital* office, sucking Pentels and gazing at the reversed T'ai Ch'i hand-outs he had given them to draw on, Ellie came over.

'Have a Polo,' she said.

They took one each, and another for later. Daisy, sucking, said: 'My mum says they're bad for our teeth.'

'You going somewhere nice for your hols?' asked Ellie politely. She had no idea where they were going; nobody told her anything.

'The Isle of Wight,' said Rosie.

'Ooh, that's nice.'

'We're going with Mum and Auntie Ann,' said Daisy, 'because Dad's writing a book.'

Ellie was about to reply: is he? But she stopped. She might be young, but she was learning.

'I want to paint my nails,' said Daisy, who was less loyal than her sister, 'like you.'

'You can't do that,' said Ellie, 'till you're a big grown-up lady.'

'When you're grown-up you can have a baby,' said Daisy. 'Are you going to have a baby?'

'I hope not!' laughed Ellie.

Daisy the chatterbox said: 'Mum is.'

Rosie hit her. Daisy yelped. Ollie came back from the lavatory. Ellie got up swiftly and moved away.

Ann came back from work, flopped down in the armchair and closed her eyes. Only one week to go before the holiday. She felt pleasantly drained of energy. Though she felt worried about Derek – he had been moved sideways at his own request, and she had recently heard that his marriage was breaking up – perversely the office was a more lighthearted place without him: a female confederacy of banter and affection. It is sad how one person's unhappiness can bring out the cruellest in those around him. Prickling, girlish resentments.

She was thinking of this, and the supper she couldn't be bothered to cook yet, and the week in the Isle of Wight from which the two husbands were going to absent themselves, saying that the sisters should have some time together – she was contemplating this when the front door opened and closed and Ken came in.

'Close your eyes,' he said.

'They're closed already.'

'Keep them like that.'

She heard him go into the hall. He had collected something; it was his scarf. He tied it around her head, blindfolding her.

'Hey!'

'Come on,' he said, taking her hand. His own felt large and dry. She stood up obediently and he led her out of the door, guiding her so she didn't bump. As she smelt the evening air – warm pavement and exhaust fumes – she suddenly remembered how when she was little she had pretended to be lame. Her parents and Viv would walk ahead and she limped behind. Passers-by would stop in the street and gaze at her sorrowfully, then glare at the rest of the family who, exasperated, would tell her to hurry up. She realized, now, that it was rare for them all to be out together; this must only have happened once. But how vividly she remembered it, the thirst for pity in a big, breezy, unfair world. She smelt next door's privet as Ken seated her in the car, and she thought for the first time: how nice was I? *There are some people,* said Douglas, *who make the world smile on them.* And the others?

'What're you up to?' she asked.

'Wait and see.'

He drove for perhaps fifteen minutes. When he turned corners she leant into them, balancing herself in her blindness. The window was open; at one point she smelt curry cooking, at another chips frying. Always fumes. With her eyes closed, sounds were clearer – shouts, a blaring radio. When they stopped, perhaps at traffic lights, she heard a child distinctly say: 'Look at that lady.' She felt alert and wary. Ken didn't speak.

The car stopped. He got out and she heard him opening her door. The hand, hotter now, took hers and she climbed out, instinctively pulling down her skirt. He removed the scarf.

At first she wondered what she should be looking at.

Beside her was a stretch of derelict concrete – perhaps an old depot yard – with yellow ragwort struggling through the cracks. It was surrounded by a high wire fence. On one side was a used vehicle lot, luminous with stickers, and on the other side was a pub.

She said: 'Don't keep me in suspense.'

He put his finger under her chin and lifted her head. Against the wire was a *To Let* placard.

They were sitting in the pub next door.

'So that's what you've been doing,' she said.

He nodded. 'It looks awful, but it's a wonderful site. Half an acre, and the nearest garden centre's way over the other side of the North Circular. This whole area's residential.'

'You never told me.'

'I wanted to be sure I wasn't being stupid.' He gazed at her; he looked so excited.

'All these weeks?' she said. She didn't tell him that the Monday before, out of a desperate curiosity, she had checked the dial on his car and worked out that he had driven twenty-two miles on a day he was supposed to have stayed in the office.

'Oh, I've been around,' he said. 'Nothing I can't tell you about disused railway land, failed timber yards and bankrupt depots for sanitary ware.'

She laughed. 'I don't believe this.'

'Our own garden centre, Annie. It could work, I know it could. You could be my financial adviser.' He paused. 'It's time I got out of that place. You know that.'

She nodded. 'I know that.'

'Suddenly I thought; well, why the hell not? I've been bored long enough. I thought: why not stop moaning about it and actually *do* something?'

She gazed at this new, bright-eyed Ken. She thought: he *has* changed. Something flashed through her mind: who's doing is this? But she pushed it away.

He was waiting. 'Well,' he asked. 'What do you think?'

She said slowly: 'We could get a grant, I expect. And a low-interest loan. And there's the house as security.'

He raised his eyebrows.

She asked: 'But why now?'

He looked down into his glass, and stubbed out his cigarette. 'Well, the way things are . . . you have your job and, well, I've been feeling you might not be wanting the baby . . .' He cleared his throat. 'And I do see why.' He paused. 'Well, I could at least do something. A new start. Make you proud of me.'

She leant over. 'You don't have to do that.'

'Don't I?'

She paused, but she didn't speak. She couldn't truthfully reply one way or another. It would be easier to talk about profit margins and thirty-year leases, which they did.

'Why didn't you tell me?' Furious, Ellie faced Ollie.

'I couldn't.'

'Why didn't you tell me she was having a baby?'

He sat down on the bed. 'There was a good reason, I promise you.'

'Who do you think I am? Your little bit of fluff, your bit on the side?' She glared at him. Her nose was sunburnt. He felt weak with pity. 'Blokes do that where I come from but at least they're honest about it.'

'Ellie –'

'You're always saying how upfront you are and all that fiddle-faddle but you're shiftier than the lot of them!'

'It's not what you think!' His voice squeaked like a schoolboy's.

'Think I haven't wanted to ask? All these months you've put me into this little box, and I can lay my hand on your brow and smooth your troubles away, think I haven't longed to ask about you and your wife and your friends that I'm never allowed to meet?' She paused for breath; he looked at her poor peeling nose. 'I'm a real person, Ollie. I may not understand half your daft magazine but I'm a real person and I deserve to be treated properly.'

'Yes,' he said. 'I know.' He too felt empty of breath. He wanted to creep under the duvet and pull it over his head. He looked at her; she was crying now and the mascara was smudged on her cheeks. Behind her was the frilled gingham curtain she had hung in front of her pots and pans. It had some broderie anglaise stitched to the hem; he couldn't bear to look at it.

'You want to come here and play houses,' she said, 'and know why? Because you can't face up to your real life, and your wife who's pregnant – what a time to leave her!'

'You don't understand.'

'Too stupid, am I?'

'No. It's not what you think.'

'I can't think, can I?' she said. 'I'm not allowed to.'

'No –'

'Yes.'

'Look,' he said, 'it's not like that.'

'It is!'

'It's not! Listen. It's not my baby.'

'What?' She sat down on the stool beside the sink.

'She's having the baby for her sister.'

Ellie stared at him. 'Come again?'

'It was all arranged. She's been, well, made pregnant by her brother-in-law. When she has the baby she's going to give it to her sister.'

To his horror, Ellie started smiling. 'Tell us another.'

'I know it sounds bizarre, but it's true.'

'You really take me for an eejit, don't you – ?'

'No!' he shouted.

'I knew you thought I was dumb, but this –'

'Listen!'

'Oh shut up! I'm fed up with your lies. Lies to your

wife, lies to me, you don't know whether you're coming
or going –'

'It's true!'

'I want a proper bloke who's straight with me –'

'It's true about my wife!'

'Save your lurid stories for your crappy, pretentious
magazine. Go on, get out!' She moved to the mantelpiece
and flung the blue china cat, his gift, to the floor. The
carpet was soft and it didn't break. She stamped on it.
'Get out!' she shouted. She stamped on the cat again. He
had to turn away; it was so undignified for her to be seen
by him. He wished the bloody thing would break.

'Listen –' he began.

'Oh shut up!'

He got to his feet and tried to grab her but she pushed
him away. She was surprisingly strong; he staggered
back.

She had given up with the cat. Instead, she picked up
his shirt and flung it at him. It missed and landed softly
on the carpet. 'I even ironed that for you!' she screeched.

One always feels safe with an aunt, particularly an
elderly one. Ann and Viv stayed with their Auntie Dot,
their mother's unmarried sister, who for as long as they
could remember had lived in a bungalow not quite overlooking Freshwater Bay. She was old, and short-sighted
now, and she had never been curious. Not once during
the week did she enquire the whereabouts of the two
husbands, neither of whom she had much liked anyway.
This was restful. She tolerated the children benignly, and
gave them unsuitably infantile gifts – slot-in plastic shapes
and a Bambi egg-cup – from the local Missionary Mart.
She seldom stirred from the house and the four of them
were free to wander the lanes – all dusty hedgerows and,
underfoot, toads, which had been flattened like cardboard.
They picked early blackberries, staining their fingers, and
climbed the slippery rocks at the beach where it always

seemed to be high tide. For the first time in months, Viv felt fit. She dreaded going home..

They arrived early in the afternoon. As they unpacked the car, Bella from next door remarked to Viv: 'You're looking bonny.'

Inside the house Viv turned to Ann. 'Know what she means by bonny?'

Ann nodded. 'Fat.' She asked: 'What're you going to tell her?'

'That I'm pregnant. That's all. Then we'll wait till it's born. We must all get together, to get our story right.'

The girls had run out to the playground. Viv started pulling their things out of their bags – pebbles, crackling lengths of seaweed, a plastic bottle. Sand scattered. Grimacing, she threw the bottle into the bin.

'We used to collect pebbles,' said Ann.

'We weren't parents.' Viv smiled. 'One day you'll find out what it's like to have lots of little pebbles, with holes in for one day making into necklaces – one day – jamming up your kitchen drawers, and shrivelled conkers under the stair carpet tripping you up, and lots of touching little presents they made at school, with glue and Rice Krispies packets, all falling to bits and yet how can you bear to throw them away?'

'Can't wait,' said Ann.

Viv sat down heavily. 'I hate coming home.'

'It's all my fault.'

'No.'

'You're doing all this for me, and look what's happened to you and Ollie.'

'It was my decision,' said Viv. 'I just wish he'd make up his mind.'

'You're the only one who seems able to make decisions.'

Viv sighed. 'What does he want?'

'He doesn't know.'

'Do any of us?'

Ann shrugged and smiled. 'You and I do. Just for now.'

229

She moved away and went to the phone. 'Must go to work.'

'Today?'

'I'll phone for a cab.'

'What a whizzkid!' said Viv.

As she stood at the phone, Ann pulled off her shell necklace and kicked off her plastic shoes. With one ear to the receiver she reached into her bag and pulled out a pair of high-heels. Viv got up and replaced the shells around her sister's neck.

'Not too much of a whizzkid,' she said.

Ann smiled. Then Viv suddenly sat down.

Ann swiftly put down the phone. 'What is it?' she asked, alarmed.

Viv reached for her sister's hand and laid it on her stomach.

'Must be all that sea air,' she murmured.

Both sisters stayed quite still. The baby was moving.

Ten minutes after Ann had gone there was a sound on the stairs. Viv froze, mid-way through loading the washing machine. It was Ollie. He looked rumpled and bleary.

'Hello,' he said.

'Why aren't you at work?'

'Been watering the plants.'

She sniffed the air. 'You've been boozing.'

'Wouldn't you?'

'Where've you been sleeping?' she asked.

'In the study.' He looked around. 'Where are they?'

She gestured outside. 'With their friends.'

'I'll just say hello to them, then I'll be off.' He moved towards the door and paused on the threshold. 'Can I—I assume you don't mind if I sleep in the study tonight? See the kids?'

'Course not. They miss you.'

He looked at the chart on the pegboard. She thought,

with fear, how quickly her best friend had become her enemy, and neither of them had quite been able to stop it. How simple to call it either the baby's or Ken's fault. But it wasn't that easy.

What little time it took. She thought: I can't even tell him about our holiday, it's too sad that he wasn't there. She realized that the range of safe topics had shrunk so much that there was very little they could say. And they had always talked so much. *Talk, talk!* he had shouted that day.

'Good,' he said, and cleared his throat. 'Ellie's away and –'

'Oh, I see,' she said crisply. 'Can't face being on your own.'

Ollie slammed out of the house. She sat down, hopelessly, on the pile of clothes. She shouldn't have spoken like that.

Then she caught her breath as, within her, the baby moved again.

Viv is dreaming of a beach. The tide is out and the sand lies flat in the sun. The sand seems to stretch for ever, right to the horizon. She herself is sitting there, trying to bury a baby. Flustered, she scoops out the sand, but as fast as she does it the hollows fill with water. Beside her the baby lies quite still. It doesn't seem to mind any of this, even the fact that it is smeared with mud. Not sand, but mud. She can't get her brain to work out why.

She is pondering this, quite calmly, when she wakes up and finds that, in fact, her face is wet with tears. She feels her cheeks curiously.

There's a movement in the bed. She reaches over. But it is Daisy, who has climbed in beside her. She puts her arms around her daughter.

18

It was the end of August; Douglas and Vera's wedding day. The reception was in full swing and the house packed; people bent their heads under Viv's drooping streamers. By now it was generally known, and indeed evident, that she was pregnant; that was all. As in all weddings, there were long-forgotten faces and small jolts of recognition: Douglas's brother, Uncle Phil, grown more portly; Ollie's Sloany sister Caroline, with her glossy black hair and big English limbs. The party had spilled into the garden. Between the bodies Rosie and Daisy threaded their way, nibbling food and sipping champagne from stray glasses. They wore Vera's new leaf dresses; Daisy's sash had come undone.

Ann filled the glass of a large, lugubrious man who nodded towards the happy couple. 'They met at our club, you know,' he said. 'I could see they were strongly attracted during our home-made wine and cheese evening.'

They were joined by another man. 'It's not a singles club, mind. It's for people with interests.'

The lugubrious man said: 'She's a handsome woman.'

Ann looked at Vera, who wore a creamy suit with flowers in the lapel. 'She is.'

'So you're Doug's eldest?' the man asked.

She nodded.

He looked at Irene, who stood nearby, munching quiche. 'But you take more after your mum.'

She nodded again. 'Excuse me,' she said, and carried the bottle away.

Uncle Phil went up to Ollie and nudged him. 'See you've been busy,' he said.

'What?'

Phil pointed to Viv.

Ollie smiled thinly.

Viv was moving from one guest to another, offering them vol-au-vents. Her Auntie Ree popped one into her

232

mouth and said in a muffled voice: 'Expect you'll be wanting a little boy this time.'

'I don't mind,' said Viv. 'Have another. Ann made them.'

She was so tense that her dress stuck to her backbone. Every now and then she glanced across at Ollie, or Ken, whom she hadn't seen for some weeks, or her children, willing them to be discreet. Now she was holding this party, she longed for it to be over.

She passed Ann. They smiled confidentially at each other.

'O K?' whispered Ann.

'Touch and go,' said Viv.

Ann gave her the thumbs-up sign and moved on.

Caroline was talking to Uncle Phil. 'I'm Oliver's sister,' she said. 'We met at their wedding, remember?'

'How could I forget?' he said gallantly. 'So how're you keeping?'

'I'm working in Brussels.'

'You've come over for this?'

She shook her head. 'Flat trouble. Got to find a new tenant.'

Ollie, overhearing this, asked: 'New tenant?'

Auntie Dot was sitting next to Vera. 'Have you ever been to Ventnor?' she asked.

'Ventnor?'

Rosie was passing by, on the hunt for food. Auntie Dot patted her absently on the head. 'They played all day on the beach, didn't you, pet?'

Rosie said: 'I can't find my pebbles.'

Irene wandered past her ex-husband and paused, raising her eyebrows. 'You look like the cat that's found the cream.'

Douglas replied: 'I have.'

★

Ollie veered towards Ann, as she passed, and spoke behind his hand. 'Could plant a crop of marrows in the lies I'm telling,' he whispered.

We're like a ballet, thought Viv, who was starting to feel dizzy: graceful, evasive action. She should stop drinking, for the sake of the baby. She must feel extra responsible for it. Through the heads, her eye caught Ken's. He was wearing an unfamiliar pale suit. He himself looked pale. He turned away.

Caroline was tying up Daisy's sash. 'At your age,' she said, 'I was at boarding school.'
'I want to go to boarding school!'
'You'd never see your parents.'
Viv was passing. She stopped. Caroline turned to her. 'I was just saying, what with Nanny Roberts and boarding school, we never saw our parents.'
'Lucky pigs,' said Daisy.
Caroline went on: 'Ollie always said they'd given us away.'
'Did he?' asked Viv with interest.
'What's the point of children? he used to say, if you just give them away?' Caroline took a slice of pizza. 'But it was what one did, wasn't it?'

Douglas patted Ollie on the back. 'Decent of you to put this on.'
'Thank Viv and Ann.'
'Better than a hotel.'
'Oh, she likes to be in control,' said Ollie, his voice slurred.

Viv stood at the kitchen sink, flicking water over herself. She felt weak with strain; her muslin dress stuck to her like cling film. The draining board was cluttered with empty quiche dishes. Ken hadn't spoken to her. Nor, indeed, had Ollie, except for the occasional 'where's the napkins?' She watched her husband; he was tall, one could always spot him in a crowd. Could anyone guess that something was wrong? He stood in the garden. Above his head pears were suspended from next door's tree. They gave him a look of poised insecurity. She remembered last year, the four of them picking the pears under cover of darkness, and Ollie saying they tasted like the wooden offcuts from his school carpentry class. It had been fun. Not perfect, their marriage, but fun.

She moved away from the sink and smiled at the nearest, unknown guest. This year none of them had even picked the pears.

Irene nudged Vera. 'You planned this?' she asked, half joking.

'Pardon?'

Irene lifted her arm; her dress had ripped. Frank was standing nearby; Irene turned to him. 'She made this for me and now look.'

Vera said: 'I told you it was too tight.'

Frank guffawed: 'So am I.'

Viv found herself next to Ken. 'More champagne?' He shook his head. 'Tell me about your garden centre,' she said.

After a moment he said: 'You're looking –'

'Fat.'

'Beautiful.' He moved away.

Douglas, maudlin now, sat on the rabbit hutch. Ollie sat down beside him.

'This is the happiest day of my life.'

'Have another drink,' said Ollie, refilling his glass.

'Remember *your* do? That weird little bloke playing the thingummy.'

'Sitar.'

'The fur really flew.'

Ollie said: 'You know my parents.'

Caroline joined them. 'I think they've got used to Viv by now,' she said. 'Got more broadminded in their old age.'

'She was a little tearaway,' smiled Douglas. 'Always up to mischief.'

'Telling me,' said Ollie.

Rosie went up to Auntie Dot. She was carrying a hamster. 'Bertie died,' she said. 'This is the new one.'

Ollie whispered to Caroline: 'Listen, sis. You really want a new tenant?'

'Why?'

Douglas sat alone on the rabbit hutch. He had taken off his tie and loosened his shirt. The sky had darkened and there was a rumble of thunder. The guests raised their heads.

Ann sat down next to him. 'All the best, Doug.'

'Go on,' he said. 'Call me Dad. Just for today.'

'Dad then.'

He patted her knee. A drop of rain fell. Beneath them the rabbits shifted restlessly.

The lugubrious man, whose name nobody had caught, was less lugubrious now. He tapped Auntie Ree on the shoulder and pointed to the bride. 'Makes you believe in divorce,' he said.

Uncle Phil squatted down beside Daisy and messed up her hair.

'You're pleased you're having a little brother or sister?' he asked.

Ann was near. She froze.

Daisy said: 'Yes.'

A moment later, when Uncle Phil had gone, Ann bent down. 'Well done,' she whispered.

Heavier drops of rain fell. The sky was threatening. The guests started murmuring and moved into the house. Irene dabbed at her eyes; she was crying.

'What's up, ducks?' asked her friend Frank, putting his arm around her.

'Weddings,' she sobbed.

Drops splashed on the rabbit hutch. The garden was emptying, but Ken still lingered by the compost heap. Ollie went up to him.

'Long time no see,' he said.

'Yes.'

Ollie, by now, was drunk. 'Let's have a little talk,' he said.

Ken tried to move away.

'Don't desert me,' said Ollie. It was raining heavily and the garden was empty. Ollie steadied himself on the brickwork of the compost heap. 'That's what my editor said to me – let's have a little talk.'

'Did he?'

'The creep.'

'We'd better go in,' said Ken.

'Maybe there's an opening for me in the dry-rot business,' said Ollie. 'What do you think?'

'I think we should go in,' said Ken, who was soaking. 'They're staring at us.'

In the living room it was so dark that Viv had put on the spotlights. Nobody could move; bodies were packed together. Outside the rain was pouring down, sluicing down the windows. There was a flash of lightning, the spotlights flickered; thunder cracked as if the sky were splitting.

Viv stood on a chair. 'Ladies and gentlemen. Quiet

please.' She was interrupted by more thunder. Her audience tittered.

'Well, we're starting with a bang,' Douglas said.

Uncle Phil bellowed: 'Haven't you had one already?'

'Shut up!' shouted Viv. She raised her glass. 'Here's to Dad and Vera.'

People toasted the couple. Vera cut the cake. Outside, it was the kind of tropical downpour that stirs, rather than depresses, the spirits. At the end of the garden the pears bobbed in the wind.

Vera cleared her throat. 'I just want to say,' she began, and started again, more clearly. 'I just like to say thank you to Vivien and Ann for this wonderful day . . .'

There were murmurs of agreement.

'I know it is the custom for the man to speak,' she went on, 'but . . .'

Douglas touched her arm. 'You say what you like, Vee, we're in a liberated household here.'

'I just want – you must excuse my English, but I am very moved.' She looked nervous but determined. Douglas nodded benignly as she spoke. 'This lovely home, this family. It is all very precious. I was only eleven years old when my parents hid me in the country, outside Vienna, with a Gentile family. So I had two childs, er –'

'Childhoods,' said Viv.

'Childhoods, yes. And my own family, I lost them all – Father, Mother, my beautiful Aunt Helga, so full of life, and her two babies. All gone.'

Everyone was listening intently to this unexpected speech. Viv looked across at her husband, who was frowning. His hair was wet. He caught her eye and looked away. She thought: I've spent this whole wedding avoiding people's eyes. She thought how sober Vera looked compared to the rest of them.

Vera went on: 'I was the only one. Sometimes I felt I should not be alive. But I was loved by my new family and I learned that life has to go on, and that it is most

238

precious. And that a family, any family, is a wonderful thing and is to be treasured.' She had been looking down at the cake, its icing cracked by her knife. Now she looked up and met Viv's eyes. 'It is to have people who love you whatever you do, even if they sometimes do not understand.' She was looking at everyone now, from one face to another. 'And I just need to say – I'm sorry to take up all this time . . . I am so happy, to be part of something again, and such lovely people. And I hope we have many more bottles of champagne together.'

She sat down. There was a silence, then a rumble of thunder. A few people hesitantly clapped, and then the rest joined in.

19 The place still looked as if he had only just arrived. In fact, it was now October and Ollie had lived in his sister's flat for six weeks. His disorder, however, had a transient, bachelor air – he had never unpacked his suitcase and the wastepaper basket was full of lager cans.

The flat was in a mansion block near the Albert Hall, an area of London he had always found boring and over-upholstered. The other inhabitants appeared either to be Arabs, or girls as well-bred as his sister, whose daddies had bought the flat for them and who had boyfriends with the sort of braying laughs that made his skin pucker. He lived with the curtains closed, in perpetual twilight, telling himself that out of suffering at least he could hammer out his masterpiece. His typewriter sat on the table, surrounded by scattered notes. He had never been so lonely in his life.

It was disorientating how many hours there were to the day when one was not at home. He had even started playing the piano again – Caroline was a gifted musician and had installed the old family Bechstein in the living room.

In fact, he was in the middle of 'Riders on the Storm' when there was a knock at the door and she came in.

'Hi, sis,' he said, swivelling round on the stool.

She put down her suitcase. 'Haven't heard you playing that for yonks.'

'Haven't played for yonks. That's why my songs are so dated.'

'You were awful in the sixties,' she said. 'You smelt of very old carpet and you smiled all the time. Must've been the drugs.'

He revolved slowly. 'I just found more things to smile about.'

'How've you been? Can I spend the night?'

'It's your flat,' he said.

'You're not expecting anyone?'

He nodded as he spun around. 'She's blonde and Finnish with long tanned thighs. She doesn't talk at all but just gazes at me in mute adoration. She demands nothing but my diminished, though still faintly pulsating, masculinity.'

Caroline smiled, like a sixth-former who has found a junior in her study. 'Shall I make us a cup of tea?'

'None left.'

'You are hopeless. Coffee then.'

She went into the kitchen. He heard her make a noise of disgust, loud enough for him to notice.

'Sorry,' he called. 'Ran out of bin-liners.'

'It's not that,' she said, reappearing. She held out three empty whisky bottles.

He nodded. 'I'm learning to be an alcoholic. It's a new life experience.'

She sighed and went back into the kitchen. He played the piano softly, thinking how if Caroline weren't his sister he'd have nothing in common with her at all. Yet he was fond of her. She had been a no-nonsense, middle-aged little girl; sometimes she reminded him of a more privileged version of Ann.

She came back with two mugs of coffee. 'Never seen so many take-away boxes in my life,' she said. 'I thought you were supposed to be liberated.' She passed him a mug. 'Bet you can't even boil an egg.'

'Look, Caro, you must realize something about my wife.'

'What?'

'We were supposed to have a sharing marriage but you can't share anything with Viv.'

'Why not?'

'She wants – she wanted to be in control. Cooking, sex, life. And she was. Nothing very liberated about that for either of us. We just used the vocabulary.' He ran his finger down the keys, playing a descending scale for effect. He felt full of self-pity today.

'Can I be frank, Ollie?'

'I hate it when people say that.'

'You're well rid of her. She sneered at us. She had a bad influence on you. You were always weak and she made you weaker –'

'Shut up.'

'What?'

He said: 'Don't talk like that about her.'

'Why not? You've always been saying –'

'I'm allowed to,' he replied. 'I love her.'

'Still?'

He swivelled his seat to face her. 'There's one thing you don't understand about Viv. None of you've ever understood it. You, or our parents, with their sherry and their platitudes, who wouldn't know a feeling if it came up and slapped them in the face; or Marcus, stuck out in Hong Kong in his boring sterile job, talking about tax evasion and what sort of stacking stereo to buy – none of you've realized one thing about Viv. She's alive.'

'So we're dead?'

'No. I'm just saying she's alive.'

Ignoring his coffee, he got off the stool, went into the kitchen and split open a lager. It was Triple Strength Export, the sort of beer that the men in his own neighbourhood, without his educational advantages, drank in the doorways of bankrupt shops. It gave his disintegration a spurious street pedigree. Besides, it got him drunker quicker.

He returned to the living room. She said: 'You might sneer at your family but the moment you're in trouble we do rally round.' She drained her coffee and took the mugs into the kitchen. He stepped aside for her. 'And you didn't exactly refuse Great Auntie Flo's legacy.'

'She left it to me.'

'Know what I'm going to buy with mine?' she asked, pulling up the kitchen blind. He winced in the sunlight. 'A Golf Convertible. It's *la rage* in Brussels.'

Ollie said: 'I've bought time.' He pointed through the doorway at his typewriter.

'Why did you leave the magazine?' she asked. 'Don't say you've turned Tory.'

He shook his head. 'Just lost my faith.' He tipped the can against his mouth. 'I've decided to discover myself instead.'

'Gawd,' said his sister, and heaved a sigh. 'It's kaftan time.'

Viv paused at the newsagent's. A *For Sale* postcard had caught her eye. She got out her biro and took down the details.

The autumnal sun shone and Mr Gupta, the newsagent, was standing in the doorway. He disappeared for a moment and came back with some *New Society* magazines. 'Your husband, he never picks these up any more.'

She took them. 'Look, why don't you cancel them from now on?' Saying the words, she felt a spasm of pain. It's arbitrary, how these things hit. After all, she was only cancelling a magazine order.

To recover herself, she pointed to the three little girls that Mr Gupta was shooing to the back of the shop.

'They're not all yours, are they?'

'Two belong to my sister and her husband, they live upstairs.'

'Do you ever forget which child belongs to who?' she asked.

He smiled politely at her joke. Well, he thought it was a joke. As she walked away, stately now in her advanced pregnancy, she thought: perhaps they would manage this business better in India.

Only those who have been pregnant know how it transforms them into public property. Strange children stroke their bellies and question them; other women confide in them, repeating in uncomfortable detail their experiences of birth, varicose veins and flatulence. De-sexed, their bodies are no longer their own, but reproductive vehicles to be prodded in clinics, preferably in front of twenty male students.

In the past Viv, unlike many women, had enjoyed this. Ollie no doubt would have attributed it to her desire to be the centre of the universe. This time, however, it made her feel uneasy and spurious. Bella next door, for instance, had had a more lurid gynaecological history even than Ann, but had managed finally to produce five children, now grown up. She liked comparing notes, and there had always been something watchful about her that Viv had never trusted.

When Viv wheeled the pram home – Ollie had taken the girls out in the car – Bella spotted her.

'Getting prepared, are we?' she asked. 'How long is it now?'

'Six weeks,' said Viv briskly, easing the pram into the hall. She shut the door behind her.

As her mother used to say, apropos of childbirth: *It goes in easier than it comes out.* Viv had to get the pram

243

out, to Ann's house. It now became dark by six o'clock and that evening, under cover of nightfall, when the car was returned, she threw a blanket over the pram and emerged from the house as furtive as a burglar. Glancing up and down the empty street she bundled it into the back of the estate and slammed the door shut.

She straightened up, breathing heavily. Her back ached. It was at moments like this, when she was doing something practical for her sister, that it hit her. Day by day she could coast along, in the slow, ruminative rhythm that came with pregnancy, and not think at all. But when it came to lugging prams – real metal, real sweat . . . Next week she and Ann were going to Mothercare. She would stand in the bright lights and buy soft white Babygros in cellophane packets, for the new human being that was kicking so insistently inside her and which she must never, for everybody's sake, ever consider hers.

'You unfold it like this. Look.'

Viv was demonstrating the pram in Ann's kitchen.

'I'd given all my stuff away after Daisy was born,' she went on.

'But Viv –'

'No, it's my treat,' she insisted. 'It was dead cheap. I got it from an ad at the newsagent's, and when I got there somebody else was about to buy it but I spun them this sob story –'

'But Viv, it's *old*.'

'Less than two years.'

'But we were going to buy, Ken and me –'

'They cost the earth new,' said Viv 'and you only need them for a few months.'

'But, I mean . . .' Ann paused. She looked embarrassed and polite, as if Viv were a neighbour who had dropped in at an awkward time. 'I mean, we wanted a new one.'

'Why?'

Ann touched the pram handle. She looked up at Viv, her face pink. 'It's a new baby.'

'My babies were new.'

'But it's . . . special.'

'All babies are special,' Viv said shortly.

There was a silence. Neither of them could think of what to say next. If she weren't my sister, thought Viv, what on earth would we have in common? This realization in the past had not worried her; now it made her heart contract in what she realized was panic.

She looked out at the extension room. Ken had finished it during the summer. It would be a place for the child to play. A sliding door led into the garden; it was one of those aluminium, double-glazed, sliding doors Viv had always considered irredeemably suburban. The sort of thing, in fact, that Ann and Ken would have. As they indeed had.

She felt jittery and went into the lounge. She suddenly missed Ollie terribly. He had always made fun of Ann and Ken's doggedly earned consumer goods, their vacuumed car and indexed cassettes. He was as snobbish as she was. Like her, he had rebelled against his background, posh though it was. He had tried to consider himself a free spirit (ah yes, but when it came to the crunch, who was?). It would have soothed her disquiet to tell him what she felt. Only somebody who knew how she felt could tell her how silly she was being.

But was she? Ann came in. Viv was studying the two shelves of books – paperback romances and *Wonderful Ways with Mince*. Some demon prompted her to speak. She said, louder than she had intended: 'This place reminds me of our parents'. They never had any books either.'

Ann paused. Then she went to the window. Outside it was dark and foggy. She closed the curtains.

She turned. For a moment her face resembled Vera's, weeks before on her wedding day; there was the same tense dignity about it. Instead of replying to Viv, she said simply: 'Thanks for the pram. It was kind of you.'

They went into the hall and stood for a moment at the front door. Viv fiddled with her car keys.

Just as she was about to leave, Ann said: 'It's not the same as our parents' house. It's not the same as yours.' She opened the door. 'It's ours.'

Viv stepped out into the street, its lamps a foggy blur.

Later that evening Ken came home, his boots covered in mud. He was in high spirits.

'Funny how I don't mind slogging my guts out after work when it's my own building site.' He pulled off his boots. 'My own mud.' He put down his sheaf of drawings on the hall table. 'Do you realize that something deeply miraculous is happening in the history of construction?'

'What?' asked Ann.

'We appear to be on schedule.'

He carried his boots into the kitchen and stopped.

She followed him in. As she had feared, he was staring at the pram.

'Viv gave it to us,' she said.

'Viv?' His voice was sharp. 'When was she here?'

'Earlier.'

His voice trembled. 'She trying to give us things?'

'Ken –' She put her hand on his arm. He moved away. She thought: my bloody sister. He went to the door and threw his muddy boots into the garden – Ken, who was usually so tidy. (Ah yes, nor did he as a rule get parking tickets.)

'Think we can't afford to buy one for ourselves?' he demanded.

'Do sit down.'

'What's she doing? What's she up to?' He was highly agitated.

'Don't be the old Ken,' she said. 'Don't spoil things.'

He stood there in his socks, saying nothing.

She tried again. 'She was only trying to help. Look, phone her.'

'What?' He stared at her, his face colouring.

'Have a chat. Thank her for the pram.'

He didn't reply.

'Well, ring Ollie then.'

'Ollie?'

'He's going through a hard time. It'd be nice. Clear the air. He's suffering.'

'Sitting in a poncy flat in Kensington writing a novel?'

'Of course he is.' Lately she had become more fond of Ollie. He might be behaving stupidly but she knew, in a way, what he was going through.

Ken looked down at his socks. There was a hole in the toe. 'That aunt of his, remember? When I put a damp-proof course in her house and she couldn't remember who I was and tried to tip me?'

Ann smiled. 'You should've taken it. We were broke.'

For a split second she didn't know if he was going to smile. It could have gone either way. Marriage has many such moments.

But it was all right. He grinned fleetingly.

Al stood at the window. Outside he heard the clackety-clack of high heels, of women with somewhere to go.

Ollie paused, then typed on.

He thought of his wife, who had demanded so much; and of his mistress, who had demanded so little. He poured himself another Scotch.

The phone rang. Ollie got up, but by the time he got there it had stopped.

Ken had flunked it.

'*. . . and the baby girl was born and there was much re-joicing. But nobody noticed the Black Fairy arriving, and suddenly, amongst all the music and laughter, she started cackling and everyone grew silent with horror . . .*'

247

Viv paused. Rosie's eyes were closing; Daisy was sucking her thumb. She looked around the room. They had bandaged up their teddies again. She went on reading: '*and she shouted: "You've made your promise, and tomorrow I'll be back and then your baby girl will be mine! And I'll take her into my tall tower in the forest and I'll lock her up . . ."*'

Both the children had fallen asleep. Viv closed the book.

It was the next evening. Viv sat in Ollie's old dressing gown, correcting exercise books. She sniffed, and blew her nose. Her bones ached.

In front of the fireplace was the electric fire; it was not worth lighting logs for one. Beside her was a tin of potato salad; from time to time she put her fork into it and ate some abstractedly.

The doorbell rang. With a grunt, she got up and padded out.

'Ken!'

'Hello,' he said. 'Just thought I'd . . .'

'Come in, it's freezing.'

He came into the living room, lighting a cigarette as he did so. His hand was trembling, but she told herself this was just from cold.

'Where's Ann?' she asked.

'At some dinner-do.'

Viv laughed. 'They'll be turning her into a Rotarian soon.'

Ken didn't reply. He stood in front of the electric fire, his back to her.

'Want a beer?' she asked.

'Please.'

She fetched a can from the fridge. She felt an urgent need to chatter. As she found a glass she said: 'Whatever will they do without her?'

'Yes.'

'They'll say, just like a woman, they never stay. Too many complications.'

Ken nodded.

'Men can be unreliable too,' said Viv, passing him the glass.

'Look, Viv –'

'How's the building work going?'

'Fine. Look –'

She grabbed the tin. 'Have some potato salad. I'll get you another fork because I've got a cold.'

'No thanks.'

She sat down at the table, indicating the tin. 'One of the secret and deeply satisfying pleasures of living alone.' She took a mouthful. 'Do you approve of what Ann and I bought at Mothercare?'

He took another drag of the cigarette and threw it into the grate. 'I've got to talk to you.'

'Let's talk about Ann and the baby.'

'I want to talk about me.'

She smiled. Her hands were clammy. 'A bad idea.'

'I must.'

'Look, we agreed –'

He shouted: 'I'm fed up with agreeing with everybody!'

His voice was so loud that they instinctively glanced at the stairs. He moved over to the door and closed it. He didn't go back to the fireplace, he walked over to the sink. This was a bad sign; people always stood at her sink when they wanted to tell her something unwelcome. She wished she had a fever and that she was hallucinating this. Then she would wake up and he would never have spoken.

He said: 'All my life I've been grown-up. Well behaved. I was the oldest little boy you ever saw. I was like a little old man, looking after my mother, swotting for grammar school. I wanted them to be proud of me because I was all they'd got, and if I was boring they certainly didn't notice because they were my parents.'

She nodded. 'I know.' She relaxed slightly; perhaps he was just going to talk like this.

'Then along came Ann,' he said, 'and I felt I had to

look after her, make her loved. Her father – well, you know . . .'

'Yes.'

'He never really loved her. Or that's what she said. I didn't know why, then, of course, nor did she.' He paused, and drank a little. 'And them splitting up. I had to be grown-up for her, I *wanted* to be grown-up, I could do that. I wanted to build her a home and look after her and give her children.' He stopped.

She waited.

'I worked away at my job, even though I hated it. I did it for Ann. And I didn't mind, I never admitted . . . well, I suppose I just thought in terms of her, and us.' He paused, and pushed a dirty saucepan further down into the water. 'And if something was missing in all this, with Ann and, you know, everything, well, I didn't have the words for it. Not till lately.' He inspected the submerged plates. 'With you. Suddenly I felt real.'

He stopped and looked up at her. She had never seen his face so naked – not even in their hotel room. She said: 'Having a baby's not going to solve everything for you and Ann, it's not going to make you really happy. Only you can.' She took a breath and moved aside the empty tin. 'You two, you're like a laid fire that's never been lit because it might waste the fuel, and you've got to insulate the house first. No house is ever really insulated.' She gestured around. 'This one certainly isn't. But Ollie and I've had some terrific blazes.' She stood up, grimacing as her back ached. 'So off you go.'

He stared into the sink. Finally he said: 'I want to stay.'

'Ken.'

He looked up. 'I've been trying. I've stayed away, haven't I, all these weeks? I've stopped myself phoning you. And, I mean, well, Ann's job. I've learnt a lot. I'm pleased she's successful and a year ago I would've been different.'

'Because you were all macho.'

'No! Just responsible.' He paused. 'We're getting on very well. It's just –'

'Don't say it.'

He said, in a low voice: 'I want you so much.'

She put down her fork. 'Fine,' she said suddenly. 'So we'll run off together, and I'll have the baby with you and we'll leave Ann, and I'll sell this house and give Ollie the girls.'

'No!' He stared at her.

She spoke gently. 'You don't want that, do you?'

He shook his head.

'But you do want me. O K. Let's fuck.'

He stared at her. She went over to him and took his hand. 'I know we're not in a nice hotel and me in my suspenders, but still.' She pulled him towards the sofa. 'And there's a bit of marmalade here somewhere . . .' She searched amongst the cushions. flinging away the old Sunday papers and various toys. She found the sticky place. 'Ugh. And I'm awfully fat and I've got stretch-marks, want to see them?' She started struggling with the cord of Ollie's dressing gown. 'And a stinking cold and Rosie'll be needing her medicine in . . .', she looked at her watch, '. . . half an hour.' She grabbed him and pulled him down on to the sofa. 'Ow!' She was sitting on a toy lorry; she flung it on the floor. 'And I must have a post-coital period correcting all those books, but still, come on, let's have a bash.'

But Ken had pulled away. He went over to the sink and stood there, leaning on the draining board, his head bowed.

Ann had removed the partition between her own small room and the rest of the office; it was more companionable that way. She could keep in touch with what was happening. Besides, it gave her pleasure to see the daily changing colour of everybody's clothes against the boring magnolia walls.

251

Gone were Derek's golfing trophies. In their place were an assortment of plants she had either bought or been given by Viv – offspring from the leggy windowsill collection. She had also bought three Van Gogh prints – the chair, the sunflowers and the bed, all of which moved her by their homeliness. Whatever her sister thought, she was not entirely unvisual.

However, there were disadvantages to the open-plan concept. It was nearly one o'clock when, with surprise, she was given a note by Trish. Scrawled on the back of a dry-cleaning receipt, it said: *To the Manageress. I humbly crave a moment of your time. I am at Customer Window 3.*

She looked across the office. Behind the customer's window she saw Ken's face.

Trish let him into the office and he came across to her desk. He stood in front of her, his head hanging.

'I can see that you're a successful career woman,' he mumbled, 'and I'm sure you've got a busy schedule ahead of you, maybe lunch with a Rotarian, I heard you went to an ever-so-important do last night, and I'm just a humble working chap, but I was wondering if I might beg a few moments of your time.'

She blushed. Everyone in the office was staring at them; Janine was sniggering.

'Quick,' she hissed. 'Let's get out.'

It was pouring with rain but she didn't mind. They sat in the car, eating Big Macs. He had brought a bottle of champagne and, parked in a side street facing a railway bridge and an expired Hillman Imp, they drank it out of plastic cups.

'I meant us to have a picnic,' he said, as the rain rattled on the roof.

'I don't care,' she said truthfully and sucked her fingers. He passed her his slivers of gherkin.

Afterwards he drove on.

252

'Where're we going?' she asked.

'Ssh.'

He drew up outside a hotel. It was a modern place, with tubs of chrysanthemums and multi-national flags.

'What's happening?' she asked.

'It's called having a long lunch-hour,' he replied. 'Managers do it.' He got out of the car and opened the door for her with a flourish.

'We can't!' she said.

'We can.'

For practically the first time in fifteen years of married life he couldn't manage to rise to the occasion. They struggled, their naked limbs bumping.

Finally they admitted defeat and collapsed helplessly on the sheets.

'I do love you,' she gasped.

'You can't.'

'I do.'

'Us men are just useful for reproductive purposes,' said Al. 'Otherwise we're redundant.'

Ollie frowned, re-read this and typed it out with a row of x's. I'm writing a story, he thought, not a thesis.

He started again. *Al stormed into the room and slammed the door. 'You don't want me any more!' he shouted.*

Ann sat down in the living room and gave Viv a carrier-bag.

'Something I've been knitting,' she said.

Viv opened the bag and pulled out a woollen object in multi-coloured stripes. 'Gosh,' she said. 'It's lovely, but won't it be a bit big?'

'It's not for the baby, silly,' said Ann. She held it against Viv. 'It's for you.'

It was an enormous cardigan.

'Your weird colours,' said Ann.

★

Viv was carrying her books to the car. Behind her she heard hurrying steps. Harold caught her up and took the books from her arms.

'When I first met Ollie,' said Viv, 'he used to do that.'

Harold said meaningfully: 'He was still a gentleman then.'

Viv reached her car. 'Then again, I wasn't eight months gone.'

She paused for a moment beside the car door. Outside the school gates a crowd of children waited at the bus stop. Amongst them were a group of sixth-formers – Yvonne, Eileen and the rest. They were talking to a very pregnant Tracey, who had long ago left school and must have come to the bus stop for a chat.

Harold remarked: 'Tracey's showing off again.' He spoke with solemnity: 'Girls nowadays are strangers to shame.'

Viv paused, then opened the car door. Harold put her books in the front, but she moved them to the back. 'Sit in here a moment, Harry,' she said, patting the passenger seat. 'Please.'

Surprised, Harold climbed in. For a moment she couldn't think how to begin. She gazed, for inspiration, at the mustard-coloured bricks of the Science Block. 'It's about me and Ollie. He's not such a shit.'

'Oh no?'

'I've been longing to tell you. You're my friend.' Sunlight shone on the hideous yellow bricks; soon it would be dark by four. She said: 'It's not just Ollie who's been having an affair.'

'No?'

'I have. Hence . . .' She patted her stomach. 'And I'm giving it to my lover and his wife.'

Harold's mouth fell open. 'You're not!'

'Don't tell anyone,' she whispered. 'But that's why I'll be back next term.'

'But the baby –'

'Don't talk about that. I just wanted you to know that it's not all Ollie's fault.'

Harold was still staring at her. Then he rallied. 'You wanton hussy!' he said.

'I'm not,' said Viv automatically. Then she realized, and smiled: 'All right, I am.'

He grabbed her arm. 'Come on, let's slip behind the bike sheds!'

'Harry!'

'All these years I've been sitting in the staffroom, slavering. What a waste!'

'You're my friend!'

'I don't want to be!' he cried.

'Oh God.'

They stared at each other. Then they both started chuckling.

'Ollie? Hello, it's Ken. Yes, long time no see. Look, I was just wondering if you fancy kicking a ball around again. Yes. We've been missing you. Yes, and a couple of bevvies afterwards. What? Bevvies. Right, good, OK.'

Ken, sighing with relief, put down the phone.

Ollie put down the phone and pushed his hand through his unwashed hair. Papers lay scattered on Caroline's table; he had been working on his book until the early hours of the morning.

Outside, church bells were ringing. He went into the kitchen and found himself the remains of some orange juice. Drinking it, he switched on the radio. It was the Sunday Service.

'. . . *and forgive us our trespasses,*' came the murmur of voices, like wind through miles of estuary reeds, '*as we forgive them that trespass against us –*'

He switched it off.

★

Beside the changing-rooms the wind tossed the bushes to and fro. It was cold. Diz, in his rugger shorts, was bounding up and down. He looked at his watch.

'He's not coming.'

'He said he would,' said Ken.

'He's not. Come on.' As they jogged to the pitch he said: 'Know what happened to the switchboard girl, with whom he was engaged in a leg-over situation?'

'No,' replied Ken, jogging beside him.

'She's gone to work for *Woman's Own*.' Chortling, Diz ran on to the grass.

Ollie had cleared the table and laid out tea for his daughters. He had also washed his hair. In one bin-liner he had hidden his dirty clothes; in another, the clanking weight of his alcoholic consumption.

The three of them had been to the Natural History Museum, one of the shortening list of places he could take his daughters on a rainy Sunday afternoon. When one had got through this list, what then? And what on earth did fathers do who lived in, say, Nuneaton? And, more to the point, how could he bear any of this?

'So did you enjoy it?' he asked, pouring out some Tizer. They were not allowed this at home.

'It was very nice,' said Daisy.

'I liked the whale,' said Rosie.

'When I was young,' said Ollie, 'they didn't have all those push-buttons and films and things. It's much more fun now.'

'Yes,' said Rosie.

He passed the plate of cakes. 'Have another one.'

'I'm full up, thank you,' said Rosie.

With a wave of panic he thought: when we've finished the cakes, what then? He felt his throat constrict. He passed the plate to Daisy.

She shook her head. 'There's too much cream. It's bad for you.'

256

'Daisy!' said Rosie.

There was a pause. Ollie looked at his watch.

'She's coming at six,' said Rosie.

There was another pause. Ollie thought: I should have bought a bunch of flowers for this table. Then he thought: but children don't notice flowers. Daisy fidgeted; Rosie frowned at her. Today she looked heartbreakingly like an older sister.

What else could they do here? He had shown them Caroline's school photo, and tried to remember some of the girls' names; they had listened for a moment and then got restless. He had found a Monet's *Bathers* jigsaw, but when they had finished there were three pieces missing; this had been, out of all proportion, dispiriting. His daughters had found the lift interesting but the other inhabitants, with some reason, became frosty about never being able to get to their own flats.

Suddenly he remembered, jumped up and fetched some sparklers. He gave a packet to each of them.

'But it's not till tomorrow,' said Rosie. 'Aren't you coming to our party?'

Ollie busied himself with searching for the matches. He shook his head. 'Nothing beats a good sparkler,' he said heartily, striking a match.

'Who's going to do the rockets?' asked Rosie.

'Your mum,' he replied. 'Haven't you heard of equal rights?'

Daisy said: 'Uncle Ken'll do them.'

Ollie paused. He still hadn't got the damned things alight. 'Ah,' he said.

At last he managed to light them both, though by the time Rosie's was ready Daisy's was nearly burnt out. Over the years sparklers, like many things, seemed to have diminished in both power and duration.

'So he's coming, is he?' he asked.

The girls stood, holding their sparklers. He grabbed their hands and waved them up and down.

257

'You can do better than that!' he said, more roughly than he had intended.

'They treat me like a vaguely kind but distant uncle,' said Ollie. He took the tea things into the kitchen and lifted the blind. In the street below, the girls were sitting in the car, trying out the headlights, then the side winkers. 'You told them what a shit I am?'

'Don't be silly.' Viv stood against the oven. She turned to look at it, grimaced, and moved over to stand against the fridge. 'They miss you.' She looked huge. She was wearing the loose tribal dress they had bought in the Portobello Road, way back in the sixties, long before she had become pregnant with anyone. 'Come to the fireworks tomorrow.'

He leered: 'See Ken and his big rockets?'

'Ollie!'

He held the bin open with his foot and scraped cream off the plates.

'Look,' said Viv, 'you can do that when I've gone.'

'Allow me my displacement activity.' He threw away a bitten jam sandwich. 'That place,' he said. 'Where's the stuffed badgers, where's my childhood security? It's all gone electronic, buttons and buzzers, it's like a mad, Darwinian Caesar's Palace, it's a sort of ecological Las Vegas . . .' He paused for breath.

'They don't think of you like an uncle.'

'. . . Put in your American Express card and out pops the meaning of life.' He stopped, panting. 'But that's your speciality, isn't it? The meaning of life.'

'Do sit down.' She gestured around the kitchen. 'What sort of life is this?'

'My sort.'

'It's not,' she said.

'How do you know? You haven't got a monopoly on it.' He glared at the rows of sequins sewn across her breast; some had fallen off. So dated, that ethnic stuff. 'Though

258

you'd like to think you have.' He pointed the empty Tizer bottle at her. 'You women, you've got the key to life, haven't you? It's all there, between your legs. Look at you, you're bursting with it, no wonder you look smug. You're at the controls.'

'Don't feel in control of you.'

He couldn't bear to look at her. He turned away and glared down at the street and his winking car. 'It's so bloody unfair. You can screw your brother-in-law and carry his child and we actually have to call you a saint!' His voice rose shakily. 'I'm the one everyone despises, walking out on his pregnant wife, and I can't even tell them why because we have to keep the bloody thing secret!'

'You don't have to walk out on me,' she said, her voice maddeningly quiet. 'Don't cut yourself off. You should've played rugger today.'

'With Ken?'

'There's nothing between us,' she said. 'I've – well, dealt with him.'

'There's that between us!' He swung round and pointed at the black, embroidered bulge of her belly.

'Are you angry because of Ken or me?'

'Leave my motives alone!' He moved to the cupboard and got out his bottle of Scotch.

'Don't drink so much,' she said.

'You can leave my liver alone too.' He stopped and looked at her suspiciously. '*How've* you dealt with him?'

'Nothing.' She looked at her watch.

'What's going on?'

'Nothing. Come home and see. This isn't a home. What do you do all day?'

'My own thing,' he replied.

'I know you need some space –'

'Stop knowing everything!'

'I'm only trying to help,' she said.

'Thanks awfully.'

She sighed, and moved back to the living room. She looked at the typewriter, put away on the bookcase. 'How's the novel?'

He moved swiftly in front of her. 'Leave it alone! It's mine!'

She shrugged, picked up the girls' anoraks, and left.

Any celebrations, even the lowly Guy Fawkes, are painful when a family is ruptured. Viv sat in the kitchen, not drinking her orange juice, and watched the shadowy figure of Ken, rather than her own husband, stoop in the garden. He was busy with fireworks. There was a shower of sparks and his stocky figure was illuminated as he straightened up.

In the grate a fire flickered. It should be cosy. Beside her, sipping mulled wine, sat her mother, Frank and her sister. The garden door was open; there was a whoosh and a polite 'aah' from the girls, who stood on the grass, looking chilly.

Viv got up to fetch the sausages from the oven. Ann stopped her. 'I'll do it.'

'Yes,' said Irene. 'You sit down.' She looked at Viv. 'You going to your classes?'

Viv nodded. 'Don't leave till the end of the month.'

Nibbling a sausage, her mother said: 'I don't mean school, ninny. I mean those antenatal things.'

Ann passed the sausages to Frank. 'She refuses.'

Viv said: 'I know them all.'

'Got to practise your breathing and stuff,' said her mother.

'I've tried to persuade her,' said Ann.

'I know all about the breathing,' said Viv. 'Anyway, I'm keeping in shape.'

'Shape's the word,' joked Frank. He was inclined to say the sort of thing to which nobody could think of a reply.

Ken came in for some more fireworks. There was only

one left in the box. He lifted it out and read: '*Erupts in a glittering explosion of multicoloured stars. Light the touchpaper and retreat.*' He smiled. There was a sooty smudge on the side of his nose, which made him look attractive. Viv had always preferred him in his working clothes, rather than his business suit. What had Ollie said? *Your bit of rough.* She passed him a glass of wine.

'Do be careful,' Ann said.

'I'm enjoying this,' he replied, and went into the garden.

'He'll make a lovely dad,' said Irene. 'Reliable, unlike some I could –'

'Reenie!' warned Frank.

There was a pause. In the fire, a log spat. Irene turned to Viv. 'It's a girl.'

'What?'

'You're carrying it so high. Just like the others. Mothers know.'

Viv replied: 'You hated being a mother.'

Irene grinned and turned to Ann. 'Don't know what you're letting yourself in for.'

Ann smiled. 'I do.'

From the garden, there was another whoosh and crackle. Beyond the houses there was a loud bang, then a distant dog started barking.

'Puking and screeching and keeping you up all night,' went on Irene. 'Still, at least you won't have the worst bit –'

'Mum!' said Viv.

'As they say, they go in easier than they come out.'

There was another bang, but it was the front door slamming. Ollie came in and stood in the middle of the room. He was swaying.

'May I have permission to join the family party?'

'Of course,' said Viv.

'Where're my girls?'

Ken had just come in from the garden. He looked at

261

Ollie, his face impeccably polite. Viv thought: how subtly power shifts. 'We've finished the fireworks,' he said.

'I want to see my daughters.'

Ken replied: 'They climbed into next door's garden.'

'So I've missed all the fun and games?'

Viv said: 'There's some sparklers.'

'No thanks.'

'You should've come earlier,' she said.

'I was unavoidably detained,' he said, speaking with care. 'A bottle and I had to partake of an ongoing dialogue.'

Ann went up to him with the dish. 'Have a sausage.'

Ollie picked one up and looked at Ken. 'You brought these? They're very small.'

'Do sit down,' said Viv.

'I'll do what I like in my own home.' His face was red and swollen and his jacket was buttoned up wrong. It saddened Viv that, whatever his drunkenness, he must know how foolish he looked. 'You're all very quiet. Been analysing my inadequacies?'

'Have some orange juice,' said Viv, passing him the carton.

'Don't be condescending.'

'Ollie –' said Ann.

'She's my wife,' he replied. 'I can talk to her how I –'

'You can't,' said Ann.

'Sorry,' said Ollie. 'I'd forgotten she's public property now. Her body belongs to you, in your different ways. It's like living with . . .', he searched for words, '. . . a gynaecological Joan of Arc.'

'You don't live with me,' said Viv. 'I wish you did.'

Ann stood up. 'Look, shall we –'

'No,' said Ollie. 'Stay and watch the real fireworks.'

'You're drunk,' said Viv.

He looked at the garden. 'At least I can make a bonfire. Fireworks without a bonfire's pathetic.' He moved swiftly, and grabbed a cardboard file from the shelves.

262

'Ollie!' Viv climbered to her feet.

'*Marx and Personal Responsibility,*' he read. 'What a little wimp I was.' He pulled the papers out, screwed them up and flung them into the fireplace. They flared.

'That's your thesis!' Viv said.

He grabbed some more papers.

'It's your essays!' she cried.

'Remember us? Campus lovebirds? Arm in arm through the concrete wonderland of Keele University.'

He stopped suddenly. His arms hung foolishly at his sides. They were all staring at him. In the street there was a battery of bangs, like gunfire.

It was Irene who spoke. 'Daft buggers, the lot of you.' She pointed to Viv. 'Starting another life, and hark at the mess you're making of your own. All this hoo-ha because of a bit of sex.' The fire spat an ember on to the hearthrug. She ground it out with her pointed black boot. 'I should know. Look what a mess I got into with you.' She turned to Ann. 'Couldn't trace Archie, could you?'

'No,' said Ann.

'It's all past, all gone. Nothing to make a song and dance about. Look at me and Frank, happy as sandboys and know why? Because we're friends, that's why. All this equal stuff you go on about, it's all twaddle. Comes the crunch and you're back in the Dark Ages.' Frank raised his eyebrows admiringly and lit a panatella. Ken cleared his throat. Ollie, standing at the bookshelves, laid his head against his Penguin Modern Classics. 'I hardly dare come here any more, and God knows what it's doing to the kids. *And* them having to keep it a secret.'

'Actually, they're enjoying that,' said Viv.

'All potty, the whole idea,' went on Irene. She turned to Viv. 'Told you, didn't I? And there's worse to come.' She paused. In the distance the dog was still barking. She looked at Viv. 'The minute you see that baby –'

'No!' said Viv.

'I know you, I'm your mother; I've seen you with your

kids. The minute you hold that baby in your arms, you won't be able to let it go.'

'I will!' cried Viv.

Irene turned to Ann, who had not moved. 'You take my advice. Don't give in your notice till that baby's back home with you. Got a lovely job, shame to lose everything all over again.'

Ann spoke to the hearthrug. 'I trust her.'

'I'm off,' said Ollie abruptly. Before anyone could speak he had left the house. The front door banged.

There was a silence. Frank looked at his watch.

Viv got up and went to the garden door. 'Better get the kids to bed.'

Ann stood up. 'I'll get them.'

'No, I –'

'Let me!' Ann spoke so sharply that everybody stared. She went into the garden.

Viv, attempting to smile, turned to Ken. 'Told you we have some good blazes here.'

20

Her time is nearly come. There is something awe-struck in the way people speak of a woman who is soon to pass out of their reach, into that closed and dangerous room, and give birth. Ollie called Viv public property, and in a sense that is true of all pregnant women – people touch them and gather round them, knowing they are doubly alive, made powerful with another being inside them. On the other hand they are also deeply private, more so as the weeks draw on and as they retreat from the world, rounded and dignified; the world keeps its distance because it is only the one woman, when her time comes, who will know what it is like to suffer.

264

Perhaps they were chastened by this. Whatever the reason, during the next two weeks both Ollie and Ken found themselves making peace, of a kind. It was Ken who plucked up the courage to visit. Stuck half-way along Park Lane in a traffic jam, he nearly turned back. Outside the Dorchester Hotel, two veiled women were being escorted into a Daimler. As he sat in the car, his palms damp, the world seemed moneyed and alien. What on earth could he say?

He said it was very nice, as he looked around the living room – piano, glass-fronted bookcase, V & A poster for a porcelain exhibition.

'You must be a closet Sloane,' replied Ollie. He looked both belligerent and surprised to see him.

'How is your sister?' asked Ken. 'Still seeing that banker chap?'

'Ken, he's married!' Ollie looked at him in mock-horror. 'Still, when does that make a difference?' There was a pause. Ollie asked: 'Like a drink?'

'Fine,' nodded Ken. 'Sure.' He glanced around again. The place was a mess. Ollie had propped up two school photos of his daughters – the sort in oval frames. Ken had never seen their hair so tidy. He looked away and tried to sound conversational. 'So what are the neighbours like?'

Ollie reappeared from the kitchen, holding two cans and two glasses. 'I've moved from one multi-racial area to another, except here nobody speaks to anyone else. Don't you want to sit down?'

Ken stayed standing. He cleared his throat. 'Er, there's something we've got to settle.' He rummaged in his pocket. 'I've been carrying this around for weeks, but it never seems to be the right moment.' He took out the cheque. 'Don't know if it'll do any good . . .'

Ollie took the cheque and stared at it.

'Please,' said Ken. 'At least it'll make *me* feel better. It's no compensation, but –'

'I don't want your money!'

'Please –'

'You trying to pay me off?' demanded Ollie.

'No, I –'

'You must be even thicker than I thought.' Ollie let out an ugly yelp of laughter. 'Christ, you really know how to rub my nose in it.'

'But –'

'Paying me for shagging my wife!'

'No!'

'How many hundreds is this per bang? Was she worth it?'

'No!' shouted Ken.

'Thanks a bunch.'

'I don't mean that!'

Ollie let out the ugly, shrill laugh again. 'Or is it the baby you're buying? Trying to put us all behind bars?'

'No! I just – oh God.' Ken shifted over, and sat down on the sofa. It had gone entirely wrong. He should have turned back in Park Lane. He said: 'I was only asking for some . . .' He searched for the word. 'Dignity.'

'Sorry, old cock. Haven't got any left to spare.' Ollie screwed the cheque into a ball and threw it into the overflowing wastepaper bin. 'Think money'll solve it? Money won't solve anything.'

Ken replied: 'That's because you've always had it.'

'What?'

He gestured around the room. 'You can take it for granted,' he said bitterly. 'It's easy for you to say money won't solve anything. You can even afford to have a shabby house.'

Ollie didn't reply. He sat down on the armchair, suddenly limp.

Ken lit a cigarette. 'And you call *me* proud.'

Ollie looked at him curiously. 'You're being very upfront. You sound just like me. What's been happening?'

Ken didn't speak. He looked at the papers spilling from the bin, like frozen boiling milk. Was that a contradiction? A tiny part of him wished that Ollie had actually torn up the cheque, but he despised himself for even noticing. Ollie was hardly going to smooth the cheque out later. Ken thought: I am boring, thinking of that at a time like this.

Ollie said: 'What's been happening? Could it be love?'

There was a silence.

'Could it?' asked Ollie.

Ken took a breath. 'If it was,' he said carefully, 'it's over now.'

'Really?'

Ken didn't reply. The room was so quiet that he was aware, for the first time, of a faint hum. It was the electric typewriter sitting on the table nearby. He looked up. Ollie held his gaze.

At last – it seemed a long time – Ollie asked: 'Want another?' He lifted the can.

'No thanks.' Ken paused. 'Yes please.'

Ollie moved towards the kitchen. At the doorway he stopped. Ken waited, alert. But Ollie's face had relaxed for the first time. He looked down at the two empty cans in his hand, and then looked across at Ken. 'At school,' he said, 'women were either tarts or other chaps' sisters. It took me years to learn how to treat a woman as an equal. And a lot of help from Viv, I'll give her that.' He sighed. Ken waited, next to the humming typewriter. 'And when the crunch comes, know what?'

'What?'

'It's back to square one. I'm just as bad as my father, and you know what *he's* like.'

Ken nodded.

Ollie smiled ruefully. 'If I'd had a son, I could've taught him how to behave. It's easier to show other people, isn't it. I wouldn't make the same mistakes my parents did.'

'All parents make mistakes,' said Ken.

Ollie looked at him. 'Will you?' he asked, and went into the kitchen.

★

267

With things eased a little between Ken and Ollie, they arranged to play rugger the next Sunday. Meanwhile, the two sisters had to get through the midwife's visit, which they had both been dreading. There would be plenty of official difficulties, and evasions, to come; this was just the first. But there was something glinty about Mrs Archer, the midwife, despite her ample figure. As she bound Viv's arm to take her blood pressure, her eyes wandered around the room. Surely Viv's scattered newspapers and struggling plants could give nothing away?

Viv had by now left school. Ann, who had taken the morning off work for moral support, busied herself making coffee. The plan was for Viv to have the baby at home, but already things were going wrong. Spooning out the Nescafé, Ann paused to listen.

'Mrs Meadows, I told you. So did Dr Stern. Home births are now actively discouraged,' said the midwife.

Viv said: 'Only because they're more of a hassle for you.' Ann, pouring out the hot water, tensed.

'No,' said Mrs Archer. 'They're more risky. If there are complications –'

Ann stopped stirring.

'Yes yes,' said Viv impatiently, 'I know.'

'Look,' said Mrs Archer. 'We've had more problems with this pregnancy, haven't we? High blood pressure, fatigue –'

'But I sailed through the other ones!'

'That's no reason. We're – let's look – seven years older now and that means –'

'I'm perfectly healthy,' said Viv.

Ann looked at the milk bottle. She didn't dare join in.

'I don't see why you're so set on it,' said Mrs Archer. 'You had your little girls in hospital.'

'It's my own body,' said Viv, in the clipped feminist voice Ann had always disliked. 'I'm not going to be manipulated by hospital policy designed for the convenience of the male medical profession.'

'You say it's your body, Mrs Meadows, but have you been acting responsibly? No. You've been a naughty girl. You haven't attended the clinic –'

Ann couldn't help it. She turned. 'Viv, you should've –'

Viv glared at her. Ann turned back, facing the draining board. What could she do? How could she afford to quarrel with her sister? She picked up the milk bottle and sniffed it. The milk was sour.

Mrs Archer was still speaking. 'You haven't let us book you into the hospital; at this rate we'll have to take you in as an emergency.' She paused. 'On the evidence of this pregnancy I cannot guarantee you a straightforward delivery.'

Ann froze. She stared at the milk bottle.

'Your neglect and carelessness hasn't helped –'

'I haven't neglected –'

Mrs Archer interrupted her. 'You've only yourself to blame.' Her voice became clearer as she turned her head. 'Perhaps *you* can make your sister see some sense.'

Ann paused and said to Viv: 'She might be right.'

Viv spoke loudly: 'This baby's different.'

'Viv!' Ann stared.

Viv paused and simply said: 'I want to have it at home.'

'What you want is beside the point,' said Mrs Archer. *Want, want.* Ann looked at the three mugs of black coffee, cooling now. All her life Viv had got what she wanted; with such ease, too, that it had never seemed like grabbing. Some people were like that. *Life smiles on them*, Douglas had said.

'You have to put the baby first,' said Mrs Archer. 'I'm here to see you have a safe delivery, and what you need now is rest.'

When Mrs Archer had gone, Ann said: 'If you go on like that they'll get suspicious.'

Viv got up, with a grunt, from the sofa. 'But hospital's so official, so many people asking questions.'

'We'll manage. Look. You have it and come back here

for ten days, like normal, till the midwife's visits end, and then . . .' She paused. 'Then we'll take it to my house.' She had never put these words so plainly. Her legs felt boneless.

'It's ridiculous. People've been giving away babies for centuries.'

'It's the word. Surrogacy.'

'But there's no money involved. Nobody knows I haven't just had an affair with Ken.'

There was a pause. Viv's hair, longer nowadays, was pulled back in a rubber band; Viv managed to make even this look fetching. She turned to gaze out of the front window, at the questions waiting for them all. Ann looked at her snub nose and the profile of her soft mouth.

'Yes, yes,' she said edgily. 'But we must wait till it's born, safely. Then tell them our version of the truth. And if it's safer in hospital –'

The phone rang. Viv answered it.

'Hi. Suzi. Yes, I'm still here, it's not due for three weeks.' She nodded. 'Yes, course I'm coming. Which pick-up point?' She nodded again. 'Right. See you Sunday.'

She put the phone down. Ann stared at her. 'You're not going?' She pointed to the Anti-Cruise poster which covered the pegboard. 'I thought that was for our benefit.'

'Course I'm marching,' said Viv.

'In your condition? But Mrs Archer said –'

'My condition gets us photographed.'

For the past hour Ann had controlled her emotions. Now she shouted: 'You can't risk the baby for –'

'Ann!' Viv glared at her. 'There won't *be* a future for this baby unless –'

'That's *your* opinion!'

Viv nodded; her silly ponytail bobbed. 'Until this baby's born, it has to have my opinions too.'

★

All week Ollie worked furiously. He was on the downhill stretch, his story had by now taken on a momentum of its own. His characters, now he re-read them, had started breathing of their own free will and for the first time in his life he felt possessed by something so mysterious that he dared not pause to analyse it. Where, after all, had analysis got him in the past?

They talked on the page, they led him on, they were his. Did a woman feel like this with a baby growing inside her? They filled him. When he walked to the supermarket he became Al, his hero, threading his way like a fox through the cars. Al had gingery hair and a watchful, weak face and problems with his wife. In the gauzy November rain Ollie walked round Hyde Park; passing the leafless shrubs he saw them with Tilly's eyes; he himself became Al's estranged wife, with her long legs and vague, distracted beauty. Nobody could possess them because they lay within himself; he had them safe.

On the Thursday evening he had a record amount of wrong numbers – his phone was only one digit different from that of a wine bar called Jingles. Exasperated, he finally took the phone off the hook.

Viv said: 'I thought something had happened to you.'

'Sorry,' said Ollie, 'I'm still here.'

He let her in; she looked at the phone. 'Ah.'

'I left it off the hook. My public keeps pestering me.'

Viv sat down heavily on the sofa. She was wearing her big mock-leopardskin coat, which he hadn't seen since last winter. It was nearly midnight. She looked pale and huge.

'Coffee?' he asked.

She shook her head. 'We must sort things out. Where's the service guarantee for the boiler, what shall I tell your parents who keep phoning, what are we going to *do*?' She paused. 'What's happening?'

He replied: 'I don't know.'

'Do you want to come home?'

He didn't reply.

She repeated: 'Do you?' She gestured around. 'None of this is real.'

He said: 'I can't come back until . . .'

He meant: until the baby is born. She understood; she had always understood him, that was the trouble. The room felt airless.

She said: 'What then?'

He said: 'Let's have another baby.'

She stared at him. He meant it; he had only just thought of it, but it suddenly seemed a solution.

He said: 'You and me, let's –'

'Let's pretend this never happened? Let's cancel it out?' Above the furry blobs of her coat her eyes were wide. 'It's real, for Christ's sake. It's happening.'

'Stop talking like a teacher.'

She paused. 'Think I've got it sorted out? Look, I'm in a mess too. I distrust my motives. I've mucked about with Ken's feelings, and yours. And Ann's. And mine. I still don't know if I can bear to give this baby up.' She stopped, breathing heavily. The Anglepoise over the table cast a pool of light; otherwise the room was dark. But when she lifted her head, her eyes were glittering. 'God knows how I'll feel if I do,' she said. 'I'll probably make your lives hell. I may never be able to see Ann again, I may never be able to bear the sight of her holding it in her own house.' She paused. 'But it's happening. We can't close our eyes. It's real. It's not a character in your bloody book.'

She got up, laboriously, and took his hand. For a moment he thought she was going to lead him away, but she was putting his hand inside the folds of her coat. She pressed it against her belly. The bulge was hard, as if,

272

beneath the wool of her dress, her body was carved. His reluctant fingers felt the lump of her navel.

They stood there for a moment, locked. Then she left him.

In the doorway she said: 'I only wanted to see if you were all right.'

21

At night Ollie escaped into his story – no, he went there willingly, sitting in his pool of light. But Viv could not escape her dreams. They stirred and disturbed her.

The week ended with storms. On the Saturday night, the eve of the CND march, she tossed and turned, while outside the house loose slates rattled and way down the road a dustbin lid rolled. When was that storm – months ago? – when Rosie had been scared by the noise and had climbed into her bed. She herself had dreamed about the trench in her allotment and an ominous sky. The whole house had been shaken, the windows shuddering, Rosie holding her tightly. The next day Ann had lost her baby.

She shifted awkwardly, the great rock of her belly obstructing her. Her mouth felt sour and dry. She slid in and out of her nightmares, as if sinking into a deep and sluggish river. She dreamed she was lost in a crowd of people, they were suffocating her and she couldn't get out. She needed to escape because when the crowd thinned she would be alone and she would have to stand on a platform and tell them something and she couldn't remember what lines she should have learnt. Of course, now she looked down, she saw she was naked. Her stomach hurt and Ollie was in the crowd, jabbering at her and pointing. The sky was thundery and she knew she shouldn't be there. She was frightened. She told herself it

273

was the bombers coming, plane after plane against the black sky, but why then was there such a sharp pain inside her?

On Sunday morning it was still blustery. During the night a section of trellis in Ann's garden had blown down; she was attempting to nail it up again. Ken was out, playing rugger. Despite her protestations, Viv had gone on the ban-the-bomb march, taking the girls with her.

Ann's hands were mauve with cold as she fumbled with the nails. She felt unsettled. Next door the curtains were closed; Mrs Maguire's mother was dying and the family had gone to Ireland. The silence was unnatural.

A flurry of rain pattered against the glass door of the extension. Ridiculously, she felt lonely; but she could not go round to Viv's, of course, because that house too would be empty.

Ollie jogged towards the pitch with the other players. Diz pointed to the windswept spaces.

'Our usual audience,' he said, 'two stray dogs and a misdirected Japanese tourist.'

Once Viv had stood there, shivering in her long-ago blue coat. Today he felt both sluggish and nervous. He had not slept well; the storm had kept him awake and he had missed her, achingly. Tonight he would go round and see her, for simple mutual comfort. If anything could be simple with Viv.

Way beyond the park a police siren sounded. The wind chilled him. In position, he jumped up and down, slapping his arms against himself, trying to get into the mood. One of the dogs barked.

Irene had a headache. Usually she relished her Sunday lay-in but this morning she felt restless. Her flat felt overheated, but when she opened the window it was too cold. She had glanced at her Sunday paper but she didn't want to know any more about Joan Collins.

274

Beyond the flats opposite she could see the North Circular; as usual it was busy with traffic. Where was everybody going, what were they doing in their cars at eleven o'clock on a Sunday morning?

She knew most of the people in this block of flats, she had lived here for years, but on Sunday morning their doors were closed. She missed Frank, who usually spent Sundays cosily with her, but he had had to go up north to visit his mother. She wondered: when I'm eighty, will my daughters ever visit me?

She was worried about Viv. If she herself were a good mother, deserving to be visited at eighty, she would be round there now, sweeping the floor and entertaining the girls. That's what you did when your daughter was just about to have a baby and her husband had buggered off. Though the whole world knew he would be back, those two couldn't live without each other.

One small advantage of this was that she could phone Viv and not feel she was intruding. She would invite herself over and they'd have a good natter; she hadn't seen her for weeks, not since Guy Fawkes.

A gust of rain blew against the window. She shivered, though it made the room no colder; she lifted up the receiver and dialled Viv's number.

But there was no reply. She must be out.

Crises dislocate everybody's plans, wiping out the hours that preceded them. But often the moment just before the violent, rupturing act remains crystal-clear long after the event. What were you doing, people ask, and themselves vividly remember, when you heard that Kennedy was shot?

Ann remembered the split-second before the phone rang. She was climbing down from the step-ladder. Just as the phone started ringing, her shakily fixed trellis clattered down behind her.

★

It was only later that Ollie, who at the time was being jostled in the scrum, remembered that in fact he had noticed a faintly unusual sight: a taxi arriving and parking beside the changing-rooms. Ordinary cars were parked there, but why should a taxi arrive? He had no time even to think of this question, what with mud-spattered legs ramming him. He was unfit, and had forgotten what a brutish game this was.

Moments later he noticed a woman running through the rain towards the pitch. He himself was running down the field, sweaty and breathless, and only had time to presume it was somebody chasing her dog.

It was Ann. Slipping in the mud, she was trying to make her way through the players. Ken had already seen her and had veered away from the others to meet her.

Ollie trotted up to her. He hadn't realized it was raining until he saw her wet hair. But it was her face he stared at.

He couldn't hear at first; the wind whipped away her words. She was mouthing at him, her coat undone.

He heard *hospital*.

'What?' he yelled.

'She's gone to hospital,' shouted Ann. 'Hurry!'

22 The waters had broken while Viv was in the coach on the way to the demonstration. Suzi, who had phoned, was looking after the girls. Then there had been the pips and the phone had gone dead. That was all Ann could tell them.

Nobody, for what seemed an age, told them anything else. The three of them sat in the waiting room, which was stiflingly hot and smelt of disinfectant and past cigarettes. Ollie had found the sister, who had said that Mrs

Meadows was in the delivery room, that it was all fine, but that he couldn't go in.

'Why?' he demanded. 'She wants me in there.'

'Not just now, Mr Meadows.'

'What's happening?'

'Please stay in the waiting room,' she said.

'I've always been with her,' his voice rose. 'It's all arranged!'

'We have to wait for Dr Khan.' She was short and severe; she looked him up and down – his muddy boots, his rugger shorts. 'Please, Mr Meadows.'

In the waiting room Ken was lighting a cigarette.

Ann pointed to his leg. 'You're bleeding.'

Ken looked down. There was a cut on his shin.

'Here.' She gave him her handkerchief.

'It's fine,' he said.

Ollie moved restlessly around the room. The only other occupant was a young black boy, who looked no more than a teenager. He was sitting there gazing at his hands.

Ann said at last: 'I should've stopped her going.'

'It's not your fault,' said Ollie.

'I'll never forgive myself,' she said.

'Ann!' Ken stood up and went to the door. He looked at his watch. Then he turned back to Ollie. 'Twenty minutes. Can't we go and ask them?'

Ollie replied: 'They told us to wait here.'

Ken opened the door. 'I'm going.'

'You stay here!' said Ollie, so loudly that the black boy looked up.

On the hour, Ken's watch bleeped. They all jumped. Ollie looked at his own watch and left the room.

Ken lit another cigarette and turned to Ann. 'Will she be all right?'

'How can I tell?' she replied.

277

'It's so early,' he said. 'There must be something wrong.'

'Do shut up,' she said.

He walked over to the window and spoke to the glass. 'I hate these places.'

She thought of a different waiting room, in a different hospital. How long ago? Nearly a year. And those other times, long before. She had never asked Ken what he did then; they had never spoken of it.

She got up to comfort him. But he started moving towards the door.

'Stay here,' she said, putting her hand on his arm. He flinched away. 'Leave it to him,' she said.

A moment later Ollie came back in.

'What's happening?' Ann and Ken asked, both at once.

'Can't find anyone,' said Ollie. 'These bloody places.'

He went back to his seat. Ann noticed, fleetingly, that though there were eight chairs in the room, they always went back to the same ones.

She said: 'Everything's going wrong.'

Ollie looked at her. 'For you?' he asked acidly.

'Ollie!' she said.

He came over and sat down next to her. 'Sorry.'

'It's Viv we're worried about,' she said.

He picked at the drying mud on his knee. Flecks fell to the carpet. 'We made it up, you know. Well, nearly. She came round and . . .' He stopped.

She said: 'I know.' They both looked at the carpet, lightly powdered with earth.

He said: 'I can't bear her being alone.'

Ann nodded. She looked up and said to Ken, sharply: 'Do go and wash your leg!'

'Got a fag, mate?'

Ken jumped. It was the black boy. 'Of course.' He passed him the packet.

'Thanks,' said the boy, taking it.

Ken looked at the packet; that was the last cigarette. He put the packet into his pocket discreetly, so the boy wouldn't see.

Five minutes later a rattle approached and the door swung open. It was an orderly pushing a tea trolley. Passing through the room he paused and grinned. 'Where's the scrum?'

Ollie and Ken, startled, looked down at their rugger shorts.

More minutes ticked by. It was so quiet. Hospitals were usually busy; what was wrong?

Ann tried to reassemble her morning, to remember it. She had been in the garden, with next door silent, her own house hushed. She herself jumpy, moving from kitchen to garden, fidgeting. The bare earth in Ken's tubs; behind one of them, the small heap of daffodil bulbs she had forgotten to plant. The wind blowing. Unusually for her, she hadn't been able to think of anything to do.

She looked at Ollie and Ken. They were both sitting, staring at their boots. They had no idea how similar they looked.

'I should phone Mum,' she said, 'shouldn't I?'

But she didn't move. None of them dared to leave the room.

Footsteps approached. A new, taller sister appeared. Or it might have been a matron.

She looked at the two men. 'Which of you is the father?'

There was a pause. She wouldn't have noticed it. Then Ollie stood up. 'Yes?' he asked.

'Mr Meadows? They're carrying out a Caesarean section.'

'*What?*'

'It's a breech presentation,' she said. 'It's routine in these cases.'

'I must see her,' he said.

She shook her head. 'They're operating now.'

For the next twenty minutes none of them said a word. Ann didn't realize it at the time; she remembered it later. She would remember, too, for as long as she lived, the pale green walls, scuffed near the skirting board; the one framed picture of Great Yarmouth; the view, from the window, of a tower block against a threatening grey sky. None of them moved, for fear of startling the others. At one point the black boy was called away – his girlfriend, they had learnt, was having twins – and then the three of them were left alone, without words.

Then there was the sound of clattering heels again, and the matron or sister was in the room and addressing Ollie.

'Mr Meadows?'

'What's happened?'

She smiled. 'She's fine. You've got a little boy.'

There was a pause.

'A boy?' Ollie repeated.

She nodded. 'You can't see your wife yet, but would you like to see your son?'

Ollie nodded. With the sister, he left the room. He didn't look back.

23 Months before, Ann had lain in a hospital bed, watching the lights coming on in a building opposite. Her head had been swimming and her stomach hurt. One by one the rooms had sprung into life, and then curtains had closed. Blue blurs of televisions. She had had no idea why she was lying in hospital but she knew she was going to have a baby.

Then she had slept, and the next morning all those little curtains had opened and her head had cleared, but there was still a pain in her abdomen. The ward had been bright and bustling; a nurse approached her bed. It was then that she realized she had no baby, only a wound.

Viv lay there, her head resting on the pillow. She looked at the block of flats opposite. It was a tower block; a man in a harness was stuck to the side, cleaning the windows. He looked as frail as an insect, with the big grey sky all around him. She knew it was Monday morning. Somebody had removed the screens around her bed; she could hear babies crying, one of them near. Her stomach ached; when she moved there was a jabbing pain. She stayed still, her eyes closed, and drifted into sleep.

When she woke the baby was still crying and she knew she must do something, if only she could think clearly. But when she turned her head, the space beside her bed was empty. There was no baby. It was another one, beyond the woman in the next bed.

She thought she must still be dreaming, because some time later, probably only minutes – who knows? – there was a girl who uncannily resembled Tracey standing beside her in a dressing gown.

'He's gorgeous,' Tracey was saying.

Viv looked at her. 'What're you doing here?'

'Don't you remember?' asked Tracey. 'We talked last night for ages.'

Of course. Tracey was here because she had had a little girl. How stupid of her to forget; Tracey must think she was mad.

'Just been to see him,' Tracey said again.

She meant Viv's son. Viv realized this now, idiot that she was. 'Did you?' she asked.

'In his incubator,' Tracey replied. 'He's gorgeous.'

'Is he?'

'Bet you're glad you had a little boy,' said Tracey. Her dressing gown was covered in sprigs of flowers – roses, were they? Small and pink. She was still speaking. 'Bet your husband's pleased.' The sleeves were edged with green lace. It had the look of a dressing gown that had been bought specially for this. 'He's kicking away,' she said.

'Is he?'

'Proper little Kenny Dalglish. He'll be bullying his big sisters soon.' How could she tell? After all, she herself would never have bought a dressing gown like that anyway. 'What're you calling him?'

Viv replied: 'I don't know.'

'Glad I haven't got a fella. We'd never agree on names.'

Each time Viv breathed, needles jabbed into her skin. She tried to keep her breaths shallow. 'What are you calling her?' she asked Tracey.

'Rebecca. After that book we did in class.'

Viv said: 'That was *Jane Eyre*.'

'Oh.' Tracey stopped. 'Yeah, it was *Rebecca* I saw on the telly.'

Ann had taken the Monday afternoon off. For some reason she didn't want to visit straight from the office, nor did she want to tell anyone where she was going. She wanted to go from her own home, with Ken.

Her armpits were damp and she felt queasy with nerves. She hadn't been able to eat any lunch. She stood at the mantelpiece mirror, applying lipstick.

Ken came into the room and said: 'He's a bit young, isn't he?'

She turned. 'What?'

He indicated the lipstick. 'To be impressed.'

They both smiled shakily. She picked up her handbag and pointed to the florist's package on the table. 'You bring the flowers,' she said.

Ollie was sitting beside her. He had brought her some flowers; like all hospital visitors he didn't know what to do with them. They lay on his lap. He had had a haircut and looked younger; he looked like a new father.

'Did you sleep?' he asked.

She nodded. 'They gave me a pill.'

He took a *Private Eye* and *Cosmopolitan* out of the carrier-bag. 'Bit of frivolity . . .'

She glanced at them. 'Thanks.'

He put them on the bedside table. 'Painful?'

She nodded. 'A bit.'

'The girls made you these.' He took out two large get-well cards – Rosie's careful, Daisy's only half coloured in. She had got bored doing the sky.

'Oh dear,' said Viv. 'Like I'm an invalid.'

'Didn't know what they should put.'

'No.'

She laid the cards on the table. He leant over and propped them up. 'Is there anything you want?' he asked.

'A cigarette.'

'You can't.'

All down the ward, men were sitting beside the beds. The place was full of flowers. There was a faint mewling sound from one of the babies. She thought: mothers are supposed to recognize their own baby's cry, but how can they when they all sound the same? She said: 'I want to go home.'

He took her hand. They sat there in silence.

She spoke suddenly, in a rush: 'Tracey must be mad. She thinks it's so frightfully romantic, all this single-parent stuff. Easier, she thinks, be your own boss; up all night with it crying and screeching, wet nappies. Course, she's right. Who needs men? Nothing but a bloody nuisance. Any woman with any tiny jot of sense'd rather be on her own. Silly cow.'

She paused, breathless. Ollie stroked her forehead. 'Darling.'

She started to weep. Each sob jabbed pins into her abdomen.

Ollie went on stroking her forehead but she stretched beyond him and grabbed her bag. Fumbling through it, she found her cigarettes and matches. He didn't stop her. In fact, he took the box of matches and lit the cigarette for her. She inhaled deeply.

'Mrs Meadows!'

The nurse was there, holding out her hand. Viv took another drag and gave the cigarette away.

Ken parked the car in a side street near the hospital. Ann checked her face again in the vanity mirror. She despised this – what on earth did it matter how she looked? She wanted never to get out of the car. Ken must think she was mad.

They got out and walked towards the hospital. At the corner she stopped and put her hand on his arm. 'Look.'

Ollie's car was parked on the other side of the road. He must still be visiting Viv.

Ken nodded. They turned back and walked down the side street again. Ken opened the door for her and she climbed back into the car. They sat there, side by side, waiting. He reached towards the radio, but then he stopped. They sat there in silence.

'How does he look?' asked Viv.

'Fine.'

'How did he look yesterday?'

Ollie replied: 'Very angry.'

'Did he?'

Ollie nodded. 'I'm not surprised.'

'You couldn't touch him or anything?'

Ollie shook his head. 'They say he's doing very well. He should be out tomorrow.'

There was a silence. Then Viv said: 'It wasn't like we planned.'

Ollie paused. 'Nothing's been like we planned.'

'Wish you'd been there.'

'They wouldn't let me in,' he said.

'I wanted you to rub my back.'

'So did I.'

She smiled. 'Remember with Rosie, you read me *The Catcher in the Rye*?'

'That was Daisy,' he said. 'Rosie was *Humboldt's Gift*.'

'Gosh,' she said. 'Weren't we intellectual then?'

There was a silence. One of the babies started crying in earnest.

She asked: 'What did you do afterwards?'

'Phoned parents. Sat in the pub.'

'Alone?'

He nodded. 'Ann and Ken invited me, but . . .'

'No.' She paused. 'Suzi had the girls?'

He nodded. 'For the night.'

Down the ward there was a burst of laughter. Viv looked out of the window. The sky was blue; it had turned out to be a lovely afternoon. She said: 'I didn't think he'd be a boy.'

Ollie picked a stray petal off his knee. 'Nor did I.'

'Funny, isn't it?' she said.

He nodded. One of the cards had fallen over; he propped it up again.

She said: 'They keep asking about names.'

'Who do?'

'Women here.'

'It's no business of theirs.'

She said quickly: 'I've always liked Thomas, haven't you?'

He frowned, gazing at his knee. 'Yes.'

She tried it out. 'Thomas.'

'Tom.' He nodded. 'Nice.'

'Straightforward,' she said. 'No-nonsense.'

'Viv –'

'Sturdy and sort of stumping up and down the stairs –'

'Viv –' he began again.

She said: 'You've always wanted a boy, haven't you?'

285

He didn't reply. He looked down at his damp knees. The flower stems were wet.

'Haven't you?' she said.

He said: 'He's not my son.'

'No.'

There was another silence. Then he asked: 'What are you going to do?'

She turned away and hid her face in the pillow. 'I want to go home.'

Viv wouldn't see Ann and Ken. When Ollie had left they went into the hospital and up to the ward, but she turned away and asked them to go.

A nurse ushered them out. They stood in the corridor. Ann was trembling; she felt as if she had been smacked across the face. She wanted to sit next to Viv and say that it was her, Viv, she was worried about. Never mind the baby. (Never mind? She would say that; she would mean it.) She had never seen Viv look so terrible – closed and pale.

'She's been a bit low,' said the nurse. 'It's quite normal.' She took the flowers. 'Aren't they lovely! What a lot. I'll put them in a vase for her.'

'What shall we do?' asked Ann.

'It's what we call the baby blues. You her sister?'

Ann nodded.

'You've got a gorgeous little nephew. Want to see him?'

Ann gazed at the ground and nodded dumbly. She dared not look at Ken.

'Come on,' said the nurse. 'You can see him through the glass.'

She crossed the corridor and stood beside a large window, waiting for them. Ann moved towards it, but Ken hung back. She turned to him.

He said: 'She hasn't even seen him yet.' His face was blank.

'Come on,' said Ann, holding out her hand. 'Nor have you.'

The nurse frowned at them. Ann blushed. Ken moved forward and stood beside her.

There were three babies in incubators; the nurse pointed him out.

All Ann could think to say was: 'He's very small.'

The nurse said: 'He's very new.'

The swimming pool was empty, except for one dogged old man in goggles. Ken swam twenty lengths and then lost count as he went on; he didn't want to stop.

When he finally climbed out, dripping, his legs bendy with fatigue, the lifeguard looked at him with a half-smile and raised his eyebrows.

'Here's to the happy father,' said Irene, raising her glass. It was later that evening, and she had brought round a bottle of champagne. 'Cheer up, you two. Thought of a name?'

Ann said: 'We thought Mark.'

Irene grinned. 'Well, if he takes after the Mark I knew, he'll do all right.' She turned to Ken. 'Does he look like you?'

'He's only tiny,' Ann said hastily.

Her mother said: 'I could tell, when you were born. The image of your father.'

There was an awkward silence. Ken was standing beside the aquarium. He rubbed the glass with his finger; then he looked up and said: 'She wouldn't see us. I don't know what she's going to do.'

'She's confused,' said Ann.

'I told you,' said Irene. 'Once it's born –'

'Don't,' said Ann.

'I wouldn't trust her,' said Irene. 'I've never trusted her, and she's my daughter.'

Ken said suddenly: 'I don't trust her.'

There was a pause. Then Irene said: 'Well you wouldn't, would you?'

★

'I feel that way about sausage rolls too,' said the nurse, taking away Viv's untouched supper. She put the tray on the trolley and began to put up the screens around Viv's bed. An orderly appeared with a stretcher bed and parked it beside Viv.

'What's happening?' Viv asked.

The nurse smiled. 'Just going to check your dressing.' While she did so she said: 'We're taking you to see him now.' She pulled down Viv's nightie. 'We've all fallen in love with him. He's quite a little character.'

They started to shift Viv on to the stretcher. She stopped them. 'No!'

'Are we hurting you?' asked the nurse.

Viv shook her head. 'I don't want to go,' she said.

'What?'

'Don't want to see him.'

The nurse and the orderly looked at each other; then the nurse turned back to Viv. 'Feeling poorly?'

Viv nodded.

'You rest then,' said the nurse, tucking the sheet around her.

Viv pointed to the screens. 'Can you leave these up?'

Surprised, the nurse agreed. They left Viv alone, screened in.

Ann stood in the little back bedroom. It was empty. They had painted it cream, that was all. They had not dared do more, though she had put up some curtains with red birds printed on them: not specifically childish.

Downstairs Ken was washing up the supper. She sat on the carpet, her back resting against the wall. Through the window she could see a square of London sky. It was too painful, to wonder if this room would ever be used. Instead she wondered about her sister, what she was thinking, what on earth she was feeling. She ran her finger to and fro across the carpet.

Down in the kitchen she heard the crash of breaking crockery. Ken had dropped something.

It was midnight, and the ward was dark. Everyone was asleep, except for Viv. She lay, gazing at the high ceiling. Outside the ward, in the nursery, a baby was crying.

Nobody stirred. The night nurse's office was lit but empty. The baby went on – a faint, insistent wail, as monotonous as wood being sawed.

She pushed back the bedclothes and swung her legs to the side of the bed. She flinched; her stitches hurt. The baby cried on. Carefully she raised herself to a sitting position, and slid off the bed. She stood, bent double. She felt dizzy, and supported herself on the side of the bed. Her head was still fuddled from sleeping; she had been dreaming of long narrow corridors and other babies crying, or perhaps that had been no dream at all.

The sawing sound went on and on; it was a different sound from the babies in the ward, or maybe that was just her fuddled head. Bent double, she hobbled slowly to the door. The pain made her breathless.

The cries came from down the corridor, where the window was. There was nobody around. She hobbled across to the window, and looked in.

The days passed strangely, in limbo. The future was blank. Like the little bedroom it waited, empty; nobody dared furnish, or fill with their own pictures, the months ahead.

So they could say nothing. Viv was pale and polite with visitors, including her sister. The baby had been moved now into a cot beside her, and the girls came and touched him with their fingertips, then lost interest and whined for some of Viv's lemon barley water. He was a sweet baby, and so far bore no resemblance to any of them.

Ollie slept at home, in the study, and seldom went out.

One evening Diz and some friends, having heard the news, rang on the door but he lay low and didn't answer. When the girls were at school he sat in Caroline's flat and tried to finish his book. For some reason he felt it must be done before Viv came out of hospital.

Ken and Ann went about the house quietly. Small talk seemed too small and plans too painful. Which left little to say. Ken, now self-employed, spent all day on his building site in a biting east wind. Trudging through the mud he thought breathlessly: I have a son. At lunchtime he sat in the adjoining pub, smoking too much and trying to chat to his chippie.

You can't trust Viv, said her mother. Viv gave people slugs instead of blackberries. *I'm a wonderful liar*, she had told Ken. She had told her parents she was spending the evening with her friend Sandra, and instead she went out with a Maltese waiter who gave her love-bites. Now she was a highly disturbed woman who had just given birth. Ridiculously, everyone had expected a girl. It might have made no difference, but nobody dared ask. The only clue to her state of mind was that, instead of breastfeeding the baby, she fed him with a bottle. Ann had not liked to remark upon this, except to Ken.

Viv was to leave the hospital the next Tuesday. On Monday, while Ollie was visiting, a woman in a tweed suit came up to the bedside. She carried a clipboard.

'I'm so sorry to interrupt. Mr Meadows? Hello. I'm Mrs Brookes, the hospital registrar. If you'd both like to register the baby now, it'll save you a visit to the Town Hall.'

There was a pause. Ollie glanced at Viv, who was fiddling with the sheet.

'Decided on a name?' the registrar asked.

Viv said: 'Not yet.'

The registrar smiled. 'Like that, is it?'

Viv said: 'It's either Thomas or Mark.'

The registrar replied: 'Could always be both.'

290

'We'll leave it for now,' said Viv sharply. The registrar looked at her curiously, stood up and moved on to the next bed.

There was a silence. Then Ollie said: 'You've got to decide.'

'Everyone's always asking questions,' said Viv restlessly.

Most of the women in the ward were new now. Viv had been there over a week; her various bunches of flowers had died and had been taken away. She looked at Ollie. 'You want him, don't you?'

'Don't ask that,' he replied. 'I can't help you.'

That day Ann spring-cleaned Viv's house, sweeping the kitchen floor and removing Ollie's old beer cans. She scrubbed the dresser with disinfectant; she washed the sheet for the baby's Moses basket, in which he would be coming home. Home? Here. Ten days, the arrangement was; until the midwife's visits ended, he would be here. Then what?

She disliked lying, but she had lied to them at the office, saying she felt ill and was staying at her sister's. In fact, she had never felt more vigorous. Damp with her exertions, she hoovered and polished. Her nerves felt taut as wire; tomorrow afternoon, at 3.30, she and Ollie would be fetching them from hospital.

Butterfingers. Scrubbing the units, she broke a cup. Clearing out the cupboard, she upset a wooden bowl of salt. It scattered on the floor; she closed her eyes, threw some over her shoulder, and wished. It had always surprised Ken how superstitious she was. *I thought you were the logical one*, he had said once. She had flared up – she remembered it, they were climbing the stairs to their flat – and she had replied: *You mean the boring one*. He had remonstrated, accusing her of jealousy, but she knew it wasn't quite as simple as that. Nearly, but not quite. He had never had a sister; he didn't understand.

She brushed the stairs: three floors of them, dust flying, from top to bottom. *The only exercise I get*, said Viv, *is sex and the stairs.* Ann's hands were grey from the fluff. *You wait*, Viv had said, *conkers under the stair carpet, tripping you up. Soggy bowls of cornflakes under the sofa.* You wait. For how long must she wait: for ever?

Viv had let her hold him. Casually, just once, in hospital she had passed him to her. But then she would do that if Ann were just an aunt. Ken had held him too.

Soft, tiny mouth. Fingernails. Perfect. All those years ago, her own little daughter had been perfect too; except she never moved.

She had put her finger in his hand, hoping he would grip it. He did. A hot rush through her body.

Perhaps Viv hadn't talked in the hospital because she was being discreet; somebody might hear. When she came home, it would all be different.

But Viv wasn't the discreet type. Ann emptied the dustpan into the bin. Some of it scattered on the floor.

'Fuck!' she said aloud, surprising herself.

Viv had packed all her stuff into two carrier-bags. Dressed, she sat on the edge of the bed. Her son lay in his cot, quietly gazing up at her. Neither of her daughters had had such dark hair. His face was a perfect oval, with a tiny pointed chin. Neither of them, new-born, had been so small.

She jumped; the sister had come up to her.

'Aren't you having any lunch?' she asked.

'No thanks,' said Viv.

'They won't be here till half past three.'

Viv nodded; the sister went away. Once she was out of the ward, Viv picked up the shawl she was going to use for carrying the baby.

I'm not quite myself, people say when they feel they're going mad. Viv felt like somebody else as she picked up the baby, wrapping him tightly in the shawl. The real

Vivien Meadows wouldn't be as cruel as this, leaving her husband and sister to find an empty bed. How could the real Viv upset them like that?

Her body felt flabby; she was short of breath. Carrying the baby and the bags, she stopped at the end bed. There was a girl there she liked.

'When my husband comes,' she said, 'can you tell him I've gone home early?'

The taxi driver actually tried to help her in with her bags. She refused, thanking him. She didn't want anybody else coming into her empty house.

The taxi drove away. She stood in her living room. It was spotless. There was a bunch of flowers on the table and, propped against it, a WELCOME HOME poster from the girls. Beside the Moses basket was a packet of disposable nappies and two new Babygros.

I have never been alone with my child. Would anybody understand?

I must be going mad. She sat down on the sofa, clutching him tightly. He mewled, his tiny, wet mouth against her ear. He started sucking the lobe, and the stud of her earring.

The room was silent. His gums gripped her skin; her body bloomed.

'Hello Thomas,' she whispered.

24

It was no better now Viv was home. Still she didn't speak about the baby. All she said was, *give me time.* Ollie's presence confused and irritated her, and he was told to stay in Caroline's flat. He went; nobody dared contradict her.

She was acting oddly, but what could anyone do? Ann dropped in each day to bring the shopping and make the girls' tea. Viv was grateful – in fact, she was gushingly grateful, as if Ann were an acquaintance at a cocktail party. Politely she said: 'Please don't, I can manage.' She sat with the girls; once she laughed so hysterically at one of their TV programmes that even her daughters were startled. She talked about the baby quite naturally, and complained that he kept her awake at night. She sounded normal, but her eyes were bright, as if she were taking drugs. She asked about Ann's office day in eager detail, looking fascinated when Ann told her the computer had broken down. She talked, all right; but she didn't speak.

By the third day Ann was so highly strung that she shouted at a man in the street who had dropped some litter. She yelled at him like a fishwife. Back home she dreaded Ken's return. As usual, he asked about Mark.

What could she say? 'He looked fine. Gaining weight.'

Some Elgar was playing. As she spoke, the needle stuck; again and again it played the same bit.

'Blasted bloody stereo!' She switched it off. The record ground to a halt. Ken flinched.

'Ann –'

'Sorry. I know how precious your stereo is, more precious than anything in the world – and your fish, and your kitchen units, and –'

'Ann!'

She paused. Then she asked: 'Do you think we live a sterile, boring life?'

'No.'

'Fixing things and repairing things and putting polyurethane on them?' she asked. 'Leafing through our Habitat catalogue, when we should be reading Tolstoy?'

'It's called home-building,' he said. 'We're building a home.' He paused. 'We've built one.'

'She thinks it's sterile and boring. I know she does. She thinks we don't know how to live.' Her voice trembled; she hated how she sounded. Peevish.

He sat down beside her. 'Listen –'

She interrupted him. 'That's why she can't bear to give him up.'

He looked at her in surprise. 'Did she say that?'

'No, but –'

'Our life's as good as theirs. Look what a mess she's made of hers.'

'Because of us,' said Ann.

'Rubbish.' He took her limp hand. 'Look, she's in a state.'

'*I'm* in a state.'

'Yes, but she's just had a baby. Women get funny then.'

Sarcastically she replied: 'From your vast experience?' How she loathed herself.

'She's all confused –' he began.

'And what's she doing to everybody else? She's playing with us, she's the same old Viv, sneaking him out of the hospital –'

'She did phone when she got home.'

Ann shouted: 'Stop defending her! I know you find her irresistible –'

'Ann!' He jerked his hand away and stood up.

'And far more exciting than me –'

'That's all finished!'

'But it does seem remarkably tactless –'

He grabbed her hand. 'Come on.' He pulled her to her feet. 'We're going out.'

She looked at him, surprised. 'Where?'

'Have a meal. Get out of this place.'

★

That night Ollie, as usual, was sitting in a Real Ale pub off Kensington High Street. Most nights he ate there: sausage and mash that almost tasted like home. Not quite, but still.

He was staring moodily at his glass when somebody slapped him on the back.

'In all the bars,' growled a Bogart voice, 'in all the towns, in all the world, and I have to come to yours.'

Ollie swung round. 'James!' He hadn't seen him for years.

'Hello, Meadows,' said James. 'All on your tod?'

'I'm with Meryl Streep, but she's just nipped out to the loo.'

James sighed. 'Oh well. Till she gets back.' He sat down. 'You always pulled the birds, even at school. "Where's Meadows?" we'd say. "Out wenching." God how I loathed you.'

'Most of the time, actually, I was teaching myself twelve-bar blues in the sports pavilion.'

'Tell us another, sonny boy. I used to pray you'd get acne.' He sipped his pint. As the years pass, most men flesh out. James, however, had grown drier and thinner; but then he was a lawyer. 'No, life's smiled on you, old chap.'

'Think so?' asked Ollie.

'Whereas *numero uno* . . . Know how much tonight's set me back? Forty-seven quid.'

Ollie asked: 'What happened?'

'This new bird, working for one of our articled clerks. I take her to the Bistro Vino, no expense spared, drinkies beforehand, pudding afterwards with flames coming out, the works, and what happens? She's got to catch the last tube to Hornchurch. Where, I ask, is the return on my investment?'

Ollie laughed – the first time, he realized, in days. 'James, I do love you.'

'Glad somebody does.'

'You're so unreconstructed.'

James sighed. 'Nowadays they don't even apologize. Once upon a time you could at least count on a grope in the taxi; you knew where you were. I'm telling you, Oliver, I'm a lost soul.' He drained his glass. 'Know my problem? Never recovered from your heartless sister. Fancy being thrown over for the EEC. Look at me. Aren't I more fascinating than the Agricultural Audit Directorate?'

Ollie laughed. What had he written? *The clackety-clack of high heels, of women with somewhere to go.* Last night he had finished his novel. 'It's called having a career.' He drained his glass. 'I do know how you feel.'

'You? You've always got it right,' said James. 'You wenched when there were wenches, and when the last wench became extinct you discovered how to be a sharing, caring, creepy, dishwashing, understanding bloody husband.'

There was a pause. Then Ollie said, 'Then why do you think I'm sitting here?'

'Tell me.'

'Are you sitting comfortably?' asked Ollie. 'Then I'll begin.'

It had been years since Ann and Ken had been quite so drunk. They staggered, giggling, into the hall. He propelled her into the lounge, and she flopped down in the armchair. He switched on the light.

She waved her arms vaguely. 'Welcome to my nice sterile lounge. Note the fitted units and overall cleanliness.'

'Mmm,' he said, looking around, 'Very nice.'

'I like to keep things spick and span,' she said, half closing her eyes. Her cheeks were flushed. 'I'm a deeply nice person.' She opened her eyes wide. 'Who are you?'

'A deeply nice man, but with unexpected pockets of violent, spontaneous, unboring masculinity.'

She frowned, looking him up and down. 'But are you worth an Indian meal? Twenty quid you've set me back.'

He raised his eyes to the ceiling. 'Oh Lord, it's one of these liberated women. What do I have to do in return?'

She stretched out her legs, kicking off her shoes. 'We'll see.'

He looked at her, his head on one side. 'You know, it's funny – what was your name again?'

'What was yours?' she drawled.

'In my experience, of necessity limited because I'm a happily married chap and deeply in love with my gorgeous wife, who incidentally bears a strong resemblance to this brazen hussy here –'

'Get on with it.'

'In my experience . . .' He came over to the armchair, sat down on the floor and ran his finger up and down her leg. 'In my experience Indian meals can only lead to trouble. They have in the past . . .' He moved his hand up her thigh, pushing up her skirt. 'Lots of trouble,' he murmured.

A baby won't solve your marriage, Viv had said, or words to that effect. Ken lay in bed the next morning. The winter sun shone through the curtains. *It's up to you two.*

His tongue was dry and his head ached. What had a girl in the office said? Ann had told him. *My mouth feels like a lizard's latrine.* If he didn't feel so awful he would smile. That girl, what's-her-name, she lived life to the full, by all accounts. Then so did Viv.

He curled against Ann, cupping her hip in his hand. He had a terrible hangover. But then, when she woke, so would Ann.

That weekend Ann stayed away from her sister. So did Ken. He said they mustn't pester her. Besides, in some superstitious way, she felt if she busied herself elsewhere Viv might make up her mind.

She put on her overalls and spent the weekend at the garden-centre site, painting the staging in the newly erected greenhouse. Ken put on the radio and painted beside her. He whistled along to an old Frank Ifield song, 'I remember you-hoo' . . . It was like the old days when they had fixed the flat together, long before the house; innocently masculine, he had made her his apprentice. They had lived off tea and doughnuts; she realized that she equated happiness with having no money. Then she realized that, in fact, she just equated it with youth.

When you're young, anything is possible. She remembered standing in another garden centre, months ago, with Viv. They had inspected the seed packets. *Ah, the dizzying possibilities*, Viv had said, smiling. That Sunday something had germinated in Viv's mind. Perhaps, if they had never gone to the garden centre and Ann had never sat on that bench and cried, there would be no Mark.

She put down her paintbrush. She longed for him so much, she felt weak.

On Wednesday Ann arranged to drop in with some lunch for Viv. Perhaps they could talk without the girls being there; perhaps it might be easier.

When she arrived the midwife was in the room. She was just putting away the weighing scales. Turning to Ann, she said: 'You tell your sister to buck up and decide.'

'What do you mean?' asked Ann.

'She's got to make up her mind about this little chap.'

Ann's heart stopped.

Viv said hastily: 'She means his name.'

Ann relaxed. Mrs Archer pointed to Viv, who sat on the sofa with Mark in her arms. 'Was she as bad with her daughters?'

'No,' replied Ann.

'Does she listen to you, or is she just as obstinate as with me?'

Ann went over to the oven and switched it on. She said: 'She won't listen.'

'I do!' said Viv.

'She doesn't,' said Ann loudly, to Mrs Archer. 'She's always had her own way.'

'She means pig-headed,' said Viv lightly.

Ann, blushing, put the lasagne into the oven. 'You said it.'

Viv spoke to the midwife, who was just leaving. 'I've always annoyed her like that.'

'Just annoyed?' asked Ann. In a rush she thought: what have I wanted of Viv's? Her gaiety, her slim thighs, the love of our dad. I want her son. She felt nauseous again, and added: 'She thinks I find it sort of appealing.'

'I don't!' said Viv.

'Charming people . . .' began Ann, and stopped. They were both looking at her. She said: 'Charming people can get away with a great deal.'

There was a silence.

'Well,' said Mrs Archer, 'you've got a charming little son, anyway.' She gave Viv an appointment card. 'Now, remember his six-weeks check-up at the clinic, and at three months his first triple shot. No forgetting?'

Viv nodded. 'He'll be there.'

She got up and showed Mrs Archer to the front door. Waiting beside the oven, Ann's heart quickened. But when Viv returned she was as polite as ever.

She gestured to the oven: 'You shouldn't have brought that, in your lunch-hour and everything.'

'I want to,' said Ann. Then she realized something. 'Hell. Forgotten the salad.'

'I'll get it.'

'No –'

'I've got the car,' said Viv. 'It'll only take a moment. Need to get out of this place for a bit.' There was a pause. Then, with a queer, sideways smile she passed the baby to Ann. She said lightly: 'Why don't you feed him? Bottle's

300

there, it's all ready. If he doesn't finish it, don't worry.' Swiftly, she took Ann's doorkeys and left.

Outside, there was a grind of gears as she started the car. Mark felt heavier since the last time. The moment his mother went he started to cry.

Ann held him tightly, pressing his hot face against hers. 'Don't,' she whispered. 'Don't . . .'

Viv sat at Ann's kitchen table. The salad was there, in a plastic bag, but she didn't move. She sat, looking at Ann's rubber gloves, laid on the draining board. The special red holder for the dish-mops. A couple of cups and plates were slotted into the rack: breakfast for two. There was no sound, apart from her own breathing. A cook's calendar hung on the wall; it still showed October. How unlike Ann, not to turn it over.

The minutes ticked by – or rather, on the silent kitchen clock, they passed. She hadn't been here for some weeks. There was no sign of the pram. They had probably put it in the empty extension; or perhaps they had got rid of it. But behind the door, wrapped in polythene, there was a brand-new high chair.

She picked up the salad and stood up. Then, on impulse, she opened the cupboard. Next to the tea-towels there was a Boots carrier-bag. Inside it was cotton wool, zinc cream and baby shampoo.

She ought to go. Instead, she sat down again and put her head in her hands.

After lunch, when Ann had gone, she put the baby into the car and drove to the garden centre. Sleet was falling and it was bitterly cold.

Ken was standing in the greenhouse, connecting the lights. When she said they should go to the Town Hall as soon as possible, to register Mark, he said quickly: 'I'm coming now,' and turned off the switches.

It was a stormy night. Sleet rattled against the windows in Viv's house, and a damp patch had appeared in the ceiling above the sink. Oblivious of household maintenance, the baby slept in his basket. Viv was watching a re-run *Starsky and Hutch* on the TV; for some days now she hadn't had the concentration to read.

The doorbell rang. She glanced at the baby, but he didn't wake. He was becoming a good sleeper, better than either of her girls had been.

Ollie stood in the doorway. He was wet, and bent double.

'Have pity on a poor chap,' he mumbled, 'seeking some refuge, some alley, some frozen doorway in this cruel concrete jungle where he can find a moment's warmth, a flickering fire, beside which he can consume his cod and chips.'

They went into the living room. 'Haven't made the fire,' Viv said.

He shivered, or perhaps he was exaggerating. 'Is there room in this inn? It's the season of goodwill.'

'Not for three weeks.' She indicated the sofa.

He sat down. She sat on the hearthrug. He offered her the open package. 'Want a chip?'

She shook her head. 'Had some lasagne, from lunch.'

He was still in his overcoat. He sat there, eating a chip, Then he asked: 'You all right?'

She didn't reply. Instead, she gazed into the red bars of the electric fire. Behind it lay the empty grate, swept clean by her sister.

'You must be sure,' he went on. 'You mustn't let anyone force you, or you'll never forgive them.'

She looked up. 'Not stupid, are you?'

'I've had plenty of time to think.'

She looked into the empty fireplace. Ann had even polished the grate. Nearby, the baby sighed in his sleep.

How quiet the room was. There wasn't even the noise

of the hamster's wheel; he had escaped, the week before, and the door hung open. The girls said he might want to come home, and who was she to disenchant them?

She said: 'I've behaved badly.'

'We all have.'

There was a pause. Then she shifted nearer and put out her hand. 'Can I have a chip?'

He gave her one. She sat, leaning against the side of the sofa. Then she reached into her bag and gave him something. He showed his greasy hands, shaking his head, so she held it up for him to read. It was the Birth Certificate.

'I've registered Ken as the father,' she said.

Ollie said nothing.

She said: 'Give us another.'

He passed her another chip. Then he said flatly: 'Well, it's done then.'

She nodded. There was nothing to say. He leant over and, with his foot, pushed a carrier-bag in her direction.

'Want to read my book?' he asked.

'Is it about us?'

He half smiled. 'Alchemized into art.' He paused, then he said: 'I've been so lonely.'

There was a moment's silence. Then she said: 'So have I.'

She suddenly moved towards him. She knelt beside him, pressed against his coat. Its buttons dug into her. He tried to keep his hands away, they were so greasy, but she grabbed them greedily. She kissed his greasy fingers, his neck, his warm mouth. He was kissing her back, numbly.

The next day Ollie moved back into his own home. He and Viv were very close; he had never seen her so bereft. For the first time in their marriage she made it plain that she needed him. They stayed at home most of the week. Out of some obscure desire to solace themselves – though they said it was for the children – they bought a video recorder and hired the sort of movies they'd never quite bothered to get a babysitter for when the girls were little. They sat, eating smoking mounds of cauliflower cheese, watching *Chinatown* and *Tootsie*.

Viv strapped the baby to her breast when she went around the house so he could feel her beating heart. It was arranged that she would give him to the Fletchers just before Christmas. She said she needed to know him before he went, and nobody felt in a position to contradict her. Perhaps it was some sort of comfort, to pass him over like a Christmas present; nobody liked to ask.

Something was called for, some event, and Ollie suggested a Christmas party for the girls. It would be a treat for them; in their offhand, spasmodic way they had become attached to the baby – Rosie, in particular, liked to half smother him in her arms – and to mark Mark's change of ownership, as Ollie put it, there would be balloons and celebration. Viv would take him to her sister's after the guests had gone.

But that was two weeks ahead. First they had matters to sort out, and a meeting was arranged for noon on Saturday. The girls were sent to play with neighbours; the sun was shining and the baby put into the garden. It would be easier to talk with the house empty. Viv, hoping to calm her nerves, lay on the sofa doing her Jane Fonda postnatal exercises while the aproned Ollie swept the floor.

'It's not so much fun cleaning out this place,' he observed, 'since your sister's been around.'

'Don't worry,' she replied, 'it'll all be back to normal soon.'

He emptied the dustpan into the bin, and asked: 'Are *we* back to normal?'

She lay back, panting. 'Hope not. Who wants to be normal?'

The doorbell rang. They looked at each other.

'Which ones?' asked Ollie.

'I'm not telepathic.'

He grimaced at her. 'Ah, but you're so intuitive.'

He went to the front door. She put away her book and sat up. It was all three of them – Ann, Ken and James.

James said: 'We met on the step.' He embraced Viv; she hadn't seen him for years. 'Hello gorgeous. How's Holloway's answer to the Earth Goddess?'

Ken stood back, watching them. James had the booming, public-school voice Ollie had long since lost. Ann went over to the garden window.

Viv, seeing her, said: 'It's all right. He's wrapped up.'

'I wasn't trying to . . .' began Ann and stopped.

'It's such a beautiful day,' said Viv.

They sat down. Ollie opened the fridge and brought out some wine. Later, Viv was to remember that moment: the sunny room, the five of them, poised. *What simpletons we were.*

Ollie poured out the Chablis. James took the bottle and sniffed it approvingly.

'You're such a wine snob,' Ollie said to him. 'It used to bankrupt me, having you to dinner.'

Ken raised his glass to his nose and sniffed it, nodding: 'Very nice.' Today he looked square and pompous; the two other men were much taller. He wore his unbecoming charcoal suit and a nylon tie. She thought: *he is the father of my child.* She remembered the scent of his skin.

James cleared his throat and put on his glasses. He had hardly changed at all, in all these years. But then he had never married.

Ollie sat down. 'As you know, James is a solicitor, and has been kindly doing a bit of research for us.'

James took out some notes. 'It's not my field, mind you, but I've been making some investigations.' He looked up at them, speaking seriously. 'I expect you're all aware of how tricky this is. We're in very murky waters indeed. Quite apart from the emotional problems.' He turned to

Viv, peering at her over his glasses. 'Now that you've had your son, are you absolutely sure you want to give him up?'

There was a silence, then the scratch of a match as Ken lit a cigarette. Viv said: 'I think so.'

James sipped his wine, then said: 'Well, let's say you are. For the purposes of this. You're all aware, of course, that you must never mention the word "surrogacy"?' He looked at them; they nodded. 'And I presume that no money has changed hands. This is in no way a commercial transaction, nor has there been any compensatory payment for loss of earnings and so on?'

Viv said: 'Not till Ken gets my bill.'

They stared at her.

She said: 'Only joking.'

There was a pause. Then James resumed: 'Nor is any professional person – doctor, midwife – aware of this arrangement?'

Ann replied: 'No.'

'Fine.' James turned to Ken. 'Now, I hear that you are registered as the natural father of young . . .'

'Mark,' said Viv.

'Mark. That's the first step.' James turned to Viv. 'Now, as the mother of an illegitimate child you have all the rights. You realize that?' She nodded. 'You can now act in two ways. Firstly, you could grant them *de facto* custody. That means they have no legal rights whatsoever. You understand?'

Viv tried to understand, but she was thinking: last time I saw James he was drunk, sitting on my bathroom floor and burbling about Ollie's sister. It was after a party. Rosie was just born, and Daisy didn't exist. She had no place in this world. How many millions of children have been born since then?

She tried to concentrate. Ollie said: 'More wine, anyone?' He stood up, refilling glasses.

James was saying: 'They can bring up young Mark

but you can still, at any time, any time at all, take him back.'

Ollie poured wine into Viv's glass. Ann said: 'Whenever she wants?'

James nodded. 'Or whenever she thinks the *child* wants. Perhaps you quarrel about his schooling . . .'

Ollie laughed. 'Or we catch them reading him Enid Blyton.'

Nobody smiled. James went on: 'Or either of you split up and' – he turned to Viv – 'you want him back, or something happens to the girls –'

Viv stiffened. 'Don't!'

'You *must* consider all this,' said James.

Ann turned to Viv. 'You must.' She hadn't touched her wine.

'Anything might happen,' said James. He looked from one face to another. 'Do you feel that custody would be unsatisfactory?' There was a pause. One by one, they nodded. 'The alternative is that Mark could be legally adopted by Ken and Ann.'

There was a pause. It was Ken who spoke. 'That was the plan,' he said, stubbing out his cigarette.

James said: 'Do you realize exactly what that means? All of you? What you'll have to go through?'

Ollie said: 'Tell us.'

'Once a child is up for adoption it is in the hands of the court.' He turned to Viv. 'Not yours any longer. And you're taking a huge risk.'

'Why?' she asked.

'The court may decide that *none* of you are suitable parents. Have you thought of that?'

Moments ticked by. In her track-suit Viv was sweating.

James's voice went on: 'It's a possibility. Certainly if there was any hint of surrogacy.' He paused. 'Now, apart from that, you, Ann – for a probationary period you and Ken will be rigorously vetted. Rigorously. You'll be visited at home and asked a lot of questions. You will be observed with the child. You will have to go to court and, in this case, with the sister connection, there's bound to be publicity. Can you face it?'

After a moment Ann said: 'Yes.'

Viv said: '*Love Tangle*, you mean? *A Family Affair*?'

James said: 'You'll have to be on your toes for all the questions.' He turned to Ken. 'And you, old chap, you'll have to pretend, of course, that you and the lovely Viv here had an affair.' He smiled. 'Not too onerous, will that be, with your mates?'

Viv spoke clearly: 'We did have an affair.'

Nobody spoke. Then Ollie got up, went to the fridge and got out another bottle of wine.

'What else was it?' Viv asked.

There was a pop as Ollie uncorked the bottle. James went on: 'And there's one more thing.' He looked at Ollie and Viv. 'It concerns you two, and you may not like it.'

Ollie refilled his glass. 'Out with it.'

'If you want this child adopted, you must stay separated.'

Everyone stared at James, who took off his glasses and put away his notes.

'What?' said Ollie.

'No!' said Viv. She looked quickly at Ollie; his face was frozen.

James said: 'You and Ollie must stay apart. And I mean apart, because they may check you out.'

'Why?' asked Ollie loudly.

'Because if you two are separated, you will be considered the less suitable of the two couples.' He indicated Ann and Ken, who sat there blankly. 'It will give them a better chance. Understand?'

26

Ollie put his suitcase on the floor and sat down. The flat smelt stale. Through the wall came some meandering Middle Eastern music; how senseless it sounded.

He sighed and went into the kitchen. He had forgotten to take out the last rubbish-bag, over a week ago: the place stank. He dumped his shopping and went back into the living room.

Stupid, warbling music. Call that a bloody tune?

His face heated up. He fetched the broom from the kitchen and banged, with its handle, on the wall. Once, twice, three times, hard.

'Shut up!' he yelled, and banged again. It chipped the wallpaper, but who bloody cared? The music continued.

When Ann arrived home she found Ken, in the extension, hammering away. He was half-way through the construction of a doll's house.

'Goodness,' she said. 'Viv'll approve.'

'Why?'

'Making him a doll's house.'

'It's for the girls,' he replied.

She went into the kitchen; he followed her.

'So how did he take it?' he asked.

'Mr Fowler?' She put on the kettle. 'He looked old and resigned, which made me feel worse.'

Ken washed his hands. 'Did he say he should never have promoted a woman?'

'Even Mr Fowler wouldn't dare say that.'

'What did you tell him?'

'That we were adopting a child, I was sorry I couldn't give the proper notice but it was all very sudden, and I won't be coming back after Christmas.' She paused and turned off the kettle. 'Don't feel like tea.'

She went into the lounge. He followed. 'Are you sure?' he asked. 'You worked hard for that job.'

She poured herself a sherry and offered him one. 'I

want to work with you.' She smiled. 'And the child-care facilities will be better.' Exhausted, she sat down in the armchair. 'He can grow up amongst growing things.'

She pictured Mark, in his pram, next to shelves of geraniums. Herself beside him, auditing the accounts. The cash till bleeping as Ken served a long row of customers. With her eyes closed, she tried to make it real.

Viv had spent the evening with the girls, decorating the Christmas tree. She had tried to be jolly. They had found the glass balls, most of them broken, and the disabled angel for the top.

Now the girls were in bed and, like every year, she couldn't make the lights work.

Ridiculously, tears pricked her eyes. In his basket Mark started crying creakily.

The doorbell rang. Startled, she went to the door and opened it. A masked, overalled figure stood there. She jumped.

'Mrs Meadows?' it said, its voice muffled. 'I hear there's something rotten in the fabric of your marriage. I've come to put it right.'

It was Ollie. He took off the mask.

Viv went into the living room and sat down. 'Christ.'

'As I'm not allowed to see you,' he said, 'I've come in disguise.'

'You terrified me.' She picked up the crying baby.

'Borrowed it from Ken's old firm. They're doing the downstairs flat.'

'I thought a nuclear war had started.'

'Sorry,' he said, sitting down.

'Don't ever do that again.'

'Where's your sense of humour?'

She replied flatly: 'I'm not in the mood.' She rocked the baby.

He flared up. 'How do you think *I* feel? Oh, it's delightful, being shoved out into the cold again to suit your

bloody sister and your erstwhile lover. Shows me where I
am on your list of priorities. As if I didn't know.'

'I'm sorry.'

'Know what I put in my novel, which I haven't dared
ask if you've read yet?'

'I haven't dared read it.'

'I wrote that men are redundant.'

'They're not,' she said.

He snorted. 'Give me one good reason.'

She replied: 'They can fix Christmas lights.'

He looked at her, then he got to his feet and went over
to the tree. Pressing the baby against her breast, she
watched him fiddling with the tiny bulbs.

Moments ticked by. Then, suddenly, the lights came
on: tiny points of red, yellow and blue. The room was
illuminated.

Ollie looked at her. His mouth twitched.

Ann and Ken usually had a silver tree – a small one,
that they unpacked each year from the bathroom cupboard. This time, however, Ken had come home with a
real one. Who were they to care about shedding needles?

The lights were on when he came in, took her hand and
stamped it with a rubber stamp. 'Hello, fellow company
director,' he said. He pointed to the number, blurred in
her skin. 'Our VAT number. For those registered together, let no man put asunder.'

She looked up at him. 'Or woman.'

He smiled. 'Or child.'

> *Hark the herald angels sing*
> *Glory to the new-born King . . .*

Ollie pushed his way along Oxford Street clutching
his parcel. It was so bulky it dug into his armpit.
Canned carols burbled from some unknown location;
people jostled him. In Selfridge's window there was a giant

Santa Claus. He looked threatening, like a child molester; he nodded his head as if to say: *I told you so, old cock.*

He felt deeply depressed. All the old wounds had flared up again between himself and Viv, as if nothing had been learnt. For the first time in his life he dreaded Christmas.

> *. . . Peace on earth and mercy mild,*
> *God and sinners reconciled . . .*

One spends lavishly when one is unhappy. Perhaps the girls at least would be comforted by their doll's house. He and Viv might make a botch of home-making, but their children could play at it. The house was large and Georgian, so far dismantled, and he had bought a whole collection of tiny furniture. Plus – he couldn't bear not to – a plastic baby in a crib.

If he were a good father he would make the furniture himself. Ken would. But how could he, when he was not only inept but absent? He was a failure. He couldn't even write a book; there was no news from the publisher he had sent it to, but that was hardly surprising. Who would want to publish something so raw and bitter, with no satisfactory ending?

Nobody could bear to make plans for Christmas Day. If Viv didn't give away the baby he could stay at home, in his proper place. They could keep that darling boy and things might get back to normal. *Who wants to be normal?* she had asked. He did.

At last he managed to get a taxi. He went back to Kensington, where the heating had broken down in the block of flats.

> *. . . come and behold him*
> *Born the King of Angels . . .*

A small group of children stood outside the tube station rattling a tin. They sang in thin voices; one boy, in an Arsenal scarf, giggled.

Ann paused. 'Who are you collecting for?'

'Charity,' said the boy glibly. Another boy sniggered.

What the hell, thought Ann. She gave them a pound. Let them keep it. She closed her eyes, for luck, as she walked on. Three days till the party; she needed all the luck she could get.

'He won't be gone far,' said Viv. 'Only down the road.'

Daisy was sitting on the sofa holding the struggling baby. Her face was set; recently she had learnt how to make herself cry.

'He's your cousin,' said Viv desperately. 'He's not really going away.' She looked at Daisy's glistening eyes and thought: everybody's always crying in this house.

'What're we having for the party?' demanded Daisy.

'I told you. A real clown, like you've always wanted. Like Tamsin had for hers. A jelly like a tortoise.' Her voice wheedled. 'It'll be fun!'

She told herself: Daisy's only holding the baby so she doesn't have to help clean out the hamster.

'You've always wanted a clown,' she repeated.

Rosie, cleaning out the cage, said flatly: 'I want Mark.'

'Don't!' said Viv.

'I want our brother,' said Rosie.

'Thanks, Diz.'

Ollie put down the phone. His blood raced.

If he'd gone out to the pub, as he'd meant to, he would have missed both these phone calls.

His legs felt so weak that he sat down.

They were going to publish his book and, after all these months, he had found Ann's father.

27

'I'm too old, Viv.' Ollie was blowing up balloons. He sat down dizzily.

Viv was getting a jelly out of the fridge.

'My tortoise! It's collapsed.'

'You've failed as a mother.'

Viv was looking under some old newspapers. 'Lost the chocolate fingers.'

Ollie inspected his balloon. 'Balloons used to be bigger than this.'

'Like policemen,' she said, still searching, 'used to be younger.' She gave up with the biscuits. 'I do want them to be happy.'

'Policemen?'

'The girls. I want this party to be special.'

Ollie half smiled. 'It's that all right.'

They were both curiously high-spirited; almost manic. When Viv dropped a knife they both jumped. Ollie had wound a streamer round his forehead, sixties style. Viv wore crimson lipstick.

If you didn't laugh, you'd cry. They avoided each other, hurrying nimbly round the room. When Viv's arm brushed Ollie's she said, 'Sorry.'

And then Ken arrived with his doll's house. He bumped it along the corridor; it was so big. A carefully painted semi.

Ollie's doll's house, thank goodness, was upstairs in his study, wrapped for Christmas. But he had shown it to Viv.

They both stared at Ken's.

'Just a little token,' he said.

Taken aback, Viv gazed at it. 'It's lovely! Very Kingston Bypass.'

For some reason, the doll's house was the last straw. She and Ollie sat down weakly, their faces rigid in their efforts not to laugh, or weep. Ken gazed at them, bemused.

★

Douglas had come to bring Ann to the party. She looked pale; she wore a rather formal, flowered dress and white high-heels. He looked around at the lounge: the illuminated fish, the lit tree. In the corner was a pram. There were no other signs that his grandson would be arriving here tonight, God willing.

She collected her handbag. They paused at the door. Suddenly he remembered this moment, it must be fifteen years before, as clearly as yesterday. Ann's wedding day: the two of them, in the bungalow in Watford, hesitating on the threshold. Behind them, the empty room; Ann's hand on his arm. *Do I look all right?* He had answered honestly: *You look radiant.* For that moment they had been close. In fact, he had enjoyed Ann's wedding a great deal more than he had enjoyed Viv's.

He said: 'She's put you through a lot of pain, that young lady. Took her time, didn't she?'

Ann didn't reply.

He went on: 'Don't think I haven't noticed.'

'It's been terribly hard for her.'

He paused, then said awkwardly: 'You deserve this baby. It's going to have a wonderful mother.'

'You needn't say that.'

He cleared his throat. 'I'm sure you'll make a better job of it than I did.'

'Don't be silly.'

He said: 'Sort of in the same boat, you and me. Somebody else's fledgeling in the nest.'

'You weren't so bad.' She linked his arm. 'Let's go.'

Downstairs the party was in full swing. There were distant squeals of laughter from the children – nine of them – and the lower boom of Smartie Artie's voice. Ollie and Douglas stood in the study; Douglas wore a party hat.

'Sorry to drag you up here,' said Ollie, 'but I have to go in a moment. I shouldn't really be here.'

'Rum business, isn't it?' said Douglas. 'Things were a lot easier before the world got computerized and the authorities started sticking their noses into other people's business.'

'There's something I need to ask you about.'

'The baby?'

'No,' said Ollie. 'Ann.' He paused and took a sip of wine. 'I've traced her father.'

Downstairs there was a burst of laughter. Viv shouted: 'Sit down, Daisy!'

'You've what?' said Douglas.

'Diz on the magazine put out some feelers – oh, months ago. Someone on a newspaper in Stockport did a bit of digging and, well, I've got an address.'

Douglas stared at him. 'Did Ann know you were looking?'

Ollie shook his head. 'I was going to ask her if she still wants to know.'

'What does he do?'

'Runs a little joke shop.'

Douglas smiled faintly. 'Very appropriate.'

There was a pause. Down below, the clown's voice boomed.

Ollie said: 'You think I should let sleeping dogs lie, don't you?'

Douglas paused; then he nodded.

The pub looks festive, its ceiling burdened with streamers. It was the Kensington pub in which Ollie had spent so many evenings.

He arrived, breathless from the party.

'Sorry I'm late,' he said, sitting down.

'Doesn't matter,' said Norah. Like many people, she was surprisingly old compared to her phone voice. She wore a fitted suit. 'We're delighted to have you join our list,' she said, shaking his hand.

'Not half as delighted as me.'

She smiled. 'I can see the reviews now. "An assured and sensitive debut", "at last, a man who writes like a woman".' They were sitting at the bar. She ordered two drinks and turned back to him. 'It's very contemporary, Oliver. And frighteningly honest. I blushed like an eavesdropper.' She pushed a cigarette into a filter-holder and lit it. 'What does your wife think of it?'

'She's a teacher,' said Ollie. 'She gave me an A-minus.'

'Minus?'

'She says I'm impossible enough to live with as it is.'

Norah smiled and exhaled smoke through her nostrils. Ollie thought: she thinks I'm joking.

'We aim to publish in September,' said Norah. 'There's something very special about it, Oliver. A ring of truth.'

Ollie thought: in two hours' time, my wife is going to get into her car, drive to her sister's and give away her son.

He said: 'Oh no. If it were true, nobody would believe it.'

They cleared up the party in silence: Douglas, Vera and Viv. Ken had gone home. Ann was upstairs putting the girls to bed. Nobody spoke, except to hold up a small plastic ring from a cracker and ask: 'Who left this?' Though it was the night before Christmas Eve there was the same sense of hushed expectancy, a holiness in the air that gave significance even to folding up paper plates and ramming them into the bin. The baby slept near the tree, his face bathed in multi-coloured lights.

Ann spent a long time with the girls. When she came downstairs Douglas and Vera had gone.

She stood in the doorway to the living room. After a moment she said: 'Always wanted to see one of those clowns.'

Viv was sitting on the sofa. 'Terrific, wasn't he?'

'Didn't have them when we were children.'

Viv replied. 'Didn't have the money.'

There was a silence. The baby sighed and shifted in his sleep. Ann said: 'Still, it wasn't so bad, was it?'

'When?'

'When we were young.'

There was another silence. Then Viv said: 'See you in about half an hour.'

'Sure you don't want Ollie?'

Viv shook her head.

Ann hesitated; then she nodded and left. Their mother was coming round in half an hour to babysit while Viv was gone.

While shepherds washed their socks by night . . .

A group of loud young stockbrokers were standing at the bar. It was nine o'clock and their faces were florid.

All seated round the tub . . .

Ollie sat alone at his table. Nine o'clock; she should be there by now.

They raised their voices deafeningly:

> *A bar of Sunlight soap came down*
> *And they began to scrub.*

His daughters sang something like that, but it sounded more appropriate when they did it.

He fetched himself another pint. Feeling in his pocket for some change, he found a scrumpled party hat. He thought: but when it comes down to it, which of us is really grown-up?

28

Viv's car is parked outside the small terraced house. On its front door there is a wreath of tinsel and holly. The downstairs lights are on; the lounge curtains are open. Inside the room there is an illuminated Christmas tree and three people: Viv, Ken and Ann, who is holding the baby in her arms.

Ann kisses Viv. Viv kisses Ken. Then the front door opens and Viv comes out. Standing on the step, Ann and Ken watch Viv as she crosses the pavement to her car and gets in. Ken raises his hand in a half-wave, but she doesn't see.

Sitting in the car, Viv turns and looks at the back seat. Something has been left behind; it is the baby's shawl. She leans back and picks it up, then she opens the car door and gets out.

But the front door is closed now. In the lounge, Ann is holding the baby and standing beside the mantelpiece. Ken moves to the window and starts closing the curtains.

The curtains are closed now. The family is complete. Viv gets back into the car and drives away.

29

It was nearly ten o'clock. In the pub the Hooray Henrys had become more boisterous and had been joined by more of their kind. He could have become one of them; he had been bred to it. It was Viv who had saved him. They had grown smutty now; there was loud talk of arseholes.

Ollie finished his crisps, scrumpled up the empty bag and put it in the ashtray. At some point he must go back to the flat. Soon he would be too drunk to do so.

When he next looked up Viv was there in her overcoat. She looked very cold.

He moved up. She sat down beside him. 'Let's have a drink,' she said.

He got to his feet, but she started to say something so he sat down again.

'Come on Christmas Day,' she said. 'Disguise yourself in a red cloak and white beard, become an outmoded patriarchal fantasy, become my regeneration myth.'

He sighed. 'Life would be simpler if you couldn't make me laugh.'

He fetched her a beer. They drank to it.